THE PEARLMAKERS TRILOGY

DUKE TATE

Copyright © 2021 by Duke Tate

All rights reserved. This book or any portion thereof
may not be reproduced or used in any manner whatsoever without the express written
permission of the publisher except for the use of brief quotations in a book review.

ISBN 978-1-951465-47-6

Cover illustration by Bernard Lee.
Map illustration by Alex Foster.

Pearl Press, LLC
PO Box 2036
Del Ray Beach, Florida
33483

CONTENTS

Foreword   v

THE HUNT FOR LA GRACIA

Chapter 1	5
Chapter 2	13
Chapter 3	35
Chapter 4	49
Chapter 5	59
Chapter 6	75
Chapter 7	89
Chapter 8	107
Chapter 9	115
Chapter 10	123

THE DOLLARHIDE MYSTERY

Chapter 1	145
Chapter 2	155
Chapter 3	163
Chapter 4	173
Chapter 5	183
Chapter 6	189
Chapter 7	203
Chapter 8	211
Chapter 9	219
Chapter 10	231
Chapter 11	241
Chapter 12	245
Chapter 13	255
Chapter 14	267
Chapter 15	275
Chapter 16	277

Chapter 17	289
Chapter 18	305

GOLD IS IN THE AIR

Chapter 1	323
Chapter 2	331
Chapter 3	335
Chapter 4	339
Chapter 5	347
Chapter 6	357
Chapter 7	367
Chapter 8	381
Chapter 9	387
Chapter 10	393
Chapter 11	399
Chapter 12	403
Chapter 13	411
Chapter 14	423
Chapter 15	429
Appendix	435
About the Author	451
About Pearl Press Publishing	453
Also by Duke Tate	455

FOREWORD

The book you are holding in your hands took a long time to get to this stage. In the book, Teddy Dollarhide says everything has a story, so let me tell you this book's story.

In 2009, while living in a vintage apartment in Santa Monica, California (a beachfront community of Los Angeles), I started playing around with a tale that combined many of the funny things that happened in my life growing up in the Deep South. If there is one thing good about the South, it is the people's sense of humor. I had gathered so many funny stories over the years that I loved to retell around dinner tables and campfires, and I just knew I could build them into a novel somehow.

When typing the first couple of pages, I was trying to teach myself how to write. It was very difficult; however, I had so many good ideas coming, I kept writing everyday with the intention to get the story down without being too hard on myself.

Fortunately, the ideas never stopped flowing, and the few stories I had from my past turned into a much larger nostalgic saga about treasure hunting, lost love, ghosts, health, and family.

At the time, the building I was living in on California Avenue was a known haven for screenwriters. Perhaps "the bug" was in the air.

FOREWORD

After 50 pages, a title emerged too: *The Golden Summer*. After all these years, I still like the ring to it.

I kept writing and writing, day after day. It was going well, but I knew I didn't know the fundamentals of the craft. So, I decided to take a break for a few days and read Stephen King's *On Writing*. That book was incredibly helpful in many ways and gave me a foundation to build on. I went back and edited what I already had with King's advice in mind. I saw how I could polish my writing to make it read better.

After two years, I finished the book. It took lots of rearranging and rewriting before I was able to craft that first work into something that read well, because the story kept getting more and more complex. That rewriting process literally took me years.

I didn't self-publish the book until 2014, under the title *The Opaque Stones*. The name was a reference to a pearl. The final book was always called *The Pearlmakers*, but I changed it right before self-publishing it. That was in the days before self-publishing was sexy, and everyone was doing it.

Even after endless editing, that first book still had many glaring errors. Not having an editing team was truly a cumbersome situation. I didn't sell as many books as I had liked, and I was always disappointed with the Amazon CreateSpace cover. Frustrated, I stopped writing for a while. After a year or so, I did work on a few other books: a murder mystery on a train in England, and another novel about a serial killer who left Scrabble letters as clues. I never completed either one, ultimately trashing them both for better ideas.

In 2019, I sat down to write a book about my journey to overcome chronic disease. After finishing the 300-page book with three separate parts, I wrote to writer Tahir Shah to ask him his advice on how to get it published. He ended up connecting me with the Tribal Publishing team, Holly Worton and Agustín Gonzalez, and the rest is history. We published those books as a series titled *My Big Journey*.

Afterwards, I sent them *The Opaque Stones* for Agustín to proof and edit. When I got it back from him, I fixed the many mistakes he found before we sent it to the Red & Black Team in Princeton, New Jersey.

FOREWORD

Agustin and the Princeton team both had a major problem with Cosby and Joey's younger brother Colt, who had a very minor role in the book, so I wrote him out completely. When the book had been thoroughly edited by three people, it finally felt complete to me for the first time ever.

Thank you, Agustín and Holly, for all your help. I am so happy I took this journey and started writing that first day in Santa Monica. It really is my passion. Thank you, dear reader, for listening.

Duke Tate
March 2021

THE HUNT FOR LA GRACIA

BOOK 1

Deep in the sea are riches beyond compare.
 But if you seek safety, it is on the shore.

— SAADI (ROSE GARDEN)

CHAPTER 1

Teddy Dollarhide's eyes sprang open as he jackknifed awake on the outside porch sofa. Beads of sweat dotted the back of his neck and he squinted through the glare of the sun. He looked around for his crew and the ocean, but only saw a pasture and a barn off to his right. Then he realized that he was safely at home and it was all a dream—but not just any dream. It was the same dream he had been having for the last fifteen years about being a crewmember on a massive Spanish galleon on its way down in a violent hurricane. He could still hear the wind, feel the adrenaline, taste the saltwater on his tongue.

Maybe one day I'll get used to it, he thought. *One day*.

Shaking the dream off, he went inside to draw the dream, a compulsion he had maintained since they started. He was a big, wide, barrel-chested man who attributed his strength to growing up on a farm and to years of sport fishing. Friends called him "Old Salt," and with his pearl hair, matching beard, and ruddy skin, the title suited him.

After scribbling down a new sketch, he went back outside to relax on the stone porch. Gazing out over the land, he reflected on the dreams, thinking back to when they started. He had been a history professor at the University of Miami when they started coming in the night, once every two months, then once a month, and eventually once or twice a week. Over the years, he couch-surfed from psychiatrist to psychiatrist and from therapist to therapist to unravel the connection between himself and the sailor haunting him, but it didn't help, and the pharmacopeia and half-wit they threw at him only turned the dreams into nightmares. Charcoal stained the tips of his fingers from his ongoing drawings of the dream, which covered the walls of his home office in Miami. Stacks of books on treasure and Spanish galleons towered to the ceiling and stuffed the interior. But in all the pages of the books, he couldn't find anything resembling the ship from his dreams and he had resigned to it being nothing more than a figment of his unconscious imagination.

One day while drawing, he got a call informing him that a distant uncle had passed and bequeathed him an Italian Mediterranean-style estate named "Isabella" that sat only 150 meters off the ocean on over sixty acres in a little town called Latchawatchee, Florida. A real estate investor, Red Dollarhide had bought the rundown mansion years ago at a killer price with plans to chop up and sell off the land. Teddy inherited the property tax and maintenance to go with the twenty million dollar estate, which was a burden considering the fact that Red had only left him a half a million in trust besides the property, having squandered his money on bad deals.

When Teddy and his wife, Sarah, were given the keys to Isabella, they were certain their plan was simply to sell it off—netting enough to settle the obligations and pocket a nice sum for themselves—but one step through the ten-foot-tall mahogany door changed everything. Netted cobwebs blocked doorways, dust caked the floors, the paint was peeling off the walls, mold blackened the ceilings, ants scaled the living room walls, and furniture hid its neglect under drop cloths. But underneath it all, the house exuded the same irresistible charm that had kept Red from selling it over all those years. And their boys, Joey and Cosby, enjoyed playing on the majestic grounds of the estate.

Sarah and Teddy couldn't let go of the house, no matter what it was worth. They spoke about cutting up and selling the land, but even that felt sacred to them. So, they kept the estate intact and did their best to make the property tax payments. Teddy made the repairs himself during their vacations there, while Sarah tended the garden, which she loved since she owned a bespoke landscape architecture business in Coconut Grove. Giving back was also a large priority of hers and she spent months every year in Africa assisting the hungry in obtaining food.

Teddy had just turned thirty-eight and Sarah was two years younger when they first visited Latch to see Isabella. Back then, they thought they were dreaming. In Miami, Teddy had started keeping a loaded gun in his bedside table ever since their house had been robbed. Latch seemed idyllic by comparison. The center of town, laid out in a square, sat a half-mile from the ocean. The Hub, as locals called it, housed a variety of small businesses and restaurants; a 1920s white-washed Spanish courthouse marked the center. A statue of Ponce de León stood in front of the building as a nod to its Spanish roots, which ran deep and wide like the oak trees that dotted the greens. Giant palms lined the streets, and flowers were replaced as soon as they wilted with the turning seasons. Traffic speeds averaged five miles under the posted limit, and children rode their bicycles in the street. A neighborhood of bungalows with wide sweeping porches surrounded the square. The grandest historic homes dotted the small bay along Route 1, which trailed out of town following the ocean north and south. In the summer, the essence of jasmine and honeysuckle filled the dense, steaming air.

On their visits, they would read the crime reports in the town's newspaper, *The Grapevine*, for a good chuckle. One week's highlights included an old lady who called the police after witnessing her neighbor drop an anonymous love letter in her mailbox and a man who had his wallet stolen by a raccoon that snuck in through his dog door.

Due to the sense of safety at Isabella, Teddy slept more hours and got better quality of sleep there. This also meant that his dreams were always more vivid; he sensed that just by being in the area, he might receive a midnight clue to their purpose.

In Miami, the dreams had begun to interfere with his teaching. He and Sarah would often take the boys sailing at Key Biscayne on the weekends, and his mind always felt the clearest on the water; he began to crave its company like a long-lost friend.

They drove up the coast to Isabella at least once a month and Sarah would always cry when they left because she never wanted to leave. One cold October Sunday, she was sobbing as Teddy turned the truck onto Route 1 and a platoon of a hundred seagulls flew up the coast in a cloud of flapping intent. The sight so astonished him that he stopped the truck and, without saying a word, slipped out to watch as the gulls began a circular ballet high above the grey sea. The dance seemed to be communicating something to him. The position of their bodies was forming a symbol, but he couldn't decode it, and then, they all stopped beating their wings for a single moment and he caught a glimpse of meaning. A second later, they flew off just as fast as they had come. Having seen Teddy draw it a thousand times, Sarah confirmed that the birds' pattern was indeed the circle with the cross and lion's head at the top from the admiral's jacket on the ship in his dream.

He took it as a sign and reluctantly quit his teaching job, bought a big boat for treasure hunting that he named *Gold Lip*, and although he was terrified of lacking employment in the face of Isabella's upkeep, decided to start a small inshore fishing business in Latch and move the family there. Sarah relocated her landscaping business as well.

The original structure of Isabella was built in the 17th century and added onto gradually over the years with a full scale make over in the Italian Mediterranean style during the 1920's. Her exterior walls were white stucco over masonry and every window and door opening was framed in coquina stone quarried in Miami's Coconut Grove. With her tower, she appeared to be an old villa in Capri, Italy.

The roof had the original barrel-shaped clay tiles that were handmade by forming them over the workers' thighs. Isabella had large stone-columned loggias on the front and the back. The 15' tall ceilings ran throughout the first floor and the ceilings in each room had either pecky cypress beams, pecky cypress paneled ceilings, or decorative plaster. Arched openings abounded from one room to the next in long enfilades while giant carved coquina stone mantles graced the living and dining rooms. Pecky cypress mantles were in the sunroom, kitchen and breakfast room. A grand wooden stair in the large foyer ascended to the second floor with its 12' ceilings in each room. Another wooden stair snaked its way from the second floor's long landing up to the tower, which had 360° views to the ocean and the countryside over the small town's rooftops.

There was a large indoor tile pool on the back of the house off the North wing that was very unusual for its day-and-age.

Isabella was a grand lady with the air of an Italian movie star like Sophia Loren–noble but earthly, with something of both the peasant and the aristocrat in her soul. Teddy and his family loved living in her, and she loved them back. She warmed them when they were cold, cooled them when they were hot, sheltered them from the rain and ocean winds, and her spirit lifted them up from the earth in which she stood. The land had a way of consoling their pain and enhancing their dreams. While shuffling through some books in the two-story library one day, Teddy stumbled upon a gold-leafed, out-of-print hardback about treasure ships in Florida; one ship in particular struck a chord with him. A Spanish galleon named *La Gracia* had been caught in a hurricane off the coast of northeast Florida in the seventeenth century and sank while carrying enormous quantities of gold, silver, and jewels. Hunters had searched for it but never found any trace—in fact, many had concluded that it was just a smoke ship and the stories were mere legends. The name and description rang true in the core of Teddy's being, and he knew it was the very ship he had been dreaming about. He googled it and found a little more history. One line made his mouth drop: "The ship went down off the coast of a little town called Latchawatchee."

The revelation floored Teddy and Sarah. They popped a bottle of champagne and, after a few glasses, chased each other around the house, laughing. And Teddy continued to fish the waters where *La*

Gracia fell, hoping that the seagulls would return with further instructions.

Meanwhile, Sarah and Teddy loved many aspects of living in Latch, but came to learn that it really was frozen in time. In an attempt to preserve the pleasantries of a slower, quieter era, the town had resisted change. When it landed on a certain travel magazine's list of the top one hundred places to retire, some residents wrote letters of disgust to the editors. Growth in the last ten years had increased housing costs as retirees and snowbirds from northern cities flocked in search of their own private tropical Mayberry. That in turn encouraged aggressive real estate development up and down the virgin Atlantic coastline.

What no one knew when they first moved there was that behind the perfect exterior, Latch had a history that wasn't written about in the pages of the magazines and rarely spoken about among the residents. The town's past covered the area like an invisible cloak of darkness, overtaking anyone who was susceptible to it; some residents gossiped, others were crooked or ignorant, and corruption had spread like a virus to a few key people in charge.

Tongues wagged about Teddy and Sarah to. They lived on modest salaries in one of the grandest houses in the area, and it was rumored that he made paper airplanes out of charity ball invitations, preferring to give a small anonymous amount on his own each month. Although the gossipers were nice to their faces, they loathed Teddy's old truck and his going shirtless around the marina and how Sarah was always bringing guests of a *lower station* over for dinner.

Nevertheless, in time, Teddy's sport fishing business became successful as it was the only one in the area and he could really spin a reel and find the fish—Sarah's landscaping business boomed, too, as she capitalized on the snowbirds. Their children did well in school and made friends with good people.

Things seemed to be going well until the four-year mark, when Sarah contracted a rare form of bone cancer and died four months later. The second her heart stopped beating in the upstairs tea room, the power went out in Isabella, and for months, the morning dew held onto the windows throughout the day. Teddy was a hollow shell of his former self; only his love for their boys anchored him in his daily life. Without her salary, the property tax on Isabella made finances tight, so Teddy resorted to drawing on even more of Red's trust to make the payments. The dreams increased, and one day at dawn, while going for a walk on the beach, he crossed the dune bridge to find hundreds of his old messengers, the seagulls, covering the sand, staring straight up at him. They squawked and then turned their heads out to the sea. In an instant, they flew off in unison toward the horizon, disappearing into the rising sun. He waited for them to return, but they never did. It was the motivation he had been waiting for to start searching the Atlantic with *Gold Lip* for the treasure of *La Gracia*, hoping to solve his financial woes.

A crew of honest hunters willing to work for a cheap hourly rate and the promise of a future cut of the treasure was hard to find. Teddy called some old buddies from Miami who agreed to join him, and he dubbed them "the Pearlmakers" after his love of oysters. Growing up in the Deep South, he had acquired an insatiable appetite for the shelled delicacies that no man could equal. He also bought an ROV (remotely operated underwater vehicle) for when they searched in deeper waters. In the six years since they had started hunting, they had found many pieces of the galleon, but nothing of significant value.

Propping his bare, calloused feet up on the stone railing of the porch, he leaned his chair back and observed the sky. The wind blew hard, whispering a secret as it curled over his ear: *a change is coming*. He took out his phone and texted the crew with instructions to meet him at the marina the following day at two o'clock. He'd decided to spend the day working in the Dog House, his work shed.

CHAPTER 2

Cosby Dollarhide, a blond, curly-headed, lanky but fit high school senior, paddled out for another wave. The previous night's storm brought big breaks, but his partner needed small ones. Dog—his short-legged Jack Russell—stood at the front of the board with his tongue blowing in the wind. Cosby turned into a three-foot wave and rose. As they rode the wave, Dog grinned and wagged. They coasted to the shore, where Dog jumped off into the water and yelped for more.

"No boy, you have to sit the big ones out." Cosby leashed Dog, then tied him to a lifeguard stand before running back into the sea. Dog yapped in a high-pitched voice.

Cos paddled out and ducked under three subpar waves. The hot sun felt good on his skin. Then he saw a wave building that looked like an eight-footer.

He turned, paddled into the wave at an angle, and dropped into the barrel; for a moment, time stopped and he felt one with the ocean, beating with the natural rhythm of the universe. When the tube rolled over him, he held his hand for balance on the inside of the cylindrical curl, which appeared like glass being blown as it moved overhead.

He was short coming out of the chute and the tail knocked him sideways. He took a huge breath before going under. The sack thrust him to the bottom in half a second, where he bashed against the ocean floor. He got caught in the undertow and dragged along the bottom like a ragdoll stuck outside a car door. At the mercy of the wave, he relaxed, knowing that tensing up could cause injury. He reached for the leash, but the force of the water was too strong. His knee scraped against something like loose jagged coral, which felt as sharp as metal. The oxygen in his lungs diminished as the pressure held him down. Feeling it ease for a moment, he reached up and managed to grab the cord attached to the board, which bobbed on the surface like a life preserver. Through the force of the current, he climbed the cord to the glimmer of light at the surface. Grabbing onto his board, he paddled to the shore, hobbled over to Dog, and fell down, fatigued. While catching his breath, the small amount of blood coming from his right knee reminded him of the scrape. Something told him that that "coral" was manmade. He had to know, but didn't want to risk going back out. Years on the water had given him a sixth sense for ocean geography, and he could guess that the area sat ten feet from where the big wave was breaking. If he swam out in between waves, he could dive for it.

The waves broke every few minutes. He waited for one to crash before swimming out and tucking his body down to the bottom, pushing hard. His fingers raked through the sand, coming across a broken sand dollar, but no coral. Not wanting to get caught in the undertow again, he swam back up for more air and a view. No wave yet. Ducking to the floor again, his hand touched something rough like coral, but longer and heavier. He grabbed it and returned to the top. Content with the find, he swam back to shore.

Although the object was covered with barnacles, through the crustacean, he made out an antique long-nosed pistol. He walked over to the restrooms and washed it at the outdoor shower spigot and sat down by Dog, flipping it around in his hands.

"This could be from *La Gracia*, Dog."

Jumping up, he grabbed his board and ran to the street where he'd parked his Cannondale mountain bike—white frame, plastered with stickers. Dog followed. He removed a white bandana from the bike's back saddle bags and wrapped the pistol in it, then placed the bundle in one of the bags.

The partners bicycled up Route 1 going north.

Most people called Cosby "Cosmo," a nickname bestowed on him by his physics teacher Tom Thompkins after he observed that the slack-jawed curly-haired blond was spaced out in class. The name spread like wildfire at school, but he didn't care. An outdoorsman who'd rather be catching a wave than parsing equations, unless it had something to do with the arc of a wave or the angle of an overhanging rock, he had little patience for numbers. But words, even foreign ones, added up for him, and he'd always aced his humanities classes.

They passed from the ocean to the oak and palm tree tailored park along the bay, turning onto Mangrove Avenue toward downtown. He was eager to show Teddy the gun, but needed to swing by the high school to check on his physics exam grade.

He coasted down the bustling street where cars lined the storefronts and people breezed by on the sidewalks, shopping and eating. The floating aroma of baking dough tugged his belly to the Malt, a vintage polished airstream on the edge of a green space that served breakfast, juices, and smoothies. He parked his bike out front. While leashing Dog to a telephone pole, he noticed a WANTED sign stapled to the front of it:

FERAL HOG TERRORIZING
FARM ANIMALS, PETS, AND PEOPLE
$25,000 REWARD DEAD OR ALIVE
CALL WILL BURNS

Below Will's name was his number; below that was an outlined drawing of a hog's head in a box—saliva seeping around the hog's great-white-like teeth. Cos shook his head in disbelief and smiled. He ripped the flyer down, folded it, and tucked it in his pocket.

At the Malt, he ordered fresh-squeezed orange juice and a bagel to go. Grease sizzled in the background as steam rose from the griddle.

The Beach Boy's "The Warmth of the Sun" played on a busted up radio that made everything sound like 1964. Watching Miss Jimmy with her red cheeks smear the rosemary butter on his toasted raisin bagel, he overheard two farmers sitting at a picnic table chirping about Half Ton over their lumberjack specials. One with a long, rough face wearing faded Carhartt overalls claimed it was the biggest living thing he'd ever seen. His friend Bill, who had his name stitched on a patch across the chest of his collared shirt stained with black oil smudges, one-upped him by claiming the beast ran in front of his truck on Dog Pound Road near the Willis Plantation chasing after a cat, and he had to swerve off to the side to miss it. Miss Jimmy handed Cos the food with a wide smile and told him she'd slipped two pieces of bacon in there for Dog, and then winked. He thanked her and exited. Dog and he ate outside by the telephone pole. An old grey Dodge truck swirled dust up in the air as it passed, and Cos swore he spotted a butterfly riding on the rim of the truck bed. They finished eating and headed toward the high school.

Yesterday was his final day of exams, and today was the last for many other students. He cruised with his surfboard in one hand and dog following his wheels through the royal palm-covered campus onto the long brick porch where grades were posted to a bulletin board. Stopping in front of it, he got off and leaned his board against the wall.

Students received a three-digit ID number to maintain privacy. He'd passed his humanities classes with flying colors, but math and science were his kryptonite, and his physics exam would determine whether he graduated—a B or better, and he was through. Scanning the grades, his stomach knotted at the clusters of Cs and Ds. He breathed a sigh of relief when he saw a B+ by his number.

"Yes! Freedom at last. I am finally done with this damn place!"

Pedaling across campus, he noticed a crowd of faculty and students staring dumbstruck at a Caterpillar crane carrying Betsy, the school mascot, out through the third floor biology window. A square leather band supported her girth under the belly. He stopped at the edge of the crowd, watching with a baffled stare.

"It's not every day you see a flying cow," a squat freshman said in a high-pitched voice.

A slim senior with dirty blonde hair walked over and stopped beside Cos. He kept watching Betsy, but smelled the lavender perfume and knew who was close by. Last month, Leslie broke up with her boyfriend of two years, Buzz Smith, and Cos had been waiting for the right moment to ask her out.

To say Cos disliked Buzz would be a vast understatement. He had no clue where Leslie and Buzz connected; everyone knew Leslie loved the Dave Matthews Band—sang the Beach Boys' "Kiss Me Baby" every morning in the shower—and in her spare time she volunteered for the Sierra Club, an environmental organization founded by preservationist John Muir. Buzz listened to bad music and cut class to dump Rubbermaid trashcans full of water out of windows onto unassuming freshman. The *arm* was the *only* explanation—she'd lost it in a car accident when she was thirteen. Some people would retreat after such a disfiguration, but not Leslie—she decided she was going to be God's gift to the world by charming everyone, and she was, but perhaps on the inside, she needed the protection of a big guy like Buzz to stop the next car if it ever came.

"Hi Cos, what's going on?" She smiled at him and pointed up at the cow with her good arm.

"Hey Leslie. It's Betsy, the school mascot. I can't believe they did this," he said, baffled.

"This is the best senior prank ever," the freshman replied.

"Why are they taking her out the window?" Leslie's friend asked.

"Cows can walk up stairs, but not down. So they brought in the crane," Cos said.

"That's unbelievable," Leslie remarked.

"Poor Betsy," Leslie's friend exclaimed.

"I don't think she knows what's going on," Cos said.

"She does seem kind of clueless," Leslie said, smiling.

"I bet she's terrified," her friend exclaimed.

Betsy lifted her tail and dropped yesterday's dinner to the ground. They chuckled and the crowd belted out. Dog barked. Leslie noticed him, walked over, and started to pet him. He leaned his head back into her hand.

"Hey Dog, been surfing lately?"

"Yep, we just got done," Cos said.

"I bet you liked that."

"He loves it," Cos said. Dog grinned. "So are you finished with exams?"

"Yes! *Thank God!* I just got out of US History."

"Congratulations! Any summer plans?"

"Oh, not much. I'm going to the everglades in July with the Sierra Club. I'll look for a job here when I get back, maybe at the Honey Bee Farm." She noticed the pistol's nose sticking out of the bandana in the saddlebag. "What's that?"

"I think it's an antique gun I found while surfing today." He picked it up and handed it to her.

"How neat, where did it come from?" She opened the bandana to examine the sea-beaten gun.

"I think it may belong to *La Gracia*, the ship my father has been hunting. Did I ever tell you about that?"

"No—I've heard he was a treasure hunter from people," she said. "You know how everyone in Latch talks." Her hazel eyes fixed on his.

"Oh, I see—they're *talking*."

"No, I didn't mean it like *that*."

"I'm just joking," He smiled and she grinned. "*La Gracia* is a Spanish galleon that sank off the coast here. Dad has been trying to find it for the last six years. The gun is from the ship, probably."

"Well, do you think it's worth any money?" she said, looking it over.

"Probably, I don't know. No, definitely. Probably worth a little. Hey, I am going back to the house to show it to dad. You're welcome to come with me if you want to. He can tell you more about the ship."

"Sure! I'd love to!"

"Great!"

"I'll get my bike. This is so cool," she said, handing him the pistol.

"Thanks." She jetted off while Dog and he waited. Virginia Matthews bounced up behind them.

"Hey Virginia, how's it going?" She walked by, spun, and backpedaled, grinning at him.

"Great, Cos! I only have one more exam left." She thought his question was a flirt and blushed a little. "What's new?" she asked.

"Some guy named Melvin likes you. He calls himself The Melvster. I said I would help him get a date. What'd you think?"

"The Melvster? No way," she said, pointing her finger to her mouth like she was trying to make herself vomit.

"C'mon, give the guy a chance. What's one date, for charity?"

She shook her head while smiling. "One too many," she said and spun forward, bouncing off.

"I told you, Melv, but you wouldn't listen." He shook his head, laughing about his potential imaginary date set up between the heartthrob and Melv—anything to take his attention off Leslie. He watched the crane lower Betsy to the ground. The crowd clapped and cheered in applause; she mooed in celebration.

"Cosby Dollarhide!" a voice screeched from behind. He turned and saw Miss Leavers, her starched shirt stuffed into a long dress. "Get that flea bag off this campus right now!"

"Okay."

"Some nerve you have bringing him here! Ten percent of kids are 90 percent of the problem, and *you're* the 10 percent, Cosby! Don't you know what happens to dreamers like you?"

"I hadn't thought about it, really." Sitting on his bike, he put on his sunglasses and stared at her casually.

"They end up broke and alone with no one and nothing, not even a stray cat to keep them company. Now get that rodent out of here!"

He shook his head and began to pedal off. Leslie rode her mountain bike over; together, they cycled off the campus and toward the bay.

"Was Miss Leavers giving you a hard time?"

"Yeah."

"Don't worry, she's like that with everyone. I saw her in a mirror once and she didn't even show a reflection."

"Good thing she can't see how scary she is."

They continued until they reached Route 1, which they followed north along the rugged ocean terrain.

After a while, he challenged her to a race to see who could make it to Orange Street first; it was an ambitious challenge, considering the surfboard. She accepted, and when he yelled "GO," they pedaled hard. Her shining hair flew in the wind as she raced past him on the mountain bike. Cos managed to keep up with her, but she beat him there by a good ten feet.

They turned left onto Orange, heading inland on a white sandy road. Green tropical plants and short trees forested the edges; scattered beach houses of different sizes and colors hid behind the vegetation. Cos saw a *Bateman and Banks Lot for Sale* sign sticking out from a spread of thick jungle and hit his brakes. Across the road ahead, four other new signs had sprung up.

The land around Isabella's sixty acres had been chopped up a few years ago, and countless signs had staked plots in the area, but the poorly designed beach houses were only a minor irritation for the Dollarhides. For three years, Bateman and Banks Realty had been petitioning Teddy to sell Isabella so they could use the acreage to overlap Casablanca, a $150 million condo development. They sent, called, and knocked with offers all the time. Teddy just folded the petitions into paper airplanes and sailed them to the trashcan, but in the last couple of weeks, his bin had become something of a hangar, and the calls were becoming more pressing, almost aggressive.

"Damn it, new signs!" Cos said.

"Why do you care?"

"Bateman and Banks want to replace this whole jungle with bad houses, and they have plans to build a condo here that's so large it'll have its own water park on top of *our* land. They won't quit harassing my father about it. If they get their way, this virgin coast will be a circus." Walking over to the sign, he jerked it up and slid it inbetween the two saddlebags.

"Oh, I didn't know they were harassing y'all. You're *pulling it up?*" she said with a slight smirk.

"We pull them all up, for our collection. They replace them quickly, but we're gonna keep doing it until they stop bothering us."

"But they have a right to buy and sell this land, you know."

"Sure, but the way they do it is wrong. Their houses are overpriced crap, and they butcher the land to build them. Dad is a free market guy, so he'd be okay with it otherwise," he said, and paused. "Now, when people come here to the beach, it's like a nature preserve, you know?"

"I see what you mean. It does feel special here, like how Florida might have been when the Native Americans were roaming around. When I am in the glades, I get that same feeling. It's kind of romantic."

"That's exactly what I am saying. Did you know fireflies still light up here at night?"

"*Yes! I love them.*"

"You know how you can see every star in the sky on a cloudless night from the beach here?"

"Yeah, well, you can't beat that," she said.

"Well, that will all change if they put big, bright condos here," he said, waving his arms at all the surrounding vegetation.

"Yeah, it's pretty sweet being able to see the stars. Did you know you can find your location from any point in the world by them?"

"Celestial navigation? Of course; it's how captains took fleets around the world before GPS."

"That's right," she confirmed.

"You're cool, Leslie. Most girls our age don't know much about this kind of stuff." His intrigue and attraction grew.

"Thanks, Cos—most guys don't know about it either," she said and blushed a little, kicking the heel of her Chuck Taylor on the ground. Cos looked at Dog.

"Dog, get to it." Dog jumped out and crossed the street, lifted his leg on the first For Sale sign and sprinkled it, then he watered the next one, and so on, going down the line.

"Gooood boy," Cos praised. Meanwhile, a black Cadillac Escalade with tinted windows slowly came to a stop behind them.

"Hey, stop that mutt!" a man with matte black Ray-Ban sunglasses yelled out the driver's window. "Those are our signs!"

Cos pushed the surfboard in front of the sign on the back of his bike and saw Stern Banks.

"Are you the little runt that's been jerking up our signs?" Stern asked Cos through the open passenger window.

"No, sir."

"You're lying to me, boy. Are you that wharf rat's son? Tell him, if he doesn't sell soon, he's going to get what's coming to him. And I am going to have that dog shot the next time I see him whizzing on my signs!"

"Dog? You couldn't catch him if you tried, mister."

"Watch me, boy." Stern stared at Cos for a whole minute to convey something he could never say out loud. Then, he peeled off, revealing his personalized license plate: SOLD.

"Wow, what a jerk," Leslie said.

"Now do you see what we're dealing with?"

"Yeah, but you *were* pulling up their signs."

"Still, it's incredible."

"I know."

They started to pedal again.

"So, are you going to the beach graduation party?" he asked.

"If my parents don't have any plans for me."

"Great, we'll hang out."

"I'd like that," she said, looking down and back up at him, smiling; he grinned and they pedaled on, riding closer now. After about 150 yards, they whipped down Windswept, following it a short way before arriving at Isabella.

From the road, Isabella concealed herself behind a twenty-foot bamboo hedge, save for a slight view through an iron gate, which was frequently left wide open for the Pearlmakers. They entered and cruised down the property's ground oyster shell road; palm trees dotted the driveway in a tightly cut green lawn. At the auto court of the house, the road circled around a hexagonal fountain.

Isabella was a sprawling Italian Mediterranean villa; the exterior wall was constructed of white stucco; terra cotta colored ceramic clay tiles cascaded down the roof. Palm trees, bananas, sago palms, and flowers grew all along the grounds. Plump fruit weighed down branches of various trees and brilliant red roses bloomed underneath the downstairs windows, the smell touching one's nose in the driveway.

"This place is unbelievable, Cosmo!" Leslie gasped, almost dropping her bike.

"Thanks—we make it work."

Hearing a noise, Dog darted off into the distance to patrol the land for varmints, which he practically lived off. He despised being indoors, leaving it for the weaker human species. Unless there was a storm, he stayed in his wooden doghouse by the barn, where he could chase the rats and snakes around the hay. Teddy fed him dog food, but he didn't eat it *really*—instead, he sometimes flipped the bowl over with his paw, scattering the dried pebbles on the ground; then, he tucked away into the shadows of his cave, waiting with patient eyes until a rodent crept up to nibble—then he attacked.

Leslie turned around and saw the barn and Dog's doghouse across from Isabella. On the other side of it sat a workshop. In front of them stood an ancient oak tree, squat and wide and host to an elaborate tree house that had two levels and a swinging bridge connecting the loft-like structures atop it. Electric current ran to it through cables, while big screened windows offered ventilation. Part of an old ship stuck off the first level to the side facing the entrance to the property and the words *Uncle Benny* had been painted across the bottom in black cursive with gold highlights.

"I love the tree house!" she exclaimed, pointing to it.

"That's my big brother Joey's place."

"Your dad built it for him?"

"No, Jojo did most of the work himself, while he was in high school. He always wanted to live in a tree. He's kind of a monkey."

"That's great that your dad let him. I mean, my parents wouldn't."

"Yeah, Dad has always encouraged us to follow our dreams. I want you to meet him. Let's go in and show him the gun."

"Okay."

They leaned the bikes up against the exterior and Cosby removed the pistol and the *Lot for Sale* sign. They entered through the tall mahogany door. At the bottom was a doggy door carved into the dense wood for Dog and their Manx cat, Bear.

"Home sweet home!" he said as they walked down the entrance hall. Fifteen-foot ceilings stretched into the air; bulky brown Spanish clay tiles spanned the floors down the hall into the living room, where they transitioned into thick mahogany planks. Antique paintings hung on white plastered walls, and mahogany timber beams criss-crossed the plastered ceilings.

"This house is *so* beautiful!"

"Thank you. It's old, but Dad has kept it up," Cosby said, looking around with Leslie's fresh eyes. "It requires a lot of maintenance, *and* Joey and I end up doing most of the work."

"That's nice of y'all."

Cos turned to her smiling, "It's *not* optional—he makes us. Since he inherited the house, he can't afford to pay people to fix it, so it's one of our duties. It's child labor, really. I should have him taken in. Do you want something to drink?"

"Sure."

"Follow me." Going down the hall, they walked through the living room and exited to the right into the dining room, which had windows that overlooked the indoor swimming pool and back porch. Cos called for Teddy, but got no reply. He continued into the kitchen.

Leslie leaned her elbow on the ten-foot-long oak island and applied Chapstick to her lips, while Cos poured them iced glasses of freshly squeezed lemonade. Cos noticed a note scribbled by Charlotte, their maid, stating she had gone out to the grocery store to get supplies for the night's dinner. The two drank the cold lemonade.

"This house is extraordinary, Cos! I just can't get over it."

"Thanks, glad you like it. Let's go see what Teddy thinks about the gun. He's probably out back in the Dog House."

She straightened. "Okay—wait—did you say he's in the Dog

House?"

"Well, it's not really a doghouse. You'll see."

They exited through the side kitchen door onto the stone porch and made toward the barn, passing the chicken coop.

"Look at those cute chickens."

"Rhode Island Reds, they're the best chickens. We let them free range. You should come over for breakfast sometime and I'll cook you an omelete. I can cook the perfect omelete."

"That would be nice," she said as they made eye contact.

"Is that a yes?"

"I'll think about it," she said, teasing him a bit.

"*All right*, playing hard to get already and we're not even dating. Just friends."

"Only friends?" she asked, hiding her concern.

"Yeah, I am just looking for a running buddy now. It's *so* nice to have a girl I can just talk to with the pressure off," he said with a straight face. She looked confused.

"I am joking, I am joking. Come on, girl." They came to the workshop and Cos knocked on the wall to the side of the screen door. A crooked wooden sign hung above the door with the words *The Dog House* burned into it; Dog came over from the yard with a bright green lizard tail hanging out of his mouth.

"Come on in!" Teddy boomed from inside.

With Cos holding the screen door for Leslie, she entered and Dog wiggled in after.

"Cos!" Teddy exclaimed with a big grin; he sat on a stool, looking up over his reading glasses, holding a plain ring in his fingers. A steering wheel from an abandoned ship leaned in the corner of the shop, an old bronze diver's helmet rested on the table, and a rack mounted on the ceiling held at least twenty different fishing poles as well as raw wood, spare ceramic tiles, and scrap wood. Tools hung from the pegboard all across one wall, along with two spearfishing bows. In the corner, a gold cage dangled from the ceiling with a blue macaw skirting back and forth. The smell of sandalwood and sawdust hung in the air.

Teddy's skin had the color and texture of worn suede, but without the lines. He rose to greet them.

"Hi Dad, this is Leslie."

"Hi Leslie, it's very nice to meet you. I would shake your hand, but…" He held up his calloused palm, showing her the polishing wax; she noticed he had so many intersecting lines, twice the average person, that he could make a palm reader dizzy.

"That's all right. It's a pleasure to meet you as well," Leslie added. Teddy paid no attention to her lack of an arm.

"It's not too often we have a nice girl around here."

"Oh r-e-a-l-l-y," she said, turning to Cos and smiling.

"No, the only thing Cos ever brings home is that damn dog, and he's usually wet and full of fleas. Not very pleasing on the eyes, either."

"No girls *ever*?"

"*Never.* One day, he trapped a female raccoon outside, but that's about as close as he's ever gotten to love." Teddy gave a wide grin, winking at her.

"Go on you two, drink it up, drink it up. I've dated, I just didn't bring them home because I was too embarrassed by someone's perpetual *shirtlessness*," Cos stressed.

"It's not me, it's you. It's not me, it's you." Teddy paused, smiling. "Well Leslie, you're welcome here at Isabella anytime."

"Thank you! I am enjoying seeing everything. I really love the house. How many rooms are there?"

"Isabella has that effect on most people. She has twenty rooms … twenty or twenty-one … I lose count. It's not just her size that gets to you, it's her soul. She's like, *alive!*"

"I think I felt that."

"Well, you're not alone."

"Can I ask why y'all call this the Dog House?" Leslie asked.

"You see, many years ago, when my beloved wife Sarah, God rest her soul, would get mad at me, I would come out here to be quiet and her friends said I was like a bad dog going to the doghouse, and well, I guess the name stuck."

"That's great," Leslie said, pleased by the explanation.

"So what are y'all getting into today?"

"Not much. I got this for you." Cos handed Teddy the for sale sign. Teddy grinned and took it.

"Thanks son, another one for the boneyard." He walked over and speared it into the hanging rack with about twenty others before turning back to them.

"Plus, you're not going to believe what I found while surfing today." Cos took the bandana-wrapped gun and unfolded it on the worktable.

Teddy put on his tortoise readers. "You found this in the surf?

"Yep."

"Oh my—very impressive, son." Focusing on the gun, he plopped back down on the stool and swung over the large magnifying lamp.

"Is it from *La Gracia*?" Cos asked.

"Probably. We'll clean the crust off, then work on dating it. Where did you find it?"

"South of the bay where the best wave breaks are. Near the lighthouse."

"Really?!" He paused, spinning it around in his hands. "The storm must have blown it in. That's about three miles south of where I've been hunting."

"Storms can move ships?" Leslie asked.

"Oh yes my dear, storms have blown in all sorts of treasures. They can carry them for miles." He paused. "You have no idea how much this means to me, son." He smiled and glanced up at Cos over his glasses and then looked back down, studying the pistol for another moment. "I'll start searching in that area right away. I knew today was going to be special. The wind told me. I keep waiting for those damn seagulls to return with another clue, but they never do. They hate me."

"Cos tells me you're looking for a ship that sunk, Mr. Dollarhide?"

"Call me Teddy or Old Salt or Salt or *anything* other than mister."

"Okay, Teddy."

"Thank you. Sportfishing is my main job, but in my spare time, I search for *La Gracia*, a Spanish galleon that went down in the late seventeenth century."

"Interesting! Everyone in my family sails. I would love to hear the story."

"*La Gracia*," Teddy exclaimed with a faraway look in his eyes, wandering into his dreams for a moment. "Admiral García Díaz was in charge of her. She was the pride of a wealthy Spanish prince who commissioned his shipmaster to build him the most impressive galleon to ever sail, but from the beginning, things went terribly wrong with construction. The weather was blazing hot and the men were in agony. A supply wagon carrying the sails from a nearby tailor got robbed and burned. Halfway through construction, lightning struck the deck, setting it on fire, and they had to start all over."

"Good Lord, Dad, you never told me all of that!"

"That's not all! Workers died, too. One fell to his death while erecting the mast; a cannon tipped over on another, crushing his skull. Everyone felt the bad vibe and the shipmaster begged the prince to stop, but he refused. Stubborn bastard. It took years of backbreaking work by hundreds of skilled craftsmen, but they finally produced a ship that took people's breath away. And she sailed off from the port of Seville to a crowd of roaring cheers on her christening. She had collected riches from South America and Cuba and was on her way to North America to gather more gold when she got caught in a brutal hurricane. Out of the vast number on board, only a few made it to shore. The ship carried over twenty-five hundred pounds of gold and an undisclosed amount of silver."

"Whoa!" Leslie said in amazement, stuck to Teddy's every word.

"And there's even more. Gold was the most common smuggled metal, so probably eight times that amount was actually on board. Her metal alone would bring hundreds of millions by today's standards."

"Wowzers!" Leslie exclaimed.

"And that's just the metal. The ship had jewels too," Cos added, nudging Leslie.

"Yes sir. It's rumored there were chests full of emeralds and pearls, and trunks containing valuable antiques."

"It's a gold cove master ship," remarked Cos. "One of the largest and least known treasures ever lost at sea."

"No one has ever found any of it?" Leslie asked, her eyes wide with the thought of riches.

"Only us," Teddy emphasized. "Even historians doubt whether our small finds came from *La Gracia*; many people believe it's a smoke ship—a legend. We have only been able to get small funding for it. No one will really back us, so we're using less than optimal equipment for it. Mainly the magnetometers and sonar and a used ROV I bought online."

"What will you do with the money when you find it?"

"Buy a house in the French Antilles, pay someone to manage this place, and put a lot into charities."

"Don't forget the Sierra Club. We do great work! I work there in the summer. Down in the Everglades."

"I'll remember it. Now, we haven't found it yet," he said, smiling at her.

"Hopefully you'll find it soon," Leslie said.

"Hopefully." He smiled and leaned back on the stool. "So, are y'all getting ready for graduation tomorrow?"

"Yep! Can't wait," Leslie said.

"Good."

"Hey Dad, I passed my final!" Cos said.

"Congratulations, son!"

"Thanks, Dad!"

The royal blue macaw in the corner sang pieces of a Jimmy Buffett song. Dog ran over to the cage, wagging his tail and barking at it.

"That talking bird is funny," she said. Cos walked over to the cage with her.

"That's old Blue," Teddy explained. "He's old now, still sharp as a tack though. Been with me through everything. Got him in Panama when I was there before college. Because of his age, he's sort of a jukebox."

"Dog, get down, leave Blue alone," Cos said.

"Fruitcake," the bird chirped again, laughing at Dog, Cos, and Leslie. Teddy turned around with a smile.

"He hates Dog and Dog hates him. Dog would eat him if he had the chance," Teddy said.

"Fruitcake," the bird chirped.

Leslie laughed.

"Oh Dad, I almost forgot." Cos took out the WANTED poster and unfolded in front of him. Teddy and Leslie both read it. "I thought you'd get a kick out of this."

"*Twenty-five thousand?!* Will Burns must really want that hog dead."

"He was first spotted near the Willis Plantation, so everyone thinks he's possessed or something," Leslie said.

"Oh, that's a bunch of crap," Teddy said.

"Yeah, I know what you mean," Leslie said.

"I am thinking about going over to the Willis Plantation to hunt him for the reward," Cos exclaimed.

"No, son." Teddy's face became serious. "Don't ever go to that place. It's got bad juju."

"But you just said…"

"I know what I said, but I was talking about the hog, not the plantation. That place has been haunted ever since the butterflies left."

"With ghosts?"

"I don't know." He paused. "You know, everything in this town was different before the butterflies left."

"I saw one today," Cos exclaimed.

"What?" Teddy's head jerked up.

"A butterfly."

"That's impossible. It must have been a moth," Teddy insisted.

"No, I am *pretty sure* it was a butterfly."

"It *was* a moth. There are no butterflies here and there never will be any, there aren't even caterpillars wanting to be butterflies—not even the stinging kind. Just stay away from the plantation, okay?" Teddy exclaimed.

"Okay, okay, lighten up, Dad; I won't go to the plantation … but I do think I saw a butterfly."

Teddy glared at him for a moment. "When does Jojo get here tomorrow?"

"10 a.m."

"Good; I probably won't see him until later in the afternoon because I'll be busy," Teddy said.

Leslie looked at her watch.

"I've gotta get home. Tonight's my sister's sixteenth birthday, and we're having a backyard cookout. I have to help set up. It was so fun hearing about the treasure and your job!"

"Certainly Leslie. It was a pleasure meeting you."

"You too," Leslie said.

"I'll let you know about the gun," Teddy said to Cos as he followed her out.

"Thanks, Dad."

Outside, Cos asked, "So are you coming to the baseball game tomorrow night? It's our qualifier for the regionals."

"I'll be there!"

"Great!"

"I had fun today," she said.

"Me too," he said, and watched her peddle off down the driveway.

THE NEXT DAY, Teddy had insisted he would meet Joey at Cosby's graduation. He was very tired for some reason and needed to rest, so he decided to take a nap on the Dog House's sofa with his cat Bear perched on his stomach.

Ram worked the bailing line of the ship. Fatigue shot through his muscles and joints, and his waterlogged shirt weighed down his arms, making it hard to lift the pail. The saltwater clouded and stung his eyes. Strong waves and winds frequently sent him and the bailers sliding back and forth across the floor like marionettes. An officer stepped down through the hatch into the humid galley and yelled to the line for a progress report. The foreman, a bearded muscle-bound man named José, answered in a booming voice, "It rises faster than we can bail, but we're doing our best!"

"Keep working!" he barked over the noise outside. "It'll let up soon!" He exited.

Instructed to retrieve the box for Admiral Díaz, who was now on the deck fighting the violent hurricane, Ram noticed Oscar, the Admiral's pet monkey, enter the room and begin rummaging around the chests, the chest key tight in his black paw. Ram watched him make his way among the sweaty bailing crew. Eventually, he came to the Admiral's chest—a tall square one decorated with a myriad of colors. He stuck the big key in the lock, turned it, and opened the lid, the way he had been trained to do a thousand times before that moment. As he sifted through the contents, he picked up each object, examined it for a moment, and concluding it wasn't the box, threw it over his shoulder; clothes, an ornate silver handheld mirror, and necklaces all went flying. Seeing some jewels packed tightly in gold urns and vases, he picked up a sapphire, bit it, and then tossed it at Ram's back. Ram turned and glared at Oscar, who showed his big teeth. Furious, Ram stomped over and pushed him off the chest. Oscar cowered in the corner and waited for him to leave, then he skirted back over to the chest and found the illustrious box near the bottom. Tucking it under his arm, he made for the hatch. As he neared the opening, a mammoth wave threw the ship to the side. He went flying back; Ram and the crew fell, too, as water rushed in.

The vessel lay sideways. The hatch to the upper deck began to draw water into the body of the ship. Chests filled with gold and jewels toppled and broke open, spilling into the rising water; pearls skated across the floor; a cannon burst out of a wooden box and rolled onto Ram's leg, pinning him down. He grabbed it in pain and opened his mouth to scream, but he didn't have the breath. Rising, the conscious crewmembers waded to the hatch, not knowing Ram was trapped in the corner.

After Ram regained some strength, he yelled out for help, but everyone had already climbed out and above to the side of the ship, which was now a makeshift deck. The saltwater crept up to his chest as he continued to cry out. After ten minutes of calling and struggling to free his throbbing leg, he relaxed with the water at his chin. Tilting his head back, he gained some inches on it. On the floor next to him, he noticed some gold coins and pearls, which he stuffed into his pant pockets. When they were full, he tore off his sleeve, made a pouch of it, and, after loading it with ten pounds of coin, tied a knot in the other end and tucked it in his waistline.

On the other side of the room, Oscar lay on a box, dizzy; he shook his wet head and rubbed the sore part that hit the wall. With the Admiral's box still tucked loosely under his other arm, he rose and climbed from one partially submerged box to another toward the hatch. As he neared it, Ram cried out in the corner. Oscar halted, saw Ram, and climbed over to him, stopping on a box. Seeing the wedged cannon, he waited. He leaned down and reached his arm deep into the water, grabbing some gold coin, which he stuffed into the front pocket of his wet white monkey shirt.

"What are you going to do with that?" Ram remarked under his breath, but Oscar just showed his teeth.

Ram saw a slim scraggly crewmember lowering in to steal some treasure before the ship went down. He made his way over to a wooden chest, busted into it, and filled a rice bag with emeralds, rubies, and what must have been ten pounds of gold. Seeing him, Oscar squealed; when the man made eye contact, the monkey ushered him over with his black paw, jerking his head toward Ram. The man waded over.

"Ram? Is that you?"

"Y-e-ss."

Seeing the cannon and the water below his lips, he tried to move the artillery while Oscar watched.

"It's too heavy, I'll go for help." He waded to the hatch and climbed out. Oscar waited with Ram. A moment later, the man returned with José and another man; the three of them together were able to hoist the cannon off Ram's leg. With the monkey leading, they helped him through the hatch. In the food storage room, the monkey came upon a blue bottle of wine floating in the water next to a few jars of olive oil, and stopped. The men became frustrated and ushered the monkey on, but he paused and insisted, mesmerized by the wine. He had once snagged a glass of wine that a sailor had left unattended by climbing through an opened cabin window. He remembered how good he felt that day, sunbathing in the crow's nest with heavy eyes. The men pressed on, while the monkey tended to the wine.

On the makeshift deck, Ram and the men passed the crew who had been dismantling pieces of the destroyed ship to use as rafts. They stopped near Díaz to watch the four rescue boats being loaded amid the pounding rain.

Díaz noticed Ram's hurt leg and assigned him a seat in a boat. "You, next."

"No, I won't go before the others who were here before me."

"What are you, stupid? You'll die floating out there with that leg! Take it!" he said, looking at him with a stern eye. Ram agreed and thanked him. He noticed the regal seal on the pocket of the jacket: a circle with a cross marked through it and a lion's head above the top of it. Díaz spun the knob on his pocket watch clockwise, but not to wind it.

"Why did you do that?" Ram asked.

"I spin it for luck!" he barked. "Wait a minute. There's something important I want you to take to shore." Ram nodded his assent. In a moment, Oscar came around to Díaz's side.

"Where's the box?" Díaz asked. Oscar shook his head in the negative and pointed down below.

Díaz grunted, almost laughing, "Have you been drinking again?"

The monkey held his fingers up indicating a pinch. "Never send a monkey to do a man's job. Well, there's nothing we can do about it now." Oscar climbed up Díaz's wet jacket sleeve to his broad shoulder, where he sat. Then, Díaz waved Ram off to two men who helped lower him into one of the overstuffed boats. The oarsmen pushed away toward the invisible coastline, belting "Good luck" to the men on the ship. The nose of the little boat pointed to the sky and dipped back down as it floated over mammoth swells. Ram looked up at the furious sky, watching it roar and rage. Sadness overtook him as he felt there was something he was leaving behind—something very important, and it wasn't Díaz's box. He couldn't remember what it was, so he closed his eyes. The world went black.

Teddy jerked up on the sofa, his eyes big and round. The sound of the storm reverberated in his mind like an annoying vacuum. He looked around his room for the wet men or the monkey, but everything was dry and empty. Grabbing his aching leg, he glanced down and saw the birthmark in the same place that the cannon had landed. He shook his head, glanced at his watch, and, realizing Cosby's graduation was thirty minutes away and that he had slept through the morning—he jumped up, ran his hand through his hair, stroked his beard and headed out the door.

CHAPTER 3

*J*oey Dollarhide forgot how hot Florida got in the summer, and this summer was even hotter than usual, with every day breaking the previous record for that date. He watched his brother Cosby receive his diploma at the graduation service that afternoon with his father, and the after-party was now underway at Lover's Bay Park, with the Florida sun beating down on the assembly like a hot bleeding furnace.

For the past four years, Joey had been at UCLA. In his senior year at Latch High, he was the best hitter in the state, taking the Indians to a regional championship, which earned him a full ride with the UCLA Bruins. His junior year at UCLA, he was supposed to be the next big ball sensation after a YouTube video of a 575-foot bomb he slugged during a UCLA Bruins versus Oregon Ducks game went viral, but he tore his ACL before the last game of the season and it required surgery. And he hadn't torn it sliding into home plate or diving for a line drive—he tore it by accidentally running his bicycle into the Oregon Ducks mascot while waving at a girl across campus. He told the coach it was a surfing accident, but an ecology student was videotaping a group falconry project outside and captured the whole thing in the background. Then, she did him the lovely "favor"—her words—

of uploading it to YouTube. Now the "Oregon Duck Hunt" video had more views than his big bomber. Although his leg felt fine now, the doctors said he could never play again without reinjuring it. Goodbye majors, hello forestry. A solid collegiate career with a depressing end, but he felt better now in Latch's arms—like slipping into a broken-in pair of leather shoes.

For young people in Latchawatchee, the aura of summer started with the graduation celebration for the seniors and their families at the postcard park on the water. All the students from Latch High attended; food vendors of all types had booths, white tents with tables were sprawled across the grass lawn. The park was the perfect setting for the event, with its wide oaks and limbs that dripped with hanging silver moss, robust palms, and manicured lawn. Violets, milkweed, and banana plants nestled in beds with a path that snaked alongside them. A Moorish tiled fountain sat in the center of the park surrounded by a rose garden featuring white, red, and yellow blooms.

As Joey navigated the maze of bodies, many dressed in black graduation gowns, acquaintances gave him an elbow pound and old friends hugged him. Some young ladies tucked their hair behind their ears and tailed him, asking if he was going to the beach party tomorrow. He told them yes with a smile, but in the back of his mind he was concerned that *she* would be there.

Annabelle "Belle" Burns had transferred to Latch her senior year from College Station, Texas. Her father was a Texas high school dropout who rolled the dice wildcatting with his savings when he was twenty-two and struck the black gold lotto. With over one hundred million in the bank twenty-five years later, he decided to move the family to Florida to semi-retire, take a stab at real estate, and manage his wells from a distance. A young but lucrative and growing real estate company based out of Jacksonville, Bateman and Banks, had contacted him in search of an angel investor. After agreeing to meet them, they picked him up at dusk on a seventy-foot Sunseeker yacht at the marina, got him drunk on Ketel One and caviar, and made a proposal. Dazzled by their big returns, Ivy-League connections, and Zegna shoes, the cowboy from Texas was sold. Maybe he felt that being connected to them somehow validated him, for with all the millions, a new last name was the one thing he hadn't been able to buy—and he wanted to be *old* money. When he wasn't on the phone, he spent his days golfing in Latch or yachting to the Bahamas. His daughters, Belle, Paige, and Courtney, lived a life of four-course meals and designer ensembles.

From the moment Joey first saw Belle swishing down the hall their senior year of high school, she struck him like lightning cracking a tree. She was a master at make-believe, and he, a seasoned dreamer. The world was her stage, and the people around her were characters in the story of her life; everyone else was a faithful audience along for the adventure. Her story was about the sea, and her blue eyes were a door to the ocean. On the stage of her imagination, anything was possible—even the mundane laws of nature didn't apply to her. Her auburn hair was like a prop, hanging down to her butt and whipping like a horse's tail as she walked. Some days it seemed a lot shorter, too—when she wanted it to be. She was five foot eight, had a big cartoonish mouth, and ears that stuck out to the sides. Joey liked how angelic she looked, but it was her creative mind that crushed him.

He'd wasted no time asking her out, but Zach Watts beat him to it. To Joey's bewilderment, they stayed together all throughout senior year, breaking up just before graduation. The next week, a friend invited Joey and Cos on a Catalina cruise at sunset and Belle came along with her friend Natasha. Joey slipped into the deep end every time he looked in Belle's aqua eyes. When the boat took a quick turn, she fell into him, spilling her drink on his shirt; he braced her fall by taking her hand, and they laughed at the touch. On the way back to the harbor, she got a chill from the wind and he let her borrow his windbreaker. She was leaving the next week for an internship in Paris, and he was going to the Bruins' training camp in Los Angeles. He called her and they quickly became friends. One day, she mentioned a Parisian she was dating, and Joey kicked over a trashcan and started dating his new best friend in Malibu, the sponsored surfer Adrianna. Adrianna was athletic, sweet, Greek, spoke four languages, and he loved her, but when he looked into her brown eyes, he wasn't in the deep end. There were things about life that he couldn't talk to her about—things he sensed Belle would understand. When he went home for breaks, he saw Belle here and there, and magic always seemed to follow them. In the spring, she Facetimed him the day after she broke up with the Parisian whom she had dated long-distance for a while after returning to the University of Texas, but Joey was still with Adrianna. Her heart dropped and she sighed, but she had trouble seeing past the long distance anyway. Joey broke up with Adrianna a couple of months later; but by the time he Facetimed Belle, she was dating someone new. Fate had been a terrible foe once again.

She was like the ocean coming to him with the tide, and he was the sand. When they connected, she would soften his rough exterior and when she rolled away, she would take a little mica with her, holding the pieces of him until they were lost in the vastness of her. And he would cling to her saltwater until it evaporated off his surface, and then, empty and longing, they would need each other again. And so the tide rolled in and out, and the sand waited patiently for the day when the ocean would rise and they could be one.

The chemistry peaked last July at a mutual friend's wedding in Montana where they made each other laugh so hard they began to cry, falling on the floor, unable to catch their breath. When they looked up at each other red-eyed and sore faced, they were both in the deep end and wanting to go deeper. He petted her hair and she closed those aqua eyes and slinked her arms around his strong shoulders, but when his lips got close, she pulled away, stood up, and ran out the door into the rain, crying, because she was still taken and he lived too far away. He followed after her, but she jumped into her car and retreated into the sea again. And her play went on, and Joey realized hers was a love story and he was the male lead. Only this time, when the memory of her left him, he wouldn't wait. He had his own story to live; the dramatic short scenes where their stories overlapped couldn't sustain him.

So senior year he dated, did some light surfing his leg could sustain on the weekends, and studied hard. He and Belle didn't talk or write, and by spring, he had learned to forget about her. When he booked his ticket home for Cosmo's graduation and a friend told him Annabelle Burns was single again, he shrugged it off with as much care as if they had told him it was going to rain.

Wiggling through the crowd of familiar faces with a big grin, he finally spotted Cos with Dog, talking to some friends.

"Cosmo!" Joey shouted.

Cos turned and saw him. "Jojo!" Opening their arms, they walked toward each other.

"Congratulations! Damn it's good to see you!" Joey said as they hugged, smiling.

"Thanks! You too. Man, I've *really* missed you."

"I've missed you too. It's a nice day to graduate."

"It sure is, but it's hot. Every day breaks a new record."

"That's what I hear. I love it though. I miss a 90-degree day."

"So you're finally done with UCLA?"

"Yep, it's been great, but I've taken a lot of shit about the duck video. Someone even made T-shirts."

"Tees? Ouch, I am sorry to hear it."

"Yeah, but I've got tough skin. Lately, I've really missed Isabella, you, and Dog."

"And Teddy?"

"*And even Dad*. We stood next to each other during the ceremony, but he had to meet The Pearlmakers at the marina afterwards and we didn't get to catch up, really. He told me he'd catch us back at the house."

"Yeah, the old man missed the sea too much. Actually, I found a pistol while surfing the other day and showed it to him. He thinks it may be from *La Gracia*."

"*Really?* Was it one of those old long-nosed pistols?"

"Yes sir, gold finished too."

"Where'd you find it?"

"South of the bay near the lighthouse. He's going to start searching there today."

"Sweet."

Joey reached down and picked up Dog by the stomach, holding

him against his V-neck T-shirt; his tongue hung out as he craned his head back.

"Hey little buddy, it's been a long time."

"Dog and I caught some good waves today from the storm two days ago. It's still a third the size of a Mavericks wave, but big for Florida. Did you hear about Hurricane Eliza?"

"Just a little on the news in the Houston airport."

"She started out as a small tropical, but she's all grown up now. Supposed to make landfall early morning the day after tomorrow."

"Ouch, that's bad."

"I know. But, it sounds like the annual beach bash tomorrow night is still on."

"Yeah, all of the alumni are going to be there. You want to break open some cold ones?"

"Of course. What's going on tonight?" Cos said.

"I just want to eat oysters with the old man and go swimming."

"Sounds good to me. Walk with me. I got to find Wolly."

"Sure, how is big Wolly?"

"The same, but bigger. He can barely round the bases now," Cos said, and Joey laughed.

Walking through the crowd, they passed various tents set up in the park. Dog trotted by Cos's side on a tight leash. Wooden booths showcased fresh pies and delicacies baked by competitive old women displaying their skills.

They passed the center of the park where a crowd gathered, gazing in a concerned manner at the fountain, which bubbled with white foam overflowing onto the concrete around it. The smell of laundry detergent burned their nostrils; Dog sneezed. Two police officers with flat tops drilled a lanky thirteen-year-old wearing an Affliction shirt and baggy jeans about the incident. Cos and Joey grinned as they walked by.

"Someone pulled another bubble bath prank with laundry detergent in the fountain," Cos said.

"Not as original as the cow—I heard about that one."

"I can't believe the boys did that, the teachers are pissed about it,"

Cos whispered, looking around. "I drove them out to campus, but they said they didn't know what they were going to do. I had no idea. Shhhhh. Don't tell anyone I was there." He looked around to the sides.

"You were there. Ha! Don't worry about it." He gestured with his hands. "If you didn't know and didn't help, you're clear."

They kept walking and passed a Disneyland-style line in front of Dan's World Famous Fried Chicken booth. Dan, a short man from Breaux Bridge, Louisiana, with a bald head that reflected light, took orders, counting them with his fingers in the air in a thick Cajun accent. His stomach was a portable advertisement for the irresistibility of his chicken and biscuits, for "that boy has tore up some biscuits," as Teddy liked to point out. Despite the restaurant's fast food décor of lipstick red booths and highlighter yellow walls, people came from all over the Southeast to try his fried chicken. A swank New York chef once got wind of it, offering Dan fifty thousand dollars for the recipe. Dan said the figure was embarrassing and called the man a "thieving yellow-bellied scoundrel" before challenging him to "just bring it on down to Florida for a fistful of manners." In fact, practically the only time Dan wasn't irate was when he was singing Broadway show tunes around the kitchen.

Cos had worked the fryer and driven the delivery truck for Dan since the tenth grade. He disliked it with a passion, but it was easy money and he was given free access to the car. As long as he made his deliveries, he could use the car for some personal things.

Cos ducked behind the crowd to avoid Dan's eye, and Joey followed. They spotted Wolly talking to Paige, Belle's younger sister, standing under a tree beside the One Hundred Egg Cake stand. She twiddled her brunette hair with one hand and laughed at everything Wolly said, touching his arm with the other hand—her biggest competition was his plate of chicken.

Joey and Cos approached as Belle glided over from the side with a plate of cake, the ground glowing beneath her step. The sight of her split an atom in Joey's sleeping heart. In one year, Annabelle Burns had passed through that mysterious realm from immature girl to confident young woman, and her new presence leveled Joey—his face went numb and his mouth felt like he had been chewing on gum for hours.

Belle tilted her head slightly forward and grinned at Paige and Wolly while she listened and ate her cake. She laughed with them, showing her big teeth. A white bandage covered her left eye from cheek to forehead; when she saw Joey and Cos approaching out of her other eye, she brushed her sun-washed red hair across her face, tucked it behind her ear, and smiled at them before looking back at Wolly and Paige. She had a radiant glow that brought a cold sweat to Joey's palms.

"Boone!" Cos yelled.

Wolly swallowed a big mouthful of chicken and answered. "Well, look here, it's the Dollarhides! My favorite family. What's happening?" he said.

"Not much, I just came in from California," Joey replied.

"Well, it's great to see you again, bud." Wolly threw his arm around Joey and hugged him close to his black graduation gown, which had the smell of John Varvatos. His hair was clean-cut.

"Wolly, you know coach told you to lay off that stuff," Cos added.

"What coach doesn't know won't hurt him."

"Congratulations on the game last night!" Joey said.

"Thanks, but I couldn't have done it without your brother. He drove in the winning run."

"Thanks, Boone. The pitcher had a weak fastball." Cos paused. "Has anyone seen Leslie?"

"She had to go home early; her aunt and uncle are in town," Paige said.

"That's a bummer," Cos said.

"You got it bad for that girl—Leslie, Leslie, Leslie, that's all I ever hear about," Wolly said.

"Shut up, Boone," Cos said. "We're just friends."

"Yeah, *okay*," remarked Wolly.

"Congratulations on graduating!" Cos said to Paige.

"Thanks, Cos! I am so glad it's over."

"Ready to be a Miami Hurricane?" Cos asked.

"Yep, dad offered to pay my way and get me a little house in Coconut Grove."

"Sweet!" Joey said.

"Hey guys, do you remember my sister Belle?" Paige asked.

"Of course," Joey said, making eye contact. "How've you been? I haven't seen you since last summer."

"Really great! How 'bout you?"

"That's great! I am doing good," Joey said. "That cake looks outstanding."

"Did you know they use one hundred eggs to make that cake?" Wolly asked.

"I kind of figured that from the name, Wol," Joey said.

"It's really good! Want a bite?" Belle asked.

"Sure!" She offered Joey the fork and he took a bite; the sugar melted in his mouth and it was even sweeter coming from her.

"Isn't it good?" Belle asked.

"Oh yeah, that's maybe the best cake I've ever had."

"Hey Cos, tell the girls about the senior prank," Wolly said.

"Shut up, Boone! I wasn't even a part of it."

"Who gives a crap!" Wolly said. "We've graduated now. They can't take our diplomas away, this isn't the Heisman you know."

"Come on, tell us … *please!*" Paige begged.

"I am not telling because I didn't even know what was going on. I just dropped them off in the chicken. I didn't even know what they were doing."

"I'll tell everyone then, y'all just promise not to tell anyone," Wolly said.

"We promise," Paige and Belle said.

"Okay, well, you know Betsy?" Wolly smiled and pointed to himself.

"That was you?" Paige said. He nodded in agreement. "Oh my God."

Belle cracked a laugh and exclaimed, "I saw her when I was visiting campus yesterday. I walked by and she actually mooed."

"She mooed in midair?" Joey asked.

"Midair," Belle said.

"Nice," Joey said.

"It's kind of animal cruelty though," Cos said.

"Is the cow hurt, Cos?" Wolly asked.

"No," answered Cos.

"Did people laugh?" Wolly said.

"I guess."

"Then it's fine. You worry too much," Wolly said.

Wolly finished off his chicken and got in line for cake. Paige and Cos joined him, inviting Joey, but he declined. Belle glanced down at the ground before looking back up at Joey.

"I like the flower in your hair. The white looks good with your blue eyes," Joey said, flirting. She blushed a little and smiled.

"Thanks—my one blue eye now. A lady at one of the booths just gave it to me. She said the Hawaiian Plumeria flower are a flower of charm and grace."

"I need to be wearing one, then."

"Yeah, you should get one." She broke a wide smile.

"Is your eye okay?"

"Yeah, it's just a little bruised. I got hit in the face with a boomerang the other day while walking across campus."

"*A boomerang?* I am sorry to hear that. That's weird!"

"Yeah, things like that happen to me."

"So I've been meaning to call you. Just—got busy, you know?"

"It's okay. I meant to call you, too. I thought about you, though."

"I thought about you too. Still in Austin?"

"Yep, I just finished school. It's been a great four years, but I am looking forward to a change."

"What are you doing next?"

"I want to go to Stanford for my MBA."

"California, really?" His eyes lit up.

"Yeah, I just love it out there. The Mediterranean climate reminds me of our family trips to Greece when I was younger."

"Maybe we can meet up sometime on the West coast."

"I'd really like that. What are you doing next?"

"I've signed up to be a forest ranger in California."

"How fun! Like putting out fires and stuff?"

"Mainly patrolling, population control, and monitoring. Possibly managing some ground fires. I'd love to smoke jump, but they won't let me with my injury."

"I've *always* wanted to smoke jump."

"You know there aren't many girls doing that."

"Yeah, well, there aren't many *girls* doing a lot things I wanna do. It just looks like so much fun."

"I know what you mean."

"Oh baby, this cake is so good!" Wolly said, coming back over with the plate close to his face as he ate. Cos and Paige followed with plates of their own.

"I guess Dan didn't make you work today?" Wolly asked Cos.

"No, he let me off."

Belle leaned down and petted Dog. "You're pretty sweet to be a surfer dog." He tried to lick her face. When he connected, she moved away. "And feisty too."

Paige looked around, then knelt on the ground, examining it.

"What are you looking for?" Belle asked.

"My bracelet is missing. The clasp was loose. It must have fallen off," she said nervously. "I've got to find it. Mom just gave it to me as a graduation present."

"I am sure it's around here somewhere," Belle said, kneeling to look with her. They looked for a few minutes—Paige growing more distressed by the second—Wolly went down to help.

"It was our great grandmother Lulu's; I *have* to find it," Paige remarked.

"Lulu's bracelet?? Oh my God, we *do* have to find it," Belle said.

"Was it gold?" Cos asked.

"Yes," Paige said.

"Good." Cos took off his thin gold necklace and held it to Dog's nose; then he said in a strong voice, "Hunt boy!" Hearing the words, Dog darted forward with his nose to the ground. He stopped here and there to sniff along a zigzagging line, in the general direction that

Paige had come from. Finding the bracelet, he picked it up and tracked back to Cos, stopping in front of him where he dropped it, waiting for his reward.

"*He found it?!*" Paige said, walking toward him. "How did he find it?"

"Good boy! He sniffs gold," Cos said. He picked it up and petted Dog. He poured his water over the bracelet to clean it and handed it to Paige, then he took out a sandwich bag of turkey jerky from his pocket and handed a chunk to Dog, who gobbled it up.

"Thank you *so much!*" Paige said.

"You're welcome!"

"How on earth did he do that?" Belle said.

"Teddy trained him to smell gold after learning about Peter Bergman, CEO of the Swedish company OreDog training Arctic canines to sniff for ore and gold," answered Cos.

Dog sat with his tongue hanging out, staring up at the crowd, basking in the attention.

"That's incredible," Belle said.

"Oh, I was so worried I'd lost it. You're an angel, Dog," said Paige.

Wolly wrapped his arm around her shoulder and she purred at the contact.

"I didn't know Dog could smell gold," Wolly said.

"Yep, that's Dog. I am glad he was here to help," Cos said, looking down at Dog, admiring his little friend. "He looks tired from this heat, though. I'm going to take him home."

"I am with you, Cosby. Can I crash at your house tonight?" Wolly added.

"*Mi casa es tu casa.*"

"It was nice talking with you girls," Joey said with a smile. "See you at the beach tomorrow night?"

"We'll be there," they said.

"Perfect!"

Belle bent her fingers forward and up and down with a smile to Joey. Walking away from her was like prying himself off a king-sized magnet.

"Hey Cos, I am riding with Joey," Wolly said.

"You don't want to ride with me?"

Wolly shook his head in disagreement. Joey put on his tortoiseshell Persols and laughed. They headed over to where Joey had parked his 1961 golden wheat-colored Chevy Impala convertible with California plates on the other side of Route 1 and hopped in. The hot leather steering wheel stuck to Joey's hands. When he cranked the engine, Smokey Robinson blasted out of the stereo; the A/C blew on high, but didn't give much cool air.

Joey glimpsed Cos and Dog in the rearview as they went into the neighborhood across the street to Dan's delivery vehicle. He and Wolly laughed as they watched him get in the 1972 Pontiac Grand Safari station wagon painted bright yellow with red trim. Dan had bolted a three-foot-tall red and yellow chicken head to the roof and a matching tail feather on the back and even installed a personalized rooster horn. Slanted red letters on the side door read "Dan's World Famous Fried Chicken" with a phone number below. Cos took a lot of criticism at school for driving it, but like his nickname, he didn't care much.

He pulled away and Joey peeled out in front of him, catching a breeze. They cruised north on Route 1 past the mansions that lined the bay toward the ocean. Dog stuck his head out the window with his tongue flying. The road hugged the coastline, and Joey felt at home when he saw the Atlantic again. Wolly suggested picking up some beer, so they stopped off at Bert's Gas and Bait Shop to get a twelve-pack of Blue Moon bottles before driving back to the farm.

When they arrived at Isabella, Teddy's brown zebu bull Five Alarm skirted off into the distance. Teddy had a bad habit of leaving the gate to the back thirty acres open, and whenever he did, Five Alarm ran wild. The group went straight for the outside cooler that Teddy kept stocked with wild game and fish from his excursions. Joey took out a handful of ahi tuna steaks, thawed them in warm water, cut them up, sea-salted them, and put them on an oval platter. Then, they went around through the ivy-covered gate into the backyard with the fish and beer. Tropical vegetation covered the area around the pool, giving it the appearance of a rainforest. A large oak tree sat between the left side of the pool and the stucco wall; a rope the boys used to swing into the pool hung from one of the branches closest to the pool's edge. A rattletrap wooden pool house was on the other side of the pool. They sat at the teak tables on the slate porch and, after grilling the fish, ate the plump pink tuna steaks with sea salt and chased it with cold coriander ale. Afterwards, they went swimming with Dog, who frequently jumped out and ran the perimeter of the 500 square foot pool, appearing like an ocean in the blessed night. Fireflies flickered at the edge of the yard near the segos as the boys swam and joked about girls and life.

CHAPTER 4

Teddy trolled on an even longitude with the old hunting location, three miles north and four hundred yards east from where Cos found the pistol. The GPS tracker beeped. Each area they had dived and come up empty-handed was marked with a red dot; any point where a piece from *La Gracia* was found was marked with a green dot.

Glancing over at the small Manx sitting on the captain's dash, his mini captain's hat crooked as he monitored the horizon, Teddy smirked.

Bear was a big thing in a small package. His back legs were longer than his front, and he had a kind of strut like a 1950s greaser. Teddy always caught him bothering the female cats twice his size, even when the season was wrong. He could climb a tree, and unlike ordinary cats who just jump out of trees, he could climb back down. And ever since his miraculous recovery from feline AIDS, Bear had a passion for the ocean that no other cat had ever known. Teddy petted him while studying the GPS.

From the dream, Teddy knew the treasure was in the hull—gold was often stored there for ballast; he also knew there were boxes of cannons in the hull for backup, like the one that rolled on his leg. They were searching for a cannon or a chest of gold, silver, or jewels —any clue as to where the hull might be.

The rest of The Pearlmakers—Patrick, Ty, and Dallas—relaxed in the back of the boat, shooting the breeze. Patrick, or "Patch," was a professor of archaeology and history at the University of Miami who wanted nothing more than to work on an offshore treasure hunt during his summers. He was wearing circular glasses, a tank top, and a Miami Hurricanes baseball cap creased heavily at the bill. A nice intellectual type who added organization to the brash crew, his extensive knowledge of Spanish history had helped Teddy correctly document, trace, and date many of the items in the catalog.

Usually the first to go down, Ty was the best diver in the group. He had curly brown hair and a face that appeared carved out of stone with a constant five o'clock shadow. In the 90s, he was a commercial scuba diver on combat pay for oil rigs in the Gulf. He had a long scar on his right forearm where a barracuda bit into him last year and wouldn't let go; Dallas was the one to spear it just before the beast could chew the arm clean off. After some stitches, Ty was in the water two days later, against his doctor's orders.

Dallas, or "Dal," was a black linebacker and a student of Teddy's at the University of Miami. He was selected in the first round of the NFL draft, but he withdrew at the last minute to study plankton instead. He went onto earn his PhD in marine biology after leaving the university and later worked on the recovery of the *SS Central America*. His strength went a long way with the lifting of heavy items underwater, and he was the whiz of the operation—Dal knew it all, knowledge he gained from his days working on the search for the SS *Central America*.

The sun swirled in the sky, its reflection skipping off the water with the ripples of the waves. The oceanfront houses in Latch dotted the distant shore. Teddy dropped the anchor. Ty and Dal jumped in the blue water, splashing like fallen boulders. They dived to the bottom to explore the midnight maze of the ocean floor.

Teddy sat back in his captain's chair, gazing out toward the endless horizon. His blue eyes squinted in the luminescent sun as he stroked Bear on the back, reflecting about the gun and the six years they had spent searching for *La Gracia*.

While visualizing the massive fortune hiding below, he dreamed about helping others. It was Sarah's dream, really—"No one should die of hunger," she used to say. She worked three months out of the year in the Sudan to bring food to villages in need, putting up with constant bureaucratic BS to thwart her efforts or divert funds, but she always stayed strong and held her position. Even through the cancer, she was optimistic. She had a natural radiance to her that didn't fade when her body did; instead, she seemed to glow even more as her time neared.

After her death, Teddy began to feel that there was some connection between health and the food people consumed. At least in his mind, he believed good nutrition could go a long way toward preventing cancer. He put the whole family on traditional whole foods and vegetable and fruit juices. He cooked a lot, exploring the benefits of certain herbs, foods, and flavors and their synergies.

Teddy swigged his Nalgene bottle of ice water and poured Bear some in a tin cup attached to a Velcro patch below the dash. Bear lapped at it and the act made Teddy smile.

He remembered how Sarah loved to sing. He used to play the piano, and they would sing together for hours. She loved plants and working in the garden with her round-brimmed straw hat, basking in the sun. She was tall with curly red hair and little bitty features. When she worked outside, he would bring her iced tea and she would wipe the sweat from her brow and teach him about each plant: what the species was and where it originated. Plants were her passion, but helping others was her religion; she would give her last piece of food to someone who needed it more.

Patch slid the door open with an ear-splitting grin, informing him that Dal and Ty found something. Bear turned at attention as Teddy rose and headed to the deck. Bear trailed him, hopping on a cooler outside to watch the crew work. Dal propped up on the boat in the water and told Patch to lower the hoister. Ty rose up after him, resting on the landing.

"Jackpot, Teddy. We've got something big!" Dal said. After raising himself up, he sat on the side of the boat with his legs still in the water. The yellow scuba tank looked like a child's backpack on him.

"Is it something good?" Patch asked.

"Is it from the hull?" Teddy pressed.

"It's a cannon, this time with *no base!*" Dal said, smiling.

"Well, if that don't put pepper in the gumbo! Are you thinking what I'm thinking, Dal?"

"It could be from the hull. A boxed cannon for backup."

"Well I'll be damned. This ain't chicken shit boys, it's chicken salad!" Teddy brushed Bear off the cooler and grabbed two ice-cold water bottles, tossing one to Dal and the other to Ty.

"What do you think, Ty?" Teddy asked.

"Well, it could be from anywhere on the ship, but I reckon it's from the hull because it doesn't have a base," Ty explained.

"Hot dog!" barked Teddy.

"Of course, we couldn't have done it without Cosmo," Dal said, chuckling.

"Yeah, the chip off the old block!" Teddy exclaimed.

"Do you think it could be from another ship?" Patch asked.

"Could be. As you know, there are no other records of ships going down here. That doesn't mean it never happened. The ocean is full of undocumented ghost ships, but I reckon she drifted over the years," Teddy said.

"Do you think it went down here or at the other site?" Dal asked.

"If the hull is here, this is probably where she finally went down, or she drifted!" Teddy barked. "Of course, we'll have to pay off our crew debts with any profits from it, nothing really to keep afterward, but at least we're on the right track. How does it look down there?"

"Pretty clean job, just sitting on the sand. We used the blower and blasted under about two feet of sand. There are a couple of reef sharks down there, though. Pass me the spear gun just in case," Dal said.

Teddy opened a large square chest bolted to the deck behind the captain's house. Removing the spear gun and some arrows, he handed them to Dal.

"The load is quite heavy, Salt. We're going need an extra hand down there to get it in the harness," Ty said.

"Patch, man the boat, I'm going down with them. Throw Dal the steel cables from the crane and feed him slack as he goes down," Teddy said.

"Okay, good luck!" Patch hollered.

Teddy removed his unbuttoned short-sleeved white linen shirt and threw it to the side. Then, he laid down the Panama hat and slung on a scuba pack. After adjusting to the tank, he kissed the gold St. Nicholas pendant around his neck and jumped into the water. Dal took the cable and jumped in after, Ty following.

They dove deep. Large underwater flashlights illuminated the murky water. When they reached the bottom, Dal pointed to the black rusty lump of coal and Teddy studied it, running his hand along its surface. His eyes smiled as he flipped a thumb up. Teddy and Dal held the arms up, while Ty wrapped the harness around it. They couldn't hold the heavy weight for long. When the harness was tight around it, they tugged on the cables hard, signaling Patch to start the crane. To the side of the box, Dal saw and picked up a blue bottle of the wine they'd dredged up six months ago. Patch started to raise the load slowly; mud dispersed into the water as it lifted from the ocean floor; they swam up with it.

They broke the surface, climbed into the boat, and removed their scuba gear. As the crane lifted it out, Teddy recognized it as one of the baseless cannons in the hull from his dreams. Patch swung it into the boat with the crane, then slowly lowered it to the floor while the men guided it with their hands.

Teddy petted the crusted piece with his arm like a long-lost friend, and they all marveled at the artillery from *La Gracia's* hull. Teddy let out a loud hoot. The crew exchanged hugs, congratulating each other. They had been searching for a clue like this for years. Teddy retrieved some Cohiba Habanos cigars from his swag box in the cabin, and they smoked them, watching the sun drop.

On the way back to the marina, while rummaging through a storage closet on *Gold Lip*, Teddy came across the box containing the twelve blue bottles of wine they'd pulled up from *La Gracia*. He shook his head, thinking about Bear and the feline AIDS a year ago. The veterinarians had sent the cat home with a medical death sentence. Teddy tried everything, but as time passed, Bear grew weaker. When the spark left his eyes and he started moping around the farm with his head down, Teddy became distraught. Sitting in his captain's chair one day over a year ago, Teddy's eyes had fallen upon one of the twelve blue quart-sized bottles. They had agreed to not open them, but thinking it would relax him, Teddy unhinged the wire cap, uncorked it, and poured a short glass of the 300-year-old ferment. The first sip twisted his face. No doubt it was good, but tart. After finishing the glass, he felt full, peaceful, light. The next day, he woke with more energy and vitality—his sinuses were clear for the first time in years. What the hell had happened?

He decided to give some to Bear, starting him on a minute dosage. Bear lapped it up. Within two weeks, some of his energy returned. Within four, he was bothering the female cats again and killing rats in the barn. A month later, the vet gave him a clean bill of health.

Teddy sent a sample of the wine to a lab rat buddy in Cambridge, Massachusetts, who gave it to cancerous mice. Within two weeks, they were cured. News spread like wildfire through the facility, and two weeks later, his friend got a death threat, his credit cards were canceled, and he was laid off. Locked out of the lab, he stopped returning Teddy's calls and disappeared.

So, Teddy recently started having his own tests run on the wine, and so far, he'd had no feedback. He knew it wasn't just the age; rather, it seemed there was an element added to it either accidentally or consciously that created a healing synergy. Whatever it was, Teddy was convinced the Spaniards had unknowingly discovered a sort of elixir.

Coming out of his reverie and closing the door, he walked back over to the captain's chair and watched as the boat chugged toward the marina.

※

HOURS HAD PASSED at Isabella when the boys heard the sound of two trucks coming down the driveway followed by the familiar screech of the Ford's brakes. A moment later, Teddy entered the backyard carrying two bushels of oysters in one hand and a plastic bucket in the other, the remainder of a Cuban plug stuck in his mouth; Dallas walked behind him. Joey jumped out of the pool, toweled himself off, and ran over to hug his father. Teddy's bare chest was hot to the touch. He greeted his son and asked the whole group if they would like some oysters. They all agreed.

Teddy took off his Panama hat, set it on the teak table, and combed his fingers through his pearl-white hair and stroked his beard generously. Then, he took a seat. He and Dal kidded the boys about swimming under the influence of the beer. Teddy took six oyster knives out of the bucket and set them on the table. He always had enough to go around because the only thing he liked more than eating oysters was sharing them.

The thick wet night grew more alive with the song of the crickets, cicadas, and frogs, and the fireflies now speckled the backyard like blinking lights on a dancing Christmas tree.

The group hovered around the table and began to shell a bushel, using their knives to eat and tossing the empty shells into the white bucket with thuds and clangs. Teddy told them the oysters were Blue Points from up north. They were small, but the briny taste was like swimming in the Atlantic on a sun baked day. They chased the saltiness with the ale as Teddy informed them about the cannon. He thanked Cos again for finding the gun. Then, he asked Joey more about California, and Joey told him while they ate and drank. Joey rubbed Dog's belly with his foot as Dog lay on the stone floor, struggling to hold his eyelids open.

The group finished off the bushel and went to see the cannon as

Teddy and Dal unloaded it into the preservation room. They expressed amazement and took a round of photos with it. Joey got a look at the pistol as well before he, Cos, and Wolly retired.

Teddy and Dal hoisted the cannon up with a Bobcat lift and set it down in a box of fresh water designed to dissolve the crustacean. They cataloged the date and time, locked up, and left.

UNDER THE GLOW of the reading lamp in his bedroom, Teddy examined through his reading glasses the ring they'd found last week wound up in tattered clothes buried deep in the sand. He concluded it was a wedding ring: a pitiful thing really, made of ivory and only fit for a peasant, worthless, the bone chipped, but he couldn't stop thinking about its history.

"Every object has a tale to tell," his father, Jim, used to say. As a teenager when he tagged along for his father's hunts after the treasure of the French pirate of the Gulf of Mexico, Jean Lafitte, around Fort Morgan, Alabama where it was rumored the pirate had buried some of his ten million dollar treasure, and they found artifacts, his dad would ask him to tell a tale for each item on the truck ride home. The game was fun, and sometimes his stories matched up pretty close to the truth when they eventually discovered where and when the item was born, who it belonged to, and what it was made out of. But Jim would always conclude by looking at him with wizened eyes and saying that "only God knows *everything* an object has seen: the love, victories, defeats, conceptions, transformations."

Where are the chests of gold? Who did you belong to? Tell me your secrets, poor ring—let me see with your ivory eyes, so I can know what you know.

He turned off the light, removed his readers, and closed his heavy eyes. What a poor ring, he thought again with it clutched in the fault lines of his hand. But he liked the way it felt against his skin, and through his pondering concluded that a wedding ring could never truly be poor because it was a symbol of eternal love—for a circle had no end and *the promise of forever* was the richest gift a person could give. The form—ivory loop, gold band, diamond setting—didn't matter: it was about the love behind it. But adding a diamond provided an indestructible symbol to the band—that was what the Greek root of the word *adamas* meant—*indestructible*—for nothing could cut a diamond except itself, and the poor ring needed a stone he thought. He fell asleep with marriage on the bow of his mind as he pushed off into the dark dreamscape.

CHAPTER 5

Teddy splashed the cold water on his face and ran it through his hair. He set the metal pail underneath the outside barn spigot, allowing it to fill. Last night's dream lingered in the window of his mind like water drops waiting to evaporate.

During this dream, for the first time, he hadn't been on the ship but in a clearing of sage grass next to a soft wheat field. The land rolled across the horizon and fell down rocky cliffs into a turquoise sea of small wooden fishing boats. He lay in the grass with a Spanish woman dressed in white. She wrapped her arm around his chest, and when he leaned his face into her ebony hair, he found it had the scent of a river and her skin smelled like milk. In the distance, there was a modest home in the Spanish style. The dream ended there—it was short, but beautiful.

Watching the water in the pail rise, he felt that same love he felt for Sarah. He rubbed the ache out of the birthmark on his leg, which was in the same spot the canon in the dream landed on his leg, turned off the spigot, and carried the full pail toward the tree house where he saw Cos sleeping shirtless in the hammock outside.

He walked up the stairs and threw the pail of water on his son. Cos sprang forward, drawing a deep breath in shock. His drenched hair mopped down in front of his eyes. Whipping around, he couldn't help smiling when he saw his father.

"Rise and shine, son! Top of the morning!"

"I was having a great dream, and you ruined it!"

"It's nine o'clock, Cosby! Time for you and Jojo to bathe the horses. Afterwards, y'all can get breakfast."

"I am tired. I stayed up too late."

"That's your fault!"

Cos was red-faced and fell back down on the hammock. "Come on, Dad. If I clean the horses *and* the pool later, can I sleep a little longer?"

"No."

Cos closed his eyes and started to drift back to sleep. A shrill ring jacked him up again; he flipped over out of the hammock, landing on his knees on the tree house porch floor.

"I am up, I am up! No more foghorn," Cos said with a very serious look on his face, holding an ear with one hand and pushing forward at Teddy as if to stop traffic with the other. "We won the game and I graduated, can't I have one day off?" he pleaded.

"I know you did, but the horses don't care if you win, lose, or graduate. Jojo is already up."

"Really? Good Lord, what's wrong with him?"

"The foghorn," Teddy said. "He fell asleep on the couch in the living room and I got him early." He giggled like a little boy.

"That explains it."

"How did you end up out here anyway?" Teddy asked.

"I just wanted to sleep in the hammock."

Teddy knelt down next to him and his tone changed. "Look son, I have some bad news. The high school received a phone call about the cow prank yesterday, a janitor who works for the school saw you in plain sight in the chicken mobile, and they called this morning. You get to keep your diploma, but they reported the episode as a disciplinary infraction to the University of Florida. Your full ride there depended on a perfect behavioral record for your third and fourth quarters. The athletic director called this morning to say they still want you to play ball if you pay your way. And there's more: the high school wants you to help pay for the damages."

"Oh no! *What?* I didn't even do anything. I didn't even know what they were doing! I just dropped them off!"

"Don't complain if you fall asleep with dogs and wake up with fleas."

"Aww man. How much do I owe?"

"One thousand dollars. All four of you have to pay that amount," said Teddy.

"What? Where I am gonna get that kind of money?

"You'll find a way," Teddy said. He patted him on the back and stood up, strolling over to the railing of the porch. Leaning his mass on it, he gazed out across the land.

"Can you help me, Dad?"

"No. You can take a loan out for school and work the rest off."

"Dammit. They can't do this to me!"

"They didn't do anything to you. You broke the rules, and it cost the school a lot and was a great inconvenience to a lot of people. What did you expect? I am disappointed and sad for you. This is your mess to clean up," Teddy remarked.

"I understand. I made a mistake."

"You're welcome to stay here for as long as you need. I want you to keep a positive attitude. We can't feel bad enough to make a bad situation better. What do we do when we fall off the horse?" Teddy turned to him.

"Cowboy up," Cos moped.

"Cowboy up, that's right—now get to those horses. Doing some manual chores today will build some good character in you." He turned and headed down the stairs. "God, it's a beautiful day."

Cos stood up and raked his wet hair back. He didn't put on a shirt, but slipped on cowboy boots and made his way to the barn, where he met Joey walking from the house. They greeted and entered the barn. Cos glided over to Caramel, the brown quarter horse, while Joey tended to Vanilla, the white quarter. The scent of manure and dry hay gave Joey a long-forgotten high.

The two washed the horses and then Joey hosed off Vanilla. Afterwards, he handed the hose to Cos, who finished washing off Caramel. Then they both attended to Earful, Teddy's white Arabian.

Cos whistled to Dog, who ran in from patrolling the yard and the two walked back toward Isabella, the Floridian sun tanning their skin. The air was dense with moisture; Joey and Cos stopped by the kitchen to get a drink while Dog went around back.

Charlotte, the Dollarhides' maid, greeted them with her kind eyes. Her blonde hair had white and silver strands through it and her skin looked untouched by the sun. She wiped her hands on her apron and tilted forward to hug Joey. Charlotte was a live-in maid and chef with her own quarters at Isabella.

"Hello sugar, it's been so long since I've seen you."

"Only since Christmas, Charlotte," Joey said.

"Well that's a *loonng* time now. You look so good and healthy."

"Thanks Charlotte! You look great yourself. How old are you now, thirty-two?"

"Oh, stop it Joey, you must be thirsty! Let me get you some fresh lemonade."

"That would be great!" Joey said.

She took out the chilled glass pitcher of lemon juice mixed with water and tupelo honey, poured two glasses and handed them to Cos and Joey. "Thanks Charlotte," Cos said and they both downed their glasses in one long sip and then refilled them from the pitcher. The drink was the perfect remedy to offset the ninety-five-degree scorcher. The boys said goodbye to Charlotte and headed out the twin louvered living room doors to the pool. Making their way to the water's edge, their feet came to an abrupt halt. Joey and Cos stood in front of the pool with an opened mouth; Dog sat beside him, confused.

"What the hell is it?" Joey said.

"Based on the weather dial in the deep end and the missing shed, I am guessing it's the old shed!" said Cos. The floating wood and grime from the former building stained some of the water brown.

"What's the shed doing *in the pool?*" Joey added.

"Beats the hell outta me," Cos added.

"Go tell Charlotte," Joey barked.

"What's it doing in there?" Cos asked.

"Never mind, Cos, just go!" Joey replied.

Cos went to the back porch, opened one of the doors, and yelled, "Charlotte, did ya know the shed is floating in the pool?"

"What?"

"Shed is in the pool!"

She walked out wiping her hands on a rag from the kitchen.

"What in the good Lord's name?" Charlotte said, staring out. Then, she placed a hand in front of her mouth.

"What happened, Charlotte? It looks like a tornado hit it," Cos said.

"I wish! That would at least make sense. The maintenance guys were supposed to demolish the old shed and take it off the property this morning. I reckon they accidentally dragged it into the pool," she replied, short of breath, and placed her hand on her chest, tapping it lightly and frowning.

"What idiots," Joey replied.

"Welcome home, Jojo!" Cos said, throwing his arm around his brother and grinning.

"Thanks, Cos," Joey said in a sarcastic tone.

The sound of a pickup truck pulled up the driveway and two hefty men got out and strutted through the gate. Charlotte turned to them, "You boys have a lot of explaining to do!" she said.

"Howdy ma'am, good day." A large blonde named Billy lifted his dirt-stained hat off his head and fitted it back.

"Explain yourselves, right now!" Charlotte demanded.

"Yes ma'am, well, you see, we had a little problem today."

"That's as plain as day," she said as they stopped in front of her.

"After my fellow Bob here got the rope around the structure, my other boy Steve drove it forward, but we was off a little bit in the calculations and it went the other way on us."

"Why didn't you come tell me?"

"Oh, we was going to, but you see, we had to go eat. We went and done picked up some of that BBQ over yonder at the Big Pit. You should try the pulled pork sandwich with coleslaw," Billy said.

Charlotte's face turned red and she stomped her shoe on the porch, "I don't care about no coleslaw. I wanna know why you haven't gotten it out yet!"

"Well, no offense ma'am, but we figured it ain't going nowhere anytime soon," Bob said, beginning to laugh a little; Billy stepped on his toe hard and he zipped it.

"You see ma'am, Steve's hypoglycemia acts up, and if he don't eat, he can't really think straight. He's liable to Smurf up and pass out on us. It's happened before," Billy said.

"Yes ma'am," Bob confirmed.

"I don't know what to do with y'all." They looked down as she paused. "Just get this mess cleaned up before Mr. Dollarhide gets back."

"Uh, ma'am, that's just the thing. We got a big hunting expedition this afternoon that we've gotta get ready for. We came back just to let cha know."

"Unbelievable! Y'all are dumber than a bag of hammers. I bet if I took both of your heads and rubbed them together it wouldn't make one bright idea," Charlotte said. Cos and Joey tried not to smile.

"We would like to do it ma'am, but this is a real special event. Last week, Will Burns spotted Half Ton on his farm and organized a group hunt for today."

"That's Belle's dad," Joey said, his voice lifting.

"You two should be ashamed of yourselves. Do you fools even know there's a storm coming?"

"Yes ma'am. It's an early hunt. We'll be here a couple of days after the storm to take care of this."

"Well, what choice do I have? You fools won't help me!" Charlotte barked, her face beet red now.

"Who's Half Ton?" Joey asked.

"He's a wild hog running loose in the area. People say he may be the longest ever, weighing *over a thousand pounds*," Cos said, exaggerating his face and voice.

"Yep, they say he's longer than Hog Kong, that hybrid shot in Kentucky," Bob said, his smile revealing a missing front tooth.

"What do you want with a stupid hog anyway?" Charlotte asked, frustrated.

"He's destroying the landscape and he's dangerous, ma'am. If provoked, he could kill someone," Billy said.

"*And* Will Burns is offering a trophy and a twenty-five thousand-dollar reward to whoever pops him," Bob said; Billy hit him again.

"*Oh*, so this is about money?!"

"Money and pride. We're sorry ma'am, we'll be back though. Y'all take care now." The two headed out the gate and back to their truck.

"Holy smokes!" Joey replied, his eyes big as saucers. "I wanna go!"

"No Joey, you're not going anywhere," Charlotte said.

"Why not? Teddy and I killed a black bear in Montana with my bow back in the day. I could pick off that hog easy enough."

"That's enough, Joey. It's time for breakfast, boys. We'll have it outside, and let's pretend this never happened," Charlotte added. "They're perfect examples of what occurs when you sniff gasoline and drop out of school."

They all sat down on the outside porch at the dining table. Charlotte went inside and came back out, setting the table with a crisp white cloth. They brought out the food, decorating the table with bowls of delicious fruits, sweet cream, tupelo honey, and freshly baked goods. When she finished, Charlotte relaxed into one of the teak chairs and wiped the sweat off her brow. She stared out at the pool, saw the weather dial bobbing with the current, and shook her head again in disgust. The boys sat around shirtless. A white '78 CJ-5 Jeep passed the truck on its way out; it stopped and Wolly hopped out. He had left early to run some errands.

"Did I miss breakfast?" he asked as he swung through the back gate.

"There's not enough. You should've called first," Joey said.

"There's never enough for Boone," Cos said.

"Oh stop it, boys. There's plenty to go around, Wolly," Charlotte said.

"Where's Dad?" Joey asked.

"He's on the back lot," Charlotte replied.

"Pass me the fruit please," Wolly said. Joey passed him a big bowl of organic blueberries and strawberries. Wolly served himself, pouring fresh cream on top.

"I love berries and cream," he exclaimed, adding a heaping spoonful of the tupelo honey to it.

Joey buttered his pancakes and drank a glass of milk. Then, he unloaded some scrambled eggs onto the plate, along with a cut tomato.

"Thank you for joining us this morning, Wolly," Charlotte added.

"No—thank you, Charlotte, for all this good food."

"How did graduation go?" Charlotte asked.

"Really great, Charlotte," Cos said.

"Yeah, it went great!" Wolly said.

"Your dad told me you lost your scholarship, Cosby," she said, looking at him with the concerned eyes of a mother. After they lost Sarah to cancer six years ago, Charlotte took over the role and had shared in their successes and failures ever since.

"Yes, it's true." He darted his eyes down, deflated.

"What?" Wolly said, looking at Cos.

"Florida found out about the prank and cut my scholarship," Cos stated. Wolly's eyebrows pointed up—Cos shook his head in the negation, indicating they didn't know about Wolly—Joey looked shocked.

"Oh, you boys didn't know. I am sorry," Charlotte remarked.

"No, I didn't know. That's terrible," Joey said. Cos shrugged.

"Well, I want you to stay positive. You'll get through this," Charlotte remarked.

"Thanks, Charlotte."

"Y'all know the weather channel says Hurricane Eliza will be here early tomorrow morning," Charlotte said.

"I know. There's a little get-together on the beach after dinner," Joey said.

"Well, I certainly *don't* want y'all going to that."

"But Charlotte," Cos said. "*Everyone* in our class will be there."

"He means *Leslie* will be there," Wolly said with a grin.

"Shut up, Boone!" Cos said.

"It's just up the road. I'll keep an eye on him," Joey said to Charlotte.

"All right—you can go, but be *very careful*, and watch out for the weather. If it starts to rain, head straight home."

"We will," Joey said.

A loud vehicle barreled up the driveway. Through the opened gate, they saw a camouflaged fire truck pass by. In a moment, a man with a strong build and a belly hanging out over his dirt-stained Levi's lumbered into the backyard, his weight shifting back and forth on the heels of his ostrich-skin cowboy boots.

"Howdy folks! Name is Bob Barclay. I am here to see about some limbs that need cutting."

"Nice to meet you, Bob. Mr. Dollarhide has been expecting you. He should be up here any minute."

"All right, thank you. I'll take a look while I wait." He exited.

After ten minutes, Teddy came around the side where the camouflaged fire truck surprised him. Bob surveyed a tree with his hands on his hips. Seeing Teddy approach, he turned with his hand out.

"Howdy sir. Bob Barclay! You must be Teddy."

"Hi Bob. Nice to meet you." Teddy noticed a protruding bulge two inches off his forehead.

"Don't let the knot get to you."

"Didn't even see it."

"Still getting used to it. I was climbing a coconut palm last year to get a lady's black cat out, and that damn cat knocked loose a big nut with its hind leg that hit me square in between the eyes. The shot knocked me off the tree and I landed on the ground unconscious. When I woke, I had this knot, and it's been with me ever since."

"That's the damnedest thing I've ever heard, Bob."

"Yeah, at first I thought it was one of those chupacabras, but it was just a cat. But that cat had it out for me. They tell you don't cross a black cat's path, but there ain't nothing about not getting in a tree with one," Bob said and laughed. "That ain't even the half of it. Ever since I went out, I've had selective tel-e-pathy."

"You mean you can see into the future?"

"Yep, I can predict the weather one day in advance." He held a finger up in the air. "I tried to get on the weather channel with it, but they said it wasn't scientific enough, whatever the hell that means. I listen to them enough to know their batting average is low."

"So tell me, do you think Eliza will be big?"

"Big *and* early!"

"Weatherman has it here around 2:30 am."

"Naw, it'll be sooner."

"I hope you're wrong."

"There are two things I am never wrong about, Mr. Dollarhide: trees and weather."

"But *no one* is right *all* the time, Bob," Teddy said, smiling.

"I suppose you're right. The truth is I don't want this telepathy. Hell, it's a burden knowing what the weather will be. I can't tell you how many fishing trips I've canceled. I even visited a head specialist to see if he could fix it. He told me he could polish the knot down, but couldn't rid me of the mind stuff."

"So you decided to keep the knot?"

"Yeah, I kinda like it. It's a good reminder to avoid things like black cats, walking under ladders, and the number thirteen, because *those* things are *real*."

"Now I don't know about all that."

"No, they're as real as anything else."

"Well I have different colored horses, and they're all the same."

"But a horse isn't a cat, Mr. Dollarhide."

"No, but a cat has as much color to him as a horse or a flower or any other thing."

"Sounds like French to me. You get tangled up with the cats then; I'm staying away from them."

"Let's get back to talking trees, Bob. The day isn't young and I want these weak limbs trimmed before the storm so the wind can't hurl them at us."

"All right, what have we got here?"

"I'll show you."

They walked around the property and Teddy pointed out weak limbs in trees.

"I want these gone before the storm. Can you do it by this afternoon?"

Bob paused for a moment to reflect, squinting to the side as he took his Florida Gators ball cap off and wiped the sweat from his forehead with a handkerchief from his front pocket.

"Oh, I reckon my crew can start right now and be finished by this afternoon. There's a hunt on Will Burns's land for Half Ton around four o'clock, so we got to be done by three."

"For the feral hog?"

"Yessiree. He's no longer staying at the Willis Plantation. Will Burns saw him on his farm in the country a good five miles closer to town. Miss Jimmy lives next door and claims he snuck in her yard at night and cleared out the chickens. Ate 'em whole, beak and all. Damn thing is possessed by Satan himself."

"I am not sure if I buy all that."

Bob's face curled up. "No, it's true. He's got the mark of the beast and needs to be stopped before he kills somebody."

"Okay, well, please get to these trees and let me know when you're done."

"Remember, Eliza will be big and early!" he said, and walked away.

"Gotcha, Bob."

Teddy walked to the backyard. Meanwhile, Bob moved the camouflaged firetruck onto the grass near the trees. The country group Alabama's "Song of the South" began to pour out of a loudspeaker mounted on the top of the firetruck. Bob raised a ladder attached to the top; he and the crew started working. The music stopped Teddy at the door to the preservation room, where he watched the spectacle for a moment. Then, he went inside, retrieved the antique pistol, and joined the group in the backyard.

"I see the gang's all here. How's breakfast?" Teddy said, glimpsing the pool out of one eye. "What happened here?"

"The guys you hired to remove the shed dragged it *into* the pool!" Charlotte said.

"How did that happen?"

"They said it 'went the wrong way on them' when they pulled it," Charlotte said. Teddy scratched his head, staring at the pool perplexed.

"Why didn't they remove it?" He turned and looked at Charlotte.

"Said they had to go eat."

"Will they be here later on?"

"Nope, they're going hunting for that hog." With each answer, Teddy became more and more astonished.

"That's bull. They're fired! I'll get Bob to do it." He walked over, sat down at the table, and rested the pistol on the tablecloth to the side of his empty plate.

"How's the food, Wolly?" Teddy said, patting him on the back.

"Excellent, sir."

"What's that music, Dad?" Joey asked.

"Oh, that's the tree man." He picked up a piece of toast.

"Does he make you pay extra for that?" Joey asked.

"No, it's a free perk. Fortunately, it's Alabama, so I can't really complain."

"Who is this guy?" Charlotte asked.

"Bob Barclay." Teddy filled a bowl with fruit, poured cream on top of it, and then served himself a coffee. "Is this Jamaican Blue Mountain?" he asked Charlotte.

"Yep!"

"My favorite. You're an angel, Charlotte," Teddy said. "I gotta tell y'all something," Teddy said, beginning to laugh. "Bob just told me that he's telepathic."

"What?" Joey said.

"Yeah, a cat hit him in the head with a coconut and he can see into the future."

"The day just keeps get weirder. Did you bring in something strange with that cannon?" Charlotte asked.

"Maybe." Teddy smiled. "He tells me he can predict the weather one day in advance and promised me Eliza will come early and be really big."

"You're not gonna listen to him, Dad?" Joey asked.

"Not really, but I want y'all to board up everything right now, every window except for the kitchen bay window."

"You got it," Cos said.

"Why leave it uncovered?" Wolly asked.

"It's impact-proof glass, and I like to have a lookout during storms," Teddy said. "And come home early tonight from that beach party. I think Bob just might be onto something."

"Okay," Joey and Cos answered.

Cos noticed the gun. "The pistol looks great cleaned up."

Teddy held it up, admiring it. "Thanks, still waiting for Patch to put a date on it, but the model was a popular one when *La Gracia* sank."

"Sweet," Joey said.

"Check out the engraving," Teddy said and passed it to Cos, who studied it.

From what they could make out, the whole body was engraved with intricate patterned lines.

"What a nice piece. They sure don't make 'em like they used to," Cos said.

"No they don't," Teddy said as Cos handed it to Joey.

"What's this?" Joey asked as he flipped out a small octagonal piece that resembled an Allen wrench from the handle; there was a hexagonal hole at the end of it.

"It's a belt tie, although I've never seen one like this."

"Hmm," Joey said.

"So what's the tale on the gun, Jojo?" asked Teddy, grinning.

"A very poor servant stole it from his master along with some bread and ran away to assassinate a man for a hefty sum. Got wet feet, and practically gave it away at the docks to a sailor."

"That's pretty good. Cos?" Joey passed the pistol back to Cos, who studied it.

"It was a vanity pistol for a rich nobleman. Only been shot once, virtually by accident, when his right-hand man was showing him how. The rogue shot hit his horse in the butt and his servants laughed at him; he had them punished in an embarrassing fashion and the pistol was thrown away in disgust, only to be retrieved by a future cook on *La Gracia*."

"Very, very good Cos; I am impressed," Teddy said.

"Thanks."

"Charlotte?" Teddy asked as Cos passed the gun her way.

"Oh, this is a stupid game, you know how I hate guns." She hurried it to Wolly, holding it with two pinched fingers by the handle like a dirty sock.

"Wolly?" Teddy asked. Wolly looked at it for a minute.

"Not sure Salt, probably went to battle, did well, and the same man was a sailor when the war ended." He passed it back to Teddy.

"What do you think, Salt?" Wolly asked. Teddy paused, studying it.

"I think it was an orphan, owned by no man, created as a humble servant, a masterless sailor on a ride to the New World to find its one true owner, but it ran into a bulletproof foe who threw it to the bottom of the ocean where it has waited patiently for hundreds of years to fulfill its destiny."

"I like that, Salt. So, has it found its owner and destiny yet?" Wolly asked.

"Must have, because its destiny is now in our hands." He set the pistol down and leaned back in the chair. "So, what else is new, boys?"

"Joey is in love," Cos said.

"Really? *You too?*" Teddy said, smiling and winking at Cos. Joey turned red and shook his head with a grin. "So what does love look like?"

"Redheaded like a firecracker," Wolly said, laughing.

"Shut up, Wol," Joey barked. Teddy laughed. "Oh now Wolly, redheads are the salt of the earth. My wife was a redhead."

They talked for another half hour and dispersed with full bellies.

Out in the yard, Barclay continued to work the trees, using a ladder attached to the top of the firetruck to reach and saw off half-broken and weak branches and limbs while his team cut the fallen pieces down to size, throwing them into the bed of a grey Dodge Ram pickup truck belonging to one of the three crewmen, who just happened to be Buzz Smith, Leslie's ex-boyfriend.

After Bob finished hours later, he handed Teddy an invoice. Teddy went inside to get his checkbook.

In the office, his heart sank when he saw his checking balance. A stack of unpaid bills sat on the broad pine desk. He put his fingers on his temple, which throbbed with his heartbeat. He walked out to Bob with his checkbook in his hand and asked him if he would remove the shed from the pool. Bob agreed, quoting him a price for that. Teddy added it to the tree removal total, wrote the man a check and handed it to him. Then, Teddy went back to the office and sat down to thumb through the bills he had been avoiding. He started with the five maxed out credit cards; he could barely meet the minimums. Then, he came to a letter marked IMPORTANT in red. Opening it, he read the notice, detailing his debt on one year of back property taxes on Isabella. Unlike his other notices, this one gave him an ultimatum of thirty-five days to pay a huge minimum he couldn't afford before the state seized the property. Making a paper airplane out of the letter, he glided it toward the trash can—it bounced off the top of the pile of other airplanes like it, ricocheted off the wall, and landed behind the desk. He jolted up, pushed the chair back, and rested his forearm on the doorframe, pushing his forehead into it. His eye caught his plans for the wooden sailing boat he wanted to build, tacked to the wall. Next to it hung a map of Florida and the Caribbean; a highlighted route ran from the coast of Latch to St. Barts. Around the map, his drawings of dreams from *La Gracia* lined the walls. Closing his eyes, he envisioned being on the boat, sailing off into the horizon, wearing his aviators with Bear by his side. After a moment, he regained his composure and ran his fingers through his hair and beard; then, he went out to the porch.

The boys spent the rest of the afternoon boarding up the windows on Isabella, while Teddy loaded *Gold Lip* at the marina and took the boat to a warehouse inland, which always charged a handsome fee to board boats during storms.

The boys placed the chickens in the second floor area of the barn, which Teddy had specifically built for use during bad storms, and penned them up. They didn't anticipate flooding, so they left the horses and the zebu bull downstairs in their stalls which was generally better for any spin-off twisters so long as there was no significant surge. Afterward, Cos returned the chicken car to Dan's, about three miles south and two miles inland; Joey gave him a ride back.

CHAPTER 6

About every fifty yards, a wooden bridge crossed over big dunes that descended to the white beach along the east side of Route 1. At the center of every bridge, there was a beehive-shaped gazebo with wooden benches inside. Cars and trucks lined the side of the dark road and the full white moon shimmered on the black ocean. A strong breeze cooled the eighty-eight-degree night, sending sand dancing across the road. The moist air told of an approaching storm.

Joey, Wolly, and Cos walked over from Isabella wearing T-shirts, chinos, and cologne, Dog trailing behind them. They took the main bridge down to the campfire. A gang of seniors ran past them, carrying a six-pack of beer, their weight drumming the wooden boards. Young ladies ahead in "beach formal" attire chatted about their summer and college plans. Lavender and white rose oil from their perfume lingered in the air, and when the boys passed through it, they experienced the essence of June.

A sea of floral, white, and pastel hues colored the sand. They slipped their shoes off and walked past the fire, which whistled smoke in the air. A crowd was gathered around it, sitting on driftwood logs and folding chairs. A senior named Jesse, a black guy with short knotty dreads, sang along to his acoustic guitar. Guys and girls chatted together in circles outside of the fire, recollecting about the past four years. Joey saw his old friend Jackson sitting on a Yeti cooler like a guard dog and told Wolly and Cos he would retrieve the beers and catch up with them; Wolly slipped him a roll of cash for a six-pack.

Joey paid Jackson for two six-packs of Sweetwater Georgia Brown. He noticed Buzz Smith at the bonfire, glaring at Cos. Wolly and Cos caught up with some old buddies behind him and Joey joined them, handing a six-pack to Wolly.

In a circle next to them, Belle and Paige socialized with Leslie and Belle's friend Natasha. Natasha had gone to a neighboring high school in Mangotan up north and had roomed with Belle during her freshman year at the University of Texas. Her brown hair was pulled behind one ear; she had round cheeks and a tiny mouth with thick lips—the top lip hung over the bottom one, furling up when she spoke. An assembly of guys came and went trying to get her number —the harder they tried, the more she lost interest.

Belle stood next to her. Baby blue and canary outlines of flowers climbed her cream dress and a new Hawaiian Plumeria was tucked behind her ear. The eye patch was gone; a bluish and black bruise from the boomerang injury covered the area near her nose, and the white of her left blue eye was a little red. Joey walked over to them, and Wolly and Cos followed. Dog ran up to the ladies, recognizing them from the day before.

"Hey Joey, hey Cosby; I want you to meet our friend Natasha! She was my roommate freshman year," Belle said.

Joey fist bumped Natasha, smiling. "Nice to see you again," he said.

"You too," she said.

"Great seeing you," Cos said, fist bumping her next.

"Thanks Cosby," Natasha said.

"Hey Dog!" Belle said.

"Oh, look at how cute he is!" said Natasha, petting him. Even Dog took to Natasha, putting his paws up on her dress.

"Get down, baby. I just got this dress," she said, pushing him down and brushing off the cotton knit.

The girls poured affection on him and he shook his body sideways in approval, wagging his stub tail.

"Dog likes the ladies," Wolly greeted them. "Beers?" He extended one to Paige and they each nodded yes. He handed each one a beer.

"Hey babe," Paige added. "Do you know Belle and my friend Natasha?"

"No, I don't think so, how do you do?" Wolly asked, tipping his ball cap to Natasha.

"Good, thanks," Natasha replied.

"So, what did y'all do last night?" Paige asked.

"Went swimming and ate a bushel with Old Salt. A perfect night," Wolly said.

"Sounds like a good time," Paige added. "How about this hurricane?"

"I can't believe this many people showed up tonight. A lot of people evacuated," Leslie said.

"*We always* stay. Teddy makes us," Joey said.

"Yeah, but your house is a fortress!" Leslie said.

"Leslie was just telling us about how incredible it is. Why haven't I ever gotten to see it?" asked Belle, looking at Joey.

"I don't know. You should come by sometime. It's a castle," Joey said and looked at Belle. Now that he could see into both eyes, he was in the deep end again and he never wanted to leave.

"That'd be great." She smiled at him, and then they both looked back at the others.

"It sounds great," Natasha said. She gave a pleasing smile whenever she glanced at Joey, while messing with her hair. He noticed and, on any other occasion, would have been very flattered.

"Count me in," Leslie said.

"You're in," Cos said, and she smiled.

"Y'all be careful! As we were leaving, the news reported Eliza is a Cat 2!" Paige said.

"Yeah, we heard," Cos said.

"This storm is going to be really rough if you're close to the ocean, even in your house. Dad has us booked at the Holiday Inn twenty miles inland so we're nowhere near the water," Wolly said.

"I hope my cousin's wedding in Savannah isn't canceled this weekend," Natasha said.

"Oh, consider it canceled," Wolly said. "I am surprised it isn't already raining here."

"Yeah, me too," Paige added.

"If everyone just hunkers down, I am sure it'll be all right, though." Wolly swigged his Georgia Brown and looked around. "Hey, is there any food here?"

"I think Zach has some hot dogs over at the bonfire," Paige said.

Wolly remarked, "Oh baby, I love a dog cooked over an open flame."

"I'll go with you. Come on!" Paige took him by the arm and they exited.

"Leslie told me about the pistol Cos found. It sounds so interesting. I wondered how his search was going this year," Belle said.

"Thanks. Yeah, Dad fished a baseless cannon out and feels he may be really close to something big. That means he's close to finding the hull, probably," Joey said.

"Did he let you see the cannon?" Belle said, smiling.

"Yeah, he lets us see everything," replied Joey.

"How neat," Belle said.

"I am sure he would be willing to take y'all out on *Gold Lip* one day if you want to come along," Cos added, fishing for Joey. Joey didn't appreciate it but stayed quiet.

"We'd love that, *wouldn't we* Leslie?" Belle said, looking at her.

"Oh yeah, Teddy is a great guy to! You'll like him, Belle."

"It's a deal. I already have my diving license," Belle said.

"Do you really?" Joey asked.

"Yep, I love to dive."

"We'll go then," Joey said.

"I wanna go," Natasha said.

"Sure," Joey said to her.

Jesse started to play Dave Matthews's "Me and You" in the background. "I love this song," Cos said. "Why don't we all go over and sit by the fire?"

"Sounds good, it's hard to pass on some Dave," Joey said.

They headed over. Joey managed to find his way next to Belle, who sat next to Paige, who leaned into Wolly, who was now working on his second hot dog. Natasha plopped down on the other side of Joey. Natasha and Joey talked and she asked him about school and life. After a while, she stretched out her legs, pushing her feet into the sand; her legs shining from the light of the fire. Jesse finished the song and transitioned into a Van Morrison song reminiscent of John Lee Hooker.

Leslie and Cos sat behind everyone with Dog; Cos rubbed her back; Dog managed to knock over an abandoned Sweetwater on a plastic trash bag and licked it up; Buzz sat across the bonfire, watching Cos and Leslie with a hot grimace. Seeing him, Cos decided they should go.

"I want to throw the ball for Dog in the ocean. You wanna come?" said Cos.

"Sure!" said Leslie.

"Come on then."

They got up and headed north along the water. Dozens of crabs skated sideways in front of them. Buzz stood up and shook his head, stomping off the other way.

When they neared the water's edge far from the crowd, Cos hurled a ball and Dog ran after it, diving into the black tide. He fished it out and jetted back with his tail wagging. Leslie threw it and he retrieved it again; they laughed at him trampling the waves. Cos tossed it again and took a big swig of his beer.

"He's having too much fun. I can't take it any longer, I am getting in too." He removed his shirt.

"What? Are you crazy? It's dark out and you can't see anything!"

"Can't help it babe, I got saltwater in my veins. Besides, there's nothing but flounder and crabs anyway out there. C'mon in! Can you wade out a little with your arm?" He got in with his chino shorts.

"Kind of. If I get in trouble, can you help me? I have my bathing suit on under my dress."

"I got you; we'll stay shallow."

Leslie finished off her beer and neatly folded her dress, placing it on the dune hill and waded in. They were out of view from the crowd, except for Dog, who sat patiently on the shore, watching them in confusion. Cos splashed her and she splashed back. He splashed harder and she splashed even harder. They both laughed and he tackled her into the warm sea. Their bodies connected in the sand with the tide coming into them, forcing his body into hers. He looked at her, hooking his arms under body.

"What are you doing, Cosby Dollarhide?" she said.

"Getting to know you better," he said with a slight smile.

"Uh-huh!" she said. His lips touched hers, and after some passionate kissing, he rose and helped her back up. They saw Dog running down the coast with Cos' shirt in his mouth. Cos called after him, but he kept going, eventually stopping to dig a hole and bury the shirt. They laughed it off and Leslie and Cos waded out past the second burst of waves. She braced herself on his soft hands.

He braced her and his nose touched her neckline where the jasmine and teak from her perfume mixed with the musk of the ocean. Her wet hand gripped around his neck and they kissed under the moonlight with salty lips. She wrapped her strong legs around his body and pushed her calves down on his butt, bringing his frame closer. In her hazel eyes, he saw a kindness in her heart that stirred his attraction. They kissed for minutes until she stopped him and leaned her head back, soaking her hair in the water; they bobbed in the ocean while he pointed to different constellations.

Back at the fire, Natasha got looser with Joey as she finished her second beer. She kept pushing her leg into his. Waiting long enough to not offend her, he excused himself. Strolling up the coast, Joey passed Dog sitting on top of the covered hole, saw the lovers in the water, and grinned. He kept walking and sat on the sand at the base of a dune where no one could see him.

After about ten minutes, Belle came that way, carrying her shoes.

"Hey Red!" Joey said. She stopped in front of him and looked around.

"Who's that?" Belle asked.

"It's me, Joey!" he said.

"Oh hey Joey, we wondered where you went."

"I just had to get away from the crowd."

"Yeah, me too. Would you like to walk with me?" Belle asked.

"Sure," he replied, hopping up and brushing the sand off his butt before meeting her. They walked along the beach, both carrying a Sweetwater beer.

"Natasha wondered where you went," Belle said.

"Oh yeah."

"Yeah, she really likes you. She told me so."

"That's flattering. I mean, she seems like a great girl," Joey said.

"Most guys fall to pieces when Natasha pays them that much attention. It seems like you ran away from her."

"She's just not my type, really."

"Well, you're the first," Belle said.

They both smiled and paused. They were a little nervous, but glad to be alone. Belle had trouble staring at his eyes without disappearing, and he couldn't stop looking at her lips, which spanned her wide awkward mouth.

They traveled into the black mystery where only the galaxy lit the sand, and then further away still from the flickering fire and the lights of the marina dotting the bay in the distance. They hugged the edge of the tide; the moist sand felt good on their bare feet as the saltwater curled around their toes. Belle savored the caramel malt.

"So, Austin has been great?" Joey asked.

"Yeah. I've met so many good friends and it's a city with a lot of flavor."

"It does have flavor," Joey said.

"It has some of the best BBQ. It's *so* good!"

"I know, Cos and I went to the Rub there once," Joey said and sipped his beer.

"I practically *live* at the Rub!"

"It's so good," he said, and paused. "So, are you dating anyone now?"

"Not at the moment. I just broke up with TJ this spring."

"I am sorry to hear it," he said, his voice almost soaring.

"It's all right. It was long overdue."

"What about you? Is there a *California* girl out there?

"Not right now."

"You've left LA, right?"

"Yeah."

"So no more baseball?"

"Nope. My injury last year cooked my chances at the pros."

"When you ran into the duck?" she said, smiling.

"Yep."

She laughed and tried to stop herself.

"You saw the video?"

"Yes, I tried not to laugh. On the phone you didn't tell me it was from running into a mascot—you said it was from a surfing accident."

"I lied. Actually, ESPN might pay me to do an ad." He smiled.

"Well at least something good will come out of it. Did you ever get the girl's number?"

"No, she won't speak to me," Joey insisted.

"Aww, I am sorry."

"It's okay, but I'll take the sympathy."

"Wasn't it your dream to play in the majors?"

"Growing up, it was always ball, but my dreams changed when I got hurt," he said, and paused.

"My dream has always been to go to Stanford; so far, nothing has changed that." They kept strolling.

"Congratulations, by the way. Stanford Business—that's *impressive*."

"Thanks."

"Are you excited?" he said as they continued down the beach.

"I am *really* excited, but the truth is my father wants me to go to business school at Texas, and he won't pay for me to go anywhere else unless it's a state school in the Southeastern Conference. If I go to Stanford, he won't even give me a *dime* for living expenses, which would make it very difficult because I would have to work. I don't want to disappoint him, but I also want to be true to myself."

"Bummer," he said. They kept walking.

"What would you do?" she asked.

"I'd follow my heart. If your heart is at Stanford, that's where you have to go. Besides, it's one of the best schools in the country. You can take out student loans and pay them back later on. Plus, northern California has incredible hiking, surfing and skiing."

"Thanks—I think you're right. I already gave my decision, but wasn't sure I'd go through with it. I haven't told my dad yet. I like the sound of all that nature. I am a nature buff myself."

"Underneath the stilettos and expensive purses?"

"I got a couple of boots and a compound bow in my closet."

"Yeah, I bet they have a lot of dust on them."

"*No*, but they got some dried mud on them!" she countered, gauging his response.

He looked smug with humorous disbelief.

"You don't believe me?" she said.

He smiled, "Not for a minute."

"I am more mountain than you, *city boy*."

"You wanna bet?"

"Yeah, I bet you can't skin a buck with a pocketknife," she said.

"So, you can't either!"

"Can so."

"Well, I'll have to see that sometime. I'll take you hunting this winter."

"No, I'll take you hunting!" Belle snapped back.

"Okay, but I choose the location."

"I'll bring my bow," Belle said.

"I'll bring my pocket knife."

They shook hands, smiling, and walked silently for a moment, still grinning.

"You're full of surprises, Belle. All these years and I never knew you hunted."

"Well there's a lot of things about me that you don't know, Mr. Dollarhide," she said, smiling. He watched the water—she watched the sand. They came across a cluster of trash and she picked it up.

"What the hell?" she said.

"It's a trashball. They wash up in LA sometimes. People need to be much more mindful of water pollution. It's so terrible to mess up your own living space," Joey said.

"Don't shit where you sleep!"

Joey stopped, "Damn! A buck-hunting, cursing nature buff who wears high heels."

"*What?* It sums it up nicely."

"I swear you're the only girl in Latch who thinks like this," Joey said.

"Is that a good thing?"

"It's a great thing."

"Then you must be the only guy in Latch who likes the way I think," she remarked, showing her teeth.

"I doubt that. There's certainly no one as special as you in Latch."

"So I am special now?" Belle said.

"You're *all right*," he said, looking away, trying to hold a straight face. She hit him on the arm and he stopped and turned toward her.

"You know I am joking," he said, and moved closer to her. "Actually, we're a lot alike." He took her beer and set their beers down, then took both of her hands. They ran into each other's eyes and she blushed and glanced down, raised her shoulders, and then looked back up at him with her forehead tilted forward.

"How?"

"Just close," he said. "You know, I've really missed talking to you."

"You should've called," she said, looking at him.

They started to kiss, but a gust of wind blew her red hair to the side of her face and a string landed in front of her lip. The wind carried the white plumeria flower of Kauai from her ear, tossing it back on the sand a few feet away. Joey went over and picked it up and smelled it; watching him, she smiled.

"I think you dropped something, miss." He reached up, placed it behind her ear again, and gently combed her hair with the inside of his fingertips. Then, he moved his hand slowly down the side of her soft cheek to her mouth, where he pulled her bottom lip down. She closed her eyes with her mouth hanging open. When their lips touched, lightning beamed down his body to the end of his toes. He pulled her tight and their mouths interlocked with their tongues dancing together in a perfect two-step. Her breath was sweet and he could still taste a touch of the Sweetwater there. A fire burst between them and the wind howled around, blowing her hair over his face; he smelled the jojoba oil in the bristles and the Bulgarian rose oil across her neckline; the wind picked up; warm raindrops fell. He pulled her head gently forward, kissing her on the forehead. She closed her eyes in an attempt to capture the moment, then looked back up at him intensely.

"That was wonderful," she said underneath her breath. Rain began to hit her face and a big drop landed on the tip of her nose.

"You have a raindrop on the tip of your nose," he said, wiping the drop away slowly. "And you're so beautiful."

She smiled. "Even with the black eye?"

"Even through the black eye."

"If you can like me like this, I think you could like me any way."

"I know I would like you any way."

They kissed again and the rain fell harder, soaking their hair. They stopped.

"Oh my God, it's raining cats and dogs!" Belle said, holding her hands up, smiling.

"It sure is! Bob Barclay was right! We better get back. We're pretty far from the bridge. Let's go!" He took her hand and they ran toward the flickering fire in the distance.

Cos and Leslie moved in from the ocean when the rain started;

Belle and Joey met them on the beach where Dog looked confused and afraid. Dog made his way ahead of them.

"Where is your shirt Cosby?" Joey asked.

"Somewhere over there, Dog buried them or something!" Cos answered.

"You two are crazy, but I like it," Belle said.

"Come on, we gotta get out of here," Joey said, leading the way.

Sideways rain battered the sand. In the distance, they could see the crowd at the campfire clearing out after dumping big gallons of water on the fire, leaving a pile of smoking ashes and black logs. People made their way off the bridge to their cars. Zach Watts, Leslie's ride, was waiting for her, but Buzz told him she got another ride, so he left. The group arrived at the bridge in five minutes and ran up the slick steps where a ranger stood.

"Do y'all idiots know there's a big ole hurricane coming? You better get on home," the park ranger who had arrived to clear people off the beaches said with a raised voice over the weather.

"Where's Natasha? She's my ride!" Belle yelled, looking around.

"Where's Paige and Wolly?" Cos exclaimed.

"They must have gone home, thinking Leslie could take us back," Belle said.

"No, Zach gave me a ride and he was supposed to wait for me!" Leslie exclaimed loudly through the wind.

"I bet Buzz told him to leave to punish us because he saw us together," Cos said.

"He wouldn't do that," Leslie snapped back.

"I think you overestimate Buzz's generosity," Cos barked through the rain.

"Look, you can come back to our house. It's stucco over masonry, and we have a generator. It's just up the road," Joey said.

"I guess my father can pick me up there. Okay!" Belle yelled through the storm.

"Sounds good," Leslie said.

The rain drenched them as they sprinted across the empty street. Cos had to carry Dog, who was shaking because he was so afraid of the rain. They ran north, hooking a left on Orange Street. On their way to Windswept, the heavens cried; their tears hurt. The group barely saw the path ahead, but managed to find the farm, open the gate, and jog down the long avenue of palm trees, which bent like asparagus in the wind, the leaves blowing sideways. The warm rain on the hot earth created a light haze, and the uplights on the palms still glowed through the sheets of water. They made it to the mahogany door. When they entered, the wind took the door so strongly that Cos and Joey together had to pull hard to shut it.

CHAPTER 7

Water dripped from their clothes and pooled on the clay tiles. Charlotte brought towels and spare clothes for everyone. They took turns changing in the sitting room off the foyer, then Joey led them into the grand den. The rain hammered the roof like a stampede of horses going to battle.

Oversized brandy-colored sofas floated in the den at angles to one another; high-backed leather reading chairs sat to the side of them. A coquina stone mantel commanded the wall facing the back porch, and a painting of a wizened man on a bald hillside hung above it. An antique Persian rug carpeted the mahogany floors running underneath the sofas. Animal skins, paintings, photos, and antiques climbed the fifteen-foot walls like ivy. The aroma of rolling tobacco and rich leather saturated the room, while sandalwood oil dispersed from a diffuser in the corner in cycles. A white sheet covered a baby grand piano crowded in another corner of the low-lit room.

The group flopped down on the couches; Dog took a spot on the floor next to Bear. The ladies walked around the room. In a minute, Charlotte entered wearing a crisp white button-up and a long grey skirt; she leaned forward slightly with her hands in front as she walked.

"Oh, you sweet things are all wet and cold. Come sit down and let me get you some hot coffee and tea. This hurricane is like an uninvited guest that topped it off by showing up early. Better call your parents and tell them you'll wait it out here. It'll blow all night."

"Oh, I can't stay, I have to get home!" Belle said. "My parents will worry."

"Me too," Leslie said.

"But ladies, you could get hurt going out in this. We can't have that. Y'all can call them and tell them you'll stay here. It's what's best."

"But..." Belle protested.

"I won't hear it. Isabella has masonry in her walls. Now, you just sit right here and make yourself at home." Charlotte's voice was like melted caramel seducing Belle into agreement.

"The house is that safe?" Belle asked.

"Yes, sugar," Charlotte answered.

"It'll be fine," Leslie said to Belle.

"Okay, I'll call them," Belle said.

"Oh good," Charlotte said.

Leslie called her parents also. She smacked on a big piece of gum, blowing bubbles and popping them quick, her way of dealing with the stress. Teddy walked in with Blue on his shoulder and greeted them. They laughed at the sight of the bird. Belle handed Teddy the phone, asking him to explain the situation to her mother. Leslie's parents, on the other hand, were okay with the arrangement and didn't need to speak to Teddy.

"Sure," he said, taking the phone to speak to Belle's mother. "Well, they were at the beach and the storm blew in early. My house is very secure. It has survived all the big ones." He paused. "Yes, *all* the big ones." He paused again. "Well, the foundation raises it off the ground five feet and the interior walls contain masonry. Plus, we're over a hundred yards from the ocean. The worst of the storm won't be here for a while, but the rain and wind are fierce. I could drive them home, but I don't think it's safe." He paused, listening. "Ok, I agree. I'll bring them home first thing in the morning. Take care." Teddy handed Belle the phone, and she said goodbye. When they finished, Teddy spoke,

"All right, ladies and gentleman. Most of you know my pet macaw, Blue." He looked at the bird. "Say hello, Blue."

"Hell-o," Blue croaked.

The room chuckled.

"And this is my best friend and business partner, Dallas, he decided to ride out of the storm with us this evening," Teddy said.

Charlotte waved at the group, smiling.

"Hey guys," Dal said, leaning back deep into one of the leather chairs.

"Belle, it's very nice to meet you and to have you in our home. I am sorry it happened under these circumstances, but I do say you make the room brighter."

"Nice to finally meet you too, Mr. Dollarhide. I've known Joey for years."

"Thanks Belle. Leslie, it's a pleasure to see you again."

"You too, Teddy."

"I am afraid I have some bad news. Eliza gained momentum due to the warm waters, and it looks like she'll touch down early and may even be a strong category 2 hurricane. A lot of people headed to the old auditorium in Lankford for shelter."

"A strong Cat 2!" Joey said. "Good grief Dad, that *is* bad news."

"Yeah, but *don't worry*, Isabella is a tank. Nothing can move her. Aside from the library upstairs, this room provides the most protection, so I'd like for y'all to sleep in here tonight. There are quilts for bedding in the closet. Ladies, you're welcome to the couches. Guys, you're sleeping on the floor. Any questions?"

Shaking their heads in the negative, they let the information digest.

"Okay, now that we got that out of the way, we might as well relax. Charlotte, will you please bring in some refreshments?" Teddy asked.

"Certainly," Charlotte replied.

"Thank you." She exited. Teddy went into the connected dining room, where he placed Blue in a cage. The power went out. Blackness blanketed the house. Dog's bark startled them.

"Well, I wasn't expecting that this early," Teddy yelled out. "Don't worry, I just need to flip on the generator." He strolled out to the garage and flipped the switch.

A moment later, Charlotte floated in from the kitchen carrying a silver tray with coffee, liqueur, and Earl Grey tea flanked by cookies and English dessert biscuits. They each approached, taking the warm beverages and sweets back to their places on the sofas. Teddy entered, and Charlotte brought Dal and him warm brandy from the kitchen.

"Thank you, Charlotte," Dal said, admiring her beauty as she glided over to Teddy.

"Thanks, Charlotte," Teddy said, taking a big sip. "Why don't you get yourself one?

"That's all right, I am fine."

"Suit yourself, but there's nothing like a warm brandy with a storm coming."

"All right, maybe just a pinch." She left.

"Eliza sounds bad," Belle remarked.

"Yeah it does," Joey said.

"What do you think, Salt? You have a lot of experience with storms," Dal said.

"I think it's time to dance!"

"Time to dance?" Dal said, smiling.

"Yes, we dance for protection. I grew up in a little town called Goodchance, Alabama, you see, and it was right smack dab in the center of hurricane alley near the Gulf of Mexico, then I lived in Miami and Key West. I've probably got ten 'canes under my belt. Never been hurt because I always dance or do something good beforehand—as a ritual, you know."

He bounced up, grinned, and turned on the stereo; Sam Cooke zoomed out of the speakers and off the walls, drowning out the sound of the rain. For a big man, Teddy jigged and glided across the room with ease, making the ladies giggle and the men grin. Taking Charlotte's hand, he led her up and they danced on the rug. The crowd watched him spin and move her across the den with grace and began to clap along to the music. Dog followed it and barked, while Bear walked alongside him.

After dancing for a few minutes, a noise sounded near the chimney and a yellow thing flew out of the fireplace. They gradually stopped dancing and clapping, and turned to watch the strange visitor. By the way it fell and climbed in the air and its yellow and black coloring, Teddy knew it was an eastern tiger swallowtail butterfly. Their eyes grew wide, their faces filling with wonder.

Dancing around the room, it eventually rested on the coffee table, where it moved its wings up and down.

"Well I'll be. No one has seen a swallowtail here in over a hundred years," Charlotte said.

"Yep, how did he get into the chimney?" Teddy said, pop-eyed.

"Probably just flew in like the birds do," Charlotte said.

They studied him for a moment as Sam Cooke transitioned into "Bring It on Home to Me."

"I think that's our cue," Joey said to Belle. He took her soft hand, and their bare feet crisscrossed the rug. Her long, wet hair was now dark auburn, and as it flipped back and forth, he wished they were alone again. Cos took Leslie's hand and led her around by her one arm. The soul of Sam Cooke insulated the room from the fury of the rising winds outside. Teddy and Charlotte started dancing again after their fascination with the critter wore off. When the song ended, Teddy flopped down in his chair and drank some brandy. They clapped and returned to admiring the stationary butterfly. Bear went after the insect, but Joey batted him down.

Teddy saw another swallowtail flutter out of the chimney. He pointed, "Look, look, another one!" As it danced, they stood in the center of the room watching it ascend above their heads. Another one followed it, and another, and another, and then they kept coming, two and three at a time—a parade waltzing into the room, over fifteen. After a few minutes, they stopped entering, the room full of a dazzling display of pulsing color. Dog barked in excitement and Bear jerked his head this way and that, looking up at them.

"Oh my God! I've never seen anything like this!" Leslie said.

"Where did they come from?" Belle asked.

"They must have sought shelter from the storm in the chimney,"

Teddy said. "But why they came back after all these years, I haven't got a clue. This is a great blessing, and a good sign for the town."

"You know this town used to be a haven for these butterflies. The eastern tiger swallowtails covered the green spaces by the hundreds—so impressive were the numbers that people would come from as far as Oregon and Michigan to see them. That was before the … well you know," Dal added.

"Before what?" Belle asked. "I've never heard about this."

"The revolt at the Willis Plantation," Joey said.

"The town secret," Leslie added.

"Now, we don't know that, Joey," Charlotte added.

"Well we know something made that place haunted," Joey said.

"But no one knows what *really* happened. It has never been investigated," Dal added. "Slaves and workers alike just disappeared."

"Whatever! Enough sadness. Tonight is a night of celebration and good cheer before the storm! Let's continue to dance until we're full of it," Teddy said.

"Nothing Can Change This Love" began to play, and the dance partners pulled each other close and swayed in the low-lit room amid the kaleidoscope of butterflies. Some landed on surfaces for a moment, only to start flying again, thirsty for the feeling of the air in their wings. Joey placed his hands around Belle's warm, round hips. They swayed back and forth in the silence of their attraction, still mesmerized by the insects.

Dal took Charlotte's hand and they embraced to the music. They had recently started dating after flirting for years, a slow fruitful harvest of kind words and gestures that erupted into an exhilarating night of sex on the beach after too much Cab Sav and oysters three months ago.

After a while, one of the butterflies landed on Belle's head while she and Joey danced. The group looked on and Leslie commented on it. Belle kept dancing with a grin, allowing it to sit there. The swallowtail spread its wings and then lifted them up again in a fluid motion; its presence tickled her skin, making Joey and her giggle. The song ended and everyone clapped in applause at the show. Belle started to walk, but the butterfly stayed on for the ride.

"He's really taken a liking to you," Dal said with a wide smile. "Joey, I think he's moving in on your girl!"

"What should I do?" she said and held her arms out with the palms up.

"I'll get him," Joey said, attempting to scoop the butterfly up, but it took off, flying across the room in a crooked line until it landed on a metal acorn post of a high-backed chair in the far corner.

The white walls now pulsed with the movement of the black and yellow wings. They took pictures with their phones while Teddy shook his head and smiled before exiting to grab a fishing net and a massive empty aquarium. With the net, he rounded many of them up and placed them in the aquarium that he set on the oversized ebony African coffee table.

Cos exited and returned with piles of quilts that were so old and soft the touch made one want to dive into the fabric, wishing life was always that gentle. Then, he brought down pillows and blankets from the hall closet and handed them to the ladies, who built nests on the deep-lined leather sofas; Cos and Joey spread their blankets on the Persian carpet.

An uncustomary chill filled the house, and Old Salt tossed some logs on the fireplace. Everyone showed concern about there being more butterflies in the chimney, but he shrugged it off, setting the logs ablaze. Charlotte brought in a warm soup made from multicolored heirloom tomatoes and fresh basil picked from the garden. The wind howled outside while they ate the soup and watched the butterflies in the aquarium.

"So, are you excited about college?" Charlotte asked Leslie.

"Yes, I am!"

"I bet your parents will miss you," Charlotte said.

"No. I think they want to get rid of me," Leslie said, laughing and looking at the butterflies, still occasionally tapping on the plastic case.

"Oh, now you *know* that's not true, honey."

"I know, but it *feels* true sometimes."

"Where are you going?" Charlotte asked.

"Miami."

"That's great. What about you, Belle, are you in school now?"

She looked at Joey before turning her head and answering, "I just finished undergrad and I am going to Stanford for business school. At least, I think so."

"That is a very good school! Congratulations!" Teddy said.

"Thank you!" she replied.

Teddy sipped his drink. Thunder clashed. Dog barked.

"*Sit down, Dog!* I swear you're as nervous as a cat's tail in a room full of rocking chairs. I am gonna give him a Benadryl," Charlotte said to Teddy.

"Now Charlotte, you know Dog has a sensitive stomach to everything except wild stuff—last time we gave him a Benadryl, he farted all night," Teddy said. The room laughed.

"Oh that's right. Well, we can't have him stinking up the place I guess."

"Salt, when do you think the storm will be here?" Dal asked.

"I reckon the eye will be here around one a.m."

"What's the eye?" Colt asked.

"The eye is the worst part," Belle said.

"No, Bellaboo, the eye is the calmest part. It's the center of the hurricane where there's no wind or rain. It's so quiet you can hear a twig break," Leslie said.

"Oh sorry, I was raised inland in Texas, so I am still a hurricane rookie."

"Dad has been in the eye before. Tell them about Key West!" Cos blurted.

"Maybe some other time; I don't want to alarm anyone."

"Aww, c'mon!" Joey said.

"No, next time."

"Teddy, I just love that painting over the mantel," Leslie said.

"Thank you, Leslie." He paused and sipped his drink, studying it.

"That's our super-great-grandpa Luke," Cos said.

"He was a forty-niner out in California during the Gold Rush," Teddy said. "The first gold bug in our family."

"Did he find any?" Leslie asked.

"A little, but he eventually came back to Alabama to be an oysterman and later opened a restaurant."

"Tell us about Luke and the cowgirls!" Cos pleaded.

"Oh, the ladies don't want to hear that," Teddy said.

"What cowgirls?" Belle asked.

"It's a great story! Tell them, Dad!" Joey said.

"Tell us, Salt, *please*," Leslie begged.

"All right, if you insist." Teddy took another sip of his drink and lit a stogie.

"It was 1853 in the High Sierras of California. Luke and his brother Sam were working a mine for six months and had just struck gold. Life in the mountains was hard. It was frigid at night, and about once a week they tangled with a bear the miners called Ole Sawtooth. Ole Saw was no ordinary bear. It was rumored he weighed seven hundred pounds and had even been shot. Apparently, he had a stomach for gunpowder too; if he could find it in a camp, he would eat it."

"He would eat it?" Leslie asked.

"He *craved it*. One day, Luke found a big sized nugget of gold in the mine and went down to the river to show Sam; Sam was supposed to be panning for gold, but instead he was fishing naked like he used to do." Teddy paused and puffed the cigar, grinning quietly to himself at the thought of Sam. The rain sang outside; he blew some smoke and crossed his legs.

"So, Luke showed Sam the nugget and they decided to go back to the mine about a quarter mile away to celebrate with wine and chocolate, but when they returned, some rough cowgirls with double-barreled rifles and pistol holsters on their belts had seized it. The leader was named Josephine. She was beautiful and had curly red hair. She might have looked gentle, but she was rough, barking orders, drinking whiskey, and spitting on the ground."

Belle's eyes grew big as she listened.

"Luke and Sam had left their guns in the camp, so they didn't know what to do." He paused and sipped his drink again, stroked his white beard, and took another puff off the big cigar. Belle and Leslie leaned forward on the edge of the sofas.

"So *what* did they do?" Belle asked.

"Well, they set up on a high bluff across the river. From there they could see the mine through a hole in the pine trees and juniper brush. Sam suggested a honey burn where a jar of honey is placed in a can and burned on a fire until it boils, producing a white aromatic smoke that sticks to the trees to lure bears to it, so Luke went into town and returned with the honey; they placed it in a can and lit it on a small fire down below. Climbing a nearby tree with a wooden post for hunting, they watched and waited. The burning honey carried a thick white smoke into the air and the pungent aroma blew with the wind, sticking to the bark and leaves. After a little while, Sam hopped down from the tree and picked up the burnt honey. Then, he mixed some molasses with it and ascended the path to the mine camp to paint it on the trees. On his way back, he heard a rumbling in the bush to the left of the path ahead of him."

"What was it?" Leslie asked.

"It's..." Cos started.

"Don't give it away!" Teddy barked. Cos closed his mouth as tight as a keyhole.

Teddy sipped the brandy and dragged his smoke with the whole room waiting. He stood up and paced the room, becoming more exaggerated.

"Out of the bushes, Ole Saw came barreling toward Sam, who dropped the can of honey, running like the wind back to the tree, climbing it faster than a monkey. Saw gunned it straight for the can, licking it with his big pink tongue. Afterward, he waltzed over to the tree and shook it like he was trying to knock a coconut loose. They held on, and after a while, Saw lost interest, choosing to follow the sugary scent into the mine.

"Luke and Sam waited, and about a minute later, they heard a shrill scream that woke the dead—those cowgirls came busting out of the camp half-dressed like they were on fire. So, Luke and Sam went back to the bluff for the night, and lo and behold, when they returned in the morning, Ole Saw was camping out in the shaft," Teddy bellowed. "Damn bear."

"How did they get him out? I forget," Joey asked.

"My dad Jimbo says they went back to town, bought a bow, and did another burn the next night to lead him out into the open, where they shot him. And that's where my bearskin came from." He gestured with his head and eyes to the grizzly skin mounted on the wall; everyone looked.

"It sure is a big skin," Belle said.

"Dad claims that's Ole Saw. Says it's been passed down from Luke. He told us all that nugget of gold sustained him for many years. But you know, getting the truth from him ain't easy," Teddy stated.

"So it could be from another bear?" Belle said.

"Possibly, but a Dollarhide never lets the truth interfere with a good story, you see."

"Thanks Teddy, that's some tale," Leslie said.

"You're very welcome." He sat.

"Legend has it Luke also learned of a John Hodges's treasure up in those mountains, but never found it. Ain't that right Dad?" Joey said.

"Now, I don't know if there even was a treasure; Jim is always spinning a yarn."

"I want to go find it!" Cos said.

"Me too," Belle said.

"If the story is true, Luke looked for it and never found it. What makes y'all think you'll find it?" Teddy said.

"I've got the gold nose, like Dog, you know. Besides, I've got good luck also," Cos said.

"It takes more than luck to find treasure, son," Teddy said. "You need stories and facts, data that hunts."

"Who was John Hodges?" Leslie asked.

"It's been awhile, tell us again Dad," Cos pressed.

Teddy slipped his buffalo-skin moccasins off, rubbing his toes on the Persian wool.

"John Hodges was a sort of legend during the California Gold Rush. He came out West to stake a claim. Legend has it his wife died early of some awful disease. Angry at the world, he became a bandit, assembling a group known as the Triangle of Ghosts who tricked and robbed people all over the West—everyday was Halloween for the Ghosts—but they never killed or hurt anyone, supposedly.

"One day, they cleared a safe of gold out from a bank and headed off into the Sierras to bury it for safekeeping—this way, they could dig it up whenever they wanted, take out whatever they needed, and bury it again. But, while traveling along the road, they happened to be seized by Native Americans, who stole it. They needed it to buy firearms for protection against white soldiers. The Native Americans buried the chest in the mountains until a later date when they planned to cash it in."

"Then what?" Leslie asked, on the edge of her seat still.

"Well about two months later, the Native Americans were attacked before they had a chance to use it. Most were killed, except for a few who fled the area never to return. I suppose that chest remains buried somewhere in the High Sierras to this day, but no one knows where. The Native American told Luke about it in a Bagby jail, I think. Apparently, Luke told the story all the time. Said he went looking for it, but never found anything."

Teddy tugged on his fat cigar, then put it out and finished the drink.

"What a story!" Belle said.

"If it's true, truth sure is stranger than fiction," Teddy said.

"It's a great story, Dad. What do you think about the treasure being there? We should go after it," Cos said.

"I don't know. If you do, be careful—Ole Saw's kin might be roaming around."

A boom occurred outside and everything went black except for the warm glow of the fire. Dog barked. Charlotte rose, reassured the group with her tender voice, and lit some candles, which radiated through the room with a soft blaze. The house started to shake a little from the force of the wind—Joey moved closer to Belle, wrapping his arm around her shoulder—Cos went into the kitchen to get some food—Leslie trailed him.

Teddy and Dal got flashlights to check on the generator while Charlotte continued to cover Isabella in candlelight. When Teddy and Dal reached the garage, the smell of motor oil and burnt metal seeped from the device.

Lightning must have struck the outside convertor, Teddy thought.

In the kitchen, Cos sifted through the counter looking for food; he spotted an apple pie in a glass container. He cut off a fourth of the pie and carried it back to the living room, where Dog was curled up on the ground. Cos entered with the treats and nestled on the sofa next to Leslie—they ate it, sharing a fork.

Charlotte unwound in the dining room with a game of solitaire by candlelight. She let her hair down and slipped off her shoes; the wool felt good on her sore feet.

"How are you doing, baby?" Dal asked, walking in from the hall leading to the garage.

"Oh, I am all right."

"You want me to get you some coffee?"

"That would be nice."

He went to the candlelit kitchen. Teddy entered and sat down next to her.

"Generator's fried," Teddy said. "The damn thing is screwed up! It's going to be a long stuffy night cooped up in here." He paused. "Dally, pour me a Pyrat, will you?" he said, directing his voice through to the kitchen.

"Sure."

In a minute, Dal came back in with the rum and coffee, handed them to Teddy and Charlotte and sat down.

"Thanks—hey, maybe Eliza will uproot more of our ship," Teddy said.

"I was thinking the same thing. This could be a good thing."

"I like your optimism," said Teddy, holding up his glass in toast. "Cheers!" Their glasses clanged.

"Did you hear gold broke a record today - $1725?" Dal asked.

"Oh yeah, we're in the right business, that's for sure," Teddy said.

"Why is gold so popular now, anyway? Sounds like fear to me," Charlotte said.

"A lack of faith in the dollar," Teddy said.

"Why don't people trust the dollar? I just don't understand," Charlotte said, flipping her cards over and moving them around.

"You see, everything changed when President Nixon took us off the gold standard. Ever since then, nothing has backed the dollar. When the government needs money, it turns the printers on at the Federal Reserve and writes IOUs to other nations and itself. It's like if we would go over to our computer and print money off the Hewlett Packard when our bank accounts get low. That process floods the market with an empty currency, creating inflation and an increased deficit."

"What's the silly debt now?" Charlotte asked.

"Over twenty two trillion and counting, and China owns a lot of it. And they're getting tired of financing our debt," Dal said.

"I didn't know it was that bad," Charlotte said. "So, what do you think is going to happen?"

"Well, the US Dollar is the reserve currency for the whole world. As long as other countries finance our debt by buying and holding the dollar, then we're fine. But, if they decide to dump it, and buy gold and cryptocurrency, the dollar will decline, and, well … you get the idea."

"Well, let's pray to God that doesn't happen," Charlotte said.

"Amen to that," Teddy said.

"Amen," Dal said.

"So, what's the solution?" asked Charlotte.

Teddy looked squarely at her with an air of seriousness and said, "The solution is for our country to *really* reduce its debt, get a hold on the Federal Reserve's currency manipulation, and return to a sounder currency like a crypto that is backed by gold. Then, the faith in the dollar will be strong. Here's to financial stability for the world," Teddy said, holding up his glass and inviting another toast. They clanged their glasses with his; Dal and Charlotte made eyes; Teddy caught it.

"You two look good together."

"Thanks, Teddy. What about you? When are you going to start dating again? Cosby will be gone soon and it's going to get lonely with just you and Colt," Dal said.

"Oh, I reckon I'll do fine. I got the animals here. I don't get lonely, anyway," Teddy remarked.

"Everyone gets lonely. I see you sometimes playing chess with yourself late at night," Charlotte said, watching Teddy.

"How do you play chess alone?" Dal asked.

"It's easy, you just move for yourself and the other person," answered Teddy.

"Oh, that's really sad, Salt," Dal said, laughing.

Teddy smiled, "But I had a dream about a woman last night."

"Really? Who?" Charlotte asked.

"I don't know. It was in another time. In Spain."

Charlotte shook her head, "Teddy, dreams are wonderful, but you can't hold them, depend on them, or share a family with them. I think you should go on some dates."

"No way."

"Yeah, you should, Salt. Charlotte set Ty up with a real nice woman and it worked out—intelligent, and a looker too."

"*Really?*"

"Yeah," Dal answered.

"Well, I am not doing it. I'll find my lady one day," he barked, crossing his arms in defiance.

"You still haven't let go of Sarah, have you? I can see it in your eyes. You're waiting for her as if she could somehow come back, but she can't. You have to move on. You may find that treasure out at sea, but you won't find love. I think you should visit the graveyard," Charlotte said.

"No," remarked Teddy.

"But you have to, Teddy, it's the only thing that'll make it real for you," pleaded Charlotte.

"I am *never* going *there*." His mouth turned up as he squirmed in his chair.

"I'll take you sometime next week. You *have* to see her grave."

"Dammit Charlotte, what part of *no* don't you understand?!" He stood up and paced around the room, slicking his hair back.

"Chill out Salt, she's just trying to help. Maybe she's right, you know."

Teddy paused, looking through the glass into the indoor poolroom with his hands on his hips. "I am sorry Charlotte, I just don't like graveyards. You pushed me," Teddy said with a soft voice.

"I am sorry, Teddy. Listen, I have a real nice friend who's a chef downtown. I think you two would make a great pair." Teddy loosened up, walked back over and sat down.

"Oh come on Charlotte, no blind dates please." He gulped the Pyrat.

"Why not? I've already told her about you, and she wants to meet you. She said you sounded real interesting, with the treasure hunting and the cat sidekick."

"*Seriously* Charlotte, why'd you have to do that?

"She's beautiful and an incredible cook. She's very nice and *besides* with all that good fish you bring in, she would always have food and you would always have a cook."

He paused for a moment, tempted by the possibility of a live-in professional chef. "I do love to eat. Just how good of a cook is she?"

"She's pretty *damn* good." Dal said, "She runs that new restaurant, Blonde, downtown."

"Haven't been there, but I like the name, I guess."

"If she can play chess, you'll have it made." Dal joked.

"Come on, Teddy," Charlotte begged.

"I'll *think* about it."

"That's a yes!" Charlotte said, smiling.

"No, that's a *maybe*."

"Come on, at least check her out first, why don't you," Charlotte insisted, showing him her facebook photo on her smartphone.

"She's very pretty Charlotte, but she's not serious enough for me. I am a serious guy you know," Teddy said. "I can tell by looking at her, she's not a big thinker."

IN THE OTHER ROOM, the younger crowd chatted.

"I think we should go to California and find that damn treasure," Cos said. "It could pay my way through college, and I could pay the high school back for the cow prank."

"I want to go! I could pay for Stanford."

"Me too!" Leslie said. "Maybe I could buy a new arm. They have these sweet robotic arms now."

"Oh babe, that sounds kind of sexy," Cos said.

"You two are silly," Belle said.

"I could pay for graduate school," Joey added, his head resting in Belle's lap as she combed his wheat-colored locks with her hand.

"I would buy a brand-new Toyota Tacoma and retire the chicken mobile," Cos added.

"But I *love* the chicken!" Leslie said.

"Really?" Cos said.

"Yeah!"

"Well, maybe I could buy it from Dan, but I am quitting the fryer for sure."

"That's bull! You're never going to stand up to Dan. He would go ape shit on you," Joey said.

"Just you wait and see, bro."

"I would give it all away after paying for school of course," Belle said.

"I would too, but hopefully there would be enough left over for a new arm and a Louis Vuitton handbag," Leslie said.

"I know, I like the Tivoli GM."

"Oh, I know the one you're talking about—with the crossed leather clasps."

"Yeah, that's it."

"I like the one that has the cream-colored leather across the top going up the handles. I forget the name, but it looks like a bowtie," Leslie said.

"Oh I know that one too, I think it's even called the Bowtie PM or something like that."

"Is it really? That's funny; it's *so* cute."

"Okay, okay. Everyone just settle down. We'll all get our share of the treasure that *we don't have*," Joey said.

"There's nothing wrong with dreaming, Joey," Belle said, looking sharply down at him.

"I guess you're right."

"Dreams are what make life worth living," Belle reiterated.

"You're so right, Belleaboo. In that case, I am getting a boat."

CHAPTER 8

Hours passed with dreams of wealth distracting everyone from the harsh winds and destruction outside the safety of Isabella's walls. A crash occurred outside and Teddy zipped into the kitchen from the dining room to see the farm drowning in water.

He shuffled back into the other room with a look of hysteria.

"What's wrong?" Dal asked.

"A storm surge has flooded the yard!"

"Oh, man," Dal said.

"Charlotte, please gather some food and take it upstairs to the library. We need to prepare in case the water keeps rising," Teddy said.

"Okay, I will get on it," she said.

"Help me put up the animals, Dal!" Teddy ordered.

"You want to go out in this weather?! Are you crazy?" Dal asked.

"No, I don't want to, I need to."

"Well you know I am your wingman, crazy or not."

Charlotte kissed Dal and straightened his collar, asking him to be careful, then exited into the kitchen to place the food into a trunk.

Teddy and Dal strapped on waders and slickers, then Teddy grabbed a very long coiled rope from the garage.

When they went outside, fierce winds blew their bodies back and tossed water against the third step, splashing it up at their legs. Rainwater stung their eyes; reminding Teddy of being on *La Gracia*. Through the sheets of rain, he saw Joey's Chevy and his own Ford truck submerged in water, a large oak limb planted in the Chevy's front windshield. Teddy threw Dal a headlamp and tied the rope to one of the stone lions' heads at the top of the front steps, then knotted it around his waist, and then to Dal's. They waded out into the warm violence as waves bashed against their torsos, sideways rain pelleting their faces.

When they reached the tree house about thirty feet from the barn, the wind picked up and Teddy slipped and fell into the water; the current carried him away from the barn. Dal grabbed onto the ladder of the tree house and dug his waders deep into the softened ground, then he pulled on the rope one arm at a time until he reeled Teddy back to the tree. Teddy hugged him and they pushed on to the barn.

It was dark and wet inside, and the horses were loud and wild-eyed.

Taking off the rope, they looped it around a wooden stall post in the barn and treaded through the water that seeped in under the crack of the door like a bad spirit. Teddy led Caramel over to the ramp he'd constructed in case this very scenario ever happened and, with Dal's help, took her up. As they led the Arabian, Earful, up next, their muscles started to fatigue, their faces turned red, and their foreheads dripped with sweat, but they continued until all the horses were upstairs. Finally, they led Five Alarm up. After retying the ropes, they waded outside back toward the house. No way they could shepherd the chicken flock up the ramp, so they let them be.

Thirty feet from the house, the speed of the wind increased and so did the current, which knocked Teddy sideways; his weight pulled Dal with him. The current took them away from the house until the slack of the rope drew tight on the lion's head, holding them steady. Twigs and debris floated into and around them. From the water, they both grabbed hold of the rope and dug their feet into the ground; using it like a lifeline, they followed it with their hands, but the rope started to give and they fell back down. The rope held them in place, but as they pulled on it, the loose knot started to unravel from the stone lion's mane.

"*What are we going to do?*" Teddy yelled through the rain.

"I don't know!" Dal yelled back, holding on tight. Teddy considered the scenario of the knot coming undone; the current would carry them onto the back thirty acres where Eliza would tear them to shreds when she arrived. Flashes of *La Gracia* came in and out of his mind. The color of the sky was that same haunting shade and the angle of the rain exactly the same, but this time Admiral García wasn't there to wind his watch for good luck and there was no boat waiting to take him to shore. The line slipped and they slid back five feet. Then, the rope caught and jiggled a little. Teddy glanced up at the front door, blocking the rain with his hand. Through the falling water, he saw Dog tugging the rope tight around the lion.

"Look Dal! Look!" Teddy said. Dal saw Dog. "Good boy! He must have come out through the cat flap," Teddy yelled through the rain.

"Good dog!" Dal yelled.

They stood back up against the force of the weather. When they jerked again, the rope was tight so they were able to make their way to the front door. Teddy picked up Dog and kissed his head. Dog smiled. "Even though Dog loves water, he has an intense fear of storms, too. The Jack Russell is a genius, though. I swear he knew we needed his help."

After entering Isabella, they collapsed in the candlelit entryway, resting their backs against the thick mahogany door. Dal rubbed Teddy's shoulder and told him they did it. Charlotte greeted them with towels and water. After drying off, they stumbled into the living room, Dog following, and flopped into chairs.

"Boy, you may not be the best fish I've reeled in, but you sure were the hardest," Dal joked to Teddy. Teddy laughed.

"That dog saved us," Dal exclaimed to the room.

"Sure did."

The group was amazed when they explained what Dog had done.

After half an hour, Eliza's first wall arrived. Isabella shook from her pressure, like an army rushing a castle. Charlotte, Dal, and Teddy rose to go to the kitchen. A boom shook the wall to the right of the mantel. A huge oak tree branch fired through a boarded up window, sending shattered glass into the room.

"Get down!" Teddy hollered. The end pierced Ole Sawtooth's hide on the wall, just missing Dal, who reacted quickly and dived to push Teddy and Charlotte out of the way. The gust coming in knocked out some of the candles, and the picture of Luke fell, crashing on the floor.

Water leaked in through the broken boarded up window while the rain rattled on the ceramic roof. Eliza thundered into Isabella through the opening like a lion roaring that never stopped to breathe. A heavy limb from the Oak branch landed on Dal's leg and he lay on the floor in pain. Teddy saw that the limb was in the same spot as the cannon in his dream; he lifted it off and helped Dal over to a chair with Dog behind him. The ladies and young men watched from the sofas, clinging to each other.

Blood seeped from the wound. Teddy went into the kitchen to get gauze pads from a storage cabinet, cold bottled water from the fridge, and a pan to wash the water into. While he was leaving the kitchen, the impact-resistant glass exploded and a piece of wood debris flew into a glass cabinet, splattering glass everywhere. Teddy kneeled and hustled into the living room.

"What just happened?" Joey asked.

"Some flying debris broke the bay window!" answered Teddy.

"Not very resistant."

"Not to a hundred mile an hour flying piece of wood. Y'all might want to stay out of the kitchen."

He poured the Perrier on the wound and Dal grimaced in pain when the cold touched his ripped skin. Teddy nodded toward his remaining brandy on the coffee table; Dal picked it up and swallowed it in one sip. Teddy wrapped his leg with the gauze and then rested in the chair beside him, assuring the group they would be safe—his confidence was contagious, and the room relaxed with him.

After about twenty minutes, the storm slowed down and everyone breathed easier.

In a bit, they heard a screeching sound accompanied by loud thuds on the boarded windows coming from the back porch.

"What's next?" Dal asked with sweat beading on his brow.

"I don't know," Teddy said. The screeching happened again. "I'll go check it out when the eye hits."

After five minutes, the winds and rain ceased. The pounding and screeching continued, amplified now by the silence.

Picking up his Browning Safari rifle from the firearm case, Teddy walked into the calm silence on the stone back porch. Water buried the pool; debris from the pool house floated all over the yard.

What he saw next stunned him. Occupying much of the width of the back porch was a white and brown spotted hog, banging its head on the wood covering of one of the living room windows and squealing.

Teddy trotted back inside and got the rope, cut it with his CRKT pocketknife, and knotted it, making a fat loop on one end. Then, he slowly approached the hog with the rifle in one hand and the rope in the other. He wanted to lead it away from the wall before shooting it.

As it turned, they made eye contact. Teddy saw a kindness there; the hog was quiet for a moment, but just as Teddy approached, it resumed banging its head and crying. Teddy backed off with the gun, which now shook in his hand. He knew that if the hog decided to attack, it could kill him—yet, he didn't *sense* danger. Waiting for a moment, he approached a second time and managed to loop the rope around the hog's neck. While tightening it, the hog turned, staring at him. He led it away from the wall; the hog resisted at first, but to his surprise, came with ease at the second tug. After getting him out to the center of the porch, Teddy prepared to fire, but the hog just stood there, looking at him. He had hunted and killed wild hogs before, but there was something deep in this one's eyes that wouldn't let him pull the trigger, something almost beautiful ... wise. Lowering the gun, he led the hog inside to the poolroom.

"You stupid hog, you see what you're making me do? This is so stupid."

Inside, he looked at the hog, and it smiled. "Do you know you have a twenty-five-thousand-dollar reward on your head?"

The group sat in the door to the poolroom, expressing genuine bafflement at the sight of the soaking wet mammoth beast, which stood there like stone. They watched it and it watched them; it smiled and they laughed; Bear and Dog sniffed it and it wiggled its caboose at them. Teddy held the gun on it while each person entered slowly and petted him. He rubbed the side of his smiling head against Belle's knee, gazing up at her.

"Is *that* Half Ton?" Joey asked.

"I reckon it is," Teddy said.

"I can't believe he survived out there," Cos said.

"No wonder Belle's dad wants him dead; he's a beast." Joey said.

"Have you ever seen a wild hog act like this?" Teddy asked Dal.

"Well, I've never seen one that big, period. He's enormous! I haven't seen that many, but *I know this isn't right*. He's acting like a damn housecat."

"Good Lord!" Teddy said. "What are we going to do with him? He'll die if we put him back outside."

"Then let him die; he's too dangerous to keep inside," Dal said.

"I know you're right, but I can't. There's something in his eyes," Teddy said. "Is there *anywhere* we could place him?"

"*Something in his eyes?* There's something in his weight and size too. He could kill someone, Salt, and tear this house to shreds," said Dal.

"I know, but I am keeping him."

"Well if you're going to be stupid, you might as well be smart stupid, so how about the garage?" Dal offered.

"It's flooded by now," Teddy remarked. Dal shrugged.

"What about the sauna?" Charlotte suggested.

"Yeah, that's just what the hog needs, Charlotte: a big bath," remarked Dal.

"I am just trying to be helpful." She shot him a glance.

"It's a good idea, Charlotte," Teddy said, and then led the hog down the hall to the tiled sauna. Half Ton's eyes thanked him when he closed the door. As Teddy walked away, Bear pawed at the door, meowing. Teddy returned to the living room where he patched the window around the tree with plastic, which he duct-taped in place. Then, he did the same to the kitchen window.

Teddy directed the young folks to the upstairs library for the second wall of the storm; Charlotte gave them the trunk of food, candles, and flashlights to carry up.

CHAPTER 9

*J*oey led them up the ceramic stairs and down the long, tiled hall to the library at the end; Cos and Leslie carried the blankets and pillows. They entered the library, which smelled like oiled wood and old books. Ascending bookcases lined three walls, filled with knowledge on every subject. The ceiling stretched for thirty feet and an iron spiral staircase spun up to an open second level that traced each wall of books around a wooden overhang.

A desk cut from one piece of staggering oak jutted out from the front wall; animal skins from safaris and hunts covered the floors. On the wall, a coat of arms from Ireland represented the Dollarhide ancestry along with antique landscapes, deer antlers, and horns from bighorn sheep.

After scanning the majestic room, Leslie and Belle spread out pallets on the floor so the room resembled a Turkish veranda.

Leslie proceeded to light beeswax candles around the room; the rays bounced off the wood-paneled walls as the aroma of the wax filled the air. She and Belle walked around with flashlights, looking at the books.

"Y'all wanna see something sweet?" Joey asked.

"Yeah," they replied.

"Follow me."

He picked up a lit votive candle and walked over to an area of the bookcase where he removed a large dictionary. Sticking his hand in the empty space, he turned and pulled a small mechanism in the lower section of the bookcase, revealing a passage just big enough for a person to crawl through.

"What's this for?" Belle asked.

"It was built as a sort of safe room from potential robbers and as way to escape fires that might block the door," answered Joey.

"Where does it go?" Leslie asked.

"It travels around to the different guest rooms on this side of the second floor each of which have a secret door through the closets, and there's a thin ladder that leads to the third-floor tower."

"Sweeeet," Leslie remarked.

Joey placed the candle down, and pulled a flashlight from his pocket, and shone it into the space before crawling through the interior wall space. They passed a fake return air grille that allowed them to see out into the room. Leslie kept tickling Cos from behind. Finally, they made it to a guest room, exiting through a tiny door in the closet behind fur coats with the faint aroma of expensive perfume from years ago, when they went to important places.

"That was so neat," Belle said.

They walked through the stately guest room and back to the library.

Belle picked out a book of Keats and flopped down on a quilt next to Joey. Leslie and Cos scanned the shelves until they came to a framed photo of a man with a bushy red moustache, suspenders, and a dirt-stained Henley; he wore a beat-up cowboy hat and rested on one knee. The photo's edges were faded and worn. Beside it were a series of small ancient journals. Cos dug his thumbs into Leslie's shoulders from behind; she tilted her head back and purred. He stopped and wrapped his arms around her waist, resting his chin on her shoulder.

"Is that Luke?" she asked.

"Yep, that's Luke all right."

"He looks like a real outdoorsman. What are these books?"

"Probably his journals from the gold mining days. You're welcome to take a look, but I think his penmanship is almost illegible."

"My mother's handwriting is so terrible that I can read anything."

She placed the butt of the metal flashlight in her thick lips and opened one of the books with her good arm. Cos kissed her neck. Her eyes smiled as she kept looking. He walked his mouth up toward her ear, kissing her again and again. Cos took the flashlight, and held it for her, looking over her shoulder. She skimmed through the age-dyed pages of pencil sketches of the Sierras. A beaver filled one page, various birds adorned others, and on another was a grizzly bear.

"Oh, that must be Ole Saw!" she said, pointing to the bear.

"Must be! Ole Saw! Ha!"

"What an artist."

"Yeah, Luke was very talented. He did a lot of the framed animal drawings in our house."

"I am going to look through this some more. Maybe we can find a clue as to where the treasure is buried." She took the books to the pallets and he went with her.

The second wall of the storm arrived, shaking the house like a drum. They took comfort in the softness of the quilts and the warmth of each other. Joey wrapped his legs around Belle's thighs, drawing her to him while she read. Cos held Leslie around the waist as she flipped through the journals.

"Look right here, in this drawing, there's a river and a point sticking out from the mountain marked with a black circle. Perhaps that was the location of the treasure?"

"Might be," Cos remarked, taking the book from her hands and looking at it. "Interesting, I wonder if Teddy has seen this. It says 'see p. 22 in journal no. 4 for aerial map.'" He jumped up to look at the other journals on the bookshelf, but none of their spines was numbered 4. It was missing. Leslie picked up another journal, which was almost a complete diary. Skimming through it, she skipped over the banal daily routines about Sam and the progress in the mine—but toward the end, a page of chicken scratch caught her attention.

"Y'all listen, listen!" The room became silent as she read aloud.

"Yesterday Sam and I got thrown in jail in Bagby after a drunken cheat started a bar fight with us at the Bearfoot Saloon because we cleaned up at poker. While in jail, the sheriff brought in a distraught Indian fellow who had been stabbed in the stomach by a white soldier who was part of a cavalry that attacked his people. In the middle of the night, he woke me, explaining that he would be sentenced to execution the next day, claimed he knew the location of a certain treasure by John Hodges's gang; his tribe had stolen and buried it. Said it was in the High Sierras at the foot of a mountain where the rock comes out toward the south side of the river so close to the edge that the traveler has to hug the water to pass the base of it. He insisted it would be back up the path roughly ten feet. He made me promise to deliver half of the gold to his people if I found it, and the other half, I could keep.

Some entries later, the journal read:

Sure enough, we found the place and dug there for two weeks, but never found the gold. We left assuming the man was either mad or mistaken about the spot."

Leslie's eyes grew big as saucers and she shook Cos.

"*Look! That's it! That's it! Look!* I was right about the drawing, that's where they searched for the treasure and thought it was but couldn't find it."

"That's unbelievable!" Belle said after Leslie finished.

"That's amazing," Joey said. "Let me see it, please." She tossed the black book to him and he read it to himself. "I don't think Dad has given these journal entries much attention. This data is like a good dog, it hunts!"

"He's always been too busy with *La Gracia*," remarked Cos. "I am only making like minimum wage at Dan's. Anyone wanna go to California?"

"Me!" Leslie said.

"Me too!" Belle added.

Joey remarked, "I don't know y'all, maybe Teddy is right. It could take weeks or months to find it. If it even exists."

"But we know it exists! We have the evidence right here," Cos said.

"But what if we go all that way and don't find anything? Old boy Luke didn't find it," Joey said.

"Why don't we just make it a road trip? We could see Jimmy and Bo on the way and then end at Camp Big Bear, which is in the area. I am sure our old camp counselor, Aspen, would lend us a cabin. We could play slaughter ball and capture the flag. *Then*, go look for it," Cos said.

"That could work," Joey

"Did you say *Camp Big Bear*?" Belle said, leaning up.

"Yeah, why?" Joey asked.

"I went to *Arrowhead*!"

"No way! Cos and I went to Big Bear, the brother camp. The area in the Sierras where Luke's mine was located is next to them, that's how Dad found out about Big Bear."

"I can't believe this," Belle exclaimed.

"Why did your parents send you all the way out there?" Joey asked.

"Dad wanted me to learn to shoot guns, ride horses, and bow hunt. Arrowhead was the only place."

"I didn't go to either, but I love road trips, capture the flag, and bow hunting," Leslie said.

"What do y'all say?" Cos asked.

"We'll think about it," Joey said.

"Well Leslie and I are going, with or without y'all," Cos remarked.

The pounding of the storm returned, the wind howled; they heard a slam outside and assumed another tree got struck—they waited for the impact, but it timbered in the yard. Soon enough, they stopped talking and lay close to each other; after a while, Cos got up to blow out the candles, sending them into darkness.

As Joey held Belle, he could feel her erratic tension. Thinking he might be too close, he asked her what was wrong. She whispered in his ear that she was very afraid of the dark and usually slept with a light on. He leaned over and sparked a candle in a glass votive; she thanked him and relaxed.

He rolled over and stared up at the distant ceiling. He placed his hands behind his head and Belle laid her head on his chest; her red hair felt like silk under his chin. She rubbed his arm with the tip of her fingernail.

"What are you thinking about Joey?" she said, looking at up at him with her big blue saucers, the left still dimmer than the right but just as electric.

"I am thinking that maybe we could go for it."

"I want to go."

"We'll think about it okay?" Joey said.

"*Okay.*"

THE SECOND WALL passed and the storm slowed down as it blew inland.

Teddy and the adults had decided to stay downstairs to monitor the potential flooding and only move upstairs if the waters rose high enough. He knocked on the library door and the couples moved away from each other as he entered. Now that the storm was gone, he insisted the ladies stay in the guest rooms. Joey and Cos' rooms were respectively downstairs anyway. "If I hear one door close from downstairs, I am coming up with Bear to sic him on some toes."

Joey and Cos laughed. The ladies agreed and exited. Teddy closed the door behind them.

Joey waited a few minutes, then rose and walked out the door.

"Hey, what did I say?" Teddy said as he leaned to the side of the hall wall where he was waiting.

"Sorry Dad, but I am a man now. I just want to talk to her."

"Talk? Yeah, sure. It's late, son."

"All right Dad—goodnight." Joey slinked back into the library. After ten minutes, he took the flashlight and crept through the passage in the wall, sneaking to Belle's room. As he rounded the corner, the light shone on Belle heading toward him in an oversized T-shirt and underwear and they both started to laugh.

When they reached each other, he set the light down, cupped her neck in his hand, and they kissed while still on their knees.

"I just couldn't stand being away from you any longer," he whispered in between breaths.

"I know. I just want to be alone with you so bad."

She sucked his lip and he softly bit hers. She pushed him back to the floor and fell forward on top of him. Leaning up, she slightly bumped her head on the low ceiling and they both laughed. They kissed and kissed for a long time and then he touched her under her shirt. Then, he glided the edge of one of his fingernails along her waistline and she grinned but stopped him, then whispered in his ear that she had to leave—the push of her breath warm against his skin. He begged her to stay, but she insisted, and by the light of the flashlight, she crawled away, leaving him twisted and tangled, crazy and thirsty. He went back to the library. They both fell asleep that night with visions of the other amid long forgotten memories of summers in the Sierras streaming through their minds like rapids in the river there.

Downstairs, Teddy slept in his room while Dal slept on one of the living room couches, resting his bandaged leg on the ottoman with Charlotte by his side. The butterflies were at peace in the aquarium, and the house was still.

CHAPTER 10

Teddy opened the front door while carrying the butterfly aquarium; Dal limped out behind him. The water had receded in the night—plants, limbs, and trees covered the land, the June sun illuminating it in a surreal haze of humidity and heat. The rosebushes under the kitchen window lay beaten to pieces. A tree lay across the driveway, and the oak limb still sat on top of Joey's waterlogged Chevy. A twister had ripped *Uncle Benny* off the tree house and slung it up the driveway where it rested, broken in two.

Teddy walked onto the grass, set the aquarium down, and opened it. With some encouragement, the swallowtails burst into the white sunlight; he and Dal watched them as they dispersed.

Walking over to the barn, he checked on the horses and the bull; they all seemed to be okay. He led each one of them down. His heart swelled with gratitude. After petting the horses, he let them out to graze. Next, he walked toward Windswept Street. Three short trees blocked the road, and leaf and limb debris littered the sand-dusted asphalt.

Returning to the house, Dal and he gazed out over the mess in silent disbelief. After surveying the land, Teddy gathered parts from the Dog House and repaired the generator and converter over the next hour. The power kicked on and Isabella breathed again. Then, he removed the plywood covering her windows so she could see.

He emailed his buddy Sam Boxfly with the Coast Guard for an update via his smartphone.

Back inside, Teddy got the rope leash and checked on Half Ton. The hog rose, lowering his head so Teddy could leash him. The act amazed Teddy. He guided the hog out the kitchen door, which Ton could just squeeze through. Then, he placed him in the horse ring to the right of the barn.

Next, Teddy woke the younger folks, leaving some clothes Charlotte gave him for the ladies at the door. Dog came in from downstairs and licked Cos's face; Cos pushed him off. The girls and guys took turns showering.

Belle bumped into Joey in the hall after getting out, dressed in an oversized Florida Marlins t-shirt, her wet hair tossed over one shoulder. He shook his head with a grin, checking her out. She smiled and pushed him lightly as they walked by—he tried to kiss her, but she dodged it, teasing him.

"This water is like bathing in a mountain stream. I love it," she said to him.

"It's well water, so it feels that way."

"That explains it. My hair loves it," she said, walking to the room to change.

The men threw on canvas shorts, T-shirts, and shoes, and Joey grabbed the two journals. Then, they went outside to survey the damage.

Teddy was back outside, standing shirtless on the hood of the Chevy, chain-sawing the limb into pieces. He idled the saw for a minute, glancing up over his gold Ray Bans.

"Your Chevy got ruined by the storm, Joey."

The group stood stupefied by the mass of fallen trees and *Uncle Benny*. Belle started crying, then buried her face in Joey's shirt; he stood there speechless.

"God, I hope my parents are all right," Belle said. She and Leslie took out their phones, but still couldn't get a signal.

Joey comforted Belle.

After a while, Joey and Belle headed off to inspect the tree house. Climbing the stairs, they dodged two broken steps. Leaves and twigs carpeted the deck like autumn in Connecticut. His hammock still hung from two posts like a weathered victory flag. They walked in through the front door to the left of the four-foot-wide trunk. The inside was a tile floor with painted white wood walls and ceilings. A mini-refrigerator sat in the entrance next to a stainless steel sink; an antique French baker's table facing the screened window served as a desk. The oak's trunk made the right wall, which curved through the space, and a signed picture of Ted Williams hung crooked from a nail in the fat bark. Cut holes in the floor allowed two big limbs to whip through the room; about an inch of water covered the floor.

"Wow Joey, I love this! It's like you're outside, but you're inside. Did Teddy build this for you?"

"Thanks! No, I built it, but Dad designed it and got me started."

He gave her the tour, taking her up a spinning staircase to a loft. Exiting onto a small porch, he pried off the board covering the screen, revealing a peek-a-boo view of the blue ocean over the small trees and houses in the distance. Some of the houses had trees on top of them, and many of the oceanfront properties were damaged or destroyed.

"What a view!" she exclaimed.

Standing there with his hands on his hips, he took a deep breath. "Yep, this is my sweet spot. It's where I used to come to get away or clear my head before a game. When it rains, you can hear it on the tin roof."

"I love the sound of rain on a tin roof. It's heaven," Belle paused. "It looks like very little damage occurred."

"This oak is pretty strong. Unfortunately, *Uncle Benny* got blown off." He looked down on the yard at it. "I'll have to replace him with something else. I'll probably just build an extension there."

Reluctantly drinking in the devastation, Belle placed her hand to her mouth and cried. Joey leaned in and held her.

"Don't cry baby, I am sure your parents are fine."

"I know, but what about Latch, it's just *so* sad."

He took her delicate hand and kissed it.

"It'll be all right, I promise. At least we're together."

After holding each other, some of their sadness drained away. In a minute, they joined the rest of the group. They stood around the horse ring, laughing at Half Ton. Colt threw one of Dog's rubber toys and the fat hog retrieved it with a smirk on his face, his tail slightly wiggling. Bear sat on the wooden fence watching his new friend in approval. Three swallowtail butterflies from the chimney perched on the fence. They flew off occasionally only to return shortly after.

"I swear this hog is domesticated," Teddy said. His phone beeped with an incoming email from Boxfly:

Glad y'all are okay. She was a strong Cat 2. Town is a mess. Windows broken, power out, electric lines and trees blocking intersections, trees on homes, people fighting at gas stations. The surge made landfall five miles south of Latch, badly flooding the Ball neighborhood and an old people's home. Stay home and if you come out, be careful! Box

Teddy knew the report would be bad, but he didn't know *how* bad. He walked over to the yard and relayed a summary of Box's message to the group, insisting that Cos and Joey walk the girls home because they couldn't drive.

"Are we keeping Half Ton?" Cos asked.

"I guess so," Teddy said, looking at the hog. "He seems to like it here, and we like him. Bear certainly does."

"Good, I like the big fellow," Cos said.

"I won't tell my father about him, it'll be our little secret. I don't know why he cares so much anyway."

"Thank you, Annabelle. Normally, I wouldn't care, but there's something about the hog's eyes, you know."

"I think I know what you mean. I see it, too."

Breakfast wafted out the open kitchen window, stirring their stomachs.

"Why don't y'all go eat. It'll set your minds at ease." Heeding his advice, they wandered inside; Teddy caught Joey.

"Jojo, wait a minute." Joey stopped and backtracked.

"Before you take Belle and Leslie home, go into my office and get the Glock, just to be safe. I don't want one of those gasoline-siphoning weirdos to hurt you."

"Sure thing." Joey started to walk off, but stopped. "Oh, I almost forgot. I have to show you something, Dad." He opened the first black journal he had in his hand to the dog-eared drawing of the mountain before handing it to Teddy. Teddy studied it, and then Joey passed him the second one, pointing to the entry describing Luke's meeting with the Native American. In disbelief, Teddy placed his hand on Joey's shoulder.

"You know, I thumbed through some of these when we inherited Isabella and all Red's possessions, but I didn't see this. You could build a hunt around this. Are you thinking about it?"

"Yeah, maybe. Cos owes the school a lot of money, and I would like to go to graduate school at some point without taking out a loan."

"Good."

"We're missing journal number four, though. Any idea where it is?" Joey asked.

"Your uncle Bo in Santa Fe took some of Red's possessions; I bet he has it."

"Great! We could go see him on the way to California," Joey said.

"Y'all have my best if you go. Just be careful." Teddy handed Joey the journals. Looking at Teddy, he saw himself smiling back in the mirrored aviators.

"Thanks, Dad."

"You're welcome, Son."

Joey pranced inside high off Teddy's encouragement and removed the Glock from the firearm case. He took out a box of bullets, loaded the pistol, and slipped it into the back waistline of his canvas duck shorts with the safety on. He threw the box away, but it missed the trashcan, skipping behind the desk. Reaching for it, he felt a paper airplane back there. Unfolding it, he read Isabella's notice of seizure if taxes weren't paid. His eyebrows pointed up; his mouth frowning.

Dal rested at the bamboo dining table with his bandaged leg propped up on a chair. Charlotte waltzed around him whistling, opening windows to let light and fresh air in. Then, she set the table with homemade jams mixed with whole fruit and honey, fresh butter, a bowl of fresh cherries, blueberry pancakes, a pitcher of freshly squeezed orange juice, and a platter of scrambled eggs. Dog was trailing her legs for a hand out. Joey entered, shook up.

Outside, Teddy got a text from Bob Barclay offering same-day tree service to his clients. Unlike the girls who had a different cell service provider, Teddy could receive text messages, but *still* could not make any calls. Teddy texted him fast to get in first; Bob responded immediately, prefacing with, "I told you it would be big."

The group ate. After finishing, they went outside and said goodbye to Teddy, who had started building a pen for Half Ton. Then, they made their way out the long driveway, down Windswept and onto Orange, and out to Route 1, climbing over fallen trees that lay like dead soldiers along the road. Dog led, sniffing the ground.

The hurricane-code houses along the oceanfront did well, while those built before the storm codes had been enacted looked like a pile of broken popsicle sticks. Demolished mailboxes slept in the grass; a fractured Chevron sign hung sideways at the station; waterlogged cars melted in the heat with their windshields cracked or blown out. The scene saddened the group.

Leslie lived in downtown, and Belle two streets off Route 1 near the bay, so the group split at the edge of town.

Joey and Belle crept along the empty park. Dead fish lifted from their natural habitat by the surge lay in the green grass, which glowed healthfully in the sun. The flowerbeds lay broken and the petals on the roses around the fountain were gone, only the thorns and empty vines remaining.

Cutting down a street, they turned onto the Burns's street and arrived at the house, dodging a limb in the driveway. The house—a two-story red brick affair, unusual for a Floridian bay home—was weathered, but high enough on an incline with a raised foundation to have dodged the flooding. A midnight blue Maybach, and a dark brown Cadillac Escalade—the color, a nod to his wife's Texas alma mater—were parked in the driveway on a slight incline. Joey marveled at the Maybach. Limbs and seaweed were everywhere around the cars.

Joey tied Dog up to the front railing and they walked up the red brick steps through the opened front door. She called to her parents. The wallpaper softened the sound. The formal entry had a wooden staircase leading to upstairs. Potpourri sat on a lowboy under a Thomas Kinkade painting of an English village with a cobblestone street in winter.

Belle's mother, Patsy, a slim lady in her late forties with brown hair and a lilac top, rushed to greet them.

"We were so worried about you, honey."

"I know, I was worried about y'all too," Belle said as her mother hugged her tight. "I am so glad to see you're all right. How did y'all do?"

"Oh, we did fine. Are you all right? You're not *hurt*, are you?" Patsy studied her with a concerned look.

"We did *fine*. I am fine, Mom—*really*. Mom, this is Joey. We went to high school together. His father was nice enough to let me spend the night. Their house is unbelievable, it's this dream house with secret passages. You gotta see it sometime."

"That sounds very interesting, honey. Hello Joey, it's nice to meet you. Thank you for letting her stay," Patsy said, shaking his hand with compassionate eyes.

Belle's father, Will, a fit man with Mediterranean skin, black slicked-back hair, tortoise-rimmed Paul Smith glasses, a Patek Phillipe tank watch with a smooth crocodile band and a navy alligator golf shirt came in from the living room and hugged Belle.

"Hi Dad, Mom says everything is okay."

"Everything is fine, sweetheart. Just a few trees down. I am so glad you're all right," he said with a long Texas drawl while hugging her.

Patsy said goodbye to Joey and ushered Belle off to see Paige. While walking away, she told Joey she would call him later.

Will extended a hairy hand. Joey took it and Will squeezed his hand as if to crush the bones.

"Will Burns. Good to meet you, Joey. Nice firm handshake you got there. You can tell a lot about a man from his handshake."

"Yes, you can. Nice to meet you too." Will's hands were cold.

"Come into my office and take a seat." Joey agreed and followed where he took a seat facing Will's desk. Will took his place in a black Eames chair behind a French Empire desk. He removed a Cohiba Habano cigar from a box and lit it before leaning back. Joey recognized the familiar smell from his house.

"Quite a storm last night."

"Yes, sir. My father got news it was a strong Cat 2."

"That's what my secretary told me. Whew!"

"I hope everyone in town is all right."

"I do too," Will said. "How did Belle end up at your house again?"

"There was a graduation party at the beach. When it started to rain really hard, we got caught in it. Mr. Burns, I just want you to know we had no intentions of her staying at my house during the hurricane."

"I know son, I am just curious. Besides, Belle is a grown woman now. She can do as she pleases."

"Thank you for understanding."

"Of course—cigar?" Will said, extending the box to him.

"No, sir."

"Cohiba. They're the best. I only smoke the best."

"No, thank you."

Will paused, "You play baseball, don't you?" He drew on the cigar.

"I played, but got injured last year. I just graduated."

"You were pretty good, right?"

"I was all right."

"Ohhh, you're being modest, son. I heard through *The Grapevine* that you were the best high school prospect to come out of Florida in years and that you played ball in Cal-i-fornia?"

"That's what some people said before I got hurt, but the injury cooked my chances at the majors."

He puffed. "That's too bad. Belle likes Cal-i-fornia. Wants to go to Stanford Business School—she got in, too." He stood, moving to the window and looking out, while gesturing with his cigar as he spoke,

"Pretty impressive feat, getting into Stanford Business School." He took another long drag off the cigar.

"Yes, Mr. Burns, I am sure you're very proud of her." Will turned around and paced.

"Yes, I am, Joey. Of course, Texas is where her sister and cousins go, and where my wife went, and her sisters and parents went. You get the picture."

Joey was quiet, shifting in his chair as Will held eye contact.

"Your father fishes professionally?"

"Yes, but he also hunts treasure."

"Treasure, *really*?"

"Yes, sir. He says that all treasure hunting *is* fishing in a way. Belle tells me you're into oil. I guess oil is kind of like fishing too."

"It's a *little* different, son," Will said with a condescending tone. "You see, I own that oil and make money each time I sell it. Drilling for oil is more like harvesting a crop than fishing. Less chance."

"Treasure hunting is not chance; it's very calculated." Joey was irritated, knowing Will was well aware of the risk in drilling oil.

"Fairytales are good things to tell children when they go to sleep at night, but they have no place in the real world."

Joey wanted to leave, but his care for Belle kept him in the seat. "I don't like people insulting my father. If you do it again, I am leaving."

"Whoa, hold on son, I am not insulting anyone, only illustrating that we're in a different business. That's all." Will plopped down again and paused, the silence uncomfortable.

"Belle tells me you have a farm?"

"Yes."

"Do you have horses?"

"Yes, three."

"You see this horse?" He pointed to a photo on the wall. "Do you know what that is?"

Joey looked at the picture.

"An Arabian, by the ears."

"Very good, you know your breeds, son."

"Yeah, well, we have one at the farm, named Earful."

"*Really?*"

"Yes."

"Well, mine is a stallion, and he lives on a farm in Kentucky. His lineage is *perfect*."

Will sucked the cigar like a straw and then blew a cloud of smoke at Joey—it hit him like a punch in the face. "Of course, they can only breed with the highest quality Arabian mare or the offspring will be tainted. It's a *pure* breed line."

"Are we talking about horses?"

"We're talking about *breeding* stallions."

"If you want to say something to me, *say* it like a man."

"I think I already have."

"Make it clearer so that I understand. Am I welcome to hang out with Belle?"

Will held eye contact and leaned forward with his elbows on his desk, punching the cigar. "Some wild horses just can't be tamed, Joey. All the treasure in the world can't make a poor quarter horse into an Arabian stallion."

"I don't have to take this from you. I may care for your daughter, but I think you're an arrogant prick." Joey got up and stormed out the door. Will smiled. "Look forward to seeing you again, Joey. Don't be shy now."

Joey slammed the front door, rushing out into the driveway. He couldn't breathe and kicked one of the bushes hard and trampled out into the street.

As he headed home, he couldn't fathom how Will and such a delicate creature like Belle were related.

Belle swung into her father's office.

"Hey Dad, what did you and Joey talk about?"

"The weather, horses, you know—man stuff."

"Well, be nice to him, I have a big crush on him."

"Really, Belle? You know he's the son of a salvager."

"He's a treasure hunter, Dad, *not* a salvager."

"Treasure, salvage, same thing. He's completely irrational. Hasn't been willing to sell that old rundown mansion or the land around it for years, even for way more than it's worth," Will said. "And he won't even wear a shirt around the yacht club. *The yacht club!* What about Lawrence? He just graduated from SMU."

"Ugh, Lawrence wears his fraternity ring to sleep at night. I like Joey, Dad. Get used to it."

"Oh jeez, I guess I'll try."

"How did the hunt for Half Ton go?" she asked, knowing the answer.

"Didn't get him, but we will, even if we have to raise the reward and get everyone in the town after him."

"What's the big deal, anyway? It's just a stupid hog."

"He's stirring things up—people are afraid, and we can't have that."

"Oh well, I am just glad to know y'all are all right from the storm. Hopefully the town will be fine," Belle said.

"Yes, I do hope so."

"I want you to know I've made up my mind to go to Stanford in the fall."

Will tried to hide the frown. "But I thought you had decided on Texas dear."

"No, *you* had decided."

"Did that Dollarhide boy put you up to this?" Will said, raising his voice.

"No, this is my decision, Dad."

"I knew he was no good. I just *knew* it. He's planting bad ideas in your head about places and things. I want you to stay away from him."

"You're not listening. This is what I want to do and I am dating Joey now, so get used to it."

Will stood and looked out the window. "You're *so stubborn* Belle, you get it from your mother. You know Texas is a better *fit* for you and our family. You'll be closer to us and your sisters."

"I am going to Stanford and this conversation is over!" She walked out as he shook his head.

Cos and Leslie arrived at her 40s bungalow in town across the street from the square. Her mother, Donna, a massage therapist and yoga teacher, sported black spandex workout pants and white On running shoes. She swung open the door with a smile, picked Leslie up, and squeezed her. She hugged Cos too, thanking him for letting Leslie stay and welcoming him in. They went into the warm living room where she brought them iced tea. The power was still out, but the sun waved in through the big rectangular windows. Leslie's father, Mike Gooch, walked in wearing tight stonewashed jeans and a "Gooch's" T-shirt with a drawing of a redfish on the front; he hugged Leslie and shook Cos's hand. He had curly black hair and a sense of gravitas. After asking about their house, they exchanged storm stories.

Mike owned an outdoor clothing store called Gooch's downtown and feared Eliza would hurt the economy, which had been weakened by a recent recession. If business lessened, he might lose the store. He explained that most people in Latch were tight-fisted with their greenbacks and refused to spend when the slightest ripple occurred in either the local or national economy; no reason to blame them, he explained—they were wise—but it distressed the retail industry there. A power pole broke the front glass at Gooch's, knocking out the display cases of sunglasses, he added. Realizing that her father would not be able to cover the tuition for her college, she decided not to mention it, and lovingly consoled him.

After some usual after-the-hurricane talk, she and Cos walked outside; he combed her blonde hair back, held and kissed her. He suggested Gooch's might be one more reason to go for Hodge's treasure. He said they could turn the hog over to Will Burns, but Teddy would be so upset—his passion ruled his decision-making, and he loved that animal. She agreed, and he promised to call soon.

When he arrived home, Teddy and Joey were building the pigpen with scrap wood from the workshop. Cosby lent a hand, and Joey kept the incident at Belle's to himself.

THE NEXT DAY, Charlotte and Dal rested in the living room on the couch with Dal's leg propped up on the ottoman. Earlier that morning, Charlotte had re-dressed the wound. She rubbed his back and hair; he proposed they go out to Ink, a new seafood restaurant at a chic boutique hotel, as soon as his leg healed and things were better. She agreed and flowed off to get them coffee. When she came back in, Dal studied her face. She was forty-eight years old and beautiful, like a Renaissance statue of a princess. When she was younger, she traveled the world as a model and had lived in Paris where she married a famous photographer—he left her for a younger woman shortly after, so she returned to her hometown of Latch. Afraid her beauty had kept her from true love by attracting a shallow mate, she retreated from it —hadn't worn make up or let her hair down in ages. She even often wore fake artsy glasses to look smarter, and then there was the extra weight like a chainmail over her figure and heart that nothing could get through. But the romance with Dal had awakened a radiance that shone from the inside, and lately she realized her beauty had always come from inside. She had always thought it was the *way she looked* that attracted people to her, but it was *who* she was that was the source of her magnetism.

Dal began to cough. After feeling his forehead, her eyebrows went up and she suggested he had an infection from the wound.

"Maybe Teddy has something, I'll go check."

"All right sweetheart," Dal said. "Hold on. I love you."

"I like you too, Dal," she said, recoiling a bit.

"I *know*, but I *love* you. Why won't you say it?"

"I don't know. I just don't like *that* word. It gives me the creeps. Besides, I care for you more than any word can convey," she said, and kissed his forehead. He frowned and let her go. She exited to the yard to get Teddy, telling him that Dal felt ill; he dropped the hammer and removed his work gloves.

"I have just the thing," he said, swinging his legs over the front of the new pen, hustling over to her with a smile. His chest and arms were soaking wet with perspiration.

"You seem awfully chipper today, considering the storm."

"I just figure, why let it upset me? So we lost some trees and have some damage. Big deal. I am more concerned about the people in Ball and the town's economy."

"I kinda see your point. So what are you going to give Dal?"
"You remember the elixir that cured Bear?"
"The wine?"
"Yes."
"Can it be used on people?"
"I've taken it."
"Is that supposed to comfort me?"
"I am still here, aren't I?"
"All right, let's do it."

They walked into Isabella and went to the living room, where Teddy placed his hand on Dal's back.

"Charlotte says you're a little under the weather?"
"A little bit. I'll be fine tomorrow."
"You look pretty sick. I have something I think will help. Will you try it?"
"I don't know. What is it?"
"Some of that wine from *La Gracia* I told you about that cured Bear. I take it anytime I get sick, and it works. Trust me."
"If you say it's safe, I trust you."
"Okay."

Teddy poured the elixir and Dal sipped it and grimaced. Rather than complain, he took it all down in the second sip.

"Whew! That's like shooting whiskey."
"It'll make your toes curl." Teddy laughed. "It just has a lil knock-back, that's all. Let's see how you do with that dose. We'll give you another tonight if needed."

Teddy went outside and finished up Half Ton's pen, then led the hog into it. The boys joked about the wild hog's docility. Bear showed endless fascination with Half Ton, who reciprocated the admiration by playing with him. After about fifteen minutes of horseplay, the oddest thing happened: Bear jumped up onto the hog like an old cowboy mounting a mustang. The broad back gave him plenty of room to ride. They laughed and pointed at him. Teddy suggested Bear had found himself a horse. They laughed again and eventually wandered off to clean up the property.

After hours of backbreaking work cleaning up debris, vacuuming and shocking the pool, and vacuuming the water out of the preservation room, garage, and barn, the group was tired and sweaty. Dusk fell and the night was wet in the high eighties. They retired.

The next day, Bob showed up early at the gate, so Teddy brought Half Ton around into one of the stables in the barn, Bear following; then, he buzzed Bob in.

Bob pulled up and hopped down off the truck to greet Teddy. A Duck Masters camouflaged trucker hat hung a little off center on his head and he had a button-up white starched shirt tucked into tight Wranglers that rode below his belly, secured by a brass belt buckle in the shape of the state of Florida. Teddy greeted him, asking how he got down the road. Bob explained the city cleaned the trees up yesterday afternoon. After walking around the property, Bob counted twenty fallen trees and quoted him an enormous amount. Teddy couldn't believe it, but the work was beyond him, so he accepted. He asked Bob to please stay out of the barn because they were breaking a wild horse stabled there.

Teddy walked to the house distressed, knowing the amount would total his personal savings. He was surprised to see Dal standing up in the dining room. The color had returned to his face in one day. Every time Teddy saw the wine work, his conviction grew.

"How are you doing, Dal?"

"I am better. I think that stuff really helped me. Even my leg feels better."

"Good! It doesn't always work that fast, but I am glad it has."

"Well, I am not well, but I am better."

Outside, Joey and Cos started to build a wall out of wood where the ship ripped off the tree house.

"So you and Belle, it *finally* happened."

"Yeah, finally," Joey replied. "What about you, how's it going with Leslie?"

"Leslie is the best," Cos said. Joey grinned and shook his head.

"It's great having you home, Jojo," Cosby continued.

"Yeah, well, I am really glad to be here. I love how hot Florida gets;

I could get used to this again. There is nothing like a good humid eighty-eight degrees."

"Well, we could get used to having you again." He paused. "You seem a little down since taking Belle home."

"Yeah, I met her father and he's real piece of work."

"A jerk?"

"Totally."

"I am sorry to hear it, but so what? You're not dating him."

"I don't know. She seems really close to him. It could be a problem."

"Don't bail yet, just see how it goes. Pass me the hammer."

"You're probably right." Joey handed him the hammer.

"Listen, I found out Leslie's dad's store is in trouble."

"Gooch's? No way, I love that place."

"I know, it's bad. Between that and my debt with the school, I am going for Hodge's treasure next week. Are you in?"

"Sure, I actually had already decided to go."

"Great! What changed your mind?"

"Look, I didn't want to tell you, but Dad may lose Isabella. He can't make the property tax payments, and he's so stubborn, I worry that instead of selling off some of the land, it'll be seized by the state and the whole property will be auctioned off—and we know who will be at the top of the bidding."

"*What?*" Cos stopped working, almost dropping the hammer.

"Yeah, I saw the letter in his office, folded up like an airplane."

"That's bad news. Do you think the Hodges's gold would give us enough to help?"

"I don't know, but if we could buy him even six months, he might find *La Gracia* in that time. He keeps saying how close he is."

"Okay, let's go to California then."

"Awesome. I can put some money together. Put your notice in with Dan and we'll shoot for this coming week. Don't tell Belle or Leslie until I figure things out."

"Deal." They fist bumped.

Buzz wandered into the barn looking for a restroom. He despised being on the Dollarhide farm. Every time he saw Cos walking around, the image of the surfer boy and Leslie on the beach flashed through his mind; he clenched his fists, his head became hot, pounding with anger. He loved her so much, and now this loser who couldn't even block a linebacker and had to play baseball instead of football was dating *his* girl. On the way to the can, he heard a loud snorting from inside one of the stables and peeked over. Shocked by the sheer size of Half Ton, he backpedaled a bit. Regaining his composure, he looked over again, smiling. Half Ton was so long, he almost couldn't turn around in the stable.

"Oh my God, this whopper is gonna make me rich *and* I'll get a shot at Cosby. Two for one," he whispered. He strutted out of the barn to his buddy Mike.

"Mike, you're not going to believe what I just found!"

"Your balls?" Mike said, unimpressed.

"No. Half Ton."

"*What? You found* Half Ton? *Where?*"

"In the barn; Mr. Dollarhide has him in a horse pen."

"Why would he have a feral hog in a stable?"

"Who cares! All I know is he's there and he's a damn beast. Just come look, and quit being so dense."

Buzz led and Mike followed. They sneaked into the barn and Mike glanced over into Half Ton's stall. He looked at Buzz with a smile that revealed his missing teeth, then he threw his arm around Buzz and they walked out.

THE DOLLARHIDE MYSTERY

BOOK 2

One's destination is never a place, but a new way of seeing things.

— HENRY MILLER

CHAPTER 1

The week after Hurricane Eliza devasted Latchawatchee, Florida, FEMA came in and repaired some of the damage and cleaned up the town. The water in the poor, low-lying Ball neighborhood eventually receded, leaving many of the houses unrecognizable. Over twenty people died, and the survivors fled to stay with family and friends or sought temporary housing in the community center. Most were left homeless. The national news focused on an enormous neglected sewage line that broke in the Ball neighborhood, spewing into the floodwater. Many of those residents were too poor to evacuate to another town and stay in a hotel and the auditoriums were hopelessly full. Some stayed put and others swam for safer areas. Of those who swam, many got ill. The sick were being treated at the community center; some had already died.

In town, cars passed along the streets and roads as people left their shelters; logs and piles of debris still lined the roads like bad souvenirs. The power had returned, and grocery stores and a few restaurants had opened.

A couple of days after the storm, people began to see Stern Banks's black GMC Yukon with tinted windows squirming the streets like a drug dealer, stopping at destroyed or injured homes to make unapologetically low offers. Some desperate owners caved, assuming the area wouldn't recover and it might be their only chance to sell. Although the move shocked some residents, Teddy was disgusted but unsurprised.

Meanwhile, the receding surge water left an alligator stranded who had gone "land shark" downtown, snooping around people's yards at night, harassing pets, and living off raccoons and possums. Although there had been reports of seeing something that appeared large and lizard-like in the shadows of bushes at night, no one had actually seen the gator in broad daylight until Miss Jimmy spotted him smack dab in the center of the road while opening the Malt; she claimed he was as white as a ghost. She ran inside and called Officer Catfish, but by the time he arrived, the albino had vanished. A few days later, he managed to snap into one of her friend's right running shoes and chomp on it while she screamed in terror and ran away from the beast. Knowing Teddy was well versed with amphibious things, Catfish contacted him to see if he could help track the beast and take care of it. Teddy said he would meet him in a couple of days, armed and ready.

Cleaning up the yard, making repairs to Isabella, and buying a new truck squashed Teddy's savings. With the ultimatum on the back taxes, he *had* to find something soon. Thanks to the *La Gracia* wine, Dal's infection was gone and his leg was healed. Now, they would be ready to hunt again soon.

The Indians forfeited their regional baseball game due to the storm, which Cos had already been blackballed from playing in due to the cow prank.

Meanwhile, Belle had been texting and calling Joey. He answered by not answering. He didn't know how to tell her the truth about what her father had said to him.

To numb the pain, he turned his attention to California with Cos. They agreed to leave in the morning. Cos had given vacation notice last week to Dan, who informed him they would be closed for two weeks anyway due to Eliza.

Joey's Chevy was cooked and had a cracked windshield, so, Cos spun a story for Dan: the chicken wagon needed an oil change and new brake pads, and Teddy would fix it for free while Cos was on vacation. Baited by the word "free," Dan agreed, instructing him to bring it back when he returned. Cos called Leslie and told her they were going to California, but Leslie said she wanted to stay at home with her family due to the damage at Gooch's.

To finance the trip, Joey cleaned out all $3,800 from his savings. In order to have a cushion, Joey swiped one of Teddy's gold Canadian Maple Leaf coins from the yellow rubber duck stashed inside of the toilet tank and sold it to a Cuban antique coin store in town; then, the brothers bicycled to Dan's to pick up the chicken mobile.

In Teddy's workshop, Joey grabbed two down sleeping bags, a pack tent, two inflatable pads, two internal frame packs, two foldable shovels, a fly rod, reel, and ties, portable stove, some gunpowder, duct tape, fuses, Teddy's Infinity metal detector to detect gold, and a big Yeti cooler. Taking their packs inside, they gathered a week's worth of clothes, the Glock, three boxes of bullets, and some hiking shoes. Then, they laid the gear out by the door and left, making two critical stops.

At Gooch's, they picked up ten Nalgene bottles, an extra tent, a double goose down sleeping bag, and a bear box. From there, they went to the grocery and filled the cart with food. They packed everything snug in the car.

They didn't plan on taking Dog, but he was onto them and jumped in the backseat. Cos attempted to leash him, but he leaped into the front seat. After five minutes of chasing him around the car, they threw their hands up in surrender. Cos put his hands on his hips, suggesting to Joey that Dog's gold-sniffing skills might come in handy; Joey thought about it and agreed.

The sound of tires crushing shells grabbed their attention. Joey spotted Belle's red Cherokee coming up the driveway—Teddy had left the gate open. Turning away, he acted uninterested and hurried back inside to get the last couple of bags, hoping she would disappear by the time he returned. She parked and got out, wearing khaki shorts and a golden tank, her red hair pulled tight into a knot. As she approached, she crossed her arms and frowned at Joey, who exited the house carrying the last bag to the trunk.

"Hi Belle." He didn't make eye contact.

"Why haven't you returned my calls?" she said, following him to the car. "What kind of a jerk are you?"

"Look, Cos is going out of town for a few days on a business trip and I got to him pack, okay?"

She squawked, "A business trip?! Cos works for *Dan's*. What is it, a special assignment to take chicken to the mayor? Do you think *I am stupid*, Joey? Why are you avoiding me?" Cos exited to the barn. Joey continued packing and adjusting the bags in the back.

"I thought we had the most wonderful night of our lives together, but since the storm, you've acted like you don't know me."

He kept going through stuff, zipping and unzipping bags for no reason. She slammed her hand against the side of the car.

"At least look at me! I *demand* an answer."

He turned, and when their eyes connected, he was back in the deep end. The black and blue was gone from her left eye, and the exquisite fibers in her irises were like those rare gemstones he once saw at a cave in Lookout Mountain, Tennessee. She was strong, too, like that mountain, and he could see distant horizons in her eyes, and even feel the wind blow there.

"Listen, Belle. There's an explanation. I just really don't know how to tell you."

"What, do you have a girlfriend? I can handle it. Tell me the truth." She paused. "Do you have a third nipple?" she said, almost making herself laugh. She slightly grinned and he almost did.

"No, there's no other girl."

"What is it, then?" She turned upset again. Joey placed his hand on her arm to comfort her, but she pushed it away. "*Don't* touch me! Tell me why!"

"Look, I really care about you, but we can't be together."

She became angry, "*Why not?* My heart has been breaking over the past week and when I think about you, I can't even breathe," she looked away, sad. "My mother thinks I am having a nervous breakdown from the storm or something because I am acting so weird, and I don't know how to tell her it's just because of some boy." She began to cry. "I don't know how to tell her it's because I am falling in love."

Joey let his guard down. "Belle, stop crying, please. Listen, when I was over at your house after the storm, your father took me in his office and suggested I stay away from you."

"He did *what?*"

"In so many words, he said I wasn't good enough for you, and insulted my family."

She shook her head in disbelief. "Oh my God, I am *so* sorry." Her tone grew empathetic, her voice softening. "As far as I know, he has never done anything like that before. You still should have told me. How does that change anything about the way we feel for each other?"

"It doesn't, but how can we be together if I have to deal with him all the time around us, attacking me, you know? That seems like a serious problem, unless you want to stay away from him, then I am fine."

"He'll get over it. We'll be in California together anyway. I *am* going to Stanford."

"You're going for sure?"

"Yeah, I decided."

Joey glanced off, took a deep breath, and paused. "Belle, you know he said some pretty bad things about Teddy."

"I am sorry, but there's a reason he acted that way. There's something you don't know about me."

"What?"

She paused for a moment, "At Texas, I dated this guy named TJ. He was nice at first, but our senior year, he became very jealous of other guys. One night he kicked me in the stomach because I was talking to a guy friend."

"What a jerk," Joey said. He moved closer and rubbed her arm.

"I know. I broke it off right away. But after that, he wouldn't stop harassing me. He called all the time, threatening me. I told my father and he became furious. Ever since, he's been trying to protect me. He keeps pushing me to date these sons of his friends."

"I am sorry, Belle. I had no idea, but he's making a lot of assumptions about me and my family."

"I know. I should have never told him about TJ kicking me."

He paused. "Look, I want to be with you, but you have to talk to him about this."

"I will, I *promise*." She took out her phone and began dialing.

He stopped her. "Not now." Moving in, he kissed her, and she wrapped her arms around his waist, tugging his body closer. Her heartbeat against his chest and his against hers; she looked down with a smile and he wiped the lingering tear off her face. Then, she turned her blue eyes up at him.

"So I was thinking we might go to a movie tonight, if you're not going with Cos," she smiled.

"A movie? Isn't it still closed?"

"Yep, but they turned the football field into a drive-in, so people can have something fun to do. Tonight, *Star Wars: The Last Jedi* is playing."

"That's awesome."

"You wanna go?" she said and glanced in the car out of the corner of her eye. "My God, there's enough stuff in here for a month at least! Where is Cos going? He's not going to California, is he?"

"Actually, yes ... well, we're—both kind of going."

"*Really?!* You have to take me, then!"

"We can't, Belle. Taking you for a two-week trip to the High Sierras isn't the best way for me to warm up to your father."

"Take me. *I am going*. He'll never know."

"We'll be gone for two weeks."

"I can say I am going to look at Texas' business school and to see my sister Courtney in Little Rock. We can stop at her place on the way."

"No, Belle."

"I am going and I don't give a *flying pig's ass* what you say." She ran over and got in the backseat like Dog, hunkering down.

Joey opened the car door and grabbed her by the feet, jerking her out and throwing her over his shoulder with a smile. She yelled.

"Come on. You're staying here." Her legs kicked up in the air and she began hitting him on the back, but kept grinning.

"I'll tell Dan y'all are taking the chicken."

"He already knows. I told you, it's a special assignment," he said with a serious tone, while swinging her around.

"That's bull, I know he isn't *letting* y'all take it."

"You *wouldn't*."

"Oh yes I would!" He set her down. As she backed away, she started to dial the number on the side of the car.

"He's not there right now."

"Yeah, but I *bet* he checks his messages," she sang and waited while it rang.

"No, no! Stop, Belle! I guess it's all right then—you can come." He smiled.

"Yayers!" She jumped on him, wrapping her legs around his waist. "I have to go home to pack and tell my parents I am going to Texas. Can Leslie come too?"

"Cos invited her, but said she wanted to stay home to help with the store."

"Are you kidding, Leslie has to come so I have a girl to play with. Besides, her parents let her do anything she wants."

"Make it quick. We can't lose any more time. It's 11 a.m. already. Be back no later than 12:30."

"We'll be here."

Joey called Teddy, who was out running errands. He answered gleefully, listened carefully to all the boy's plans, thought hard, and wished them good luck and a good trip.

Belle called Courtney in Little Rock and gave her the plan. Courtney agreed, and Belle told her parents. At the thought of Texas over Stanford, Will offered his American Express. She packed her internal frame backpack and picked up her bow and arrows she used for hunting. Then, she called Leslie, who changed her mind about going after Belle enticed her with dreams of California and adventurous days on the open road with the two handsome guys. They met up at Leslie's house. Leslie's hair was knotted in two side ponytails with a yellow bandana tied over the top. She wore linen shorts and a tank, grinning ear to ear with exuberance; she packed and then they headed to the farm.

Cos hugged Leslie; Joey loaded their packs into the car. Belle walked over with a Bear Archery Carnage bow and a set of arrows.

"I told you I bow-hunted."

"Damn, you weren't lying. This might actually come in handy if Ole Saw's kin are around. I'll pack it there for you." He grabbed it and slid in the back. First, he looked at the route on his iPad Google Maps app. Then, he spread out a roadmap on the chicken's yellow hood and carefully highlighted the group's route. Cos leaned on his forearms and took off his Ray-Bans.

"We'll go up Route 1 to Highway 57 to I-10 and take it all the way to Alabama, where we'll stay with our granddad Jim. In the morning, we'll get on 10 and travel to I-55, taking it north to Jackson, Mississippi. Then we'll jut over to Little Rock, Arkansas."

"Where do we go from there?" Belle asked.

"We'll take I-40 through north Texas to Oklahoma, where we'll stay for one night. Then, we'll head onto Santa Fe to shack up with Uncle Bo, Teddy's brother, then to Las Vegas for a night, and finally to California."

"How long?" Cos asked.

"It'll take five days to get there. Then, I figure three to four days to find the treasure, plus the return. Looking at least twelve days," Joey said.

"Let's get cooking," Cos said.

He got in the backseat next to Belle, who wore blue mirrored gold aviators, and was blowing bubbles and popping them sharply, and had her elbow slung out the window; she looked at him and patted the seat beside her.

"Keep me company, Cos."

"Okay." Cos sat down, grabbing his Panama estancia hat from the back.

"I like that hat."

"Thanks! Gotta dress for the West."

THE DOLLARHIDE MYSTERY

Alive with the momentum and the promise of wealth, Joey maneuvered the chicken out the driveway. They relaxed into the plush seats, which Cos equated to floating on a cloud, but no one else went that far. Dog perched on the armrest between, scanning the road ahead. Joey hit shuffle on his itunes and Jimmy Buffett's "A Pirate Looks at Forty" flowed out. They motored north on Route 1, admiring the ocean view between homes. The AC was no match for the ninety-eight degree weather, so they rolled the windows down. The wind blew their hair back and the sun hugged their arms.

After a while, Route 1 turned inland from the beach, and the landscape changed from low trees, oaks, and sand dunes to pines and grass fields. They followed it until Highway 57, which cut through north central Florida. Horse and dairy farms dominated the landscape and an occasional orange grove spread for acres, imprinting the air with the smell of citrus. A broad wooden stand on the roadside had a big sign above reading in orange letters on a white background:

FLORIDA'S BIGGEST NAVEL ORANGES.

Joey pulled in and Cos and Leslie hopped out to get two netted bags of oranges from an old farmer wearing a straw hat with holes in it. Indigo clouds floated behind the violet sky ahead of them, warning of rain. They distributed the fruit in the car and hit the road again, heading north. When they reached the clouds, a tropical shower fell.

Around Tallahassee, they hit the first sign of hills. They connected to I-10, taking it toward Alabama. Out of the city, the hills dwindled into flat plains; for the next hundred miles, the car and repetitive scenery provided a meditative landscape for good laughs and nonlinear conversations.

When Cos took a turn driving, Joey joined Belle in the backseat and they talked about various subjects together—the arts, politics, old movies—each topic a wormhole to a galaxy of humor and exploration.

The sun faded and the group stopped at a rest area to raid the Yeti for swordfish sandwiches. Joey whipped out the Tabasco sauce, passing it around.

Dusk arrived, and the group piled back into the car, rolling into the darkness. While driving, Cos announced they would be in Pensacola in about an hour and a half, and then it was another hour and a half to Mobile.

Joey gazed out into the darkened roadside while Belle rested her red head on his shoulder; he rubbed his hand through the locks. Leslie slept with her face pushed against the front passenger window, Dog dreaming in her lap.

CHAPTER 2

*E*arlier that day, sheets of rain fell outside the window at Dr. Wyman's office. Teddy lay on the leather lounger like a beached polar bear with his eyes shut. The lights were off, but a dim light seeped in through the window. The soothing sound of a tabletop waterfall ran in the corner. The soft-spoken British therapist guided Teddy through the hypnosis, starting out with guided imagery that placed him in an elevator going down, further and further into the subconscious.

As the elevator descended, he drifted further away until he exited the steel sliding doors into another realm. Dr. Wyman asked him to describe what he saw.

Images flashed. He related them. The place seemed like Spain hundreds of years ago. He saw a beautiful woman whom he loved very much and her family who disapproved of their relationship. They desired her to marry a nobleman instead. In a grove of lemon trees, they met, picnicking on the grass where they fed each other olives, fresh fruit, and cheese. She drew a circle in his palm; the touch sent a jolt through his body in the office, causing him to grip his hand into a fist. He went far into her amber eyes, seeing past the iris and into her heart. She turned and lay into him, while he traced things on her back over her paper-thin white shirt and she tried to guess what he drew. Teddy fidgeted in the chair.

"I was only going to be a deckhand to Admiral Díaz on *La Gracia*, but the pay would have been enough to make me a wealthy man. I knew her parents would agree to our marriage if I had the money, even if it was a long time for us to wait."

"Go on. What did she say?"

"She *begged* for me to stay. Said the trip was too long and dangerous. Wanted to elope. But I assured her my plan was better for our happiness. Before we left, she pulled on my earlobe and I pulled on hers—that was our thing, a way of saying 'you're it, babe.' That was also something Sarah and I did."

"Interesting. What happens then? What do you *see*?" The image choked Teddy up a little and he ran his palms along the leather.

"The day we sailed out, the sun was obscured by a cloak of grey. She stood on the shore in the distance and waved goodbye. I couldn't see her tears, but I knew they were there. I could feel them like ice in my veins. My heart told me I was making a mistake, but my mind said it was the only way. Eloping would mean leaving the area and never seeing her family again. I couldn't do that to her, even if *she* wanted to."

"What happens next?"

Teddy paused and reached into his mind, struggling to get the words.

"It's just ... images of the crew sailing. I remember some of the men got sunstroke and a few others died of scurvy. *La Gracia* was a majestic galleon with a broad stern that gained tremendous speed with a good wind. Its misfortune was due in no part to the crew, who were happy and harmonious, and it wasn't due to the boat either—no —if there was any omen, it was the problems during construction, the grey sky, and the pain in my heart."

"We've never gotten this far before—what else do you see?"

Teddy paused and saw an image of the man holding the plain ring up on *La Gracia* on a hot sunny day, smiling as he surveyed the vast sea.

THE DOLLARHIDE MYSTERY

"The ring!"

"A ring?"

"The ring we found in the ocean here! I had it on the boat and was going to give it to her when I returned. It was a wedding ring."

"Anything else?"

"Nothing else, doc. My mind is tired."

"OK, very good work."

He walked Teddy back up the elevator and into the room where he opened his eyes and readjusted to the surroundings. The sound of the waterfall trickled back into his awareness. He sat up and ran his hands through his pearl hair.

"When do you want to work again?" the doc said.

"I don't. It's too painful."

"But, it's cathartic Mr. Dollarhide."

Teddy paused. "I just don't understand why you can't help me find a clue as to where the treasure went down. That's what I need to know. Rings and love are great, but they can't pay my bills. I am drowning in bills."

"I am a therapist, Teddy, not a money sonar."

"I know, I know. It's just so frustrating," Teddy exclaimed.

"Well, maybe we will find a clue next time."

"OK, one more session." Teddy always agreed to just one more session, but every session, he saw a little more, and wanted to return again when it ended. He stood up, paid the man, shook his hand, put on his raincoat, and, regaining his composure, walked out. The rain had stopped and an avalanche of fire burst through the clouds. He walked down the slick street and over to his new wet Ford. An image of Spain and the woman with the amber eyes lingered.

He got his alligator-trapping gear out of the truck bed and carried it down the sidewalk to the Malt to meet Officer Catfish for the gator hunt.

Catfish and Teddy met seven weeks ago when Teddy called the police department to inquire about a restraining order against Bateman and Banks because of their harassing petitions. Cat submitted the complaint to the sheriff, Doc Waterhouse, but still hadn't heard back. Teddy questioned why he never received an answer—Cat explained that Doc suffered from CRS, or "can't remember shit" disease, and was always forgetting things. Teddy thought it was more like CDS, or "can't do shit" disease, and didn't trust the sheriff, who now had that year's silver Jaguar parked in his driveway. Two years ago, the three-story maximum for new buildings built on the ocean had mysteriously disappeared—no committee voted, no town hall meeting, *no explanation*—one day, a nine-story pink condo was being built along southern Route 1. And just like that, Teddy's land became a target for Bateman and Banks.

Cat was from Mississippi, and since Teddy was from Alabama, they had a deep Southern chemistry—the kind that brothers share—and a natural friendship blossomed. The sheriff had a judicial way about him. Everyone called him Catfish because he had a gringo moustache that was bushy and narrowed to a point at the ends, plus a ravenous appetite for the whiskered fish that he satiated at least four times a week—his freezer door often didn't close well because of the catfish surplus.

Teddy spotted the Ram truck with the siren on top in front of the silver Airstream trailer. Catfish sat behind the wheel, wearing a short-sleeved khaki uniform with a stiff brimmed hat and silver mirrored Ray-Bans. Sam Boxfly, also a member of animal control, was in the backseat grinning as he watched the big man approach. Teddy threw his stuff in the back and got in. Miss Jimmy waved to him from inside the Malt, and he saluted back.

They drove onto Palm Ave., a neighborhood street just past the square, cruising at five miles per hour. Teddy and Box leaned their heads out the windows, scanning the bushes for any sign of the white beast.

"So what are we dealing with here, Cat?" Teddy asked.

"Eleven feet, four hundred pounds, mean and fast. A house cat has even gone missing and an older lady was attacked."

"People call him Crazy Legs because he moves so quick," Box said.

"He may be quick, but a four-hundred-pound albino is easy to spot," Cat said.

"Yeah, well his party is getting ready to end. No gator kills a Latch pet, attacks a woman and gets away with it," Teddy said.

"Yes, this is a peaceful community and it's going to stay that way," Cat said.

"Are we really going to put a bullet in him?" Box said.

"Of course. It has to be done," answered Cat.

"But he's an albino, they're so rare."

"That was before he chomped on a Nike, Box! His status has been officially downgraded." Cat shook his head.

"Cat is right, he's gotta be stopped," Teddy said, still focused on the plants.

"I just hate to see a creature that special get killed if it's not necessary," Box whimpered. Teddy looked at him through the reflection in the side mirror. From his expression, he sensed that Box didn't understand certain things about nature, life and death.

"Box, you're acting like a total space bunny. This is a four hundred pound meat-eating machine. It's a predator. We're not talking about an Egyptian hairless cat that belongs in some petting zoo." Right after uttering those words, Teddy thought about Half Ton and sighed.

"I guess I see what you mean, Salt. It's kind of like that feral hog, he's dangerous as hell."

Teddy thought about Half Ton's gleaming eyes and Bear riding on his back. "Well ... hogs aren't as bad. Just try to remember the distinction between predators and prey—sharks and dolphins."

"I got it."

Teddy quietly wondered if animals had souls and how it all worked. Perhaps some of them, the ones closer to us, were here learning and growing at some level. Clearly some were more able to relate emotionally and live among us, while others seemed hopelessly disconnected and dangerous.

They cruised the streets up and down the gridded neighborhood near the bay. On Jungle Lane, Teddy saw something squirm in the bushes under some banana palms and ordered Catfish to stop. They pulled over and watched the bushes. A long white beak poked out of the green leaves like an arrow, pointing toward a fluffy tan cat dreaming in the front entryway of a neighboring ranch house. The gator took slow gentle steps so as not to wake fluffy. Teddy reacted fast, reaching into his insulated bag to remove the iced beef lung, which he secured on the end of a 12/0 forged fishhook. He hopped out and left his door open, picking up the snare loop out of the back. Box followed him carrying a .22.

"I don't know if that .22 will pierce his skull, Box, and you'll need to shoot him in the back of the head behind the eyes," Teddy whispered.

"It's all we got, so if he comes at us, I'll aim there and just keep firing. Do you really plan on getting him with that hook?"

Teddy raised up the beef lung, "This isn't chicken shit—it's chicken salad. Just watch and learn."

Teddy threw the baited hook to the edge of the bushes in front of Crazy Legs. He was on it quick. When he bit, Teddy jerked the hook in and pulled the rope slowly through the hole in the snare loop, luring Crazy into it. His eyes were clever and bloodthirsty. The cat next door awoke from the noise to the reality of his situation, cried out, and galloped off. Crazy rolled, trying to knock the hook loose, but it was no use. So, Teddy tightened the snare around his neck, tossed a roll of black electric tape into his mouth, and mounted the beast's white back, grabbing the gator's chin with both hands, raising its head back. With the black tape, he wrapped the snout over and over again, using half the roll. With Crazy muzzled, he was as dangerous as a tank full of rubber-banded lobsters. Box and Teddy led the beast up a slant walk into the bed of the Dodge. Cat thanked Teddy and dropped him back at his car, throwing him a salute before driving off to bring Crazy to his fate. Everyone knew he had to be killed because he had attacked someone and killed someone's pet.

Getting in the Ford, Teddy sensed that the town felt a little safer with Crazy gone. Teddy drove down Mangrove Street, observing that the town looked better, but a depression still covered the area—the theater marquee had missing letters and others leaned crookedly—fallen tree limbs still lay scattered on the sides of the streets. Heading toward the water, trees leaned on some of the houses of families that had evacuated and hadn't returned. Teddy could see the ocean through the park—a view once obscured by the tops of trees.

Having only seen the Ball neighborhood from the protection of his television screen, he decided to turn south on Route 1. After driving for five miles along the ocean, he turned inland on Sea Dog Lane and drove for a little while before making a left on Hope Street going into Ball. A few reporter vans were the only signs of life that hadn't been sucked out of the area. Waterlogged houses and cars waited for no one, and a scraggly yellow dog jogged down the street to nowhere. The yards and flowerbeds were torn up, fences knocked over, and telephone poles leaned sideways. Many of the low ranch houses had trees on them; some had cars rammed into the sides. He got to the end of the road at the corner of Slingshot Avenue. A black boy in cut-off jeans and a white T-shirt perched on a rock on a slight hill about thirty yards away. He stared at Teddy with umber eyes, kicking some dirt up with his black high top Chuck Taylors. Teddy got out and walked up the hill, looking back out over the devastation. He waved to the boy, but he didn't wave back. The hot sun blinded his eyes, so he put on his gold aviators and scanned the horizon. After a while, he headed back to his car and got in. The boy watched him as he drove off.

BACK AT THE FARM, Teddy boomed into the dining room where Dal and Charlotte were chatting.

"How's the leg, Dal?"

"Butter and biscuits, baby." Dal stretched his leg out on the floor, hot dogging the healed wound.

"How do you feel?" Teddy asked, walking over to the coffee pot and pouring a cup.

"Great! I think the wine even helped my overall energy. Thanks again."

"I've never seen anything work that fast," remarked Charlotte. "It's a miracle."

"Good science can seem like a miracle," Teddy said, swinging around a chair and taking a seat. He sipped the Jamaican Blue Mountain coffee slowly.

"So, what do you say? You wanna hunt today?" Dal asked.

"Yeah, I just saw the Ball neighborhood and it gave me motivation. Those folks lost everything, and I want to help out when we find something. Have y'all seen it?"

"No," Dal said. "But I like your idea to help."

"What a shame." Charlotte shook her head and paused for a moment. Then she asked, "How did it go today with the rescue?"

"With Crazy?"

"Yeah."

"We trapped him."

"Oh, that's great. I overheard some folks at the Malt saying that a cat had gone missing."

"Yeah, well, Crazy had his last meal," Teddy said.

A horn honked twice. "That's Patch. Teddy, ready to go?" Dal said, getting up and walking almost normally now.

"Always."

"Still on tonight for Ink at eight?" Dal asked Charlotte.

"Eight o'clock," Charlotte said.

"I'll be here," he said and kissed her on the lips. "I love you," he whispered in her ear.

"Dal?!" she replied.

"Okay, okay—I won't say it," he said. "See you tonight."

"See you."

CHAPTER 3

*I*t was about nine p.m. when Cos noticed the chicken running sluggish and read the fuel gauge on empty. Only a few trucks and cars passed in the black night, and there hadn't been an exit since Pensacola. A sign ahead indicated a gas station four miles away. They exited onto Spider Hollow Lane. Along the vacant road, they passed tilted shacks with cars and the occasional busted sofa in the yards. They approached a stop sign before railroad tracks where a leaning green sign to the right read "Bees Nest, Alabama, pop. 238." Across the street sat Sambo's gas station with only the letters S and O lit up on the sign, so it read SO. An eerie fluorescent glow seeped from the inside. It was the only light in town except for the exterior fluorescent, which cast a blue spell on everything around it. The station still had the old-timey pumps, only it wasn't trying to be retro. A thirty-foot-tall by one-hundred-foot wide castle of flat tires was piled in a field of weeds to the side. Cos waited at the stop sign.

"We're going to break down right here if we wait any longer," Joey said with a serious tone. "Thank God for our smartphones!"

"I don't like this place. I think there was another gas station the other way. Let me check my GasBuddy app," Cos remarked.

"She's sputtering, man. C'mon on, we're just getting gas!" Joey insisted.

The chicken coughed again; Cos accelerated, rolling over the tracks and pulling into the station to the first self-serve pump. A wide-bellied man sat inside watching a small television behind the counter. Two of the other signs said "full service," but there was no one to pump the gas.

Peeking through the window of the car, Cos spotted Joey rubbing his hands through Belle's hair. A gentle breeze blew. He smiled and thought that Bees Nest wasn't that bad after all.

Finishing up, Cos went inside to pay. Along the window to the right of the door, stacks of tires were piled to the ceiling, which struck him as odd since it wasn't a real service station, hosting little more than a pathetic excuse of a garage. Boxes of stock flooded the floors in the disheveled aisles; a box of dried ramen noodle packages was spilled down one of them.

The man behind the counter was overweight and bald with thick-rimmed glasses. His bottom lip hung out and his ears protruded like an antenna from a head shaped like a soccer ball. Vanessa White's soothing voice came from the TV in the background.

Cos walked to the counter and greeted him, "Good evening."

The man gave him the classic mule skinner stare while ringing up the total. Cos handed him the amount and the man counted the dollars, saying nothing. Cos wondered if the sun-washed curly hair or the Patagonia AC shirt were too outdoorsy for the attendant or maybe the guy was like that with everyone. Cos didn't know, but the guy's death stare rattled his last nerve. The man checked him out and handed him the change, holding his gaze.

"Thank you, sir," Cos said, trying to be as polite as possible. The man said nothing, just watched him leave; then, returned to *Wheel of Fortune*. Cos hurried back to the car and got in.

"And THAT was weird."

"What?" Joey asked.

"A total psycho behind the register. He gave me the muleskinner stare. I wanna get out of here fast."

THE DOLLARHIDE MYSTERY

"Sorry to hear it," Joey said. As Cos pulled off, the left side of the car wobbled. "What's wrong?"

Cos leaned his head out the window and saw the left back tire flat. "Dammit! We got a flat."

"When did that happen?" Joey asked.

"Just now, I guess. The clerk probably went telekinetic on it with his death stare from the register."

Cos stopped the car and got out. The tire was weak now. He traced the ground back to the road. Kneeling down, he ran his finger over two tiny one-inch-long bent nails. Suspecting foul play, he carried them back inside.

"Excuse me sir," Cos stammered and placed the two bent-up nails on the counter. "I ran over one of these and now my tire is flat." The clerk picked one of them up and looked at it like he was examining a chunk of meteorite that just fell from the sky. The man knew no one important came to the station late at night, and the sheriff and one trooper in town practically always used pump five across the way, and never drove through that area. They sort of knew about "the nail trick" anyway. It was one of *those places*. The man craned his neck around from the stool, looking outside.

"This got yur tire?"

"Yes sir."

"Never seen it before."

"But what about the stack of tires outside, and there were two of these nails? Some coincidence."

"Well, I can replace the tire."

"*Uhhh, yeah.*"

"All right. Tire like dat ul run ya eighty-five dollars and two dimes."

"*What?* I am *not* paying for it!"

"No money, no tire."

"I want *you* to make this right."

"Okay." The man slowly stood, picked up his rifle for protection against armed robberies, and walked outside in front of Cos.

He had on a see-through white undershirt and black Dickie pants that rode high above his belly button, hanging on by a pair of miserable stretched-out suspenders. Although the sight of the gun alarmed Cos, his curiosity followed him.

The man greased over to the chicken's other back tire as casually as if he was going to point at a light bulb that needed to be changed, cocked the gun, aimed, and fired. The back tire boomed with a violent expulsion of air. The blast startled everyone in the car, waking up the ladies, who ducked down. The attendant then turned to Cos with the smoking gun in hand.

"Well now you gurt two flat tires ... that ul run ya a hundred and seventy-one dollars and four dimes." He smiled a toothless mess, while staring at Cos, who had hit the pavement when the gun fired. Cos got up and ran around to the driver's door.

"Now, are we gonna have any more trouble here?" the man said, approaching the driver's door with the gun.

"No sir, I was just leaving." He got in and cranked the engine.

"What the hell was that?" Joey said.

"I don't know! I think he just snapped! Too many lonely nights in Bees Nest."

"Go, go, go!" Belle commanded.

Dog barked in the commotion; Cos accelerated and the car barely wobbled off on the two blown tires. The attendant turned back to the station; as they left, Cos leaned his head out the window and yelled, "You still owe me two tires, mister!"

The comment enraged the clerk, who charged after the car, his belly shaking. He fired at them again as the chicken barely winged back onto Spider Hollow heading out of town, riding on metal now. The shot took out a small piece of the chicken's tail with a loud crack. Cos rolled forward, shocked, his hands visibly shaking; everyone in the car ducked down; the tires were hopelessly torn piles of rubber now and the rims went flying. The attendant, howling through his smirk, planted in the center of the dark lonesome road and threw them a one-finger victory salute.

"You should've seen the look on your face when he shot that tire! I wish I had a picture," Joey said, laughing.

"You wouldn't find it funny if it was you out there."

"I was right there with you, Cosby."

"Were you scared?" Belle said.

"Scared? You wouldn't believe it Belle! I saw my whole life flash before my eyes. I swear," Cos said, his voice shaking.

"He was just trying to scare us," Belle said, being the voice of reason.

"Well it worked!" Leslie added.

"Let's just get off this road. I feel like I've slipped into some ghost machine time warp with strange weirdo people from nowhere," Joey remarked.

Although the chicken acted like it was in fourth gear, it carried them far enough away to change the shot flat with the spare in the trunk. Thank God Dan kept one. Then, they wobbled to the nearest gas station along the frontage road, almost damaging the axel before they could change the other popped tire.

Afterward, they drove for twenty minutes and reached the exit for Goodchance on Highway 89. Taking it, they rode south along the bay. Holly trees and streetlights lined the median, which ebbed and flowed over sweet hills. They exited at a sign marked *Scenic View*, and ancient oaks with grey moss that nearly touched the ground and southern coastal vernacular houses tucked in between them on sprawling lots passed by. After a couple of miles, the houses dropped off and forested areas sprang up on the left side; across the street, the bay was visible for miles. At the top of a hill, they passed Wild Bill's, a wooden bar designed to look like an old western saloon. Tied to the front porch columns, a huge plastic banner read "Friday Night: Live Music, Crawfish, and one dollar pitchers." Cars swamped the parking lot and surrounding green spaces. A bouncer sat on a stool at the door checking IDs.

"Look at that," Cos said, pointing. "Crawfish! Gotta love the Gulf Coast." He suggested they come back after checking in with Jim—their grandfather, Teddy's father—and Joey and the ladies agreed.

The winding road became flat and straight as it entered downtown Goodchance. Joey cruised through the intersection on Main and turned right onto Peanut Lane, a street of sweet bungalows wrapping around the downtown. He pulled the chicken into the driveway of his grandfather Jim's bay-front home. Half of the bungalow was blue, and the other half was stark white. Weeds and brush overgrew the yard like the Tasmanian rainforest, and the lot was sandwiched between two chipper houses with well-groomed lawns of equally well-groomed people—except for their hatred of Jim's yard, which grew wild like the kudzu around the way.

Darkness blanketed the sky, but automatic streetlamps illuminated the area. They unloaded, finding their way through the partially bushed path to the porch. Construction debris and sawdust littered the porch, two Rubbermaid trashcans stuffed with empty paint cans and scrap wood flanked either side of the door, and an old claw-foot bathtub sat at an angle with mildew on the inside.

Jim had been renovating the house for ten years now, starting the day after his wife died. He did all the work himself, stopping each project before completion only to start a new one. When people in town or his neighbors caught him, they asked when he would finish something like the painting or mowing the yard, and he always gave them a definite date and time: "Oh, Monday at around 1:30 ... Wednesday around 4:00 ... next Sunday at 9:14 p.m.," but when they drove by or looked out the window, it was never finished. When they asked him again, he gave them a new deadline just as certain as the last one. He wore his 108 citizen complaints with the city council like a badge of honor, but the council rarely enforced anything. Now the disappointed citizens just asked Jim for a time because it was the only way they could remind him of their irritation.

Joey wiped his feet on the "Welcome Home" mat. The ladies followed the boys with trepidation. Belle crossed her arms and shrank her shoulders. Joey assured them it would be okay, that Jim was awesome. Joey pushed the metal rooster's beak for a doorbell and waited while it rang. He knocked, but there was no answer. They went around back.

At the fence, they found Jimmy "Jim" Dollarhide, age eighty-five.

Hearing them, he turned and approached. Although his hair and clothes were straight and neat, there was something open and free in his eyes. After being introduced to the ladies and catching up, he informed them he wanted to show them something.

They went with him into the backyard covered with patches of wild grass. They passed a garden and an obstacle course with a wood climbing wall, rope course, and hurdles. Jim was a weirdo, the ladies thought as they walked on down a path that cut between a very thick brush that revealed a circular clearing forced by an old oak tree. A tire swung under it and a lean man with a hooked nose, bony face, and reading glasses relaxed in a lawn chair examining a quarter-sized rock with a magnifying glass under a spotlight; a pot smoked on a smoldering fire near him.

"I'd like y'all to meet Palmer, my best friend, roommate, and chess mate, although he's usually the one in checkmate."

"Oh, that's a load of rubbish, you old mule," Palmer turned to them. "He just can't stand that he always loses. You see, he doesn't know how to play with the queen—if he could master the queen, he would win, but as it is, he's just a pawn."

"Jealous tongues tell jealous lies. Don't listen to it wag!" Jim said. The four laughed.

"What are y'all doing back here?" Cos asked, surveying everything.

"A couple of days ago, Palmer mixed a rare earth mineral into our broth of base elements, and we got something."

Jim held out his hand to Palmer, who placed the stone in his palm; Jim twirled it in the light.

"What do you think it is?" asked Joey.

Jim studied it, then passed it to Joey. "You tell me."

Joey looked at it, "Is it gold?"

"We'll see soon. No, but maybe. It's a great piece of silver, and I am rich!" Jim exclaimed.

"Show it to Dog," Cos said.

"Oh yeah, Teddy and his gold-sniffing dog," Jim said, and placed the nugget at Dog's nose; he barked at it with a big smile.

"Well I'll be. Looks like it might be something, if that mutt's nose is right," Jim said. "How 'bout we go inside and eat, and I can show y'all to your rooms. How do oysters sound?"

"Sounds good!" they answered.

Jim led them into the kitchen where he pulled a bushel of oysters from a second fridge in the laundry and then set them on the dining table with four oyster knives and four rags. He slid the trashcan over to them with his cowboy boot.

"Still wearing boots, Jim?" Joey joked.

"Yeah, it drives my doc crazier than a march hare, and sometimes my back aches, but I am never stopping. When y'all bury me, it'll be in boots."

They laughed and began to shuck the oysters. Belle already knew how to do it, taking pride in opening them with the first turn of the knife. Cos shucked Leslie's oysters for her, a sweet, romantic gesture that wasn't lost on her. The group ate the marshy oysters with their sweet aftertaste and chased them with iced well water. After eating two dozen or so, they began to feel relaxed and satisfied.

Once finished, Jim gave them a tour of the house and led them into the living room, which consisted of a square couch and a recliner, a shelf of books lining one wall, and a painting of a bald eagle on the wall to the left—a wooden square poker table crowded a corner underneath two windows, and a chess board with a game in progress sat in the middle. Two deer skins sprawled on the floor, their white tails sticking up a bit.

"It's been awhile since y'all visited," Jim said.

"About three years," Joey answered.

"Yep, Palmer moved in about two and a half years ago. We started rooming together so we wouldn't have to go into a home. It's a resistance pact: he's got my back, I got his. If I leave the stove on, he catches it; if he trips, I am there to pick him up. You see."

Jim led the ladies into one bedroom and the men to another. Afterward, Palmer and he sat down to play Texas Hold'em poker while Joey unloaded their bags from the car.

After showering, Belle dressed in Seven jeans and a green Marc

Jacobs top; Leslie wore jeans also and an ecru V-neck Polo tee. The guys wore loose fitting Patagonia natural shorts and T-shirts. They walked into the living room where Jim and Palmer hunched over the card table in the corner drinking wine and playing Hold'em. Attracted by the goldfish snacks, Dog sat between them, watching the play go back and forth between the hand and the mouth. Jim tossed him a goldfish every couple of minutes.

"Go on old man, show em. What'd ya got?" Jim asked with eager anticipation, taking a swig of his merlot.

"Three cowboys." Palmer flipped his cards down with a smirk.

"Dammit!" Jim threw his jack with an ace high to the middle. "I think that new memory pill is helping your game too much. It ain't fair."

"Face it, Jim, you're a sore loser. You'll just have to wait until next month to get your social security check before I whip ya again." Palmer chuckled as he raked the chips toward him.

Jim saw the company to the side. "Where are y'all going at this late hour?"

"For a bite to eat," Joey answered.

"At Wild Bill's?" Jim asked.

"No. We'll probably just pick up some burgers, those oysters weren't enough for our appetite," Joey said.

Jim studied him. "Have fun at Wild Bill's. Promise me you won't drink and drive. If you need a ride, call Mary Jo White, she volunteers to pick people up who've been drinking and drives them home for free. She's on Google under Mary Jo Goes."

"That's nice of her," Belle said.

"That's Goodchance, my dear. Nice folks are easy to come by."

"Mary Jo, got it," Joey confirmed. "But we're not going to Bill's, I swear. It's twenty-one and up. Little bitty Cos can't get in," Joey said, smirking.

"All right then, have a good time," Jim said. The group turned to leave. "Wait, I kinda like that chicken car—I'll trade you my '62 Ford truck for it?" Jim said.

"We can't. It's Cos's boss's car." Joey let it slide.

"I am not even gonna touch that one."

"He let us borrow it," Cos said, reaching.

"*Sure* he did." Jim shook his head. "Y'all have fun, and remember: Mary Jo if you drink."

"Got it," Cos said.

CHAPTER 4

*E*merging from behind the stage into an outdoor dirt area that resembled a dude ranch, the group spotted picnic tables set up along the wall of the bar with steaming boulder-like pots packed to the baking brim with crawfish. A sign read "$5 A Plate with a side of Boiled Peanuts." Loose chickens roamed around the grounds pecking at grit, and a goat loitered, chewing on patches of grass, his ribs showing under his white coat. Due to Cos and Leslie being underage, they had to sneak in through a loose board in the back fence.

Some guys with groomed haircuts, button-ups, and blazers hid cowboy boots underneath blue jeans, and when the ladies, equally well tailored, went in and out of the bar, the guys held the door open. Another group that seemed to have come from a wedding was wearing slacks and dress shirts, the buttons on the men's necks undone and their coats missing; the ladies wore dresses and pearls, some carrying their high heels. The crowd had a good humor; deadhead bikers from the Florida panhandle and various townie barflies weaved in and out. Groups gathered in circles, chatting and laughing and telling stories in an animated fashion.

The gang trotted over to the crawfish table where a round-faced man with flushed red cheeks and dimples asked if they wanted some mudbugs in an incomprehensibly thick accent. Joey and Cos plated up; "Don't mind if we do," Joey said.

The ladies commented that they looked gross. The man suggested they were tourists; any good local knew they taste damn good and that everyone needs some of that Vitamin Red found only in the head of a mudbug. Belle politely declined again, but Joey challenged her masculinity and she immediately got a plate, making a point to fill it up so full it sank in the middle. After trying them, she agreed that they were pretty damn good. Leslie shuddered at the idea, sticking with boiled peanuts and beer.

After a while, the goat took an interest in Leslie, circling around her before nudging her with his horn, which he followed with a buck that just missed her butt. The man tending the crawfish stand told her not to worry: "that just means he likes you."

"Oh good," Leslie said.

"C'mon, let's go inside," Joey said, holding the door open.

"Time to mess up a perfectly good bar scene," Cos added, walking through with the ladies following him.

The inside of Bill's had wooden walls with no insulation, similar to Joey's tree house. A screened rectangular hole spanning the length of the wall offered ventilation; a swamp cooler hung from the corner blowing out semi-cool moist air, and a single ceiling fan provided the rest of the temperature control. The walls sweated in the June heat and humidity. Often mistaken for earth, the wood floor had multiple layers of dust; a hazy cloud of cigarette smoke stuck to the ceiling in strings like vaporous bubble gum. Up front, the band on stage played folk renditions of classic rock and country songs; their banjo player infused the place with an Appalachian twang. People broke the capacity, sitting at tables littered with beer bottles, while others stood. As they entered, another group got up from a booth against the wall and they took a seat.

They finished off their crawfish. Then, Joey headed to the bar to get the drinks. The bar wrapped around a half rectangle facing the stage. The bartender smiled and pointed to Joey, "Hey! You're the Duck Hunt guy?!"

"Yeah, unfortunately, that's me."

"No, man. Own it. I love that video!"

"Thanks," Joey said, a little red-faced.

"It's a real pleasure to meet you. I haven't been this excited since Lyle Lovett showed up. Will you sign the wall?" He pointed to an area behind the bar where celebrities had thrown their John Hancock.

"I'd rather not."

"Aww c'mon, if you do, the drinks are on the house. Jimmy Buffett signed it!"

Hearing Bubba's name broke Joey's resistance; he took the marker and gave his best John Hancock as close to Bubba's name as he could get. He wondered if he would ever escape his YouTube fame after this. After a round of photos with some eager co-eds and other employees, he ordered and returned with scotch for himself and Belle, and beers for Leslie and Cos. They chatted and drank while the band played. After a while, the lead singer, a middle-aged man with a thick grey moustache and long silver hair that glittered in the stage light, announced they would play "Orange Blossom Special," and the fiddler stepped in. Guys and girls danced in the open spaces between the stage and tables. Joey led Belle out and they began to follow the crowd.

Cos exited to the bathroom, unaware of the group of vultures that had been circling their table. The leader, a short hyperactive sort with brown hair and a belt buckle bigger than his ego, tipped his cowboy hat to Leslie and leaned in with a big smile, introducing himself as Skeet, telling her she was "a stone fox."

She insisted her boyfriend would be back, but he persisted, explaining that he had a girlfriend and didn't care. One of his friends swooped in on the other side. They took a seat at the booth and closed in on her.

As Cos walked to the bathroom, he saw The University of Alabama's football team, The Crimson Tide, memorabilia crowding the back wall. At the entrance, there was a framed photo of Coach Bear Bryant with his houndstooth hat and studious eye.

After finishing, Cos exited and a towering guy with a twenty-inch neck who could have been the son of Paul Bunyan and Wonder Woman came up, asking if he could borrow a quarter to continue his video game on Big Buck Hunter Pro. Cos emptied his change into his hand; the man thanked him and patted him on the back. Cos stumbled back a bit from the touch.

Cos saw Skeet sitting next to Leslie, and slid into the booth across from them. Skeet put his arm around her and she recoiled with repulsion. Cos wanted to tell the bouncer, but knew they might get picked up for being underage. Skeet flipped a toothpick over itself with his tongue.

Cos intentionally spilled his beer in Skeet's direction, running into his lap. Exploding, Skeet brushed it off.

"I know you meant to do that, you surfer freak. Do you have any idea who I am?" He pointed at his chest.

"No idea."

"Skeet Boomer! Number one steer wrestler in the state of Texas for the last three years. No one messes with me, especially not some sissy boy."

"Well Skeet, I am an avid aficionado of the circuit, and I've never heard of you."

Skeet's face turned red and he lunged forward, but his friend held him back. Pushing his pal out of the way, he continued for Cos's throat, but he got jerked back from behind by Big Buck Hunter, who turned him around, elevating him by his shirt.

"Is there a problem here?" the guy asked.

Skeet whimpered, "No."

"Good." He dropped him down. "Now, leave these nice people alone." Skeet scurried out of the bar with his friend.

"Thanks, man!" Cos enthused.

"No problem. Y'all have a nice evening. Thanks again for the quarters—I broke my all-time high!"

"Sure thing," Cos said, and the guy walked off.

"Nice move with the beer," Leslie said. They fist bumped and laughed about it.

"Thanks. Teddy always tells us nonviolence is the way to solve things, but sometimes you gotta do something."

"Who was that big guy?" Belle asked.

"I don't know. I gave him some quarters for the hunting game and I guess he loves me now," Cos said.

"Well, that paid off," Leslie said.

Joey and Belle returned from dancing with love covering their faces.

"What happened here?" Joey asked.

"Some jerk was hitting on Leslie," answered Cos.

"Cos knocked his drink into the guy's lap and boy did he light up!"

Joey exited to grab a rag from the bar.

"Really?" Belle asked, smiling.

"Yeah, Skeet Boomer was his name," Cos answered, and shook his head with a smile. Joey returned and wiped the table down, then slid next to Belle.

"What a name!" Belle said, and nestled up to Joey's chest, sipping the scotch.

"Don't you know scotch is a man's drink?" Leslie said.

"So what!"

"Well it's gonna put hair on your chest if you don't watch out," Leslie insisted.

"And a moustache too," Cos said.

"She already has a moustache," Joey said, laughing. Belle frogged him on the top of the arm, smiling.

"Ouch, babe."

"She hits too. You *really* are a man," Leslie said, smiling. "Ha! *I knew it!*"

"You want some, Leslie?" Belle made a fist, her smile now showing her full mouth of teeth.

"No way, I am not tangling with a tomboy like you."

"That's what I thought," Belle said. "So, let's talk about the treasure."

"Okay, I am so excited I don't know what to do about it!" Leslie said.

"How are we gonna find it?" Belle said.

Joey took out their map of the Sierras from Gooch's and spread it on the wooden bar table.

"Camp Big Bear is in the Sierras about five miles northwest of the valley the river runs through. When we get there, we'll stay for a day here," Joey pointed to a place on the map, "recharge, and then hike out. We know the treasure was along the river on the right side in the valley, which would make it somewhere in this area," he ran his finger to another point on the map. "But we need the other journal from Bo's to see where this exact spot is."

"When we find the loot, what will we do with it exactly?" Belle asked Joey.

"I don't know. Uncle Sam gets a cut off the top, found treasure is taxed as income. Then, we have to set up a contract with the camp since it's on their land, probably give them 10 percent. Then, we take 50 percent of what's left, and the other fifty will go to a charitable organization for Native Americans. We have to keep Luke's promise. That's the way I see it," Joey said.

"How much do you think it will be?" Leslie asked.

"No way to know. Let's just hope it's there."

"Oh, it's there all right," Cos said.

They finished up their drinks and left, forgetting about Skeet. The air outside was syrupy like the people in lower Alabama. They walked down the hill to the chicken, but Cos was a little funny and Joey stopped him, suggesting they call Mary Jo. He dialed her number and a very old lady answered, agreeing to be there shortly.

Up the hill, Skeet and his friend Jethro watched them from the interior of his black F350, which had an airbrushed mural of a blue and yellow cobra on the back windshield with *Skeet Boomer No. 1* written in rope cursive on top of a storm cloud. A lightning bolt fired from the cloud into the cobra's head, electrifying it with a golden hue.

In ten minutes, a pink scooter meandered down the street at fifteen miles per hour with a line of honking traffic behind it. It pulled over and an old woman wearing a long blue dress with white polka dots that furled around the neck got off; she removed the helmet, revealing her white afro and oversized glasses, and slowly asked Joey to load the folding scooter in the back of the chicken. The group watched on with amazement as she hunched forward and turtled toward the driver's seat after Joey handed her the keys. They got in and she began relaying her life story, starting with her birth in Mobile. She swung out at a snail's pace, leaning forward on the wheel, squinting at the road.

"When I was little bitty, we didn't have video games, didn't have the Pods, didn't have Ephones, didn't even have TV," she went on and on, occasionally interjecting *"all we had was each other."*

The F350 eased down the hill after them.

While talking, she drove fifteen miles per hour, traffic blaring horns behind them. When they reached downtown, she ran a red light, just missing a car. She explained she thought it was green, confessing she was a bit colorblind to the green and red spectrum. The group held on for dear life in silence as they watched with horror. When she hit Peanut Lane, she turned into the wrong lane of traffic, steady at fifteen mph. The approaching truck honked and they warned her, but she didn't understand. Cos pulled the wheel a bit, jerking the car into the right lane, and they dodged a mishap.

When they escaped the car at Jim's, they relaxed. Joey removed her scooter, unfolded it, and thanked her. She congratulated them for not drinking and driving; they waved goodbye and breathed a sigh of relief as she scooted away.

The black sky read midnight. The lights in the windows were off, except for a reading lamp in the living room where Jim rested in his favorite chair, smoking a pipe. They walked into the house and the alcohol caused the ladies to laugh; they tried to stop, but that caused them to laugh even more. Jim greeted them with a smile, asking if they had fun. They answered yes. Tired from the trip, the ladies wandered off to bed. Joey and Cos trailed them down the hall, hoping to spend more time with them, but they assured them that nothing, not even a kiss, would happen under their grandfather's roof. Joey tried stealing a kiss from Belle, but she leaned back and blocked it with her hand, shutting the door in his face while smiling.

They went back into the living room, deflated. Joey asked Jim if Palmer would wake up if they played a game of cards.

"Palm couldn't hear a gun go off if he was in the barrel. Go right ahead and play dem cards."

Outside, Skeet parked a couple of houses down. He and Jethro crept low into the driveway. Jethro talked loud and Skeet slapped him on the back of the head, ordering him to be quiet. They stopped at the chicken's gas tank, where Skeet unscrewed the top of a bottle of Old Crow bourbon.

"This will teach them to never wrangle with a true cowboy."

Next, he removed the gas cap and started to pour it, but chatter from the cracked window above stopped him.

Inside, Cos shuffled the cards with the fluidity of a Bellagio dealer, splicing and folding them. He dealt. They agreed to play with Goldfish crackers to make it more fun.

Skeet overheard the word "treasure" and his ears flipped up like a rabbit. He hugged the side of the house, motioning Jethro over.

"Where are y'all going tomorrow?" Jim looked up from his book.

"Little Rock," answered Joey.

"I love Little Rock," Jim said. "Are y'all taking that car all the way to the Sierras in California where the Hodge's Treasure is buried?"

"Yep," Joey said.

"What makes you think you can find the treasure where Luke failed?"

"We found missing clues in his journals," Cos answered and hustled off to get them. When he re-entered the room, he handed them to Jim, who studied them.

"Well, I'll be. I never knew there was a documentation of this conversation with the Native American. Got no idea why. Never saw this map in journal four either. I can't believe Luke never told anyone there was a *damn map!* I surely would have hunted it."

"That's probably why he never told anyone," Cos said.

"He didn't want you to waste your time," Joey said.

"I guess he knew we would all go for it," said Jim.

Outside, Skeet gestured to Jethro to follow him out the driveway.

Jethro had a befuddled look on his face, being half deaf from working at the firing range in Lubbock, Texas. Back in the truck, Skeet stared at him with a big grin.

"Did you hear that?" Skeet asked.

"Naw."

"These boys know where a treasure is in California, and they're going to find it."

"Really?"

"Yep, and *we're* gonna tail em, let em dig it up, and then snatch it from em." He swooped his hand through the air.

"That don't seem right to me, Skeet."

"What's right, huh? That we bust our butts on the rodeo and don't have nothin to show for it while some sissies get rich diggin up a box?"

"So, you're saying this is our due?"

"Hell yeah, this is our due. Our *reward* for all the work we've done and never been paid for. It's like a gift from heaven," Skeet said, holding his arms up to the sky in praise. "We were meant to come here tonight and hear this."

"Good point. Maybe we were. Could I get that Dakota rifle I've always wanted with the treasure money?"

"With this treasure you could buy anything you want buddy. Besides, we can spot that damn chicken car from a mile away, that's the goofiest thing I've ever seen."

"You're right about that. What are they doing driving a chicken around anyway?"

"No clue, bunch of losers if you ask me," Skeet barked.

"All right, let's do this!" Jethro said, his eyes glowing and his mouth widening to a huge grin. They agreed, leaving for the Brown Pelican Inn with a plan to wake early and wait up the street from Jim's house.

Inside, Joey and Cos's poker game proceeded with Dog looking on, planted on his hindquarters. Cos tossed him goldfish from the bowl every other hand.

"I swear that dog doesn't *know* he's a dog," Jim remarked.

"They say the Jack Russell is one of the smartest dogs in the world," Joey said.

"I guess brain size doesn't mean much, 'cos he has a little bitty head," Jim said.

"Must not, because he's as smart as a whip. In the house we have to spell words because if he hears a keyword like *walk, eat,* or *go,* he knows," Joey said and glanced at his cards, shooting Cos his best poker face. Jim laughed.

"It's true. He's like Google. I'll check," Cos said, glancing at Jim.

"Your grandmother was the same way, only her keywords were *shop* and *shoes*," Jim said—Joey and Cos laughed.

Jim looked at the clock. "It looks like it's my bedtime, boys. I may be young at heart, but my body is old."

They said goodnight and Jim exited to his bedroom. They finished playing into the night by the light of the swinging lamp, Joey winning with a flop of aces. Then, they shuffled back to the bedroom.

CHAPTER 5

*M*iles of vacant forest closed in on Belle. Like a runaway train, she scrambled through an ominous presence permeating the still air. A bare hollow tree in front of a dilapidated wooden shack with a crooked tin roof and walls the color of the sky stood ahead.

She felt someone behind her, but craning around, only saw the bare-branched trees. The foreboding house felt like the only shelter from the doom. As she neared the tree, she got jerked up in the air in a net. Swinging five feet off the ground, she called out for Joey, but she only heard the door to the house creak open.

She looked around, but the tree obstructed her view. A slick raven landed on the net, pecking at her through the holes. She wiggled like a caught fish to escape the pecks. A second bird approached and pecked, then a third, and a fourth. A withered lady with eyes as hollow as a well, a hunched back, and a nose punched into her skull approached from the side with a smile that grew in its wickedness as she neared; she wore a dark cloak and had long gnarly hair, every morsel of nutritious life gone from her ages ago. Standing in front of Belle, she glared at her, touched her with a foot-long finger, and began to draw the air out of Belle's lungs.

Belle half-woke unable to breathe—her body paralyzed—in two states of consciousness at once. She could see a fleeting glimmer of the dark shadow flying through the room of Jim's house; it stopped to hover above her. The being from her dream was a figment in this world, her shredded cloak blowing in the wind of the fan, her mouth a black hole with silver blades for teeth. Belle was helpless and the being knew it, drawing the air from her chest. She had to wake up—*"Wake up!"* her mind screamed to every part of her body. She forced herself back into consciousness, jolting forward, gasping for air. Sweat soaked her neckline and forehead and stuck her pajamas to her skin.

Jim's house confused her; she looked out the window in a panic for the woods and the woman, but there was only the neat wood house next door. She could feel the invisible phantom in the room, but couldn't see it. While running into Joey's room, she stubbed her toe hard on the door but kept running.

She dove into bed with Joey, squeezing him. He woke and when he glanced into her eyes, she was miles away and he couldn't go there with her. Rubbing his hand through her red hair and kissing the top of her wet forehead, he started to reel her back from the distant dark dimension.

"What's wrong, sweetheart?"

"I had the worst nightmare—it feels like there's darkness all around me."

"I am sorry, but you're safe now."

"No. The dreams never end and they never will. I have them all the time, ever since TJ."

"Really?"

"Yes."

"We should ask Jim about this! He knows all about this kind of stuff. It's only 1 a.m. Jim rests a lot, but he sleeps with one eye opened."

"No. I don't want to trouble him. It's late."

"No really babe, he can help and won't mind."

"I guess I'd be willing to *talk to him*, but only if you think he won't get mad."

"No way."

Joey got up and led her by the hand. Light simmered through a crack in Jim's door. Joey knocked and Jim beckoned them in. He leaned up in bed reading a book, a painting of pelicans perched on marina pilings hanging above him.

"Granddad, sorry to bother you so late, but Belle just had a bad dream."

"Well, it just so happens I couldn't sleep anyway. Come sit down sweetheart." She sat on the end of the bed. "Now, do tell me about it."

"I have these dreams—nightmares—ever since I dated this guy." She looked down and rubbed her temples, then told Jim the nightmare in vivid detail.

"I am so sorry to hear that."

"Can anything be done to stop it? Like alchemy for bad dreams?" Joey asked.

"I do believe I have just the thing that might help." Jim leaned over, picked up a brown leather box from his nightstand, and sifted through it, eventually removing a wooden beaded necklace with an exquisite rose crafted from various gems and rare stones.

"Take this and wear it. This rose was made by a Franciscan monk in Italy and given to me by a very special priest. It *will* protect you for now."

Belle took it and clasped it around her neck. When it touched her skin, Joey swore her complexion slightly brightened. She leaned forward and kissed Jim on the cheek, thanking him. A tear fell from her face.

"Don't cry, my dear."

"I've just struggled with it for so many years. If anything could help, I would be so relieved."

"You'll be fine now; however, it might take a special kind of person to completely break the spell for you, like a priest, or Tahoma."

"Who?" Joey asked.

"You're going through Santa Fe to see Bo, right?"

"Yes."

"Well, there's an old native there named Tahoma whom Bo knows. He works as a cook at a restaurant called Gourmaize. I imagine he's the kind of person who could help with this sort of thing."

"We will surely look for him when we go. Thanks, Jim."

"No problem," he said, and lifted up his book again. "Good evening. Hope it helps."

Belle and Joey returned to his room; Belle asked to sleep with him and he agreed. She kissed the rose for good luck, detecting the subtle fragrance of the flower and a feeling of the monastery in Italy where it was made. She fell into a deep sleep, waking in a sprawling green pasture abundant with apple trees—a flowing stream with the clearest water ran by and roses of every shade waved in a gentle wind.

The next morning, they woke to the sound of a Weed Eater outside and the scent of cut grass wafting in through the open window. Belle told Joey it was the best night of sleep she had experienced in the last year and kissed him on the lips. She got up smiling and swished into the next room to wake Leslie. Joey waked Cos, and the four went to the kitchen to get breakfast.

Through the kitchen window, Joey saw Jim outside just finishing up his morning obstacle course: climbing a wood wall, two hundred push-ups, and a rope course. He came in wearing aviators, a T-shirt, and shorts.

They each grabbed a bowl and placed fresh blueberries on top of some yogurt. Dog patrolled the yard for varmints to eat for breakfast.

"So tell me Belle, how did you sleep?"

"Excellent, thank you. The necklace helped soooo much." She touched it.

"Glad to hear it. You can keep it."

"Thank you, Mr. Dollarhide."

"You're welcome my dear."

They finished the yogurt and packed the car before saying goodbye to Jim. In the driveway, Joey jokingly asked, "Hey Jim, if you ever make that silly gold, what's the first thing you'll do?"

"Open a jewelry store!" he said with a smile, his hands stuffed in his pockets. They waved goodbye as they headed out of the driveway.

It was a nice Saturday morning with low humidity; Joey put on some John Hiatt to guide them into Mississippi.

Skeet and Jethro followed about five car lengths back in the black Ford, eating an egg McMuffin and listening to some bad country. Skeet knew generally where they were going, so he wasn't too concerned about his proximity as long as he could see the comb of the chicken truck.

CHAPTER 6

Teddy and the Pearlmakers spent the first part of the day hunting the sea around where they had snagged the cannon, but they left empty-handed. Teddy wondered how the boys were doing and promptly sent Joey a text. Joey replied that the group had indeed had a wonderful time with Jim in Goodchance and were now making their way to Mississippi. Midafternoon, Teddy heard a knock on the door. When he opened it, a man with slicked brown hair, a blue seersucker suit, and smooth skin with whitened teeth smiled and introduced himself with an extended hand. Teddy looked at it with disgust, and then glanced back at him.

He knew it was one of the land sharks: a baby shark sent by the great whites back at the cove. He started to close the door, but the man stuck his fin in the crack, begging Teddy to listen.

"If I listen, will you promise to leave and never come back?"

"Mr. Dollarhide, I won't have to come back because we're going to make you an offer you can't refuse." He smiled. Teddy didn't believe him. They would be back again and again, but he let the man continue anyway.

"We have plans to build a state-of-the-art condominium here. Let me show you." He pulled out a mocked-up glossy brochure with two people playing tennis on the front and held it forward.

"I know all about it, they've told me before a thousand times," Teddy said, refusing the brochure.

"Casablanca will be a 150-million-dollar community equipped with tennis and racquetball courts, a spa, a gourmet market, and a shuttle to the marina."

"Well it's *not* going to be anything *here*."

"Mr. Dollarhide, listen to me, there isn't an available plot of land large enough on either side to build it. This is the *only* location with enough free acreage that's close enough to the ocean and not too far north from town for it to work." Handing him an aerial shot of the land, he pointed to a white line already marking the condo's perimeter over Teddy's land.

The nerve, Teddy thought, staring him down.

"We're willing to make you a very generous offer of twenty million dollars."

"No." He began to shut the door, but the baby shark leaped forward, sticking his nose in the door.

"What about thirty million?" Teddy listened for a moment. That was an unbelievable amount.

"What would you do with Isabella?"

"Who's Isabella?"

"The house, DAMMIT!" Teddy barked, amazed by his ignorance.

"The house … oh … the house would have to be taken out because the condo has to overlap it."

"The city wouldn't even allow it, she's a historic home."

"Well, let's just say there are ways around that. So, how about thirty million? What'd you say Mr. Dollarhide?" the man added with a sly smirk. With that, Teddy picked up a cane from the hat rack and raised it above his head, charging toward the man, who backpedaled down the stairs to his car.

"*Get off my property you dirt bag!* Tell your boss I am never selling! Not ever! Not for a billion dollars! You hear me?!" his voice thundered, shaking the leaves on the tree.

"Okay, I get it," the shark replied. Rattled, he got in his car and swam off.

Teddy went back inside to the living room. Sitting down in his chair, he took a deep breath and exhaled. He slid a Zino Chubby Tubo cigar out of the black box and chewed on it while opening *Sherlock Holmes: The Valley of Fear*. The hours passed and he fell into a deep sleep with the Zino lodged in the side of his mouth and the book in his lap.

While sleeping, he dreamed of the woman in the field again, never wanting it to end, but she said goodbye as he sailed into the horizon on *La Gracia*. The time lapsed in images, and next, he was soaking wet in the hull of the ship. A loud bang and he twirled around and saw the monkey, Oscar, sifting through a chest. Another bang, and this time he woke in a sweat with his leg aching and the taste of rich tobacco in his mouth. Hearing the sound a third time, he realized it was the door and he jerked up, setting the Zino down. He glanced at the clock, which read half past eight. The house felt empty, so he assumed Charlotte had left. The rain pattered outside. *Must be another shark*, he thought. Still shirtless and barefooted, he got his Winchester .22 from the office and loaded it on the way to the door.

He peeked through the mahogany door's metal view box and saw a woman in her forties with olive skin and drenched black hair wearing a fashionable black dress staring at the door with a yellow canvas duffle that had leather handles and a matching carry-on laptop bag. *They sent a female shark this time*, he thought. Cracking the big door with his brow furled, he poked the barrel out into the night.

"What do you want?" he barked. "I told the last guy never to come back." She moved back, startled by the gun and his temper.

"I am sorry—I guess I-I shouldn't have come." Frightened, she jogged off.

She spoke with an accent, definitely European, Teddy guessed Italian or Spanish, and realized sharks in Latch didn't talk like that. Lowering the gun, he stepped out.

"Wait a minute!" he called, but she kept running. "Wait, please wait! So you're not with Bateman and Banks?" She stopped and turned.

"No, my name is Alicia. My car broke down up the road; I am from Spain," she said apprehensively, the rain falling around her.

"I am Teddy. I am sorry. It's nice to meet you, Alicia." With the gun now at his side, he walked out into the rain to her. "What can I do you for?"

The rain pounded down as she started to explain how her car broke down on Route 1. Her eyes glanced at the gun and back at him.

"Wait, let's go inside where it's dry."

"Okay," she reluctantly said, and trailed him to the door. He turned to usher her in, but she paused.

"Can you please put the gun down?"

"Oh certainly, sorry about that. I thought you were one of the sharks coming to take my land; they were here earlier." He set the gun in the umbrella holder. She entered with trepid steps.

In the entry, their eyes met and seemed familiar; they paused in silence and he took her coat, and they held the gaze.

"A shark?" she asked, visibly nervous.

"Oh yeah, these guys are real lowlifes, and they keep trying to buy me out," he said as he hung up her wet coat. "I am okay with salespeople, but when someone says *no*, it *means no*."

"I see, but don't you think the gun is a little much?"

"No, just the right amount. They call and knock all the time—I never get any peace! I leave the damn gate opened during the day so the Pearlmakers can come in with ease, but it lets those bastards breeze in also!"

"But don't you realize that your resistance creates more conflict?"

"Resistance? My dear, it's *their* fault."

"I bet if you would just forgive them and show them you're less agitated, they would go away."

"I'll forgive them when *they leave me* alone." He paused. "So, you say your car broke down?"

"Yes. This was the only lit up house within walking distance. My phone is out due to the weather." She held it up, showing him. "You see, no bars."

"It's spotty out here. Let me check mine—no signal either. This means we won't get through to the rental car's emergency line. You're welcome to wait it out here if you like."

"Thank you, I think I will."

"Why don't we sit down in the living room where it's more comfortable?"

"Sounds charming."

Teddy put on a white linen shirt, leaving it unbuttoned, and led her into the living room before exiting into the kitchen. She walked around, admiring the animal skins, pictures, and souvenirs, eventually stopping by a picture of Sarah and Teddy on a sailboat in Key Biscayne. He strolled in from the kitchen with two glasses of Monterey Pinot Noir and handed one to her.

"Thank you. Is that your wife?"

"Yes, that's Sarah and me. She died years ago."

"I got the feeling you were still married."

"I guess I still am. I mean technically we never got divorced."

"She seems very special to you," Alicia said, picking up on the sadness in his voice.

"She really was." He looked at Alicia with a reserved smile. She smiled also and glanced back at the wall to a picture of Joey and Cosby.

"Are those your sons?"

"Yes, those are my wranglers." He sipped the wine.

"They are handsome young men." She sipped the wine.

"Thanks. They got their mother's looks, I'm just an ole bullfrog."

"I wouldn't be so modest," she said. "You're handsome in a masculine sort of way."

He smiled, "Thanks."

"So where are they now?"

"On a road trip to California; I miss them already. Can't keep them here after a certain age though." He ushered her to the couch and sat on the other one.

She looked at her cell phone and saw that she still had no service.

Teddy got a signal and managed to call an emergency rental line, but they informed him they weren't driving until tomorrow due to the harsh weather. He relayed the news to her.

"Why don't I drive you to take a look at your car and see if I can fix it for ya?" Teddy said.

"Okay, thank you. Are you sure?"

"Absolutely."

"Sounds great, thank you very much."

Leaving his shirt unbuttoned, Teddy threw on a rain jacket and the two hopped in his truck to drive out to her car. Amid sheets of blinding rain, Teddy popped the hood on Alicia's rental car and tinkered with the engine. He came back to the truck and informed her the starter was cooked.

"Where were you staying tonight?" Teddy asked.

"I don't have a hotel yet. Is there a good one nearby?"

"I am sorry my new friend, but they will probably all be taken by reporters and townsfolk's relatives." Teddy paused to think. "You know, perhaps you could stay in one of the spare bedrooms here. I don't want to put you off."

She laughed, "Well you did greet me with a shotgun."

"I know, I know, I am truly sorry. Let me make it up to you by allowing you to stay here."

"Okay, I guess that could work. That's very kind of you," Alicia replied and they drove back to the house.

In the living room, Alicia looked around some more and Teddy picked up their glasses of wine, returning hers to her.

"There's something so special about this house. It's friendly," Alicia said.

"Thank you. Isabella is a very special house." He paused and took a sip of the wine. "So tell me why you're in Latch. You don't look like you're from around here. Way too well dressed."

"I am taking my necklaces to jewelry stores in the area to see if they will carry my line."

"Interesting. I am a jewel finder, you're a jewelry maker—we have something in common," Teddy said, glued to the beauty. The strange woman's eyes fixed on his—they were different in color than the woman in his dream, brown not amber, but he realized they were the same eyes, and his fascination grew.

"You're a jewelry finder?"

"Sort of—I am a treasure hunter."

"Interesting, I've never met one before. What are you searching for?"

"A ship that went down off the coast here."

"Here, right here?"

"Yep."

"How did you find out about it?"

Teddy tasted the wine and straightened up. Focusing on the lady, he wondered if he might still be dreaming. Over the years, his dreams had a way of melting into reality like snow into water; he had sometimes thought that one day he might dream forever. Or maybe he would wake up with the Zino stuck in his mouth. But this didn't *feel* like a dream. No. He had never tasted tannin or the cognac notes of rich tobacco on his tongue or felt an attraction that fierce in a dream. No. He had never been this lucid in a dream, and maybe, just maybe, he had never been this lucid in his entire life.

"Well, the dreams started many years ago." He gazed off into the room, his tone lowering. "I would see myself on a Spanish galleon full of treasure that goes down in a hurricane. After I inherited this house, I learned that such a ship went down in this area, so I started hunting it. Only recently did I start dreaming about a Spanish woman in the countryside." He glanced back at her. "That's when I started enjoying them and didn't want to wake up."

"Your *dreams* told you about this ship?"

"Yes."

"And the Spanish woman was a lover?"

"Yes. Hold on a sec." He rose softly and went to his office, opened a drawer, took out the plain ring, and walked back over to the couch with it, where he placed it in her hand and dropped down even closer to her now.

"What's this?"

"It's a ring from the ship ... it was going to be my wedding ring for the lady when I returned from the New World, or so I think." He smiled and ran his fingers through his white hair and stroked his long beard. He was trying to put the pieces together: what did her being here mean?

She flipped the ring over, studying it.

"Have you found the rest of the treasure?" He noticed a green freshwater pearl necklace around her neck.

"No, we're still looking, but we're getting closer. I mean we're *really* close now."

She slid the ring on easily.

"Perfect fit—not too big, not too small."

He smiled and paused, watching her. She slid it off. He opened a drawer on the side table and pulled out a charcoal drawing of himself and the woman in Spain he had recently drawn, and handed it to her.

"Wow, you are such a talented artist!"

"Thank you," he said. "That ring finger is too pretty to be so lonely. Why aren't you married?"

"I just haven't found the right person that I relate to on every level. You know—mental, emotional, physical, and spiritual. Sometimes it feels like I'll never find anyone, and at other times, my faith is strong."

"I have the same feelings." He smiled.

She handed the ring back to him and he reluctantly took it. He felt calm around her, and now that he was closer, she smelled like Christmas mornings at home.

"So, what do you like to do in Spain?"

"Ride horses. There's an Arabian I ride at the stable near our country house; I am a member of an equestrian farm."

"Really? I own an Arabian," Teddy said and paused to sip the wine. "He's named Earful. You'll have to ride him."

"No way! Earful is an appropriate name," she said. "I would love that. They're my favorite horses."

"What are you doing tomorrow?"

"Well now I am doing nothing, with this car and all."

"We'll go tomorrow then."

"Okay." They fell silent for a brief moment.

She broke it. "So you had a really bad storm here, no?"

"Yes, we had a hurricane. Many trees got knocked down, some people's houses and businesses were flooded. Some people got really sick and need help."

"I saw it on the news. I am so sorry."

"Thank you. They've done a good job of cleaning up, but it has devastated the tourism, except for the hotels. One neighborhood was totaled."

"That's *so* bad. I understand."

"It'll be okay with time." He paused. "Let me now show you to your room in the Birdhouse. It'll be fun!"

"What's the Birdhouse?"

"You'll see."

After picking up her things, he led her up the ceramic stairs where they wandered the hall past the library to another staircase that spiraled up, ascending into a tower that had white stucco walls, pecky cypress beams, terra cotta clay tiles and windows that opened to a view over the property to the ocean. A queen bed sat in the middle with Bear curled on it at the foot. Alicia strolled over to the window, gazing out into the misty night. Teddy turned on a zebra foot lamp. She watched him out of the corner of her eye and found his gentle air and broad shoulders attractive. A light rain trickled and a wet breeze blew in through the shutters, tickling her chest. Teddy went to the closet and reached for a white cotton quilt with periwinkle blue geometric stars to go with the bed linens. Realizing it was Sarah's favorite—the one his mother sewed—he put it back and selected a butter-colored one with blue squares. He cut his eyes at Alicia, who was still staring out the window, then he looked back at the quilt and paused. Spinning around, he put it back, took the blue star one, and set it on the bed.

"I bet you can really see the ocean from here in the day," she observed as he walked over.

"Yeah, it's an incredible view. Sometimes I just come up here to be quiet."

"I bet." She smiled at him.

He grasped his hands behind his back. Her pearl necklace caught his attention again, "I love your necklace."

She pulled up on it and looked down at it, "Thank you, it's one of mine."

"It's beautiful."

"Thank you."

"Pearls are my favorite jewels because a living thing makes them, you know," he said.

"I know, *and* they're from the ocean."

"*I* am from the ocean too. Sometimes I feel like she's my mother," he said, watching the night mist with a smile.

"Me too."

"It's because it takes care of you—you know—the water."

"Yeah it does."

"Rocks you, feeds you, cleans you."

"Sets you at ease," she added.

"Easily," he paused. "Why don't I take you out on the boat before you leave?"

"I would like that very much." Their eyes met again and they smiled.

"Good."

They gazed back out over the ocean. Bear stretched on the bed, then stood up to yawn. He purred and meowed toward Alicia.

In a minute, they exited and went back down to the living room. Bear followed. Teddy offered her a second glass of wine; she accepted; he filled her glass and she sipped it, noticing it tasted like sandalwood and cranberries; they sat.

"So will you tell me about Spain? I've never been there."

"What do you want to know?"

"What the dirt feels like in your palms. What it smells and tastes like. I've only been to Italy and France."

THE DOLLARHIDE MYSTERY

She sipped her wine.

"Well, it's very special where I am from. It's a Mediterranean climate, warm and arid in the day and cool at night. The air is weightless and the lack of moisture gives it a surreal quality, like glasses that sharpen your perception. People love life. In the morning, I go to a bakery near my house where Pablo makes fresh bread with his own yeast. The line starts outside fifteen minutes before they open. The food in almost all the cafes and restaurants is from local farmers and is very good. We follow simple lives, rich in joy and prosperity. The ancient architecture reveals a history of beauty and wisdom. In the afternoon, we take breaks to snack and visit with friends. For recreation, we cycle, go to the theater, and see art." She paused and stared down. "My family's jewelry store, started by my great grandfather, may have to close if things don't improve soon from the recession." She trailed off, her mouth frowning.

"I am sorry to hear that. Spain sounds very, very special indeed. I would like to go there."

"You should go."

"I think I will; maybe I can find that little spot on the hillside from my dreams with the ocean below." He sipped the wine.

"Ha! It sounds like where I live."

His eyes got bigger. "*Really?*"

She was somber. "Yes." She paused for a moment. "I am sorry. Now I've made myself sad talking about the economy."

"Well, do you like to swim? Sometimes the water washes my troubles away."

"Oh yes, I am like a fish. I swim every day in the ocean when the weather is good."

"Let's go for a dip in the indoor pool, then."

"Okay, but I don't have a suit."

"We have some spares for guests in the indoor pool room."

"Let's do it then."

They made for the indoor poolroom. He showed her where the suits were and they both exited to change. When Teddy returned to find her in the swimsuit, not staring was like ignoring a visual symphony unfolding before his eyes—her long legs, curvy figure, and dark skin were something to behold. The pool lights glowed through the water that rippled from the fountains along the wall. Rain beat the glass ceiling above as he waded in the shallow end, her walking in behind him.

"Tell me more about the ship."

"My crew and I are six years in now. We've found over fifty artifacts, but nothing of significant value. Cosby just found an antique pistol in another location, and after trolling in that area for a day, we found a baseless cannon."

"Is that good?"

"Yes, well, we're certain the treasure is in the hull along with some boxed-up baseless cannons, so we may be close to finding it. Join us for a hunt one day! I am confident you'll bring us good luck."

"I would love to!"

"Great, we'll ride horses in the morning tomorrow and hunt after lunch, maybe."

"Sounds English, if we were hunting birds. I love shooting birds. I suppose I will suspend my business plans for a week or so."

"Okay girl, hunting birds is boring after you've been hunting for mantiques and jewels in the deep blue sea."

"What's a mantique?"

"Body armor, antique pistols, swords," he said.

She smiled. "I see—old manly stuff."

They swam closer to each other in the shallow end. The three stone lion heads on the wall spewed water that bounced off the surface.

"I am glad your car broke down tonight," he remarked.

Alicia laughed, "Glad my car broke down?" She moved closer to him. "You have a special way with words," she said in a sarcastic tone.

"Well, let's just say I am glad you're here now, however it happened," he said, running into her eyes.

"Me too."

In Alicia, Teddy recognized an old love that had been buried and was being unearthed; all they needed to do was wash the dirt away, and they were already wet.

She looked at him and smiled, and he could tell she was ready to be kissed. He was old enough to see the signs. He moved toward her. Bringing her moist head close to him, he kissed her lips and slid his fingers across her slick shoulders. She smiled when it tickled. Their tongues touched for a moment and he started to remove the strap of her bathing suit. She pulled it back up.

"We just met, Teddy. And I don't do this. I don't even know you," she said under her breath.

"I know, but I feel like we've always known each other."

"But it's so fast. We don't want to burn the candle too quick. A lit wick without wax burns quickly."

"I understand. Thank you for the kiss."

He stopped and waded away from her a bit. He watched the fountains for a little while, and she came over and kissed him again and he touched his nose to hers.

"But what about the candle?" he asked in between kisses.

"I think there's enough wax for us to burn slow."

Traveling into his mouth, she closed her eyes, slipped the straps off, and wrapped her legs around his thick waist. Cradling her in his arms like a glass egg, he carried her through the cascading water to the wall. Pressed against it with the waterfall enclosing them, she slid his shorts off with her toes and he circled his finger around her chest before kissing it. They merged in the warm water as time disappeared.

Afterward, they held each other for a moment. He tugged on her earlobe and she tugged on his; she smiled because she knew what it meant without him explaining—it was something her parents did. Floating over to the steps in the shallow end, they talked and didn't talk, and he rubbed her back, tracing images with his fingertip while she tried to guess what they were.

In a while, they got homemade chocolate ice cream from the kitchen and took it to the Birdhouse. After feeding each other and laughing, they embraced a second time and sat facing with their legs wrapped around one another. The storm howled outside through the opened shutters. He took a white feather out of the bedside table drawer and brushed it over her skin. Quivering with delight, she went to him and they made love into the night to the rhythm of the rain on the roof, sweating until the sheets were wet. When sleep knocked, they stopped and fell into a slumber with their bodies and spirits tangled like the vines of ivy climbing the outside of Isabella.

CHAPTER 7

*E*arlier that day, deep in the land of mud and cotton, the saltwater foursome cruised along to the music of Roy Orbison. Belle perked her lips, applying lipstick in the passenger mirror. Teddy always told the boys that Mississippi's culture was one of the secret spices in the American gumbo that eluded outsiders, even though they wondered why the soup tasted so good. Receiving mainly negative attention for its rocky racial history, it was the birthplace of modern music, Teddy would explain, and had made a significant albeit widely unappreciated impact on literature and the arts.

The chicken came to a gas station outside Brookhaven that used to be a general store; swallows of dust swooped around the car. Joey, Cos, and Belle went in; Leslie waited in the car with Dog resting his head on her leg.

They bought glass-bottled cokes, a Sonny Boy Williamson CD, and a Mississippi mud pie with a tagline that read "A fudge concoction of love."

Behind them, the black F350 had continued to trail six cars back, but no one suspected the danger of a lurking attacker there. The black 350 would gas up on the far side of the gas station when the chicken stopped, watching carefully to make certain the chicken didn't leave too early.

After leaving the store, they headed up I-55 and stopped in Jackson for a late lunch. Belle suggested the Magnolia. They went and the rich penetrating aroma of fried catfish and fresh turnips filled the eatery where men wore ties and suits and well-dressed women softly decorated the tables. After finishing, they headed back to the road. Leslie drove now, and the highway gradually cut through hills, pastures, and ranches, eventually arriving in Little Rock.

Courtney, Belle's sister, lived in an old 1920s house just outside of the city on a horse farm. The house shared the land with a white wooden chapel that sat up the hill to the left at the end of the driveway. They got out, and Belle knocked on the door. A strawberry blonde with a large mouth and kind eyes swung it open and squeezed Belle tight. Courtney and Belle exchanged pleasantries; Belle introduced the group.

The men unloaded the bags and Courtney took them through a tour of the modest house she shared with her three roommates. Will Burns had wanted to pay for a nice apartment downtown, but Courtney had insisted on her independence. Accommodating Leslie and Cos first, she had no guest bedroom to offer Belle and Joey except an outside porch with three old metal beds lined up and big fans circling on the ceiling. She showed them, apologizing.

"Courtney, don't apologize, this is perfect! I love sleeping outside anyway!" Belle said.

"Thanks for understanding, Belle," Courtney remarked. Joey and Cos marveled at the sisters. Wealth and luxury hadn't spoiled them in the least; in fact, they seemed more understanding, flexible, and adaptable than anyone they'd ever known—for all Will Burns' faults, if there was anything he had done right, it was to teach his girls self-reliance, respect, and manners.

They went back to the living room, where Belle and Courtney caught up. After a while, they packed a picnic and headed out through the field to a stream in the woods.

Gigantic trees as old as the countryside were all around. They slipped their shoes off and walked to the edge of the stream to sit and eat. Cicadas sang. Dog frolicked after squirrels scaling the giant trees. After eating, Leslie, Belle, and Courtney talked while Joey and Cos lay by the running water. When they got ready to leave, Courtney pointed out a waterfall up the way.

Back at Courtney's, everyone went inside except Joey, who got some extra clothes out of the car. It was dusk and a flurry by the candlelight through a window in the church was followed by a crashing sound that caught his attention. Suspecting foul play, he unsheathed his Swiss army knife, which almost made him laugh, but he went with it and wandered over.

When he entered, oak was in the air and the walls waved with alternating yellow and white candles. Creeping over to where he had seen the commotion, a mad rooster ran by him and he saw a planter knocked over at the window. His anxiety eased.

A man with white hair and a goatee came around the corner.

"May I help you?"

Joey was startled. "Oh, no sir, I just saw the flutter in the window and thought someone was in trouble."

"That's just Bob, our pet rooster. Sometimes he gets in through the front door. Damn bird," he said. "What were you gonna do with that Swiss army, whittle a stick?" He laughed. Joey looked at the pathetic dull knife and smiled.

"Name is Jack."

"I am Joey."

"Nice to meet you. What brings you here?"

"I am staying next door with my girlfriend's sister."

"Great! One of Courtney's friends, come sit with me on the porch awhile."

"Sure."

The man led him to the back porch of the church, where he sat in a rocking chair and crossed his legs, showing his cowboy boots; he lit a Natural Spirit, then offered one to Joey; he declined.

"You don't seem like an average preacher, Jack."

"And you don't seem like an average young guy."

At that moment, a frail woman in ragged clothes emerged from the darkness outside and knocked on the screen door.

"How can I help you ma'am?"

"I've lost everything to drugs and have nowhere to go, but I wanna get clean. Can you help me?"

"If you can help yourself."

"I can do it. I am ready this time."

"There's a room with a cot around back, I'll bring you some clean clothes and food in a minute. Tomorrow we'll go to the treatment facility."

"Oh, thank you so much! They said you were a good man and you would help me."

"Not good, just here." She exited. "So what brings you to Little Rock?" he asked Joey.

"We're passing through on our way to California."

"Where in California?"

"The Sierras."

"That's God's country," Jack said, and then slowly tugged the cigarette. "What's there?"

"A summer camp I used to go to."

"You're going that far to visit an old summer camp? C'mon—what are you *really* going for?"

"Just the camp."

"That's a long trip down memory lane."

Joey noticed Jack's tan skin was smooth like spread peanut butter.

"Yeah, it is. Would you tell me about the Sierras and what it's like? It's been awhile," Joey asked.

"Oh, it's awesome. Lots of wildlife and beautiful nature. Good fishing, too. Are you hiking?"

"Yeah."

"Then beware of bears. Do you have a bear bag?"

"Yep."

"Use it."

"I will. So how did you get to be a preacher?"

"In college, I had a crush on this girl named Jasmine Hope who left town. She quit me and it broke me good. So, after graduating, I decided to follow my kid brother to Africa to become a diamond miner." He paused.

"A diamond miner? Goodness."

"Goodness is right. We made and lost a lot. The strife I saw caused me to become a missionary in my spare time. When I returned to Arkansas, I became a preacher. It turned out Jasmine Hope was a single chef in Little Rock. We met one night at a Shakespearean festival, and this time, the chemistry was molecular. Been together ever since." He held up his hand, turning his wedding ring with his finger.

"That's incredible y'all got together after everything."

"It really is," he said, and then paused, studying Joey. "Look, I know you're searching for something, Joey, you got that wander in your eye."

"Oh, California, no, we're just going for fun."

"I mean you're looking for something in life. If you really care for the girl, fill that void yourself—don't ask her to do it."

"What do you mean?"

"I mean only you can fill yourself up, and when you're whole and she's whole, it'll be perfect. Look at what happened with Jasmine and me. When I was younger, I wanted her to make me happy, but no one can do that. Love of another starts with love of one's self."

"I see your point. Sometimes I think we're so perfect together that I forget where she ends and I begin."

"Kinda like when you ran into that duck. You took your eye off the road in front of you."

"Wait, how did you—"

"I am sort of a baseball fan. I love that video, though. Funny as hell. Just stay on your path, and if it's meant to be, you'll wind up on the same trajectory."

Joey reflected on Jack's words. "That's great advice—thanks, Jack."

"Anytime. So what are you doing now?"

"I am going to be a ranger in Yosemite this summer."

"Sounds great! Is that what you want to do with your life?"

Joey looked at him and thought about it. He had always wanted to play ball; when that fell through, he was left aimless. He stared into the dark pasture for a moment.

"After that, maybe I'll go to business school … or become a treasure hunter like my father."

"You know, there's still a lot of buried gold in those California mountains. Why don't you hunt for some this summer?"

"I think I will, Jack."

"You know, my dad is an offshore treasure hunter," Joey said.

"Well, there's no offshore up there," Jack said.

"Yeah, I know that."

Jack polished off the cigarette, rose, and patted Joey on the shoulder with a kind touch.

"It was such a *gift* talking to you, Joey." His eyes twinkled. "If you ever need to talk, call me." He handed Joey his business card. Joey took it and stood.

"A preacher with a business card?"

"If anyone needs one, we do," Jack replied. "God's got a line also. It's called prayer. If you ever need help, just ask."

"Sometimes I ask, but nothing happens."

"Maybe you don't see it. Help comes in different ways at different times, but God always knows the best way."

"Thanks for the advice, Jack. I enjoyed hearing about your life."

"You're welcome. Before you leave, there's something I want you to have. Wait here." He went inside and returned with a book.

"This is a very old, out-of-print book I bought in Africa about legends of African treasures. Every hunt starts with a story. Take it." Joey took the gift, noting that it sounded like something Teddy would say.

"Thank you, Jack."

"You're welcome." Joey left.

Back at the house, the group passed the hours watching TV. Afterward, Joey climbed into the bed on the outside porch next to Belle. Big white canvas curtains were partially drawn over the screen that wrapped around the porch. The ceiling fans and the occasional breeze through the canvas openings offered some relief from the heat. Leslie and Cos slept on the other side of them. Joey sparked a candle on the table and cracked open the dusty book. He flipped through it and Belle leaned up, looking along with him. Stories of gold buried in jungles filled the pages. One, about a trapper who stashed a bag of diamonds in the coffin of a famous trained gorilla, really fascinated them. Toward the end, he stopped on a drawing of a hulk-sized diamond covering the page and read the opposing print, which described how it was given by the African Khalfani as a gift to a Spanish prince who apparently lost it on a ship at sea. Joey wondered if it existed and if it might be worth Teddy looking into. Teddy talked about the 530 karat Cullinan Diamond—the "Great Star of Africa"— all the time. The stone described in the story was even bigger; it could possibly bring hundreds of millions, exceeding the entire bounty of *La Gracia*. He dog-eared the page before closing his eyes.

At dawn, Belle woke him with her finger over her lips and he followed her, tiptoeing past Dog, who slept on the floor. They were both damp from sleeping in the wet heat. Sneaking out a door on the porch, they ran through the pasture to the woods and then to the gurgling stream. They peeled off their pajamas to their underwear and jumped into the cold water, laughing but not speaking. As the sun began to rise, Joey waded with her to where the waterfall hit the water. They kissed at its edge. In her eyes, he saw service to others and the subtle sound of laughter and in his eyes, she saw honor, gentleness, and a new horizon. They moved through the falling wall of water to a stone embankment covered in patches of green moist moss that grew up the walls. He lifted her up on the ledge. She wrapped her legs around him and leaned down to kiss him. They kissed for a long time, touching with moist hands. He ran his fingers up her wet thighs.

Dog raced up to the side of the waterfall from the bank and yapped.

"We've been caught," Belle observed and laughed.

"I want to stay."

"Me too," she said.

They kissed again, but heard Cos and Leslie's voices and stopped.

"There is always later," she whispered to him.

"I want now." But when Cos and Leslie entered the water, they both swam out. After swimming for a bit, they dressed and left.

Back at the house, Courtney cooked. After they ate, Joey called Patch instead of Teddy because he was much better at searching the internet and gathering information and left a voicemail about the African diamond. Courtney and Belle had a bittersweet goodbye. As they pulled away, Joey saw Jack in a window of the church, waving to him. Joey threw him a casual salute and smiled.

CHAPTER 8

In Latch, Alicia and Teddy were radiant in the morning. The heat and sun filtered in through the opened shutters on the windows. The morning dew reflected the sun off the grass in the yard.

They showered together. When they got out, he picked out a long-sleeved white linen shirt and modeled in the bedroom mirror, his strong arms and shoulders filling it out. She dressed in beach clothes. He combed his wet hair back and smiled. He hadn't worn a nice shirt in ages. He kissed his St. Nicholas pendant and tucked it in under the shirt, pulled on a pair of white Levi jeans, and rolled up the legs.

The sky was blue and the light was bright. The rental car company, when called, agreed to send a tow truck to pick up Alicia's car and said she could pick up a new one in town whenever she wanted.

After eating, they proceeded to walk on the beach and wade in the waves. While shell hunting, Alicia found a perfect sand dollar.

"Do you know why they're called sand dollars?" Teddy asked.

"No."

"They're symbols of the coins lost by the people of Atlantis. If you save it, wealth will come your way."

"Neat, I'll take it," she said and tucked it in her pocket.

Around noon, they headed to the house. He let her ride the Arabian, Earful, and he mounted Caramel, the brown quarter, and they trotted to the beach preserve a couple of miles up the road where they walked along the ocean for three miles with the surf brushing the horses' hooves. Around noon, they returned to the farm along Route 1.

Dal and Charlotte had stayed in town at his place the night before, preceding their dinner date. They were sitting on the back porch now; as Teddy and Alicia rode up, they came around front, curious about the dazzling Spanish stranger. Teddy introduced her and they all agreed to go to lunch. Teddy and Charlotte went inside while Dal and Alicia waited outside, talking.

Teddy moved through the house whistling with a big smile. Charlotte bird-dogged him.

"Teddy Dollarhide, come back here. Who is this woman? What on earth has gotten into you?"

He kept walking. "What's wrong, Charlotte? I thought you'd be happy I finally met a woman. This one is *very* special, too."

"She's a *stranger*, Teddy! What is she doing already sleeping here? There's a bikini in the upstairs bathroom!"

"Oh Charlotte, this is the best day of my life." He kissed her on the cheek to throw her off. She looked stupefied. He went through the drawers in the kitchen, not closing them. Charlotte stomped her foot with her fists on her hips.

"What is going on here, Teddy Dollarhide?"

"Oh Charlotte, she's *the woman* from my dreams," he said, still looking through drawers.

"What the hell are you looking for?" she asked, frustrated. "You're like a bull in a china shop."

"The beard trimmer—I stashed it somewhere in here. Remember the woman in the dream I told you about?"

"No, your dreams all sound the same to me."

"Charlotte, why won't you listen to me? *This is her.* She showed up last night. And for the first time since all this started, I don't so feel crazy anymore."

THE DOLLARHIDE MYSTERY

Charlotte's frustration turned to sympathy when she heard his sincerity. His tough exterior had softened for a moment, revealing a gentle side she hadn't seen since Sarah was alive.

"Well I want you to be careful. We don't know who she is."

"I know who she is. First, you want me to date and get a woman. And now that I have one, you don't approve. I don't get it, Charlotte."

"I just don't want you to get hurt again, that's all."

"Just be happy for me. I am in love again!"

"In love? You know I *hate* that word. There really is something wrong with you."

"*Right* with me. There's something right with me." He landed on the beard trimmer. "Aha! Got it." He exited, heading toward the bathroom. "We're leaving in ten minutes, get ready," he hollered back.

The wind blew through the trees in the yard as the group climbed into Teddy's Ford. They cruised Route 1 to town where they parked at the Pantry, a hole-in-the-wall with a reputation for Georgian soul food.

As they entered, the Temptations played. A wide white woman with a stark white apron and a hairnet took their order with pursed lips. She had a habit of saying "baby" too much, using the word as often as possible, even referring to the restaurant's cat, Fleetwood, as "baby Fleet, or just baby"—and there wasn't *anything* baby about Fleetwood, who was easily the size of two cats. The smell of cooked corn hovered over an "L" shaped buffet with hot metal trays offering turnips with ham, mashed potatoes, cornbread, fried chicken, biscuits and gravy, yams, meatloaf, fried okra, and buttered corn on the cob.

Alicia loved the food. Teddy picked the Pantry because he knew soul food could bring friends and strangers together like glue, and Charlotte was already warming up to Alicia like the cold butter slipped in the middle of the hot baked cornbread. She laid her kindness on thick, complimenting her and asking about her life; Alicia was as sweet back to her as the sugared yams she was eating.

"Down here, we do everything too much. Eat, drink, sleep and laugh. You name it, people are loud and proud," Charlotte proclaimed.

"You are a passionate people, no?" Alicia asked.

"I think that would be the polite way to put it," Charlotte said.

"Well, I think it is swell," Alicia said.

Teddy caught wind from a neighboring table of an update on the outbreak that had infected residents of the Ball neighborhood. Parasites were believed to be the cause. The afflicted were being treated at the community center with antiparasitic drugs, which had worked for a few, but many were still deathly ill. Five had died already.

"What else will happen?" Teddy said disgruntled by the news.

"Hey Salt, that wine you gave me might work," Dal said.

"You know, it just might."

"What wine?" Alicia asked.

"There's some old wine we dragged up from *La Gracia* that seems to cure multiple illnesses."

"Really? Like what?"

"Well it cured my cat of feline AIDS and took care of Dal's foot," Teddy said.

"Can it cure cancer?" Alicia asked.

"It worked on some cancerous mice in Cambridge," Teddy said, and insisted he would take it to the shelter the next day.

After eating, the whole group met Ty and Patch at the marina. In *Gold Lip*, Alicia sat up front with Teddy and Bear, giggling at the Manx's captain hat. Dal and Charlotte rode on the deck with Dal, Patch, and Ty; Dal pointed out places on the shoreline for her.

Alicia petted Bear as the boat cruised out to the point marked on the GPS where they had found the last cannon. Teddy looked at her with last night on his mind and saw it in her eyes too.

"I am glad you're here."

"Me too." She pulled out the sand dollar and studied it.

When the boat hit the target area, Teddy shut off the engine; Ty and Dal geared up and dropped in. The ladies lounged in the captain chairs on the deck, drinking iced mint green teas with sage honey and lemon wedges. Charlotte sharpened her Spanish by asking Alicia various words and phrases—her southern drawl an insurmountable obstacle to mastering the Spanish accent. Alicia poked fun at her, while helping.

The divers came up empty, so Teddy decided to move the boat to a deeper location just a little further out and dropped in the ROV. Teddy drove the ROV with a remote-control handset, watching its camera through his iPad app viewer. After navigating it for some time, Teddy couldn't believe his eyes when he saw on the screen a small narrow piece of the horribly decayed wooden ship sunk into the sand, protected by a large anchor lying on top of it. He almost dropped the remote handset, becoming completely exhilarated when a slight front arc to it revealed it was probably a piece of *La Gracia*'s hull. He broke the news to the crew and ladies who hooped and hollered yells of enthusiasm. Teddy, Dal, and Ty put on their oxygen tanks, masks and headlamps and grabbed the lamp, vacuum and blowers and jumped into the water while Patch stayed on the boat with the women. They floated through the blue belly of the ocean until they reached the floor, which they combed with the underwater floodlight and headlamps until they reached the small decaying shell. Around the ship, they found a hot zone of nothing artifacts, which they worked around for a while by blowing up and vacuuming sand. After some time, lo and behold, they found a heavy chest that appeared to be full submerged in the sand. Teddy beckoned Ty over to it; Ty used his shovel to dig around it.

The large metal box was caked in a thick crust. Dal flipped a thumb up to Ty, who swam up and announced the discovery. The ladies both clapped and Patch's mouth dropped to the floor.

"Let's wait and see. Too early to say if it's chicken salad or not. But it's metal!" Teddy said to the group.

Patch rigged the crane and Ty dove back down with the metal rope and harness. At the bottom of the ocean, he and Dal wrapped up the rectangular box and tugged on the rope, sending Patch the clue to start reeling. Following it, they guided the box up to the surface.

At the top, Teddy and Patch craned it out of the water while Ty and Dal got into the boat to help guide it in. Bear watched closely. Once it thudded on the deck, they celebrated with a round of high fives and hugs. Teddy retrieved six Cohiba Habanos and passed them around; even the ladies accepted. While enjoying them, they studied the box. The heavy weight was a good sign. The crust being too thick to break into on the boat, they had to wait to see what the box was hiding. They then went back down to retrieve the anchor which had the name of the ship *La Gracia* written into its ore.

Relaxing in the boat, they talked and celebrated with concrete proof that they had found a piece of a real ship, not a smoke ship. Teddy went inside to retrieve a bottle of the historic wine and poured everyone a little in some plastic red solo cups.

As they all toasted, Ty asked, "Hey Teddy, what's *the story* on the wine? You never told us."

"I thought you didn't know?" Alicia asked.

"He doesn't. It's a game we play. We try to guess the history behind the object," Dal answered, drying his wet head off with a towel.

"Interesting," Alicia said. "So what is it, Teddy?"

"I don't know, but I see pirates—lots and lots of pirates!" Teddy joked, then wiped his hands clean with a towel and headed to the cabin.

Teddy turned the boat around and motored toward land. Alicia joined him in the cabin. Taking an ice cube wedge from her tea, she held it in between her teeth and fed it to him; they kissed as the sun set in the western skyline, sealing a perfect day.

Back on land, they unloaded the trunk into Teddy's truck and the anchor and took it to the farm. Alicia and Charlotte went inside while Bear and the crew proceeded to the preservation room with the bounty. Dal picked up the automatic saw. With the precision of a neurosurgeon, he ground around the box in an even line and then cut up on the box, removing rock-like chunks of concretion. Teddy, Patch, and Ty watched like kids on Christmas waiting for someone else to unwrap their biggest present. Hell, if this was Christmas, then Alicia must be Santa Claus, Teddy thought.

Dal echoed his thoughts, glancing up from the cutting, "I think the ladies brought us good luck today; we need to keep them around."

"They're Pearlmakers like us, and believe me, I am planning on it if Alicia will stay."

After thirty minutes of work, Dal jerked opened the trunk. The edges creaked like a rusty door and more grit fell onto the stainless steel table. Everyone gathered around and peered into the case, wanting to touch the gold coins revealed within. Pearls were haphazardly thrown in also, like a rich man's bounty. They celebrated, immediately ordering a case of wine, cheese, and party blow horns from the Wine Stop. What a mistake it was to not find this sooner! Each person, including the ladies, was given a chance to scrape their hands through it. The chest was poured out onto a large metal working table and each item valued mentally and combed through carefully. All the coins were of a similar gold mint, weighing roughly an ounce in their minds. Dal picked up the other bounty from the Wine Stop, while Teddy replaced the contents of the chest, placed the chest in the walk-in general safe with the other valuables, and locked it with his key. With the vault door closed, the crew retired to celebrate.

CHAPTER 9

It was midnight and everyone in Isabella slept soundly.

Buzz and Mike softly closed the doors on his Ram; Buzz took a bandana out of his pocket and wiped the sweat off his forehead. The Dodge's AC didn't work; he'd rigged a small fan on the dash, but it did little good in the ninety-degree heat. He grabbed a long, coiled rope out of the truck bed. The tobacco packed in Mike's mouth caused his bottom lip to hang forward; he spat on the ground before raising his tall slender frame over the iron gate. When he got to the other side, Buzz tossed him the rope. Like a sumo wrestler trying to master the gymnast's pommel horse, Buzz climbed the gate and fell hard onto the ground oyster shells inside. Mike laughed; Buzz got up and socked him on the arm.

The moonlight reflected off Buzz's shaved head. The black T-shirts and blue jeans camouflaged them as they slithered up the palm-lined driveway underneath the quarter moon. Isabella was asleep, her eyes closed—lights off and shuttered.

They proceeded to Half Ton's pen, where he slept outside in the mud like a whale. After looping the rope, Buzz tossed it toward the hog's neck, but missed, hitting him in the head. Ton stirred with a peaceful gaze, turning his head slowly to take them in.

Buzz made another effort at lassoing the hog and missed. Ton watched them, amused.

"I think you would suck at calf-roping, Buzz. The damn thing is a behemoth and you still can't hit it."

"Shut up. You didn't even know what a behemoth was until I told you. If I wanted your input, I'd ask for it."

"Okay, but get him soon—I don't like the way he's just looking at us with that stupid stare," Mike said before spitting a stream of brown juice on the ground.

Buzz tossed the rope again, and this time, it landed around Ton's neck. He yanked it tight; Ton continued to sit still. Buzz really yanked back on it, digging the rope deep into the forest of a big brown spot of hair.

"You got it, Buzzard!"

The lasso produced a malicious grin on Buzz's face as he began to reel the hog over to the pen gate. Half Ton's tired eyes opened wide and alert as he stood.

"Would you look at him! He's like a force of nature," stated Buzz.

Mike opened the gate and Buzz attempted to lead Ton out. Ton dug his feet deep into the mud and stared them down like a bull on a rodeo clown. Buzz pulled again, calling him. Nothing.

Wading into the stall, Buzz leveraged his 250 pounds of muscle and weight into a tug, but it was like trying to pull an Escalade. Ton played with him, taking a step forward and launching Buzz into the manure. As Ton stared at him, Buzz could almost hear him laughing, and sprang up in a red rage. Mike began to encourage Ton by baby-talking.

"Here little piggy, come to Mikey. Come on."

"What the hell are you doing?" Buzz said, wiping the manure off his arms. But to his dismay, Ton took one step and then another, his eyes brightening.

"Well I'll be damned. This pig is a big baby!" And he began to sweet-talk Ton as well; Ton trotted over to them; Buzz petted him with a wicked grin as he led him out of the stall.

Awakened by the commotion, Bear rose from his position on the roof of the tree house. Spotting Half Ton in trouble, he leaped into action and ran into the house through the doggy door. When he reached Teddy's room, the door was shut. He pawed at it, but Teddy didn't wake. Frustrated, he ran outside and around to the back porch, hopping over the gate. Standing under the dinner bell, he grabbed the rope connected to it with both paws and jerked hard, ringing it over and over again.

"What the hell is that?" Buzz asked.

"It's coming from the house, but I don't see anyone."

"Sounds like a shit storm blowing in, and I don't want to be here when it hits—let's hurry!"

"I hate to say it, but you already got hit with the shit storm, Buzzard," Mike said, laughing at the manure on Buzz. Buzz leaned over and punched him again. They jogged down the driveway with Half Ton in tow.

The bell shook Teddy out of a dream about *La Gracia*. He got up and splashed cold water on his face. Alicia woke and asked why he was up. Hearing the bell again, Teddy told her something was going on outside for sure.

"Come back to bed," she begged, sleepy eyed.

"No, I gotta see what all the ruckus is about, I will only be a minute," he insisted and hobbled outside to the porch in his underwear. Through the courtyard gate, he glimpsed the thieves running down the driveway with Ton. He was terrified they might be robbers and might have also taken the gold he and his crew had found earlier that day.

Back inside, he donned pants, jumped shirtless into his cowboy boots, and grabbed the Winchester by the door along with a box of ammo. After explaining the situation to Alicia, he kissed the St. Nicholas necklace, locked the doors behind him, and sprinted outside after them.

Bear galloped behind him. Teddy yelled "Stop!" as the men approached the gate. He ran as fast as his large frame could carry him. The gate opened automatically from the inside as it always did when the sensor was tripped. Buzz had been too scared to drive through the gate originally because the truck engine might have woken someone in the house. They trotted Ton through.

Teddy fired a shot in the air to scare them, but they kept moving. They turned the corner and Mike loaded the hog into the trailer, which sagged under his weight. Buzz started the truck and Mike hopped in. The tires spun as it lunged forward, throwing rocks. Teddy and Bear bolted through the gate which opened again as they approached. Once in the street, he fired at the tires, but clipped a taillight instead. Though unable to make out the license plate, he thought the vehicle looked like Buzz Smith's grey Dodge.

"Dammit!" he said, kicking rocks in the pavement with his boot as he watched the truck head down the road. Bear pranced back and forth in the road, jacked up on adrenaline, looking disappointed in himself and the loss of a great friend.

"C'mon Bear, let's hustle. We'll get your buddy back, I promise. I know where that ole bastard lives."

Teddy tossed on some clothes and woke Dal, who was staying in Charlotte's quarters again. He dressed fast. Bear watched. They marched into the wet heat with the cat behind. Teddy hitched his empty trailer and he and Dal climbed into the Ford.

"Bear, you stay here and keep a watch on things," Teddy commanded, and then drove off. Bear meowed as he watched them go.

After cruising a short way, they exited onto Highway 59, following it inland to the country. The small trees near the ocean gave way to taller pines, elms, and oaks; the branches of some canopied the road in a few places. After miles of horse farms and nice subdivisions, the houses thinned out, transitioning into land and a series of run-down shacks. On the left side of the street, they stopped at a wooden house with a light on in the living room. The Dodge lurked in the driveway with the rusted trailer and its busted taillight. No one was in sight, but Half Ton was still standing in the bed.

"They must be looking for a place to put him in the backyard. Let's go for it!" Teddy said.

Dal jumped out and unhinged the trailer while Teddy went over and led Half Ton down the incline of Buzz's trailer and loaded him into his own truck's trailer. Buzz came out front, spotted them, went back inside and returned with his shotgun.

"Dem boys got chur hog, Buzz," his brother, Jeremy said.

"Oh hell naw," Buzz said, running after them.

"Let's get them!" Mike said, coming out of the living room. Buzz's father was knocked out in the back after putting away a bottle of Wild Turkey and screaming at the wind out in the yard for about an hour.

Teddy and Dal pulled out. Buzz fired at the Ford's tires, but missed. Buzz got in his truck—Mike jumped in too—and they whipped out. The two trucks flew down the deserted highway.

Buzz pulled out so fast that a stack of books slid into Mike's lap from a cubby in the dash. He looked at them, attempting to pronounce the titles.

"*Catcher in the Rye, One Hundred and Fifty Ways to Prepare Pasta, The World is Flat*. What is this bull butter?" Mike asked.

"Give me those." He snatched them out of Mike's hands and tossed them in the back.

"What were those?"

"Books, ain't you never seen books before?"

"Like for reading and stuff?"

"No, for propping doors open, you idiot. Goodness." Buzz handed the shotgun to Mike. "Shoot the tires."

"Okay." Mike leaned his lanky frame out the window, spit his dip, and fired at the Ford's tires.

Back in the Ford, Teddy was incensed, "I can't believe these boys are firing at us! I have a right mind to go straight to Catfish's office."

"You want me to call the law?" Dal asked.

"No, not yet," Teddy said. "I have a better idea. I know these roads like the back of my hand."

"K.O.B."

"Yep, they don't call me king of the back roads for nothing," Teddy confirmed.

After some miles, Teddy took a sharp right, launching off the pavement onto a small gravel road that cut between two cornfields. Half

Ton slid around on the attached trailer and decided to lie down. Buzz tailed the Ford, a sandstorm of dust obstructed the visibility ahead, so Buzz used Teddy's taillights as a compass. Teddy's truck was a newer model than Buzz's, and the two engines were keeping a similar speed even though Teddy was towing Half Ton. Buzz asked Mike to save their ammunition until they had a better shot. Teddy got a little distance between them and drove through the tall cornfields to the edge of a thick wood ahead.

"Salt, you *know* where this road goes, right?"

"Yeah, I know."

"I don't want to go there."

"It's nothing to be afraid of, Dal," he said, hiding his own feelings behind a façade of confidence. "We're not going into the house, just in the driveway long enough to lose these boys. We can cut through the property and come out the other end onto Dog Pound Road, then back on Sundown to Highway 59."

Dal shook his head. "What choice do I have?"

"Not much, there's nowhere to turn around now."

Buzz trailed behind them, his high beams blinding Teddy in the rearview. Mike turned to Buzz with an alarmed face and asked, "Do you know where this road leads?"

"Yeah, I know. So what?" Buzz said, taking a large swig out of a flask.

"So, I am not going to the Willis Plantation. Stop the car and let me out!"

"You're a big wuss, Mike, I swear."

"What about T-Bone?"

"T-Bone was nuttier than a fruitcake."

"He came down here on a bet and had a stroke. He's been in an institution ever since. After that, the sheriff started warning people not to come here."

"You're dumber than a bucket of rocks. I don't believe *any* of it. Not *one* lick."

"Don't call me dumb again. There's a reason this is the only hundred acres in Latch selling for fifty thousand. No one will touch it. They couldn't give it away."

"The only things that are real are the things *you can see.*"

"Well, T saw something."

Coming to the end of the moonlit field, a line of tall trees made a boundary along the edge like an army of soldiers guarding the blackness behind them. The Ford slowed down to ten miles per hour as they neared the rickety gate.

"Teddy, I *really* don't feel good about this. I've got a knot in my stomach."

"Yeah well it's spookier than I thought it would be," Teddy said in a serious voice.

The open gate had paint peeling off it. Down the long road, an abandoned house with empty holes for windows warned trespassers to stay away. Teddy kissed his pendant; Dal crossed his chest. They entered the gate. Driving along the road, the tree branches twisted and coiled like alien beings starving for daylight and water. The temperature dropped and Teddy put his hand on the window, which was now cold to the touch.

The house was so rattletrap that homeless cats and rats had left it for better shelter. Teddy laughed to settle his fear.

"I am *not* laughing," Dal said. "This is *not* funny to me."

When they neared the house, it pulsed with a living death. The paint peeled and dark decay scaled the sides. They took a left fork, going deeper into the forest.

Buzz took the turn and continued to follow; he swore he saw the outline of a person in the window of the house looking down, but Mike told him to shut up.

Teddy glanced in his rearview. Five feet behind them, the Dodge hugged their tail. Teddy pushed the gas to the floor, throwing dust and gravel. He got ahead about thirty feet, then thirty five, then forty, and began to feel good about the distance; then, the headlights in his rearview suddenly blinked out.

That was odd, Teddy thought.

"Dal, look in the rearview. Buzz's lights are out."

Dal looked. "That *is* strange."

"Should we go back?"

"Go back? What kind of *space juice* have you been drinking? They were shooting at us!"

"Yeah, they fired chicken shots at the tires. They weren't trying to hit us. What if something happened to them?"

"If something happened, I *really* don't want to go back. And how do you know it isn't just a trap?"

"Good point."

"Damn, you white boys are always walking into some dumb stuff. It's always some white dude who wants to go communicate with the spirits."

Teddy laughed. "I just want to do the right thing here."

"Then keep driving!" Dal pointed ahead. "Damn."

Teddy headed down the gravel road and saw Dog Pound Road ahead. They barreled out of the property onto it. He drove a little way before parking on the side of the road.

"Why did we stop?" Dal asked.

"I want to see that those boys make it out of there. I may not like them, but I don't wish them harm."

"You're crazy, Salt, you know that?" He paused. "But this time, I think you're right."

Buzz and Mike sat in the dark, their truck having lost all power before coming to a dead stop.

"What the hell just happened?" Mike asked.

The battery powered on and the radio turned on with it and sped through the stations, passing a news station, then retracing back to stop on it; the volume increased, the windshield wipers clicked on, and the warning lights flashed; the security alarm went off.

"What the hell," Buzz said, taking a big gulp off his flask, which now visibly shook in his large hands.

Mike was speechless. Buzz held the flask in front of him, and he finished it off.

"Let's make a run for it," Buzz said.

Mike was mute. Both doors locked. Buzz tried to start the

engine, but nothing happened. Phantom shapes curled around the car in the darkness outside. Mike picked up the shotgun and cocked it.

"Did you see that?! What was it?" asked Mike.

"I don't know, but I am getting out of here. I am a hunter and I know we are being tracked. I can feel it. We're sitting ducks." Buzz removed the keys, but the engine cranked without them and the Dodge started moving backward to the house. Buzz lifted his cowboy boots up and sent his legs through the driver's side window, knocking the glass out. The truck moved faster and he jumped out the window with the gun, landing in a ditch. The Dodge accelerated in reverse to twenty-five miles an hour. Mike crawled over to the driver's window and leaped out, hitting the ground hard. Meanwhile, something knocked the gun out of Buzz's hand and howled. After bouncing to his feet, Buzz raced over to help Mike up. With their hearts racing, they headed down the driveway. The truck stopped and began to move forward, accelerating quickly toward them. They made for the distant streetlight at the road ahead, running at full sprint. As the truck caught up to them, they began to run in a zigzag; the possessed machine darting forward at Buzz, who jumped to the other side, barely missing the bumper. Mike joined him. They ran through the wood with the truck following alongside them—a dark phantom with solid white eyes was at the wheel, cackling like a hyena with a mouth full of silver razors.

Teddy eyed his watch. "What's keeping them?"

"I don't know."

"Well I ain't waiting for paint to dry. I am going to see," Teddy stated. "Are you coming?"

"Yeah—it's the right thing to do."

They peeled back down the gravel road until they saw the Dodge's headlights approaching in the distance. Realizing it didn't plan on stopping, Teddy hit his brakes and the Ford slid to a halt, slinging gravel. He threw it in reverse; meanwhile, the lights kept approaching. To the side, Buzz and Mike tore through the brush. When they saw Teddy's truck, they headed straight for it.

Mike slammed into Dal's window and banged his hands on it, yelling "*Help us!*"

"Get in the back!" Dal answered through the glass.

"Those boys look like they've seen a ghost," Teddy said.

"I told you this was crazy."

Buzz and Mike hopped in the trailer with Half Ton, who was lying down. The renegade Dodge's lights were only fifty feet away now as Teddy ripped backward. As the truck gained on them, the white-eyed phantoms surrounded the outside of the Ford and its trailer and Teddy could only go about 25 miles on hour to keep the trailer steady and all. Buzz and Mike lay down now beside Half Ton on the trailer floor with their hands covering their heads. The phantoms climbed around the side of the trailer, reaching at them with their snarled hands—Teddy and Dal saw them in the rearview and became scared. When the apparitions prepared to attack Mike and Buzz, Ton rose on all fours, made a loud shrill snort wilder than any hog has ever made. The phantoms all grabbed their holes for ears in pain. They tried to attack but bounced off the air around the trailer and disappeared into the forest. The Dodge in front of them also came to a stop, its lights flipping off. Teddy stopped the truck. Everything felt still. He asked Dal to slide over and drive. Getting out, he hustled over to the Dodge—it was empty. He hopped in and turned the key—it cranked. He drove forward as Dal accelerated in reverse. They emptied onto Dog Pound Road, where Buzz and Mike got out of the trailer.

"What happened to y'all?" Teddy asked as they stood in the empty country road.

"Our truck ... it ... came after us," Buzz said, regaining his breath.

"What the hell were y'all thinking? We almost got killed. Shooting and shit at us. You worked on my land boy," Teddy said.

"Listen, y'all saved our lives. Let bygones be bygones," Buzz said.

"Look, " Teddy said, pushing his index finger into Buzz's chest fiercely. "Stay away from my hog and stay off my land son. Is that clear?" Teddy glared at Buzz.

"Yes sir," Buzz said, looking up sheepishly.

"Okay, do you boys know what the hell those shapes in the night were?" Dal asked Mike and Buzz.

"Ghosts, I guess," Mike answered.

"But, I don't believe in ghosts," Dal said.

"No way Dal, they're real. I told you that. What about me and the ship?" Teddy asked.

"Okay," Dal shook his head. "But why on earth did they leave?"

"Something about the hog. Right when they got close to him, they couldn't handle it—maybe he affected them somehow," Buzz said.

"Well I'll be," Teddy said, glancing at Half Ton through the back window. "I knew that hog was special." He paused and glanced back at them.

Teddy got in his truck without saying goodbye to Mike or Buzz and they sautered back to the Dodge before peeling off.

At the farm, Teddy placed Half Ton in his pen and poured some milk in the trough. Bear came down from the tree house and climbed up on the fence to welcome his brother home. Half Ton gave him a tired smile. Teddy petted Bear and then told them both goodnight before climbing in bed with Alicia. He woke her to quietly tell her what happened and she freaked out and jumped out of bed, pacing the room. Teddy assured her it was just a bunch of young loafers who didn't wish them harm really out for Half Ton's reward money. The ghosts, he said, were confined to the Willis Plantation and wouldn't leave its haunted grounds. She insisted they should call the police anyway, but Teddy said he didn't want *anyone* knowing about Half Ton, not even the police, and the poachers were just boys really and would never come back. At that, she threw her hands up in the air exhausted, and crawled back into bed with him, holding his body tight.

CHAPTER 10

"Good morning, Salt." Dal said, sitting at Isabella's kitchen island as Teddy entered the room. Ty and Patch sat perched on the island barstools on either side of him.

"Good morning boys."

"Where's your lady?" Dal asked.

"Still asleep," Teddy said. "When did you boys get here?" Teddy asked Ty and Patch.

"About an hour ago. We are eager to classify and organize the gold coins from the chest today. What do you say Salt?" Ty asked.

Teddy poured a glass of fresh squeezed orange juice from the island and drank it. "Sure, let's do it!"

"I just can't *believe* we found a chest, a chest! Finally!" Patch said, excited by the riches.

"Finally," remarked Ty.

"And that's just the beginning," Dal said.

"So, you ready to work right now, Salt?" Patch asked. Teddy set the glass down and thought for a moment.

"I want to, but I can't. I must take the wine to the community center today. I promised myself I would go do it, and I don't want to slow us down with the cataloging."

"Okay—Dal told us about Half Ton and what you guys went through last night. That's just so crazy!" Ty said.

"Yeah, I swear, the strangest things happen to you Dollarhide," Patch said, shaking his head.

"Tell me about it. I am just glad we got that pig back."

"I hope Buzz doesn't tell Will Burns about this; he's a powerful man," Dal said.

"He won't," Teddy said and paused. "Besides, Half Ton is family now; he's part of the tribe, and I stand by my tribesmen, even to Will Burns." He paused again and then addressed the group, "So can y'all catalog the gold today while I go to the center?"

"Sure, boss," Patch said. "We got you man!"

"Perfect."

TEDDY LEFT a sweet note for Alicia by her bedside table and kissed her on the cheek. Driving to town with the wine he had stored at the house, he stopped by the grocery store to pick up some food. At the counter, he overheard the radio announcer chirp about a tropical storm heading into the Gulf of Mexico. As he left, he noticed Mangrove Street looking a little neater. He called the bank, informing his account manager he would be able to make the back taxes on Isabella due to a discovery and let out a "wooha" afterwards.

A mile inland, he parked out in front of the convention center, picked up a book and the glass bottle containing the wine, and hustled inside.

The homeless residents of Latch filled the open meeting hall area. Metal cots lined the geometrically patterned carpet floors. The room, normally used for conferences and company meetings, had never been so disorganized. The air was stale and reeked of synthetic air freshener. Hopeless faces, expecting absolutely nothing from the world or each other, passed around him, and Teddy thought maybe, just maybe, he could help them improve their attitude with the wine.

A sign above a door indicated the infirmary and he moved toward it. The same cot beds lined a second room full of Ball neighborhood residents who had swum in the sewage-contaminated floodwater; some curled brutally on their sides in pain.

A brunette nurse with stylish glasses and a big mouth dressed in broken-in blue scrubs moved around the room waiting on people. Teddy caught her attention as she came over to the nurses' station to write something down on a clipboard.

"Excuse me, ma'am," Teddy said.

"Yes?"

"How are the patients doing?"

She looked at him with kind eyes. "Not too well, honey. They all have parasitic infections and haven't responded to the medication, and frankly, we have nothing else to offer."

"That's too bad."

"Do you have a relative here?"

"No, just a friend."

"What's their name?"

He bumbled for a moment, searching the room for an indication of a name. Any name would do. Behind the nurse's head, he saw a patient list tacked to a clipboard and picked the first name, Andy Matthews.

"Mr. Matthews."

"Oh, Andy is such a sweetie. He's resting now," she said.

"Okay, can I wait by his bed until he wakes up? I brought a book with me."

"Sure. I'm leaving now, but Miss Judy is on duty if you need anything."

"Okay, thank you."

She exited.

Teddy took a seat by Andy's bed. The black man in his late sixties lay on his side, his knees jutted up and his thin bony hands clenching his stomach. Even in his sleep, his weathered face could only form a grimace. In the cot on the other side of him, a middle-aged white woman snored, a metal table against the wall between them.

Teddy opened Volume 1 of the complete Sir Richard Burton translation of *A Thousand and One Nights* and read in silence. Out of the corner of his eye, he saw a man in a seersucker suit sitting across the room talking to one of the patients. He appeared to be showing the man papers and explaining something. When the man turned his blonde head, Teddy realized it was Walker Bateman, and to his dismay, Bateman got up, carried his chair over to the next patient, and sat down, showing him papers.

What in the world is he doing here? Teddy thought.

After the nurse left, he leaned forward and touched Andy on the shoulder; he didn't wake, so he shook him harder until Andy began to move. One eye opened, then the other.

"What time is it?" Andy said, looking at Teddy. "Who are you?"

"Hi Mr. Matthews. It's a quarter after ten. My name is Teddy Dollarhide. I am here visiting. I think I might be able to help you."

"Help me? Doctors say they've tried everything." Andy leaned up on his side, moving his mouth around. "My mouth is dry," he said looking at Teddy. "Can you hand me that water please?" Teddy handed him the water and he drank. "You were saying?"

"There's an old bottle of wine my crew and I found in the ocean while hunting for treasure that seems to cure things. I am a treasure hunter. Would you be interested in trying it?"

"*A bottle of wine?* Do I look like I need a drink?" he said, perplexed. "Have you ever tried it?"

"On myself for small things, and a friend's infection. I also cured my cat with it."

"*Your cat?*" He started to laugh, but it was too painful, so he smiled instead. "Do I look like a cat to you? Lord have mercy on me, I've seen it all now." Relaxing flat on his back, he looked up at the ceiling; then, he glanced back at Teddy. "What's your angle, man, why are you here harassing me with this crap about a cat cure. Sounds like snake oil. If it's so good, why don't the doctors know about it?"

"Well, no one knows about it yet; we just found it."

"That's hard to believe."

"But it's true." Teddy looked at him with a firm eye. "Besides, what choice do you have, my friend?"

Andy narrowed his eyes at Teddy. "Man, I feel terrible. I guess sometimes you just gotta bite that bullet and take a chance. You got any?"

"Yeah. But, the nurse might not like you taking it because of liabilities. They're so concerned about getting sued, you see. I told her we're friends and that I am just visiting. I brought some in a bottle—here." He showed Andy the bottle. "Hide it and take an ounce twice a day for the next couple of days; if you get well, we'll know it works and we can help the others." Teddy handed over the glass bottle to Andy, who poured it in a paper cup and knocked it back. "Good man," Teddy said.

"Whew! That tastes bad."

"I know, but it's good. I'll call to check on you the day after tomorrow. Tell the nurse I'm coming, okay?"

"Hey, tell your cat I said hello," Andy said and chuckled.

"I will. It's going to work for you the way it worked for ole Bear, I promise."

"All right, but a cat has nine lives. A man only has one."

"Believe me, this cat had already died at least eight times; it saved him in the bottom of his ninth life."

"That's good to know."

Teddy leaned in and hugged him, feeling Andy's bones on his back merging together with nothing to cushion them. Then, he slipped him his business card. Turning, he saw Bateman at another patient's side down the line and paused, watching him.

"I wish that jerk would leave us alone," whispered Andy.

Teddy turned to him, "He came to you too? What for?"

"He wanted to know if he could buy my house—or what's left of it. Can you believe that? The nerve some people have. I am in here dying and he's trying to close a deal."

"Good Lord."

"Offered me half of what it's worth too, the little snake."

Teddy shook his head. "Damn land sharks. I gotta run. Take care, Andy."

"You too."

Teddy exited and returned to the farm where Alicia and he ate

Blue Point oysters on the back porch. Though desperate to join the guys in cataloging the gold coins, he simply had to eat first or he was going to faint.

§·

AFTER A SHORT STROLL on the beach, Teddy checked in with the Pearlmakers in the preservation room. With a wide-mouthed grin, Ty informed him they were halfway through and had counted roughly six million dollars' worth of gold in the chest, including the numismatic value of the coins. Teddy cried and hugged them. The group celebrated by popping a bottle of champagne and lighting more Habanos cigars. They placed the gold coins neatly in various drawers in the walk-in safe.

Teddy asked about potential buyers and Patch pointed to an Excel spreadsheet on his silver Apple laptop of the top people to call.

"I'll call first thing in the morning to see if we get any early bidders. Y'all can finish cataloging the rest tomorrow. And I need to get a better safe, pronto. This is just too valuable to be playing games with. I'll have to max out another credit card I guess. So be it."

"Will do, boss," Ty remarked.

Teddy exited and called Joey who answered after the first ring. Joey told his Dad he and the crew were just passing through Texas. And Teddy relayed to him the incredible news of the chest. Joey couldn't believe The Pearlmakers had found a chest full of gold after all those years of snaking around the Atlantic. He broke the news to Cos who yelled out the passenger window like a dog taking in a cool breeze. The boys and girls, however, concluded that they would all still go for The Dollarhide family treasure, in lieu of the new bounty.

Later that evening, Dal, Teddy, Alicia, and Charlotte celebrated over a glass of Merlot and a game of Scrabble. Still a little shaken by the previous night's events at the Willis Plantation, the word game relaxed them.

Afterward, Dal retired to Charlotte's room. Alicia and Teddy chased each other to the Birdhouse, where they kissed on the bed. He enjoyed the texture and softness of her sweet tongue; when he finished, he kissed her face and then her neck and breasts; when he neared her abdomen, the tenderness of his lips unfolded her, and she took the lavender-infused coconut oil off the bedside table and straddled his lower back, massaging the aromatic slick into his thick body. He almost fell asleep, but she rolled him over and they made love. Afterward, he wrapped them in a blanket and she laid her head on his chest. After a moment, she started to cry.

At first, he thought nothing of it, but became concerned when it continued. "What's wrong, baby?"

"Nothing."

"Nothing never sounded so sad. You can tell me anything, you know."

With tears rolling down the curve of her cheeks, she took a deep breath and looked away.

"What is it?" he asked and twirled his finger around in her hair.

"Two months ago, I became dizzy and passed out in the kitchen while making tapas. My mother rushed me to the hospital. They ran tests. At first, they thought it was my blood sugar. I left okay, but continued to have dizzy spells and splitting headaches. The tests for diabetes came back negative. The doctors ran further tests. Everything came back negative. Then, I had an MRI, which found a tumor the size of a marble on my brain stem."

"I am so sorry to hear that," he said, alarmed but remaining calm.

"Its location makes operation difficult, and surgery carries with it a risk of death in many cases. The prognosis was eight to twelve weeks to live." She started to cry further. Teddy pulled her body close to his, wrapping his arms tight around her. "They said I could do chemo or radiation, but the chances of it helping in such a short amount of time were slim in my case. I knew if I did the treatment I would be in a lot of pain for the remainder of my short life, and I wanted to feel love again before passing into the light." She broke down, stuffing her furrowed brow in her hands.

"I am so sorry, baby." The news shocked Teddy.

"Oh, I don't want to lose you. I am not afraid of death, but I am scared of losing you. I hardly know you, and I love you so much already."

"I know, baby. I understand." He wanted to cry or run or scream out in defiant opposition to this wicked twist of fate. All things happened for a reason when it was something a person could see past, but Alicia's impending death caused Teddy to feel like a silver ball on an arbitrarily haphazard roulette wheel that always landed on the wrong number. As he looked up at the stoic dealer getting ready to rake his heart away, he felt slung and bounced around, tricked and conned. He couldn't stand losing another loved one to this dreaded disease. Not this time, he thought. He took her beautiful hand to his mouth, closed his eyes, and kissed it; then, he gazed deep into her eyes.

"I love you, Alicia. Don't give up hope. I'll stay with you through this storm and we'll make it out together. Let's forget what the doctors say about the time and focus on getting you one hundred percent well again."

"But *what* can we do in a month or two? It would have to be a miracle!" She couldn't stop crying and leaned up with her back to him.

"Miracles happen every day. We can try the wine."

"I am not sure the wine could work on *this* on me, even though it worked on rats, cancer is so … so … serious, you know. That's why I never mentioned it after you mentioned the wine the first time." She began to cry. "I should've never come here. We've fallen in love and we'll have to say goodbye again, only unlike your dreams, it'll be real this time." She put on her robe and ran down the stairs to a guest bedroom. He sprang up and followed her.

"Wait baby, please, *wait!* This doesn't change the way I feel," he said, hearing her cry from inside the door. "Please open the door, Alicia. Talk to me. Just talk to me."

"I need some time alone tonight. We can talk tomorrow," she said from inside.

"Okay. I love you. Good night," he said, reluctantly.

After tossing and turning in pain for half an hour, he submitted to the night, staring up to the sky for help, like an injured soldier begging the heavens. As the ceiling fan looped around on high, he followed every turn. Then, he wondered if the wine could actually work on her—it *had* to. Rolling onto his side, he fell into a deep sleep. In the Spanish countryside, he held Alicia as they watched birds circling in the periwinkle sky. She was healthy and he decided to hold that reality of her and bring it with him when he woke up again.

CHAPTER 11

After climbing over a wooden fence on the north end of Teddy's land, Jimmy sneaked through the property, his bug eyes surveying the area. Big Ham was right behind him. Their clothes were as black as their guns, from their shirts to their boots. They approached a clearing and, in the distance, spotted the sprawling stone estate. They were so quiet that not even Half Ton or Bear woke from their slumber. They ran toward a structure with a flat roof attached to the left of the barn.

At the first window, Jimmy wrapped a bandana around the gun and broke the glass with it. He raised his muscular body through the window onto a wooden desk. Crawling to the floor, he instructed Big Ham to keep watch outside. As he crept across the room, the odor of rich tobacco touched his nose and a half empty bottle of champagne caught his eye. *Not the cheap stuff*, he thought—they had something to celebrate.

Antiques filled the room. Tubs lined the floors and tables, one next to another, full of water and artifacts. What appeared to be a silver metal vault-style door to the left really got his attention. No code pad. He breathed a sigh of relief and quickly drilled the lock. Teddy wasn't prepared for this, but he had always worried about his security if they ever found gold—he just hadn't been expecting trouble this quickly. Inside the safe, Jimmy noticed a pile of gold coins on a stainless steel work table that became the new focus of his attention. His closed lips broadened to a wide smile. With the tip of his blade, he lifted the top on an empty chest nearby and shined a mini-mag flashlight in it; he quickly filled it with the coins. Then, he opened up the drawers of the stainless table and saw hundreds of other coins in hard plastic cases labeled with dates and numbers. He began emptying them into the chest also.

The chest was full and very heavy, but for a hobby cage fighter who spent two hours a day in the gym, it was manageable. Jimmy slid it out the window to Big Ham, who lowered it to the ground. Jimmy went back to the wooden desk by the window and left a note for Teddy pinned to it with the tip of his bone-handled hunting knife. Then, he exited. After carrying the chest a short way, Jimmy fell to one knee and grabbed his temple in pain. Big Ham stopped. Jimmy cursed the migraine, gritted his teeth, and stood up, lifting the chest again.

"Hurry up, Jimmy!"

"It's this damn town! The headaches won't stop, ever since I came back. They're like the metal wheels of a freight train running over my brain." He forced himself up and the two thieves carried it to the other side of the land, lifted it over the fence and loaded it into the bed of his orange F250.

Will Burns hadn't been able to sleep that night after learning about the possible financial juggernaut of Casablanca covering Mr. Dollarhide's land from Stern Banks, and decided to take a night drive in his smooth Mercedes past the old man's property and see the scale of it for himself. He just happened to be passing in the night right as Jimmy and Big Ham were loading a chest into the orange truck. While Will did find the activity a little irregular, he figured it was just some country boys poaching for racoons.

Jimmy and Big Ham got in and sped off into the night. Jimmy hit redial on his cell phone. Stern Banks picked up. Stern Banks had received a tip from an insider at the bank that morning that Teddy

THE DOLLARHIDE MYSTERY

Dollarhide had come into some money, so he'd called Jimmy, his gun for hire, to drive up from Miami to relieve him of it. Jimmy, a classmate of Stern's in high school, had been hired by Stern for many odd jobs. Recently, he had even done "the knee-cap thing" with a metal Louisville slugger bat a couple of weeks ago on a man who had sued Bateman and Banks for harassing him over his ocean front property in the area. The guy stopped the lawsuit immediately and sold his ocean front property to Bateman and Banks for their asking price. He was simply too scared to call the police after the metal bat.

"Banks here."

"I got the chest and left the note."

"Good."

"Stick around in the area in case we need something else."

"Got it."

Jimmy clicked the phone off and sped down the Florida coast. He headed to the Sea Breeze, an old motor lodge overlooking the ocean in Spanish Palm, a town ten miles south of downtown Latch. Across the street, a bar and restaurant named Cap'n Sam's bustled with young people who wandered in and out, laughing.

CHAPTER 12

*I*n the morning, Teddy woke early and made breakfast in the kitchen. From the living room, Blue echoed his song. Alicia strolled in wearing a rose-colored silk robe and hugged him.

"Good morning. Are we okay now?"

"Yes. I am sorry about last night. I just had to sleep it off."

"I understand." He paused. "I got to thinking, and I think that wine I told you about might help."

"You think it could work?"

"Maybe. It can't hurt you."

"If you trust it, my faith is in you."

"You'll drink it three times a day, every day. I'll divide up the dosages and keep them in the fridge. We'll start today."

"Okay."

He placed his arm around her. "I am so glad you're willing to try it. We must keep a positive attitude and have hope."

"But I need to take the necklaces to stores. My parents are counting on me." Her eyebrows pointed up and she frowned.

"No Alicia, you must rest. Stay here with me at Isabella for now and see how you do. Then you can take the necklaces. I'll go with you and help. Pretty soon, we'll go."

She paused, thinking about it. He hugged her. "Thank you, Teddy. I think you're right."

"Good. Then, when you get well and you've sold your necklaces, we'll go to St. Barts for a vacation."

"Oh, I would absolutely adore that—I've never been there, but I've heard it's wonderful," she said, looking up at him.

"I've never been either, but I've read stories and books about it."

While they talked over breakfast and her first drink of wine, Teddy noticed that the hope of the wine seemed to ease her anxiety, although he could tell she was still not convinced it would work.

Teddy slowly sipped his green tea, blowing on it to cool it down. He informed her he had to go to the hypnotist for another session. Afterward, they would take *Gold Lip* out and she could go into town, but she stated she wanted to rest. He kissed her and left for the preservation room to call on some buyers.

On the way, his phone rang. He answered to the sound of a familiar voice. Andy Matthews thanked Teddy, informing him that he was much better now.

"That fast?"

"Yes, I know, it's like a miracle."

"What did the nurse say?"

"She forced me to leave. Assured me it was the medicine."

"Due to legal issues, doctors are financially liable, which causes them to be very cautious; in some ways, it's really a shame they have to be so concerned. Treatments have to be tested thoroughly first, so they're not really acting irrationally, given the system."

"I see what you mean, but we still have to try to help the others," Andy proclaimed.

They agreed to meet in the afternoon so Teddy could give him more wine for the others.

Teddy unlocked the door to the preservation room and flipped on the light. Out of the corner of his eye, he noticed the sun coming in through the north-facing window at a different angle than usual. Seeing the blown out glass above the desk, he panicked and moved toward the safe door, but it was drilled and ajar. Lo and behold, the catalog drawers in the safe lay on the ground empty too; he placed his hand on his forehead and stared at the floor.

Then, he walked over to the broken window. On the wooden desk, the hunting knife pinned a handwritten note down. It read:

You know what you have to do.

Worried and shocked, he gasped, then he ran out of the door to the main house, where he called Catfish to report the episode.

Inside, he collapsed into one of the living room chairs, blankly staring into space. Alicia came in from the other room. Seeing his expression, she asked him in a very soft voice what was wrong.

"They took the chest," he whispered with glazed eyes.

"They what?!"

"Someone took it, last night. They broke in."

"Oh, my goodness!" she gasped and paused. "But it was only a tiny piece of the treasure, right? You'll find the rest soon, I am sure of it. No insurance on it yet?" she said, rubbing his pearl hair back.

"No, not yet, it wasn't reported yet. It's six fucking years of work down the drain."

"But you know where the hull is now, so you can find the rest of the treasure. That was just a fraction."

"Yes, but I am running out of time." Alicia didn't know what he meant, being uninformed of the debt on Isabella.

"Just keep up hope baby and you'll find more. I'll get well and you'll find it," Alicia said, and hugged him. "And then, we'll go to St. Barts like we talked about. And it will all be as it should be in our dreams."

"I would love that. At least I have you my darling." They held each other.

"Through the storm together, isn't that what you told me?"

"Yes, baby." They kissed.

Catfish arrived shortly, filled out a report, took the hunting knife, and, after gathering some samples, informed Teddy he would be in touch soon.

Teddy rested a while and then called the boys from his lounger. Cos answered and Teddy explained what had gone down quietly. He also told them about Alicia's inoperable brain cancer and the wine and how everything was going to be alright with her and the hunt. Teddy said they all needed to be patient. Then, he told him how much he loved them and said goodbye and as soon as Cos hung up, overwhelmed with emotion, he started balling his eyes out.

"What's wrong sweetheart?" Leslie asked from the back seat.

"Yeah bud, what's going on?" Joey asked.

"The landsharks took the gold! They took dad's gold guys for crying out loud! Ahhh!" Cos cried.

"What?!" Joey said and swerved off the road applying the brakes. "You serious bud?"

"Do I look like I am making it up bro?" Cos said, staring at him through blurry eyes. Joey stared forward and banged his hands on the steering wheel. "Dammit!"

"It's going to be okay guys," Belle said, rubbing Joey's upper right arm from the back seat. "Everything will be alright soon. Let's keep going and find this treasure," she said. Joey touched her hand with his left hand gently. Then, he got out of the car, slammed the door and walked forward into the open space where he stared into the horizon. Cos got out and approached him. "It's okay bro, Belle's right. Let's calm down and take what's waiting for us in California. It's our duty."

Joey stared for a moment longer and then said, "I guess it's in our stars after all man."

"Yeah man, we Dollarhides have saltwater in our veins and stars in our hearts. You know that."

IN THE EARLY AFTERNOON, Teddy drove to Dr. Wyman's office in town. A group of young girls and boys chased each other on the sidewalk, laughing. Many of the businesses had reopened. The letters on The Aquarius theater marquee had been fixed and an old Humphrey Bogart classic, *Key Largo,* was playing. The Aquarius always recycled old timey flicks.

Dr. Wyman welcomed Teddy into the office, ushering him to have a seat on the lounge chair. Teddy relaxed into the leather. When the doctor walked him into the hypnosis, he slipped off into a light sleep.

❧

AT HIS HOUSEBOAT in the marina, Patch had begun to research the diamond after receiving the message from Joey a few days prior.

As he sipped his coffee, he moused through Google entries, scanning for the best results. For obscure things, he had learned that sometimes the best results would be three Google pages back, and when hunting treasure, it was that extra digging that paid off. After visiting ten pages, he found an entry giving a detailed legend fabricated into a short story about a diamond from Africa.

The story, a legendary tale of what really happened, titled "The Prince," opened in a grand appointed court with detailed frescos of exceptional quality across the ceiling. At the front of the room, a man wearing royal threads sat on a gilded throne with tufted red velvet cushioning. Viziers and assistants were on both sides of him in a line wearing drab pants and shirts and plain haircuts. The musk of frankincense filled the space.

The general of the prince's army, Felipe, marched down the center of the court, where he bowed before the prince.

"Your majesty, may I present to you the largest diamond in the world, courtesy of the African Khalfani as a gift for protecting his country," Felipe said and held a box forward, unlocking it with a key to reveal a perfectly cut diamond the size of an apple. The austere assistants gasped in awe, their mouths dropping. The sunlight whispering in through the windows caught the diamond and it emanated a shimmering brilliance. The prince's eyes sparkled as he fell to the ground, kneeling before the stone the way others kneeled to him. Grasping the box, he held it up deep into the light.

"Aww, it's the most beautiful thing I've ever seen." He paused. "What did they name it?"

"'The Prince,' after you, sire."

"After me? Really?" He held it down, still mesmerized. "Very good. Send him a fleet of men to stay at his port and protect our ally, and take gifts of gold, chocolate and spices." He paused, thinking.

"Yes, your sire."

"I want you to give this illustrious stone to my shipmaster on *La Gracia* and have him take it on our next voyage to the New World. On the way back, instruct him to deliver the diamond to the lady Isabella in Southern Spain as a token of my love. She refuses to marry me because she is waiting on someone special to her. Thus, I shall give her something special she cannot refuse."

"If I may ask your highness, why not just insist the lady marry you?"

"No. She must *agree* to marry me—I will not force her. Have the stone placed in a special box that no man can open without a special key."

"Yes, your majesty."

The prince handed him the box and said, "Guard it with your life."

"Yes, sire."

"Very well," the prince said, sitting down again on his throne.

The assistant bowed out and exited the court with his companions.

Patch was now on the edge of his seat. He had heard Teddy mention the name of the legendary Prince diamond many times before, but couldn't believe there was a story about it being aboard *La Gracia*. Maybe, just maybe, the story was written based on some records from a Spanish library, and a clue like this could break their treasure hunt wide open. He texted Teddy the info about the diamond with the emergency abbreviation they used: *chknsld, meaning, "it's chicken salad, not chicken shit."*.

In Wymann's office, Teddy checked his phone, read the text, jerked forward, and slipped on his leather flip-flops.

"I gotta go, doc!"

"But we're only halfway through."

"It doesn't matter. It's chicken salad!" He ran over to the doctor with a big smile and flung his arms around him.

"What's chicken salad?" Wyman squeaked, squirming in the chair.

"If it ain't chicken shit, it's chicken salad, which means something *really good*," Teddy exclaimed, hugging him.

Wyman looked violated as Teddy exited without closing the door; a moment later, he came back to close it.

He skipped out to his truck where a crowd gathered on the hot sidewalk, looking to the street and pointing. In the middle of the street, a lone butterfly danced in the blazing sun, hovering over passing cars like it was in a parade. Other than those in his living room, which they had set loose the day after the storm and the one Cos saw on the truck, it was the first butterfly to be seen in the town since they had disappeared so many years ago. A sixth-grade science teacher observed by its coloring that it was indeed a queen butterfly, not an eastern swallowtail. Teddy saw the black boy from the Ball neighborhood selling hydrangeas on the street a block up; he went to him and greeted him; the boy had a big smile on his face that showed all his teeth, and his eyes were full of hope. Teddy selected a light blue flower and inhaled its fragrance deeply. The boy smiled at him and Teddy winked; he left and climbed in his truck.

Back at the farm, Teddy found Alicia planting the empty garden plots to the side of Isabella with new flowers. She had on khaki shorts, a white button-up shirt, and leather sandals. Her long black hair rolled over to one side around the front, and an ivory driftwood pearl necklace was around her neck. He carried the hydrangea to her.

"Aww, thank you Teddy. I love hydrangeas."

"You're welcome! Thank you for planting the garden."

"It's nothing. I love working in gardens, and the ground here is so fertile, it's just waiting for my seeds! Are you feeling better now about the chest?"

"I am very irate about it, but there's nothing I can do except to sell the house. For now, I am forgetting about it and focusing on us and this diamond."

"Diamond? What diamond?"

"Well, you're not going to believe this, but I just got a text from Patch about an enormous diamond that may have sunk with *La Gracia* —it could be the biggest in the world."

"*What?!* That's great news!"

"I know, right?" he said, and paused. She covered her mouth in exuberance.

"Wow, good luck!"

He smiled, "Thanks." He paused, gazing into her kind eyes. "Have you thought about how long you will stay here with me? I mean, after your recovery?"

"I haven't thought about it. I could go whenever the treatment is over," she replied.

"Go? No, please stay here for as long as you can."

"Thank you. I'd like that. My visa allows me to be in the USA for up to ninety days," she said. "And I feel so at home here with Isabella and you."

"You *are* home," he said and kissed her.

"Come with me, I want to show you something," she said, taking his calloused hand and leading him inside to show him some of her necklaces, handmade with rough pearls, beads, and exotic gemstones, which she had just unpacked. He asked if she could make jewelry out of some of the coins from *La Gracia* when they found more, suggesting they might even sell them.

"I would love that. I've already had my supplies shipped to me from my US distributors. Which room should I work in?"

"Pick any room in the house for a studio."

"*Any room?!*"

"Any room. Make it *every* room! If it's your stuff, I don't care. All that is mine is yours."

"Oh Teddy, you're just a really big sweetheart underneath that tough exterior." A tear came to hear eye and she kissed him on the cheek.

After a little debate, she chose the tearoom on the second floor looking out over the pool. Her favorite room since arriving, she often went there to gaze out the broad window at the banana palms guarding the back of the pool—they moved in the wind in a way that made her feel good.

Meanwhile, Teddy got a small blue-tinted bottle of the wine elixir and put it in his goat-leather shoulder bag. He called the Pearlmakers to rendezvous at the marina. They had all received a text from Patch about The Prince diamond and were eager to move their sea legs.

In *Gold Lip*, Teddy broke the news about the stolen chest. The crew became furious. Teddy said he knew it was the land sharks who stole it. Had to be. Ty suggested they approach Stern Banks directly with force. Teddy calmed them down, insisting they not do anything irrational. He repeated Alicia's consolation that the chest was only a fraction of the bounty, and insisted they would find The Prince or more gold soon now that they knew the location of the ship. The crew reluctantly agreed, and sour faced, pushed off into an overcast eighty-five degrees. The clouds held moisture high above them. Patch said the legend about the diamond that caused women to faint and men to cry was still just a legend until they got more proof.

"No Patch, it's not a legend, the damn thing is real. I can feel it in my leg, and it had a ticket on *La Gracia*—a ticket that went to the bottom of the ocean right here. No word of this to anyone. All the hunters from South Florida will swarm the coast if they hear of it."

"My lips are sealed," Ty said.

"Mine too," Patch said.

"Not that anyone would believe a legend like this, but I am not saying anything either," Dal said.

"If you believe it, someone else would too," Teddy said.

"Well, I guess you're right," Dal said.

"You know, the ancients believed that diamonds were splinters from the stars," remarked Patch.

"Is that right?" Teddy said, putting on his gold aviators and showing his pearly teeth. "A big ole star splinter stuck in the sand. Well, we're gonna tweezer it out! Ain't that right, boys?"

"Sure is!" Ty said. The humor relieved the sour mood of the crew and they all laughed.

Then, Teddy silenced them by placing a finger to his lips. Through the open window in the cabin, the satellite radio reported that the hurricane in the Gulf would pound the Texas coast tomorrow evening. Teddy shook his head at the news and walked into the captain's quarters.

The ship's engine rumbled as they glided to the search area. Ty and Dal dropped the ROV in and Patch controlled it with the remote control, while Teddy relaxed in the captain seat with his hands locked behind his head. After searching with the bot for hours, they came up empty-handed, but the vibe in the water told them they might be on the right track, so they marked the location on the GPS.

On the way home, Teddy detoured to the Ball neighborhood and parked. Andy Matthews was waiting there. He walked over to greet him with a face that shone with the radiance of perfect health. He embraced Teddy, who gave him the bottle of the wine and asked him to keep in touch.

CHAPTER 13

*E*arlier that day, Belle drove while Leslie sat in the passenger seat with Dog in between them, his tongue slopping out. They sang and grooved to Motown songs, while Joey and Cos relaxed in the back and stared at the cactuses in the distance whose stationary green arms waved back at them.

As they rolled west on a barren desert highway, dust billowed in the air as the breeze blew it up in sheets. The vast sky swirled with bluish-grey cirrus clouds and the sun shone high above them. The arid heat baked the metal box, but the wind blowing through the window cooled them.

They had stayed in Oklahoma the night before, and it felt good to be one step closer to the Sierras. Outside of Albuquerque, a gas station sold Native American souvenirs like stone jewelry and handmade belts. Shortly after it, they spotted the exit north for Santa Fe. After taking it, they turned into a McDonald's.

Belle collected their list as they waited in the drive-thru. Joey wanted a double quarter with cheese; Cos got a Big Mac and ordered Dog a double patty with no bread, which Joey explained that would be a "Flying Dutchman 2×2" at an In-N-Out burger in LA.

As Belle ordered, the car watched the spectacle in front of them—a waxed gold 1988 Chevrolet Cavalier convertible marinating in Billy Ocean's song, "Caribbean Queen." The owner was seven feet tall and had slicked-back brown hair and knock-off Gucci sunglasses. He danced to Billy wearing tan racing gloves—the kind with the holes in the knuckles.

Watching him, Belle was so distracted she accelerated forward and the chicken head got pulverized by the clearance bar, flying off the back of the wagon onto the ground five feet behind.

"What the hell was that?" Leslie said.

"Oh my God! The chicken's head!" Cos said, getting out. Joey couldn't help laughing as he joined him.

"It's not funny, Jojo, this is Dan's car! He's going to kill me."

Through the opened car window, Belle hollered, "I am so sorry, Cosmo. I really didn't mean to, I was just so distracted by the Billy Ocean."

"Relax, Cos, it's going to be fine," Joey said.

The hit damaged the paint on the front of the beak and the bottom of the head where it had been fastened to the roof. After inspecting it, Cos concluded it could be fixed with some expensive work.

"Aww, that's bull, Cos. We can patch it together with a little paint and some glue at the shop when we get home. Dan will never know the difference," Joey said.

"I sure hope so."

From the other side of the parking lot, Skeet and Jethro witnessed the whole thing and were stupefied and wide-eyed now.

Joey picked up the head and placed it on the seat between him and Cos.

"How's it doing?" Leslie asked, craning back from the front seat; the busted-up head stared back at her.

"I think it'll be fine," Cos said with his hand resting on the top, almost petting it.

Belle drove forward. After handing them the food, the attendant spotted Joey in the backseat.

"Hey, it's the duck hunt guy!" Another attendant came over and looked out the window.

"Oh, it sure is. A living legend."

Joey shook his head. "Just go, Belle."

"Hey, could I get your autograph?" the second lanky guy asked.

"Just go," he said again.

"Joey, they just want your autograph. Go for it. Relax."

"Okay, I guess."

"Great, give me something he can sign," the second attendant asked the first. The first attendant handed him a folded Happy Meal bag. He passed it and a pen to Belle, who handed it to Joey.

"Sign it to Ben," the second attendant asked. "I'll give you a free milkshake," the guy proposed.

"Go for it!" Belle said again.

"Okay, okay, make the milkshake a large vanilla, okay. How's that?"

"Sure thing."

He signed the side of the Happy Meal and handed it back. The guy passed him the milkshake.

"Thanks a lot, Joey!"

"Sure!" Joey said and smiled, looking forward.

Belle laughed and they drove off. They stopped at a rest area up the road, where the flat landscape expanded for miles. A brown hill in the background ascended and descended along the horizon. The sun waned behind it and the air became cold the way the desert does at night. After finishing their food, they resumed the trek to Santa Fe. Sun-washed adobe buildings made up the New Mexican hill country. They drove onto Bo's as daylight left.

Cos's phone rang.

"Hello." He paused. "Oh hey *Dan*, how's it going?" He paused again. Everyone in the car laughed. "Oh yeah, the car is just great, we're getting it fixed up real nice. She'll be like new soon." He paused. "No sir, I wouldn't think of taking it out at night. I would *never* do an irresponsible thing like that." He paused. "All right, take care." He hung up and exhaled. "Great timing, Dan."

"He had no clue?" Leslie asked.

"I don't think so," Cos said.

Belle and Joey smiled and laughed.

They climbed the hill winding up to Bo Dollarhide's ranch, which sat on ten acres of mountains outlined by a wooden fence. At the entrance, a cow skull hung with an iron sign reading *The Wrangler's Roost* swinging above it in the wind.

Skeet passed the ranch and parked his truck up the hill, where he still had a view of the house, but they couldn't see him. In the car, Skeet talked about money and gold, and what they would do with the expensive treasure. They wanted to retire on the beach in Alabama, get flashy new cars, and all sorts of luxuries. They thought about women too, and how women would come to them when they had more money. They laughed and joked about the chicken head dismemberment and what to do to completely disable the car once they got the treasure in California. They would sleep in their car another night, drink whiskey, and watch the Santa Fe sun set over the mountains in the distance.

BO WAS A TRUE COWBOY, always raising horses and training bulls. He used to ride bulls professionally until Hurricane Frank tossed him bad, leaving him with some souvenirs—a scar on his right arm in the shape of the state of Kentucky and an injured back. He got used to the scar, but not the back pain, and although it was excruciating at times, he refused to take pain pills. The suffering caused him to explore other remedies and he eventually cured it with physical therapy and yoga. Afterward, he started training bulls. Bo still reminisced about Frank, calling the old tanned Brahman his friend and compass.

Belle whipped into the entrance, throwing dust into the air; she parked in front of a wooden ranch house with a broad porch and a tin roof. There were some rocking chairs under the eave. They got out and put on sweaters and jackets before knocking on the door.

Bo answered with no shirt, just jeans and a cowboy hat. He had a bushy grey moustache and enough chest hair to pass for a sweater. Like Teddy, he was strong, but had an ectomorphic body.

"Who do you think you are, coming here?" he commanded, looking at them with a confused stare.

"It's us Uncle Bo—Joey and Cosby ... *your nephews?*" Joey said with a stunned look. He had spoken to Bo a few days ago and had just phoned, but no one answered.

"Never heard of you."

"You know, Jojo and Cos, Teddy's boys?"

"No idea." His expression was serious. Joey became worried.

Then he broke the face and his eyes became warm, "C'mon in! I am just playing with y'all. Make yourselves at home. Give your Uncle Bo a big ole bear hug." They embraced and entered to an open floor plan. A painting of a Native American soldier hung on a knotty pine wall and a long dining table rested on the left with a broad hearth to the side; an old black stove and a fireplace provided heat; multicolored Mexican wool blankets and quilts rested on the back of two sofas in the living room; and delicious smells emanated from the kitchen.

"Nice to meet you ladies, I am Bo."

"I am Leslie."

"I am Belle." He shook their hands.

"You remember Dog. Can he stay inside?"

"Can you vouch for his character, Cos?" Bo asked with serious eyes, sizing Dog up.

"Yep. He doesn't like the indoors much," Cos said, smiling. "But he's a pretty good dog."

"I don't like the indoors much either so guess what......he can stay!"

An iguana walked in from the kitchen to greet them.

"This is my pet lizard, Popeye. Don't let his lazy eye bother you."

Popeye had an Alabama Crimson Tide bandana, Bo's alma mater, tied as a sash around his neck; he stared up at them with his good eye, the other one trailing to the side. He eyeballed Dog with apprehension. Dog watched him closely, unsure of what to make of him.

They had a seat in the living room on the suede couches each one topped with a deer skin. Popeye joined, plopping his belly off the rug onto the cold floor. Bo left and came back in, passing them each a glass of Riesling and starting a fire in the earthen chimney.

"I have some quilts laid out, and there are pillows in the closet. This couch folds out and there's an outhouse outside. Watch out for the cockroaches though, they're everywhere!" Belle and Leslie turned to each other in horror. Bo pointed at them and grinned, laughing to himself, "Gotcha! I am just joking, ladies. Relax. The bathroom is just down the hall and it's roach-free." He paused. Then said with a glint in his eye, "Sometimes." They laughed.

"This is perfect, Bo," Joey said.

"I am glad you feel so. I am getting Brawny ready for the rodeo—he's the bull in the ring outside." He paused. "So y'all are really going for Luke's treasure?"

"Yep," Joey said.

"That damn thing has been buried for over a hundred years, just waiting. I'd love to go with you and taste the thrill of the hunt again." Memories of Teddy and his past gold hunts with Jim at Fort Morgan for the treasure of Jean Lafitte danced in the flames as they bounced off each other, warming the room.

A very tall Native American woman with straight black hair braided in thick knots and smooth skin floated in from the kitchen wearing a violet silk dress. She carried food to the table, swishing over to them after. Her marble eyes were the color of honey.

"This is my friend Ooljee, you can call her Moon for short. She's my love."

"Hi, it's very nice to meet you all. I've heard so much about you, Joey and Cosby." They said hello.

"They're searching for the treasure I told you about."

"Oh, how interesting. Do you know what tribe it was?"

"No, we're not sure," Joey said.

"Well, I wish you great luck. Will you be joining us for golf tomorrow morning?"

"Thank you, ma'am. Sure, why not? I love to hit the links," Joey said.

Bo smiled, "These aren't just any links."

"How so?"

"You'll see," he laughed. "It's a great course though, really." He laughed some more.

"I am making dinner, are you all hungry?" Moon asked.

"Well, sort of. We just ate, but I could eat again," Joey said, tempted by the aroma of baking corn and sweet cream. The group agreed with Joey.

"Great, it'll be ready in a bit." She exited.

"Uncle Bo, one reason we are stopping here is dad told us you have some of Luke's diaries that we believe contain an important aerial map pointing to the exact spot where the treasure is located. Do you think we can see them?"

"Oh, I don't have them anymore. I had to use them as kindling to start a fire."

"*Really?!*" Joey said, his heart dropping.

"Yes…..it's a crying shame…..but…..I *might* have saved one." Bo broke his straight face, laughing.

"You are an evil man Bo, an evil, evil man," Cos said.

"I just love playing with y'all. Yeah, I got em." He got up and retrieved three black diaries from the bookshelf that matched the ones from Teddy's library and passed them to Joey. He sat down again, sipped his wine, and watched Joey thumb through them.

"Do you see what you're looking for in there?"

Belle, Cos, and Leslie surrounded Joey as he flipped through the first one to page twenty-two; where he only saw writing on it. He put it down and picked up the next one; more random journaling on twenty-two—but on the third unmarked one, he saw a drawing of the Sierras with various points marked with stars, and in one area by the river's edge, there was a black circle.

"That's it!" Leslie said, pointing at it. "That's it! A black circle, the way it was described in the other journal."

"Yep, that's what we're looking for," Joey said.

"Let me take a look." Joey passed it to Bo.

"So *circle* marks the spot. I saw this many times, but never knew it meant anything. How do you know this is it?"

Joey took out the journal with Luke's description of the interaction with the Native American and passed it to Bo, who opened to the dog-eared page.

"Incredible, truly incredible. You boys have enough for a hunt here."

"That's what Teddy said."

"This calls for a toast!" He said and raised his glass and they followed. "To your good fortune!" They drank the sweet Riesling with the fire crisping in the background.

Joey gave Teddy a late call, informing him they had indeed found the missing journal at Bo's and after praises by the old man, handed the phone to Bo who talked to his old brother. They talked for a bit about good times and said goodnight.

Something foul touched Joey's nose and he glanced around the room trying to call the culprit's bluff. Next the odor hit Belle, who craned her neck around, trying hard not to make a face. Popeye fled the room, glancing back at Dog with a suspicious eye. Joey spotted it and realized the Flying Dutchman hadn't agreed with Dog.

"So, what are you doing these days, Uncle Bo?" Joey asked again.

"Training bulls and raising horses." He paused. "And reading about plants in my spare time. I have something I want to show y'all tomorrow. Something very special to me."

"What is it?" Joey asked.

"It's better if I just show you. You'll see."

"Okay, tomorrow then," said Joey.

"Tomorrow."

Moon was setting the table in the background and Joey asked Bo, "Have you seen Frank lately?"

"No, I haven't, but he's still on the rodeo circuit. I got a picture of him over the mantle that I look at and say a prayer of gratitude to every day." He nodded to it and they looked up at the photo. "I love that damn bull."

"Cosby told us what happened in the car. You're not bitter about what he did to you, are you?" Leslie asked.

"No. He taught me all my lessons. Besides, forgiveness is a well that never runs dry, and I drink from it constantly." He sipped his wine.

"Well I would be so upset," Leslie replied.

"I was for years, but it only hurt me. Old Frank just kept bucking and twirling, winning trophies, while I moped around. Then one day I realized it was time to set it down. It had gotten heavy, carrying him around."

Moon interrupted and ushered them in to eat, serving bison meatballs with butternut squash dumplings and gourmet black bean and corn soup.

"The food is so delicious. What's your secret, Moon?" Leslie asked.

"I just try to be happy and in a loving state when I am cooking, and it seems to make the food better. It sounds simple, but I swear it works."

"Makes sense to me," Leslie said.

"So this is black bean soup with a side of love and happiness?" Cos asked.

"You got it," Moon said.

"So, the other day Jim called and told me y'all want to see Tahoma?" Bo said.

"Yeah, actually, we might want to." Joey looked at Belle to gauge her reaction.

"Well, my dreams *are* so much better now," she said, thumbing her necklace.

"So maybe we don't need to," Joey said, looking at Bo.

"Well, whatever. If you want to see him, he's downtown off Canyon Street at the restaurant Gourmaize. He's a good friend of mine. Tell him I sent you."

"Good to know."

After dinner, they retired to the living room.

Bo and Ooljee went to bed early since they had to wake at 4 a.m. Joey put on the John Wayne classic *El Dorado*. Belle loved that movie, stating she could "watch John Wayne swat flies for two hours." Dog continued to pollute the room and they eventually had to isolate him like hazardous waste in the laundry. Belle rested on Joey's chest while Cos and Leslie relaxed on the other couch.

Joey fell asleep around the time Robert Mitchum's character in the movie sobered up; finding himself in a hard brown desert with a thunderous black sky, big and guarded, the stars like white crystals dotting it, and a moon hanging there, he traced the empty land in circles, not knowing which way to go.

Suddenly, Belle appeared by his side. And in the middle of the desert, a tiny Native American with long hair braided at the sides, as black as night, wearing a suede outfit with long beaded jewelry, approached with kind eyes. He walked up to Belle and pulled a tiny cloud of charcoal smoke from her body in his hand; containing it in his cupped hands with great care, he slowly took it and blew it into the wind where it scattered. Joey noticed a life enter Belle's face immediately that wasn't there before, and she smiled. The Indian looked content.

"What was that?" Joey asked.

"Hate," his voice said. He now had sand in his fist; as he spoke, he let the sand slip to the ground, and then the dream ended.

Joey jerked awake, pulling out of the dream. The credits rolled on *El Dorado* and he was in the living room with Belle asleep on his chest. His eyes darted to her, and then to Leslie and Cos, who all slept peacefully. He brushed Belle's red hair over her shoulder and ran his fingertip in circles around her pale neckline. The feel of her relaxed him into a beautiful sleep.

In the morning, Joey woke to Popeye staring at him out of his lazy eye, the Crimson Tide sash drooping in his face. Belle relayed that she'd had the most peaceful night of sleep in her life, implying the necklace must be helping.

"Must be," Joey said, not telling her yet about the dream.

After breakfast, they played a round of golf. Bo had ten holes of the baldest course in North America. Not one blade of grass: just hard dirt. The ball bounced like a racquetball off it. Bo outfitted his golf cart with off-road tires, speakers, a phone port, and a cooler rack just to make it all the more fun.

He pontificated about everything from bulls to politics. Bo had always been a thinker, which Joey and Cos liked about him—whether they agreed with him or not, he never failed to leave them with grist for the mental mill. They knew it was better to have reflected on something than to have accepted it as true just because others did. After completing the ninth hole of the most sideways game of golf in their lives, Bo pointed over the hill to the ground below, where a tall glass greenhouse sat.

"There it is—follow me."

The group followed him and Moon down a trail to the greenhouse below. They entered to row after row of short green trees with strange drumstick-like pods that resembled fat string beans lining the floors and tables.

"What are these?" Belle said, touching one of the pods.

"The Moringa plant—the tree of life."

"Never heard of it. Why is it a tree of life?"

"They call it that because it's the most nutrient-dense plant in the world."

"Sounds like a miracle to me," Belle said.

"It's a blessing for sure," Bo commented.

"It could potentially go a long way to solving malnourishment in America and Africa," Moon said.

"Then why have I never heard of it?" Leslie asked.

"Yeah, I've never heard of it either," Belle said.

"Well, there are a few charitable organizations promoting it. I think in time you'll hear more. Sometimes, things are like that. Humans have knowledge but don't use it," Bo said.

"Have you told Teddy about it? Mom would have loved to know about this," Joey said, looking closely at one of the strange pods.

"No, I haven't told him yet; I've only been studying it for a year now. I wanted to make sure it was as good as the research says."

"You know Dad wants to help solve hunger in Africa and at home with some of the profits from *La Gracia*. I am sure he'd love to know about Moringa," Cos said.

"So, the old toad is picking up where Sarah left off?"

"Yep," Cos said.

"Good man," Bo said. "Here." He went over to a shelf and returned carrying a bottle of oil, a bag of brown powder, and a bag of seeds and handed them to Cos. "Take this home with you to Teddy. Tell him to look it up, and I'll mention it next time we speak as well."

"Will do."

"Y'all better get on the road if you want to make good time."

"Yeah, thanks again, Bo!" Cos said.

"You're welcome." They said goodbye, headed back to the chicken, got in with the injured plastic chicken head, and proceeded out of town. The road appeared different than the one in Joey's dream—more banal, but clearer. He put on his shades, hit play on the Beach Boys, and adjusted the rearview mirror. They would stop in Vegas for one night, and then go on to California.

Skeet followed them when they pulled out, the foursome still unaware of his hung-over but eager and conniving presence.

CHAPTER 14

*A*licia worked on a French baker's table covered with glass bowls. Pausing for a moment to sip some carrot juice, she gazed out the large paneled window to the banana palms. They waved in the breeze, drinking in the sunlight. Her heart swelled as she watched Teddy perform his morning stretches under the palm trees. She finished the glass and set it down to work again.

Her stones and materials had been delivered overnight. Each bowl had a different type of stone, bead, or pendant, creating a tapestry of colors on the table. She had aquamarine, rose quartz chips, and carnelian briolette in some bowls, and Peruvian opal rondelle, nuggeted citrine, and black obsidian chip in others. More contained emerald-cut imperial topaz and Russian alexandrite. But her favorite bowls shimmered with various shapes and sizes of pearls—a potato-shaped one, another like a black-eyed pea, and a perfectly round one like a marble. In addition to the variety of shapes, she had multiple colors: green, brown, black, purple, pink, golden, and white. She liked the rough freshwater stick pearls that looked like tiny white chips of driftwood the best.

She wore a pink potato-shaped one and stood, stringing the jewels, occasionally adding an antique pendant or an ivory, stone, or pearl pendant. She had five pearl pieces finished already, which she had placed in a velvet-lined box on a shelf. A second piano, a baby grand, sat covered with a white sheet in the corner.

This was the first glass of carrot juice she had completed since Teddy insisted she start drinking it yesterday. Her very first glass was disgusting to her, but now, she found herself wishing there was more in the empty bottom. The juice increased her energy—perhaps her body was calling for it through her taste buds. She already felt a little stronger from the medicinal wine, but still had waves of lethargy and headaches as a painful reminder of the harsh reality.

Watching Teddy, she realized that finding him might have been the best medicine. Unmarried and childless at forty, she wasn't young anymore, and lately, she had started to wonder if she would ever find her soul mate. To be with him now was like a healing tonic, cathartic in nature, and although she didn't recall dreaming about him, this felt too familiar; maybe, once in the distant past, she had dreamed of him and with time forgot, the way people's dreams sometimes slipped back into that dimension whence they came without ever becoming a reality. Dreams or not, she was here and they were like two pieces of twine being woven into a rope.

When Teddy finished the exercise, he glanced up, caught her eye, and with a smile that only she put on his face, waved and she waved back with a big grin. A moment later, he walked into the room and grabbed her from behind; she started laughing like a silly child while he tried to kiss her. He looked at the necklaces and jewels.

"They're really wonderful, sweetheart."

"Thank you." She looked back at him, smiling.

"Where will you sell them?"

"Well, I was wondering if there might be somewhere in town that would take them on consignment. Before I broke down, I was going to drive down to Melbourne next, and then on from there."

"Probably not here, due to Eliza," he said. "But we might find a store in Palm Beach, the ritziest island in Florida. We'll go soon."

"It was actually on the top of my list."

"It's a rich place, you shouldn't have a problem. How are you feeling now?"

"A little better. I can't believe the wine is actually helping!"

"I am so glad to hear it. You're going to the top."

His arms felt good around her, and she didn't want him to leave.

"I still have waves of lethargy and headaches."

"Well, I am sure they'll pass honey." He let go and started to exit.

"Stay here with me. Don't go." She turned and looked at him.

"Okay, I'll stay for a while." He sat in the corner, looking out the window, sometimes watching her work while they chatted about things.

After half an hour, the phone rang; the caller ID read "Private No." He took it in the hallway. A man with a calm voice asked if he could speak to Mr. Dollarhide.

"Speaking."

"Stern Banks here."

"Yes?" Teddy said with an undertone of disgust.

"Have you reconsidered selling your land Mr. Dollarhide?"

"Are you serious? One of your sharks robbed me! I can't believe you have the audacity to call again! You fucking prick!"

"I have no idea what you're talking about, Mr. Dollarhide. All I want to know is if you've considered our proposal."

"No, I've been too busy replacing the broken glass in my workshop."

"It doesn't have to be like this, you know. It could be easy."

"Are you *threatening* me?"

"Don't be ridiculous. I am just asking you to consider where you can go from here. We're offering you thirty million for a property you can't pay taxes on and have to maintain with your own labor. Make no mistake about it, this will happen; it's just a question of how and when and whether you'll be a *winner* or a *loser*."

"You're a wicked man, Mr. Banks."

"Do you have any idea who I am?" Stern's voice rose.

"I don't care."

"You should. My driveway is so long you have to stop and pump gas halfway down it."

Teddy hung up at that and banged his fist on the wall. The phone rang with another private number. He picked up and started to yell, but this time it was Andy Matthews, informing him that he had almost been arrested for trying to administer the wine at the community center. Teddy thanked him for trying, then told him to stop and honor the nurse's wishes. He agreed, and Teddy hung up, deflated. He called Catfish and informed him about the call from Stern Banks. Cat explained that they hadn't found anything yet and couldn't proceed without hard evidence. Teddy hung up and shook his head. Alicia stuck her head out the door into the hall.

"Is everything all right sugar?"

"I gotta get out of town today to clear my head babe. Do you feel well enough to take the necklaces to Palm Beach with me today?"

"Sure! I am always up for a good road trip."

THE DRIVE to Palm Beach was quiet and nice. When they arrived, they marveled at the historic homes and mansions with manicured edges reaching twenty feet high lining the streets. Not one cigarette butt or straw wrapper littered the grounds of the whole city. They stopped on Worth Avenue, took Alicia's five necklaces, and walked around. Due to the exceptional quality of the work, it didn't take long to find a jewelry store willing to take them.

Afterwards, they strolled Worth Avenue window-shopping the designer stores. Teddy tried on a Zegna suit, promising Alicia he would come back and buy it one day. She saw a huge diamond ring and modeled it. The sun closed with the shops. They decided to eat at Mint, a little bistro on Worth. They got a table in the corner by the opened shuttered windows looking out onto the streets, ordered a round of oyster shooters for appetizers, and split a smoked salmon pizza and a bottle of Merlot. The talk turned to her family.

"When you asked your mother to send the jewels, did she mention her finances?" Teddy asked.

"Yes. She says things are very slow, but they have some time."

"How much?" Teddy said and sipped the wine.

"Maybe three months before they have to close."

"Things will improve before then. I promise we'll find The Prince and use some of the money to help them."

She smiled, "That would mean a lot to me, but I'll understand if you can't. God will provide."

"We're going to find something soon, I just know it."

They watched the people breezing by outside.

After eating, Teddy got a quilt and pillow out of his truck and they drifted to the deserted beach under a star-speckled sky. They nudged in between two dunes, lying on the quilt together. With her back pushed into his chest, he smelled gardenia in her hair and the milk from her skin. Looking at the waves crashing, they harmonized in silence with the wind talking between them. After a while, Alicia spoke.

"Tell me about Sarah. How did she die?"

He paused, questioning whether or not to tell her the truth.

"Cancer."

Alicia looked back at him shocked, *"Really?"*

"Yes."

"What kind?"

"Not the kind you have. She died of bone cancer."

"I am so sorry."

"I am too." He watched the sky, petting her head. "I am forgetting her now already."

"No. Don't forget her. Please. You can love me and still remember. Always remember. I won't be jealous."

"I don't know. Maybe we have to forget for a while in order to move on."

"Well, if you have to for a short time, it's okay—just not forever."

"Okay, I'll try." He paused. "What about you? Did you ever love another?"

"Yes, once," she almost whispered.

"Tell me."

"It's been a long time since I've thought of him. I was fourteen and he was a few years older, a baker in a café where I worked. I was so nervous I couldn't speak around him. But I could tell by the way he looked at me that he liked me. He was a painfully shy boy, and one day, we ran into each other on the beach by accident. We didn't even speak, just looked at each other and smiled. He took my hands and we kissed; it was my first kiss and his too—he didn't tell me, but I knew. I could tell. Afterwards, he walked away and I never saw him again."

"Never again?"

"No, not him, just a shattered piece of him. He didn't come to work the next day or the day after or ever again. But I saw the shattered version of him about ten years later. I had been with a few other men after him, but I had pined for him the most and sought him out, traveling hundreds of miles. When I found him, he was a hopeless drunk and a winless gambler. As I stood across from him in the tavern with his shirt stained of vodka and his oily hair, I looked on him with pity, keeping my identity secret. I had this image of the boy from the beach as a strapping man full of character and wisdom, but he was someone else, and so was I. I felt nothing ... nothing but sympathy."

"It's funny how people can become other people," Teddy said, reflecting on her story.

"Yes it is. I am glad though because you're the one I was looking for all along."

"Thank you." He leaned in and kissed her. Then, they burrowed under the quilt, their bodies tangling as he slid off his linen shorts and she lifted her white dress up. After making love, they dressed again and the ocean breeze soothed them into a deep sleep.

The sun woke them the next morning at daybreak. Sand coated their backs from the wind, and they went swimming in the ocean to bathe. Afterward, they walked over to the Ocean Dunes Hotel for breakfast, where they sat outside in the morning sun and sipped Cuban coffee and read the paper. The front page detailed the Cat 1 hurricane that pounded Texas's coast. Teddy shook his head and flipped to the next page, where he saw an article about a group of sick hurricane survivors from the Eliza flood of the Ball neighborhood that were cured with a strange remedy of aged wine that a "happy homeless-looking man" had given them.

Teddy grinned wide as he showed Alicia. She clapped in celebration and commented that she needed to take her morning dose. She took a small blue bottle of the wine out of her purse and a shot glass, poured a dose, and knocked it back. He turned to the next page for a lighter note. A story talked about an old University of Mississippi Rebels and University of Alabama Crimson Tide collegiate baseball game where the Rebels crushed the Tide and he laughed, thinking how mad Bo would be before throwing the paper aside.

"The other day, I saw a blip on the news about a queen butterfly that paraded down the street. The man said Latch used to be a safe haven for swallowtail butterflies. Where do you think they all went and why?" Alicia asked.

"I saw that queen as I was exiting Dr. Wyman's office. It was beautiful. It's rumored they migrated after something bad happened at the Willis Plantation, which left a sort of curse on the whole town, but no one talks about it."

"Really? That's so odd. What happened?"

"No one really knows. A lot of slaves disappeared along with some people who worked at the plantation. People suspect some of the people were helping the slaves escape and they all got caught by Mr. Willis and were killed. Whatever it was, the butterflies left."

"Maybe one day they'll all return."

"I hope so. During the hurricane, a flock of swallowtails came in through Isabella's chimney."

"Really?"

"Yes, but they left afterward. I let them out."

"Maybe they'll return too."

"I hope so."

CHAPTER 15

Jimmy leaned back in his chair on the balcony at the Sea Breeze with one of his black cowboy boots pushed against the railing—the wind blew his silk shirt back as he watched the water crash on the shore across the street past Caps. He glanced at his gold Rolex Daytona. A queen butterfly headed north in front of his line of vision, and he shook his head in disgust. He hated butterflies—a useless species, he thought. They didn't create anything, they weren't like bees that made honey or birds that could sing. What was the big deal? He raised his Glock and lined up the crosshairs with the fluttering insect. He wanted to pull the trigger and watch it get blown apart; he would if he were in private, but he couldn't, so he lowered the firearm. He popped two Advil—he had taken four already, but they didn't touch the headaches, which had started last month and had been getting worse and worse ever since returning to Latch. He could hardly focus on his assignments, they were so bad.

His phone rang to a soft Mozart symphonic ringtone, which hurt his head even on the lowest volume setting—he grimaced and answered it.

"Yep."

"We have an itch we need scratched."

"What and where?"

"Get this, my wife ran into a lady named Charlotte who is a maid for the Dollarhide's and she informed her that the mark's sons have gone to California to look for some buried treasure. If it's large enough and they find it, he can make his property tax payments before the foreclosure. That *can't* happen."

"What?! Buried treasure? They're never going to find it. This isn't some fairy-tale. It's the real world."

"No, it was their relative's treasure and they have maps. And let me tell you something, these Dollarhides are resourceful little rats. Why don't you tap the older boy Joey's phone so you can track these fuckers."

"Got it, scratch the itch by making sure they don't get the treasure. Where?" He spun the Glock around his finger.

"Some camp in the High Sierras near Bagby. Bear something."

"Big Ham and I will take the first flight out tonight."

"Do whatever it takes this time to make this seizure happen. But don't kill anyone, okay? I am serious. We're not vigilantes, just professionals who apply force every now and then."

"Okay, okay *Mom*. Goodness!"

"Good!"

CHAPTER 16

After spending the night in Las Vegas, on the outskirts of town, far from the hustle and bustle of the bright neon lights of the city, the group climbed a mountain with pine and eucalyptus trees flanking it on either side on a narrow road. Dusk approached. A crisp mountain wind pushed the scent of eucalyptus through the chicken's windows. They entered Bagby; the old gold miner's town, once home to a few holes-in-the-wall and transient miners, but now it too had a Pizza Hut and a Walmart. Some relics like the Bear Foot Saloon and the old town hall still dotted Main Street; the original jail, hangman's loft and all, was recently converted into a library, which bothered more than a few locals.

They stopped at a red light behind a baby blue '57 Cadillac with fins and a bumper sticker announcing *It's hard to be humble when you own a poodle*. They laughed and passed on to an even smaller road that snaked into the mountains, where the elevation popped their ears. After fifteen miles, a wooden fence appeared on the right side; they hugged it until they saw a stone rectangular sign announcing "Camp Big Bear."

"I am so happy to be in California!" Belle exclaimed. "I can't wait to move here!"

"Yeah, it's good to be back." Joey smiled. "Would you roll up the windows, Cos?"

"Why?" Cos asked.

"It's just a little cool."

"Okay!" Cos rolled them.

"No, I like it," Belle said. "Texas is just so damn hot all the time! Even though I love it still."

"Leave it, then," Joey said.

Cos obeyed the lady.

Skeet and Jethro trailed a little way back.

Joey had notified his old counselor, Aspen, that they would be coming, and the gentle giant offered one of the empty cabins. They entered the gate and headed down a gravel road that turned into dirt. The mess hall, a two-story log building with a wraparound porch, appeared on the left with a short stone embankment where the road was cut out. A tetherball pole stood near the main building, and a tiny wood hut provided campers with refreshments when they broke from activities. On the right, the roofs of log cabins peeked up from a declining hill between pine bristles.

Skeet and Jethro didn't enter but passed the camp and drove down an empty gravel service road along the perimeter, where they parked.

A pudgy-faced boy with a bowl haircut and no shirt, painted in green, brown, and red like an Indian warrior, jumped off the stone wall and rushed to the headless chicken, holding his hands out in front. They stopped.

"Hey, did you see which way he went?" His cheeks jiggled when he spoke.

"Who?"

"*Moon pie!*"

"No, we just got here," Joey answered.

"But, he ran right in front of your car! *Surely* you saw which way he went? I am chasing him."

"Sorry buddy, we missed him. Who's Moon Pie anyway?" Belle asked.

"You must be as blind as a bat because he ran right in front of you."

He shook his head. "I can't talk now, I gotta go or I'll lose him." He darted away.

"I guess we'll find out who Moon Pie is eventually," Joey said. "He sure wasn't here when we were here."

"No, I've never heard of him," Belle said, looking around at the place where she, Cosby, and Joey had all spent time during their youth.

"Yep. That's the dining hall to the left. Y'all do remember Daisy's cooking?"

"How could I forget?" Belle said.

"She made the best pies," Cos said.

"The chicken and dumplings were my favorite," Belle said.

"I love this place," Leslie remarked. "It's like a cute little mountain retreat for young people."

"It may look cute, but it's where I became a man," Joey said.

"Nice babe, I love that," Belle said.

They kept driving, shortly passing tennis courts on the left and a thick forested area to the right. A field opened after the courts, and a cluster of brown, orange, and red streaks and bushels of feathers marched in front of the car. Joey hit the brakes and one of the boys, an Asian boy painted with swooshes of green and wearing a Native American headdress, ran around to the car window asking if they had seen Moon Pie. Joey replied no, telling him a boy told them he saw Moon Pie along the main road near the mess hall. Joey asked who Moon Pie was, but the boy impatiently jetted off back down the road, waving the other Native American dressed lads to follow. Joey drove again. The dirt path led to an open-air log gym. They parked behind it.

"All right ladies and gentleman, we'll walk to the cabins from here."

They all got out and stretched—even Dog—and grabbed their gear from the back of the wagon. The summer mountain air was clear and still as they trekked past the gym through the green grass in the open field, listening to the songs of the crickets. Fireflies danced over the grass like they did at Isabella. The sun had just left, but it wasn't dark yet, and a cobalt sky full of brilliant white stars lit the way. The path became a thin trail before reaching the cabins rising on a short hill.

Meanwhile, Skeet and Jethro were making their way through the woods into the backside of the camp on foot.

Joey led the way. Walking up the incline, he pointed out his old cabin, Fox Hollow, with a grin. The trail carried them to a wooden cabin at the top of the horseshoe where the glass windows glowed with electric light, distinguishing it from the boy's cabins around it. Joey walked up the steps and knocked while the group hung back. A twenty-year-old Spanish counselor with a shadow of facial hair and a Grateful Dead T-shirt opened the door and greeted him. Joey asked for Aspen, and he turned and called.

A tall, physically fit counselor in his early forties, Aspen came to the door wearing circular glasses; he had a long nose and his light brown hair was as neat as his crisp Big Bear shirt. When he saw Joey, a big grin spread across his face and he bear-hugged him.

"Joey and Cos, I haven't seen you guys in forever. I can't believe you're here!"

"I know. It's good to see you too. You look really good, man!" Cos said.

"Yeah bro!" Joey said.

"Thanks! You guys look good as well."

"How are things?" Joey asked.

"Great! I work here in the spring and summer, and in Bagby as an ER nurse the rest of the year," Aspen said.

"Sweet," Cos said.

"What about you two?"

"I was planning on doing some ranger work in Yosemite starting in mid-July," Joey answered.

"Solid. You should come by and visit sometime," Aspen said.

"I will."

"Nice. Do it. What about you Cos?"

"Playing ball and catching waves, that's all bro," Cos said.

"Sounds stellar man, the cabin is ready. Why don't you guys put your gear up and we'll go see Tuck about the treasure you mentioned?

Just follow the path around the side." He came further out and pointed to a thin trail off to the side of the cabin.

"Thanks again, Aspen!"

"Sure. I'll meet you here in five." He glanced at his black Ironman Timex.

"All right!" Joey said.

Joey led the group up a footpath that sliced through the brush. Trees canopied them and he turned on his flashlight. He thought they might catch a glimpse of Moon Pie—whoever or whatever it was. They continued for about a half a mile before reaching a lone cabin in an opening. The name "The Eagle's Nest" was burned into a wooden plaque above the screen door.

Skeet and Jethro, who had been watching them from a distance through some brush, happened to see the flashlight in the distance, and moved toward it.

Walking through the door, they were hit with the cabin's scent of dust and pine. Seven metal beds, each containing its own wooden shelf for clothes to the side, were the only furniture sticking out from the barren wood walls. A screened window ran along the top part of the room for ventilation.

They dropped off their bags and went back to meet Aspen, who waited out front. He hugged Cos and they introduced him to Dog, Leslie, and Belle. Then, he led them along a shortcut to the mess hall.

"So, how did y'all do in the hurricane?" Aspen asked.

"Pretty good. It was bad, but things are getting better. You know how time has a way of making things right," Cos answered.

"It certainly does man," Aspen said. They walked over a small bridge and continued into an opening surrounded by trees, with Dog trotting along.

"Did y'all see any campers running around?"

"Yeah, two of them asked us if we had seen Moon Pie. Who's *that*?" Joey asked.

"He's our escaped camp mascot. They're hunting for him. Some dress like Native Americans for the hunt. Do you remember Bear Eleven—or was it Ten when you were here?"

"Ten! The racoon mascot? Yeah of course I remember!" Joey answered.

"Damn good coon," Cos said.

"Well, Moon Pie replaced Bear Twelve after he died last summer of a heart attack. He got too excited at a Slaughter Ball game that was a real barnburner. We changed Bear Thirteen's name to Moon Pie after his escape three months ago in the off-season. Mr. Wallace, the camp owner, instructed every camper to hunt for him tonight by cabin; whichever group finds him gets hand-churned ice cream and a movie."

"Well that certainly explains their determination!" Belle said, smiling.

"Yeah, there's nothing like ice cream to light a fire under some boys," Aspen said. "Plus, everyone wants to see Moon Pie back on the sidelines and at the front of reveille."

"Just a raccoon?" Leslie asked in wonder, still trying to learn about the new place her friends were so intimate with.

"Yeah, just a coon, but a damn clever one," Aspen said.

They kept walking and chatting until they came to a small forest of trees, where they took a path down a slight hill to a timber house that sat on a small lake. The butter colored moon was big and shone off the water, its reflection alive in the ripples. The path ended at the beginning of the back porch where bright light radiated through the windows, and big glass iron wall sconces burned on the porch.

Aspen had told Mr. Wallace they would be coming over. He knocked, and Miss Daisy answered. A woman in her fifties with black hair and round cheeks, she greeted him with a wide smile and kissed him hello on the cheek. Then, she asked them to wait outside for Mr. Wallace.

They sat in the rocking chairs, soaking in the view of the lake and the moon.

In a moment, Tuck Wallace came out with a brown and white English pointer named Shadow that inspected them and Dog, sniffing and wagging. Tuck shook their hands, then sat in a rocking chair between Joey and Belle and brushed off the shoulders of his tweed blazer; he pulled the center forward around the waist and rested his right arm's leather elbow patch on the chair. His white hair was parted to the side and maneuvered back and over with old-timey goop like a fifties movie star. His moustache was clean but bushy, and he smelled of aftershave.

"What a beautiful night," Tuck said.

"It sure is," Belle said.

He paused, looking out. "The moon looks like butter," Tuck observed.

"Just like butter," Joey confirmed.

"It's making me hungry," Tuck said. They smiled. "I think I'd like to spread that moon on a hot sweet potato." They laughed. "So Aspen, I guess the boys haven't found Moon Pie yet?"

"Not yet, but I am sure they will."

He nodded yes.

"The group here was wondering how Moon Pie got his name," Aspen said.

"You want me to tell it?" Tuck said, looking at them.

"Please," Joey said.

"Moon Pie used to be the thirteenth coon named Bear in a line of faithful camp mascots. I am sure you remember the Bear when you were here?"

"Of course so, how could I forget Bear Ten?" Joey said.

"Damn good coon. Let me start by saying there's nothing I love more than my wife, Daisy. A short second would be the camp and the Texas Longhorns, my alma mater, and I guess I should include things like air and water—they're pretty damn important. But above all of those and right below my love for Daisy is the candy moon pies. Daisy orders me a case a month, and we also give the cleanest cabin each week a single box of twelve pies of the flavor of the week. I only eat one a day—that's how I keep my figure. I guess it's the delectable combination of marshmallow and chocolate that drives Bear to the pies, but I don't know what has caused him to act *so crazy*." He paused, rocking gently in the chair.

"When did he escape?" Leslie asked.

"One night, Daisy, God bless her heart, left Thirteen's cage open by accident. Well, you see, after we went to bed, he crept up on the kitchen table where I had a box of the chocolate goodness, and that bad raccoon proceeded to devour three on the spot, dragged the remaining box out the doggy door, and never came back. Ever since, he has been on the hunt for pies, doing whatever his little coon mind can figure to get to them: chewing through screens, picking locks on doors, and *even* climbing in car windows." He shook his head and looked off again.

"Why not just trap him?" Leslie asked.

"Oh, *we tried!* Good Lord, how we've tried! We even used a vanilla moon pie as bait in a trap—those are his favorite—but he didn't fall for it."

"Wow, he must be smart," Belle said.

"As a whip!" Tuck said. "We've learned he doesn't care much for the banana flavored ones, but he likes most other flavors. This evening, he grabbed a box of peanut butter crunch off the back of Aspen's truck when he was unloading groceries."

"And I didn't even see him," Aspen said, smiling.

"*Of course* you didn't see him!" Tuck stressed. "He's like greased lightning."

"I can shoot him for you with my bow. I've got a perfect kill shot," Belle offered.

"No thank you. Can't do that unless he becomes violent. Pie has devoted three years of service to us. Shooting him would be like executing a decorated soldier just 'cause he went AWOL."

"I understand," Belle said.

"So what are you going to do if the campers don't find him?" Leslie asked, rocking her chair back and forth.

"We'll give them thirty more minutes," he looked at his crocodile-banded watch. "And if he doesn't show, Shadow and I are going to track him."

They chatted for another twenty minutes and the conversation came to treasure. Joey was apprehensive about broaching the subject of contracting Luke's treasure out to Tuck since it was on Camp Big

Bear's property and he feared Tuck might send them away and hunt it himself, but talking to Tuck, he realized he was the kind of man he thought he was: the kind who ran a camp like Big Bear for years, the kind who awarded kids with homemade ice cream and wouldn't shoot a pest raccoon because he was family. Not only was he not a thief, he was practically a saint of some sort. Joey explained everything about the treasure and showed Tuck the map. The whole thing tickled Tuck, who almost couldn't believe it. Joey asked if he knew where the point was.

"I most certainly do. You literally can't miss it. Follow the Red Ridge Trail and you'll come to it. I sure hope you find it and make your ancestor proud." He looked at Joey and Cos with a twinkle in his eye.

"Let's make a contract. We'll pay you ten percent of the total treasure," Joey said.

"Sounds good to me. Aspen will draw one up and have it ready for you in the morning."

"Wonderful," Joey said. Aspen nodded in the affirmative.

At that, an assistant head counselor rounded the corner, explaining that no one could find Moon Pie. Tuck stood and Shadow rose with him, following close behind him, pausing when he paused. He went inside to get ready and offered them the restroom.

The hallway was full of framed photos of counselors and campers. As they studied them, Leslie waved them over to one. The most antique picture featured an older woman standing by a horse. She had long, straight, golden white hair—the kind that was once red—with a cowboy hat covering it.

Tuck came out with a .22, a steel trapping cage, and five moon pies. They asked him about the photo. He told them it was of his great-great-grandmother, one of the first female gold miners in California. Sometime after getting scared to death by an enormous grizzly bear that invaded a mine she had found, she decided to settle down in the area and start a school for children. She named it Big Bear, after the beast. Over the years, when schools developed in the surrounding town, the Bear evolved into a summer camp.

"My other family members migrated to Texas over the years, except one of my mother's sisters, whose family had always lived here to run the camp. When she died, I was the only living heir willing to move up here and run it."

"What was her name?" Leslie asked, gesturing at the photo.

"John," he answered.

"*John?* That's a man's name!" protested Belle. Joey stared at Cos and they both didn't blink.

"Her parents tried to have a boy for years, but kept having girls. On their fifth child, they agreed the next one, girl *or* boy, would have a boy's name, and they picked John." He paused, loading the .22. He looked at the shiny slugs in his hand and shook them around. "Of course, her friends all called her by her middle name, Josephine, because she never cared for John—John Josephine Wallace. She was some kind of tomboy. I guess we better get going before it gets too late."

They all looked at each other astonished, thinking back to the band of ladies that tried to steal the mine from Joey's ancestors. Belle started to speak, but Joey shook his head no. Considering the fact that Josephine was an outlaw, it might not have been the most pleasant information for Tuck to learn. They kept the secret to themselves and said goodbye, and then Aspen led the group back. As they passed by the log cabins, laughter from counselors' stories muffled out. They said goodnight to Aspen, and he agreed to meet them for breakfast at six thirty in the morning.

BACK AT THE CABIN, Joey lit an oil lantern and hung it from a hook on the ceiling. The light cast shadows on the walls that moved as it continued to sway; the bullfrogs and crickets sang even louder outdoors; they picked their beds. Rain fell, so Dog came inside and hit the floor.

They chatted for a bit and ate their moon pies. Joey only ate half and put the rest in its wrapper to the side. Tired from the long day, they retired. The rain fell harder; a cold air that often waited until early morning came in through the screen. Meanwhile, Skeet and Jethro surveyed them for a moment longer before returning to their truck for the night.

Joey and Belle got close in the double goose down sleeping bag on one of the bigger cots, and he thanked God for it. He held her from behind with his knees pressed into her legs. Her hair touched his nose and the jojoba made his legs weak; he pressed his nose to her neckline, smelling her. They stayed like that for some time before he pulled on her right earlobe slightly.

"Why did you do that?" she asked, craning her head back, smiling.

"It means I love you," he whispered. Her smile got bigger and she pulled on his earlobe too, and then they kissed.

On the other side of the cabin, Leslie and Cos joined their sleeping bags on the floor. Her blonde hair brushed his face as they kissed. Dog held guard at the door, glaring out into the darkness. After a while, Dog's eyelids became heavy and he slipped into a dream with the rest of the group.

The wind howled, waking Joey in the middle of the night. He rose and felt a presence in the air. The rain-drenched leaves shook in the wind with lightning strikes flashing on them in the black night. At the door, he saw two beady, glowing eyes staring at him through the screen.

Remembering the attack phrase Teddy had taught Dog, he yelled, "Dog, wake up! It's meal time!" Dog woke, his ears pointing up. The others stirred in their bags.

"Good boy! *It's meal time!* Get him!" He pointed to the screened door. Dog hopped to his feet, growled, and pawed at the door, knocking it back enough to stick his nose in and open it, but Moon Pie blackjacked him, knocking the door back in his face like a Samurai warrior. Dog yelped and cowered back. Inside, Pie bolted straight for Joey's side table. Dog went for Pie, but the coon clawed at his nose drawing blood. *YELP!*

Pie climbed the table, and Joey, realizing he was dealing with a trained assassin, went after him. Placing the crescent vanilla moon pie in his mouth, Pie made for the door. He was out before he came in. A shirtless Joey hustled after him into the cold rain where Pie sat in the foot trail ahead with the lightning around him, staring at Joey while eating. They stayed like that for a moment before Pie headed down the trail into the brush. Joey went inside to the warmth of Belle.

CHAPTER 17

The next morning, they woke to a blaring horn. Dog popped up like he'd been ejected from a toaster, and barked.

"Shut up, Dog!" Cos said. His ears went down slightly and he stopped, but stayed alert.

"What was that?" Leslie said.

"Reveille," Belle answered, yawning and stretching under the sleeping bag.

Joey leaned up, his wheat hair matted down, his eyes hard to open. The rain was gone and the sun hadn't yet knocked out the frigid air. Separating from Belle's warmth took a willpower that could only be summoned by the prospect of money.

They filed out one at a time, scurrying to put on clothes. Skeet and Jethro woke before dawn and were hiding in the bushes around the cabin, waiting and watching for the four to leave with their packs.

The guys and girls walked to the counselor's cabin, where they used the private bathroom to shower. Skeet and Jethro waited for them to return. Afterward, the foursome returned to their cabin, where they dressed in tees, shorts, and trail shoes. Then they proceeded to the dining hall for breakfast.

Cos tied Dog to the tetherball pole. The mess hall was a massive room featuring exposed lacquered oak beams and matching oak floors with long wooden tables and equally long benches sitting before them. Breakfast filled the air. Aspen joined the group at the door, smiling with his hair slicked back, still wet from the shower. They loaded their plates with Daisy's help and started to chow down with Aspen, reminiscing about their adventures and sharing camp stories. All the tongues in the room wagged about Moon Pie, but Aspen brought up the subject of another wild foe.

"You need to be careful out there. There is this one Grizzly—Chuck—that has been harassing our campers on their campouts. The forestry service warned us he has attacked a few tourists in the nearby park. Apparently, he has a fiery tooth—likes gunpowder, so pack up your bullets."

"We'll be careful," Joey said, smiling at the group.

"You have a bear bag, right?" asked Aspen.

"Of course," Cosby replied.

"Use it. *Don't* forget. Might as well hang your bullets too." He laughed. Then, he informed them the campers would be going on a two-day overnight. When they finished eating, they thanked him and filed out with the campers. On the second-story porch, Aspen unfolded the contract Tuck had drafted in regards to the Hodges treasure that might be buried on his land and had each person autograph it; then, he told them goodbye, wishing them good luck.

A group of campers came out and recognized Joey from the YouTube video. They all wanted his autograph. He signed some of their camp sashes with a Sharpie. Afterward, they went back to the cabin.

Before setting off into the mountains, the crew packed up all the gear from the Chicken they would need: foldable shovels, tents, sleeping bags, fishing rods, etc., then Cos rubbed his gold necklace into Dog's nose a couple of times. Then, they hiked out through the field past the gym. Skeet and Jethro followed a long way behind, watching them occasionally through a pair of binoculars. The group continued over the dirt road to a trail through the woods.

After a half-mile, they reached a swinging bridge over a stream.

On the other side, they arrived at a small clearing on top of a hill that looked out toward mountains reflecting into a river that split a forest of pines in the lower valley. With the sun shining in the brisk mountain air, they hiked down the southern footpath marked *The Red River Trail*. The other path went through a forest, eventually following the north side of the river.

After so many days in the car soaked with Dog's farts, their muscles enjoyed the exercise. Flies swarmed and honeybees buzzed in the air. Joey led. Cos whistled songs while the ladies tried to guess them.

The smell of eucalyptus, the hawks gliding around the valley, and the otters playing in the river reminded them of Teddy's stories about Luke and Sam fishing and running from bears. They knew that somewhere in the mountains where a stubborn wind blew, Luke's spirit circled with the hawks, guiding them to the treasure.

By early afternoon, they reached the foot of the river and stopped for a short lunch of jerky and trail mix. Dog barked at the fish, ducking his head in to grab one. After many attempts, he managed to snake out a small trout. His tail wagged with pride as he pranced over to them like a frolicking doe, displaying it to each person. Then, he sat down and ate it whole.

Sitting in the grass with the sun feeding his skin, Joey ran his hands through the green blades and looked at Belle's red hair shimmering in the rays. A painted lady butterfly with its patterned camouflage and large wingspan flittered around and landed softly on top of Belle's hand, just like at Isabella when one landed on her head; everyone commented that she must actually be a butterfly because of their attraction to her, and Cos suggested Joey must be one also because he was so drawn to her. After a while, it left. Cos skipped a rock in the river and Leslie grabbed the tail of his shirt from behind, jerking him to the ground for a kiss. In a bit, the group washed their faces and hands in the stream; then, they took the thin trail along the river as it crooked upstream into the valley of the towering mountains.

They passed a big waterfall, and by late afternoon, they reached an area where the base of the mountain jutted out to the water's edge, tightening the path along the river. On it, a small circle was carved at the base, stained black, possibly with tar or ash. Up the trail, there was another big waterfall—beautiful from a distance, but full of jagged rocks that stuck out like spikes on the wall and at the base. Dog sniffed around the area, wagging his tail.

Seeing the black circle, Joey scrambled forward and kneeled down by it, comparing it to the journal. The rest of the group filled their canteens and soaked their bandanas in the river. Joey traced his finger through the mark.

"This is it!" Joey said with a big grin, feeling the energy of the place.

Belle rushed over and put her arm around him with a smile, "Oh my God! You're right."

"This is a piece of family history," Joey said as he stood. "From this point, the chest should be buried ten feet west." He walked back down the path using his size twelve hiking shoes as a measuring stick and brushed an X across the spot. Cos removed the Infinity metal detector from his backpack, turned it on, and gunned the ground. The device gave a favorable reading, beeping in rapid waves.

"This is where we'll start. Ladies, at ease. You can go swimming or whatever. We have to get this hole at least four feet squared."

"I am digging with you guys," Belle insisted.

"Okay; if you insist, babe," Joey said.

"Well screw that, I am just going to relax in the sun and catch some rays!" Leslie said.

The men took off their shirts. Cos untied the folding shovels, handed one to Joey and another to Belle, and they began to throw dirt.

Seeing them stop, Skeet and Jethro decided to take a trail up the mountain to a higher lookout point until the work was done. Skeet tossed a wad of dip in his lower left cheek and leaned on a slanted boulder with a vista of the scene below. Jethro opened a can of tuna and ate.

Leslie went swimming in a shallow spot where she could still stand along the river where the water was still, the water cold against her suntan. Dog started out monitoring the digging, but his interest waned when he heard the splashing in the water and he jumped in the river with Leslie, who found a stick for him to chase. They made a game out of leaping as far as possible off a boulder that jutted out into the river.

After four hours of digging, they had almost finished the square. A pile of reddish-brown dirt sat in a mound. Again, Cos gunned the Infinity down in the hole. The device beeped even louder now, and they felt certain the chest lay just below. The sun fell over the mountainous horizon and the sky became less light, almost ethereal. Dog jumped down into the hole, barking and wagging his tail. The ladies started a fire near the base of the rock away from the river. Brown dirt covered every inch of Dog's hair.

"Boy, that dog is happy," Joey said, laughing.

"He smells the gold," Cos said with a sly smile.

"Ya think?" Joey asked in a sarcastic tone.

"Yep," Cos said.

"It's a shame to stop when we may be so close," Belle said.

"But it's getting dark. We have to," Joey said, wiping sweat from his brow.

They put up the gear and went swimming to wash the sweat off. Skeet stopped watching, and he and Jethro spoke about times on the rodeo and bar fights they had lost. Dog joined the group in the river; Belle covered the hole with a large plastic tarp so he couldn't get back in. The ladies set up the tents. The campfire crackled, sending a trail of smoke into the mountains.

Skeet whittled a stick into a point, turning to the side every so often to spit a load of dip on the ground. They couldn't light a fire without blowing their cover, so they unrolled their sleeping bags on the dirt and climbed in fully clothed.

The mountains got very cold at night in the summer, and the young women and men hugged the fire and each other to stay warm, retelling stories from camp and high school. When the stories ran out and their mouths hurt from smiling, they retreated to the tents, laughter squeaking out over the roar of the river.

Before bed, Belle realized she had lost the rose necklace while swimming and worried about bad dreams. Joey assured her the spell was probably broken and wanted to tell her about Tahoma, but didn't know quite how.

In the middle of the night, Joey woke to a commotion outside the tents. He peeked out and saw an enormous mound of brown fur with grey flecks rummaging around the campsite. His mistake flooded through his mind: so distracted from the allure of treasure, he forgot to put the food in the bear box. He watched the bear, praying it would lose interest. He got the Glock out and loaded it just in case. Chuck swaggered around the camp, sniffing and poking. When he reached the entrance to Cos's tent, Joey stuck the tip of the black steel out the plastic tent flap and waited. His hand began to shake and he steadied his aim with his other hand.

The grizzly smelled the tent before turning and walking back toward the fire ring. He sniffed the ground around it and then shuffled back to the trail and left. Joey fell down on the bag in relief. He immediately put the food up in the bear box and he wrote "Bear Box" on his hand in black marker so he wouldn't forget it tomorrow.

A frigid morning came early. The men woke first; Cos assembled his fly rod and fished while Joey started a fire. Joey relayed the previous night's events with the bear and Cos wondered if it might be old Sawtooth's kin (the bear their distant relative tangled with). In a half hour, he'd snagged two beautiful native brown trout and a rainbow trout and handed them all to Joey, who fileted them on a rock near the river so he could run the blood into the stream to discourage predators. The blood stained the rock burgundy; he threw it and the guts into the stream, then cleaned off the filets in the mineral-rich water. Cos seasoned the trout with a mixture of cayenne, garlic, pepper, and salt and cooked them. The taste of the riverbed in the fish lifted their spirits. They left the rest for the ladies.

By the time Belle and Leslie awoke, the hole was done. When Joey told them about the bear, Belle oozed enthusiasm at the thought of nailing him with a kill shot from her bow, but Leslie was truly alarmed.

Dog came around and barked at the empty hole, implying there was something there. They rested on their shovels, their bodies and hair covered with sweat-soaked dirt. Joey got the foldable Infinity metal detector out, unfolded it and gunned the area, which still beeped loud.

"This detector is bothering me, and why is Dog barking!" Joey shouted.

"Maybe Dog would bark at any hole," Cos said.

"But this is chicken shit, *not* chicken salad, Cos," Joey said, looking at Dog. Dog smiled. "Chicken shit." He shook his head.

"Maybe we overestimated his intelligence," Cos said.

"I don't know. Show him your necklace again."

Cos removed his gold necklace and held it to Dog's wet nose. He sniffed and ran around the hole, pointing at it with his head, and then looked back at them, barking in a frantic state.

"Should we keep digging?" Cos asked.

"I don't know," Joey said.

"Maybe it's over to the side."

The ladies came over and consoled them. Joey and Cos concluded the treasure must be a little further up the path and started a new hole next to the other one. The Infinity bleeped loud in the same way it did over the other one. They agreed Dog's gold hunting abilities were turning out to be inaccurate at best but trusted the Infinity. After digging all day on the new hole, they broke to eat and dip in the stream to cool off.

The ladies hiked around the area, fished, and swam. Belle was an expert fly fisher and hooked four glorious trout.

By dusk, they had completed another hole. When they hit the dirt bottom and the Infinity beeped even louder, they were baffled. Their arms and legs ached with pain and their hands had calluses and small blisters on them. Frustrated, they went swimming again—but the water polished off Joey's ink reminder about placing the food in the bear box.

Belle prepared a fish stew with the trout, which they ate while sipping wine, and then retired to the tents. The boys fell asleep fast—having no reminder and little mental clarity, Joey again forgot to tie up the food.

Up on the bluff, Skeet had been watching every thirty minutes or so. Seeing the empty holes, he assumed they'd found the treasure. Getting impatient, he told Jethro they were going to move in. They went down to the camp, creeping over to the holes to check for treasure; Jethro lifted the tarp and climbed all the way down into the first one.

A voice kept telling Cos to wake up in his sleep. He managed to open his eyes, and heard whispers in the distance. Slipping on his trail shoes, he left the tent and walked toward the shadow with a flashlight.

When Skeet heard the footsteps behind him, a smile twisted across his crude face as he unsheathed his buck knife and waited.

"Hey! What the hell are you doing in our camp?" Cos asked. Skeet turned, and Cos looked stunned when he recognized the face from Wild Bill's.

"It's *you*? How did *you* get here?"

"We followed that stupid chicken all the way from 'Bama. We've come for the treasure. And you're gonna give it to me." He flashed the knife with an awful smile. Cos backed off, holding his hands in the air.

"Look, we don't want any trouble. I am sorry about the bar, really."

He spit on the ground. "You're sorry I got a knife."

"The holes are empty, see for yourself." Cos began to back-step and Skeet lurched toward him, crouching over with the knife. Jethro wiggled out of the first hole and scampered into the second. Skeet swiped at Cos with the knife, cutting his shirt across the chest. Cos backed off fast and grabbed an onyx stone, threatening to throw it. Skeet lunged at him and Cos released it, but Skeet dodged it and tackled him to the ground. He held the blade to Cos's throat with his other forearm pushing down on his neck.

He yelled to Jethro, "Anything in there Jet?"

Jethro lifted up the tarp. "Just some dirt."

"Where's the loot? It's not in the fucking holes."

"I told you already, we didn't find any," Cos gasped. Skeet spit in his face.

"You're lying to me, boy," Skeet said, pushing harder on his windpipe. "I want that damn treasure."

Suddenly, a crash came through the bushes to the side of the path about fifty feet away. Skeet maintained his hold, but turned his head to look. Seizing the opportunity, Cos knocked the knife out of his hand and kneed him off into the path. The gigantic bear Chuck galloped up the trail straight for them. Cos hurried back and dived for Joey's tent, waking Belle and Joey. Belle was up fast and, after hearing Cos's explanation, got her Carnage bow out. Chuck ran toward Skeet with the force of a dislodged boulder on a mountain. Skeet crawled toward the first hole to take cover and yelled to Jethro to stay in the second.

Belle fumbled, but managed to load an arrow. Cos watched over her shoulder, while Joey stirred. She set her mouth and narrowed her blue eyes before firing at the bear's right shoulder. The arrow flew over the beast and into the river. She got another and nocked it, her hands shaking. Joey was up now, watching from behind, and decided not to draw the gun.

The formidable beast must have weighed as much as two black bears; he continued forward with his body mass swinging back and forth under his titanic weight. He was close to the hole when she fired the arrow, which soared off into the night, grazing the bear's left ear and landing in the river.

Dammit, she thought. She remembered what her father Will taught her: to play music in her head to focus when shooting. She selected something calm and soothing, Claude Debussy's *Clair de Lune*. Skeet dived into the hole under the blue tarp just before Chuck reached it, clawing off the tarp and pawing down at him with foul-breathed saliva dripping off his fangs onto Skeet's shirt. Leslie was awake and alert, looking out her tent. Joey held the Glock in his hand behind Belle; Dog was next to him.

Belle got an idea: she took a bandana and wrapped it just below the head of the arrow with the cloth and tied it, leaving the tip exposed. Then she soaked the cloth in some gasoline from the portable stove and lit it, then nocked the flaming arrow and fired.

The arrow planted beautifully behind the beast's arm. He roared and whipped around, glaring at the tents. The burning part of the stuck arrow spread, devouring the fur like kindling. The pain drove Chuck instinctively to the shallow part of the cold river, where the water sizzled it.

Belle's hands shook as she lowered the bow. Her hair stuck across her forehead and Joey hugged her.

"Nice shot, babe!"

"I told you I was good with a bow."

"Well, you weren't lying."

Cos' kinder heart sent him running out to the hole to pull the guys out in case the bear returned, but Skeet snapped out and forcefully lunged at Cos pushing him back to the river's edge.

"We just saved your life!"

"Like I care, you dirt bag. I wanna get that treasure or I'll have your head!"

Belle was already out of arrows as she could only carry three on the bow's arrow holder itself.

Joey pointed the gun, but didn't want to shoot. He yelled, "I have a gun, you bastard!"

"You are too big of a pansy to shoot me," Skeet screeched back at Joey before leaning down to pick up the knife quickly and then swiping it at Cos who dodged it to the side. Close to the edge, Cos' right foot slipped, sending him off the ledge into the river. The temperature had dropped since the sun left and the cold water jolted him. He sank deep and the current began to draw him downstream, but he managed to grab onto a loose root coming out of a naturally made shelf where fish nested in the bank of the river wall. Running out of air, he pulled up the shelf toward the surface. Reaching for a second hold, he touched something square with bulky edges up in the nook. He opened his eyes, but it was murky and the water stung them. He let it go and lifted himself up.

He gasped for air at the surface, holding onto a tree root from the dirt bank. Skeet and Jethro thought the current had washed him downriver and went for the tents, where they assumed the treasure was hidden. They didn't know Chuck had waded out of the water, thirsty for blood at the scent of his own; when he spotted them, he charged. They ran, following the river upstream with him on their tail, growling a beastly moan. They went around to the holes, and when he caught up to them, the river was their only choice—they jumped in—the current caught them and took them past Cos, who watched from the embankment, amused. The bear jogged along the river's edge, tracking them like a bloodhound.

Cos figured they would float far downstream before reaching a low current or beaching on the stony shore, or maybe not until after the waterfall—perhaps Chuck would follow, or he might even come back. He knew *they* would be back as long as they were alive.

Cos raised himself up and informed his crew that he'd located something manmade on a shelf in the water. Joey and the ladies were ecstatic; he and Joey plunged into the river together. They grabbed ahold of it but it was too heavy to lift to the surface. While Belle Leslie held their large flashlight for them, they rigged ropes around chest. Then Belle lassoed the rope around a small tree trunk and helped hoist it from above. Dog was hysterical, barking and pointing at the chest when it hit land.

"Wow!" Belle said, combing her hand along the side of the chest. "Is this it?"

"Must be! Let's open it and see what's inside," Leslie said.

Joey and Cos shook from the cold water. They dried off while Belle and Leslie packed up the tents to leave the area. The weight of the chest was such that the only way they could carry it was to rig two long limbs under each handle. Their packs were too heavy with the extra weight, so they had to ditch the tents and a few other nonessentials.

Their headlamps lighting the way, the trail took them upstream, further into the mountains. They desperately wanted to go back to Camp Big Bear, but needed to open the chest in a new location and divide the treasure. They cut away off the main path onto a pitch-black trail, which was wide enough that they could walk with the chest. After traveling a quarter-mile, they crossed an old overgrown railroad track. In the clearing, there were two hitched abandoned boxcars, overgrown with wild plants and weeds. The red metal walls had the faded words *Pacific* across the side. Another word after it had been worn off by the elements. The clearing seemed like a good place to camp, so they set the chest down and started removing their sleeping bags.

Rain began to fall hard and fast, and having ditched their tents, they headed for the boxcar. Joey swung the big sliding door open and dust rose into the wet air and thick rope-like tails scurried to the corners. He shined the headlight through the door into the dark and dusty interior.

"Looks dry as a bone. Let's hoist the chest up," Joey said. They slid the chest in, which screeched along the wood floor. Joey entered first, with Belle right behind him. He complimented her lack of fear. She thanked him, explaining that her fears seemed to be gone.

"It was sexy how you took out that bear with the torched arrow," he said, smiling at her.

"Well, I got more where that came from."

"Would y'all cut it out!" Leslie cried, stopping at the door. "You might not be afraid, but I am! I hate rats."

"C'mon Leslie, Skeet will never find us in here," Cos said. "I'll get the rats out, and in the morning, we can go back the northern route. Skeet will never suspect it. They'll most likely be waiting for us on the same trail."

She waited at the entrance, getting soaked. Belle shined a headlight in the corner where the rats should have been, but they were gone now, having fled through a hole into the neighboring car.

"Look Leslie, they're already gone. I thought you were a nature buff?" Belle said.

"I am—I just hate rats."

Joey laid down the pack and sat up against the wall. Belle leaned into him. Cos filed in across from them. Leslie entered with her flashlight in her hand in addition to her headlamp, shining the light up and down the dust-covered walls with a look of pure hysteria. She closed the door behind her, leaving a small opening for air, and took a seat close to Cos.

Cos lit a small Sterno fire and the ladies unfurled sleeping bags, using them as covers to shield from the cold. Cos and Joey inspected the chest, which had a lock. The mud on it was like wet chunky cement.

Joey ran his hand through his curly wheat-colored hair, pushing it back and studied the lock. The rain sang outside.

"What do you think?" Cos said.

Joey didn't say anything, but pulled out his Leatherman, attempting to jimmy the lock open. No luck.

The ladies slowly lost interest and began to humor themselves by flicking Dog's stub tail with their fingers, acting innocent when he turned to confront them. He was at full attention in front of the chest, cocking his head to the side from time to time in an attempt to decipher Joey's actions. Joey decided to blow the lock. He took some gunpowder, duct tape, and a fuse to create a small bomb that he attached to the lock. He motioned them to move out of the car until after the blow. He lit the fuse and ran out after them.

BOOM!

The lock blasted loose; they reentered and he glided over to it, waved the smoke away, and attempted to open it. The top gave a bit but was stuck around the edges, so he used the butt of the Leatherman to knock off some of the mild crust and pry the top open.

The ladies' interest returned as they surrounded the chest, waiting to see what dreams it held for them. Leslie thought of her father's store—Stanford flashed before Belle's eyes.

Lifting it, he shined the mag on the contents. A thick layer of moist mush topped it off. He removed his shirt and used it like a sponge to soak up the mud. Below, he saw gold with water around and between. He and Cos pushed the chest to the open boxcar door and tilted it, draining the water out. The action revealed bricked gold bullion, stacked side to side and top to bottom. Joey's mouth dropped open and Cos's eyes widened.

"Oh let me see! Let me see!" Leslie said, getting a view over Belle's shoulders.

Joey and Cos moved their heads over, making the contents visible to the ladies.

"Good Lord!" Leslie said.

"Ain't that the prettiest thing you ever did see," Belle joked.

Joey held up a bar, inspected it, and passed it to Belle.

"Your gold, madam."

"Why thank you," Belle said.

"Madam." He handed another to Leslie.

"Why thank you, sir."

Joey smiled and threw an arm around Cos.

"I can't believe we actually found it bro!" Cos said.

"How much do you think it is?" Belle said.

"Each bar is a pound, and a pound is worth about $27,200. This chest must weigh at least 150 pounds. Can you do the math on that?" Cos said.

Leslie took out her iPhone and ran the numbers. "A little over four mill split four ways!"

"Yes and no—taxes will take a chunk, we give Tuck ten percent, and donate half. Hopefully, there's no Uncle Sam finder fee other than the taxes," Joey said.

"Well, we may not be millionaires, but the money will go a long way," Belle said.

"Why on earth was it in the river?" Cos asked.

"To hide it I am sure," Joey said.

They talked awhile until Joey finally closed the trunk and he and Belle climbed into the double bag. Cos and Leslie bagged up also, and Dog plopped in front of the chest as if to guard it. Joey lay on his side, staring out into the rain with a feeling of satisfaction in his heart. Belle and Leslie fell asleep fast.

A cool wind blew through the cracked door from the outside—when it hit Joey's bones, he thought about the hot weather in Latch, and Teddy. Being back in California had made him realize that although he loved it, it was far from the warm waters and his dad. The treasure gave him options. He could go to graduate school in Miami and buy a boat like Teddy, live on it, return to business school, and hunt in his spare time.

He would be far from Belle, though, if she went to Stanford in Palo Alto, California. He glanced down at her and thought it was not an option. He remembered what Jack had told him. *Maybe* he could convince her to come with him. He looked over at Cos, who lay awake with his hands folded behind his head. He smiled as he stared at the boxcar ceiling with Belle asleep by his side.

"Hey Cos, can you believe we found it?" he whispered.

"No."

"Me neither," Joey said. "How you think dad is doing, should we call him now?"

"Let's call him the morning. It's so late and I don't want to frighten him. Although, he is tougher than a one-eyed alley cat."

"Yeah, he's got *grandes bolas* right bro!"

"Hahaha, of course! That honcho has big balls for sure."

"I sort of hate that about him sometimes though, you know?"

"I know what you mean. He can be tougher than wilt leather sometimes, but it's all a big act. He's really just a big baby, a kid at heart."

"Yeah," Joey paused, watching his brother. "Cos, I've decided to leave California."

"Really? Where are you going to go?" Cos said.

"Maybe Miami."

"*Without Belle?* I thought she was going to Stanford," Cos whispered.

"Hopefully she'll come with me, but don't tell her yet."

"Great. I'll enjoy having y'all around in the F-L," he said. "Hey man, not a word. Since my scholarship is bust, maybe I could move down to Miami with you, play baseball with the Hurricanes. With this gold, I can certainly settle my debt with the school," Cos said.

"Sweet, we could start a treasure hunting biz together with our capital."

"Sounds good to me, but I'll have classes."

"So will I."

"Alright," Joey said.

Joey looked up at the ceiling.

"Goodnight, Jojo."

"Goodnight."

Joey's new plan gave him a sense of being in control. He hated the feeling of not knowing what was going to happen next or how things would work out. He could see him and Belle on a boat off the coast of Florida and it felt good. It felt right.

CHAPTER 18

*E*xceptionally groomed men in suits and women in cocktail dresses filled the yacht club's meeting hall to capacity. Varying items for auction spotted tables along the walls, the proceeds going to charity for breast cancer research.

Teddy hadn't worn a monkey suit in years; he kept loosening the tie around his neck, which felt like a dog collar. They had been invited to submit one of Alicia's necklaces for auction after a treasurer of the charity saw her wearing a pearl necklace in town and inquired about it. Teddy was reluctant at first, but Alicia insisted they go, and he had to admit it was worth coming just to see her in the black sequin dress. Everyone important in town was there—Walker Bateman, Stern Banks, Will Burns, the mayor, Sheriff Waterhouse, etc. They socialized, and Teddy managed to avoid Walker, Stern and Will throughout the night—he was concerned Will might somehow sense Half Ton on him. Buzz had not told Will Burns where the hog was because he was afraid that without the animal in his possession, Will would never part with the reward.

Mesmerized by the pearl necklace Alicia brought, a crowd eventually gathered around it, outbidding each other. Each lady claimed she "just had to have it." Eventually, Alicia got pulled over to talk about it.

Teddy pried himself out of the estrogen-infused circle and made his way over to the piano in the corner, where a slender man with a delicate voice sang some Chet Baker songs while tickling the ivories. Teddy dropped a rolled-up twenty-dollar bill in the tip jar, and the man winked at him. After a few more songs, the man got up and exited to the restroom; echoing chatter permeated the room.

Teddy walked over and tapped one key, and then looked around to see if anyone saw him, like a mischievous little boy, before tapping another one. The sound made him smile.

Maybe it was the martini or Alicia, but he couldn't help sitting down on the still warm bench at the old black eighty-eight. He felt good, like being in the pilot seat getting ready to fly home. He took off his tie, rolled it up, pocketed it, and started to play Billy Joel's *A River of Dreams*. His voice was as smooth as marbles and deep like an iron well. The audience fell silent, mesmerized by the fact that the vehicle carrying the beautiful sound was a little too worn on the outside to make something so pretty. Even Will Burns's face became serious; he wafted over closer to see if it was really Teddy Dollarhide playing.

"Is that the wharf rat with the pet cat?" he asked George Boozer, a prosecuting attorney with two chins and a helmet of grey hair.

"I think so. Damn, he can sing. You never know what people have inside them until you see it."

As he neared the end of the song, Teddy's eyes began to moisten. After he finished, everyone clapped loudly and the piano man smiled and bowed at him, slipping his twenty back to him.

They stayed for the sit-down auction, and Alicia's pearl necklace went for five thousand dollars. She and Teddy gasped and smiled. Her store was getting better.

When they returned from town happy, the sky was a midnight hallowing blue with electric lightning flashes in the distance and some rain.

The Pearlmakers' vehicles lined the auto court around the stone fountain. Teddy parked, and he and Alicia headed to the preservation room.

They entered to Patch, Ty, and Dal standing around a new metal coffin on the stained concrete floor.

"Salt! Glad you're here! You gotta see what we pulled up."

"Is it chicken salad?" Teddy asked.

"It's definitely *not* chicken salad," Dal said. "But it's neat."

"What is it then?" Teddy asked. As he and Alicia approached, they saw the skeletal remains of a person in the metal box.

"Aw man," Teddy said, grimacing.

"Oh, gross!" Alicia said, and turned around with her hand over her mouth.

"We found the box today and it was so short, we thought it was a treasure chest at first. Hell, we just had to bust it open, it was locked so tightly," Ty said.

"What are skeletal remains doing locked in a metal box?"

"I don't know. What looks like the remains of some shredded parchment was below it. I think they trapped this dead man in there because they were afraid of spirits. Spooked, you know," Dal said.

"So, they were superstitious, just like you, Dal. Who knows? Maybe he would've crawled out of a wooden box, or perhaps he was trapped in it and buried alive, and the wooden boxes didn't have locks on them, you know," Teddy said.

"Well, they could've at least nailed one shut," Dal said, examining the bones closely. The figure was still dressed in his sailor clothes and there was a holey cape bunched up on top of his midline that appeared as though it was once red. On the chest of the cloak was stitched the symbol from Admiral Díaz. Patch donned gloves and held a light on the skull, pointing out an indentation.

"This looks like an injury of some sort—like he was struck with a bar or something."

Teddy studied it. "What are you saying, Patch? That there was some foul play on *La Gracia?*"

"I don't know. I just know an injury like this is seldom accidental," Patch said.

"Anything could have happened. Something could have fallen or rammed into the sailor's skull," Teddy said.

"C'mon, Teddy, what's the story?" Ty asked.

"An iron rigging on a loose sail swung down and hit him in the head probably. No way there was foul play on our boat boys!" Teddy said.

"Good one, but what do we do with the body?" Patch said.

"Call Cat and report it. He'll be surprised to see the remains of a body lost at sea for this long," Teddy said.

"Okay, I will," Patch said.

"Thanks, guys—see you." Teddy and Alicia exited and headed through the falling rain back to Isabella. Darkness arrived.

Charlotte offered the group almond cake, but Teddy, Dal, and Alicia weren't hungry after seeing the corpse, so they just sat at the dining table, drinking tea and coffee.

"How are you feeling by the way, Alicia?" Charlotte asked.

"Better every day."

"So the wine really is working?" Charlotte asked with perplexed eyes.

"I am afraid I am going to jinx it by saying anything," she said, and then whispered, *"but I think so."* Then she knocked on the top of the wooden table with her right hand and laughed.

Teddy smiled and said, "I told you that stuff works Charlotte. Damn wine is a miracle I tell y'all!"

"I am so happy to hear that," Charlotte said, and took a seat. "Did the boys find anything today?"

"Oh, just a body," Alicia said.

"Oh my God," Charlotte exclaimed. *"Don't* tell me about it. I don't want to know."

"Hey you asked baby," Dal said.

"A body," Blue, Teddy's pet macaw, repeated in the background.

"Shut it, Blue," Teddy said. "You're gonna scare the girls." He grinned and winked at Alicia.

"Oh guess what?" asked Alicia.

"What?" Charlotte answered.

"Teddy played the piano tonight, Charlotte."

"You played?!" Charlotte said shocked.

"Yes, and it was beautiful," Alicia said.

Teddy blushed, smiling and said, "Thank you. What can I say, it just came out of me like the wind."

"It's because of Alicia. I can't believe you two hooked up from a past life or something."

"Now I don't really know about past lives, Charlotte," Teddy said, giving her a sharp look.

"But Teddy, how do you explain your dreams?" asked Alicia, sipping her tea.

"We just have a connection to these other people, that's all."

"But you told me you feel like you were really there," Alicia said. "And I feel as though I've always known you."

"Yes. But it doesn't matter. Sometimes past lives can be another excuse for people to not live their life today. I believe each life is a sacred gift from God. If a person thinks they get endless chances, they might not make every effort to be a better person in this life."

"So you're saying people are generally lazy, and if they're given another reason to be so, they will be, regardless of whether it's true or not?" Charlotte said.

"Precisely. If people take responsibility for their life, they can do and be anything. Their dreams are their only limitation."

"I think life is a gift too, but I *still believe* that sometimes we come back. I think there are lessons people don't always learn, so they get sent back by an angel or something—but not every time," Charlotte said.

Dal came in and joined them; they had coffee and chatted for a while. Afterward, Teddy and Alicia went swimming as the rain thudded the glass roof; then, they went to the tearoom where Teddy removed the sheet covering the second piano, the baby grand. After brushing the dust and cobwebs off the keys, he began to play. Alicia snuggled up next to him and they sang standards for an hour.

In the middle of the night, Dal, Bear, and Teddy all woke at the same time. Lightning was outside the windows. They converged in the dark living room from different directions, pausing together. Bear meowed.

"Do you have that feeling?" Dal asked.

"I think so," Teddy said.

"Like someone is here."

"Yes, all around," Teddy said.

They followed the wet droplets of water that formed footprints down the hall toward the big mahogany door. They opened the door, walking out into the light trickle of rain. Across the drive, they saw a light on in the preservation room and headed that way with Mr. Bear following.

"Did you leave the light on, Dal?"

"No. In fact, I saw Patch turn it off."

"What the hell then. This ain't gonna be good."

When they got to the preservation room, the door was cracked. Teddy slowly opened it and saw a set of wet footprints formed by droplets coming from the bones in the box. They followed them to the box.

"It's empty, Dal. How the hell do bones walk away?"

"I don't know. First the Willis thing and now this. I am getting scared, Salt."

"Me too. And I hardly believe in ghosts."

They heard the sound of a door slamming outside and ran out. The barn door creaked as it swung open; the silhouette of a man with a long red cape ran out toward the back thirty acres.

"Look!" Teddy shouted. "Should we follow it?"

"I am not following it," Dal replied.

"But we *have to*," Teddy said. Dal reluctantly went. Bear barreled out in front as they followed the man who stopped behind a tree, glancing back at them for a moment. Even from a distance through the rain, they could see his eyes, hollow plugs of his former self, but still staring through the souls of them both.

"Go away," he uttered before jogging off.

"I am getting out of here," Dal remarked.

"No. It's harmless."

"He just talked to us. I can't handle this Salt, I am going back."

"Think of it like a hologram or something, it's not real."

"Then how is it talking?"

"Okay, fine, I'll go by myself! It's amazing to see a man as big and strong as you acting like a little baby. Where are your *grandes bolas* like we talk about?"

"I got them right here in my pants boy! And my *bolas* are big enough to know the difference between being smart and being afraid. And it's about time to be smart," Dal said and shook his head.

"Come on Dal, I ain't got time to talk about *bolas* with you and what they know," he said and kept walking.

"Whatever," Dal said and reluctantly followed Teddy with Bear continuing forward.

"I thought you were staying."

"I would, but I can't let you go alone, smart big balls or not."

As they ran after the man, he began to sprint; they trailed him through the pasture to the edge of a thick forest and into and through the wood brush; then he hopped the wooden perimeter fence near the road and sprinted down the middle of the barren road, ghostly cape blowing in the wind; Bear gunned it under the fence, staying right on his heels. Dal climbed over the fence with Teddy trailing him. Ahead, a lone truck of drunken teenagers swerved out from a side street and headed down the road, but the sailor was invisible to them; as they passed through him, he held a bottle of wine above his head as it was still in the laws of the earthly universe and his body was not. Afterwards, he hid the bottle back inside his cape. The truck also ran right over Bear, who splayed under it. After it passed, Bear rose and galloped forward. Dal and Teddy trailed shortly behind Bear and went all the way down Sand Piper Street to Route 1, and then over Route 1 to a bridge over a dune and down to the white sand below, all the while slightly gaining on the ghost.

As he headed down the stairs, Teddy yelled, *"Wait! Stop!"* But the man waded into the sea and disappeared without a ripple. Along the horizon, they spotted the ghostly image of a ship in the violent sea, wisps of gnarly fog were vaporing off it. They stood at the edge of the ocean, hands on their hips and watched the solemn waves, wondering where the spirit disappeared to with the single bottle of wine he had stolen from Teddy's stash in Isabella and why he wanted it?

The next morning, it was ninety-eight degrees outside. The ghosts of the previous night had vanished into the sea with the day's humidity, for it was now dry and clear.

Teddy and Alicia played with Bear in the bed and then headed down for breakfast. Alicia claimed she was feeling better than ever, and a nice coloring had even returned to her face that hadn't been there when she arrived. Teddy and Dal informed the ladies about the night's irregularities, and Charlotte claimed she was leaving if things got any weirder. She believed that they were just too tuned in to the hunt and were seeing things because of it. That it wasn't real. *It couldn't be.*

Teddy and Dal went out with the Pearlmakers, while Alicia stayed back and made necklaces.

He returned that afternoon, empty-handed from the hunt, but with a bushel of Louisiana oysters. He and Alicia ate them on the outside porch with tall iced glasses of sugary mint tea. And he continued to leave Alicia in the dark about his debt on Isabella and the sprawling estate.

AT THE BREAK OF DAWN, Teddy and Alicia decided to ride horses to the pond on the back acreage. They let Half Ton loose to go with them. Teddy took Caramel and Alicia rode the Arabian, Earful. They wore old T-shirts and blue jeans with the legs rolled high. The big hog trotted alongside them the whole way with a smile on his huge head. Half Ton waited at the edge of the pond while they swam for a half hour.

Teddy said to Alicia, "Did you know babe that 3.14% of all sailors are pie-rates?"

She just laughed and said, "That's funny big boy, but what do you know about pie except the kind that comes on a plate!"

They both laughed so hard they couldn't stop, then rested on the bank, and when they decided to go, Alicia stood, but out of nowhere, her legs buckled. She fell, hitting the ground with a thud. He rushed over to her side with his heart flashing sirens.

§⁂

THE MONITOR HOOKED up to Alicia's heart blipped up and down. It was 9:45 am. Teddy watched it with an owl's stare. He held her hand and kissed it. Remembering Sarah's final days, he almost cried.

A tall slender man with salt and pepper hair and wire-rimmed glasses entered; he was soft and gentle like someone's favorite uncle, and he spoke in a deep tone. Teddy stood and shook his hand.

"Hello Mr. Dollarhide. I am Dr. Clark." For an emergency room doctor, he was very calm.

"Nice to meet you. Can you help her, doc? Please," he begged with pleading eyes.

"We'll do our best." He studied the records, pushing his glasses up on his nose. "So the nurse said she just fainted?" He glanced up over the glasses at Teddy and back at the records again.

"Yes. We were just swimming in the pond. She was laughing and everything was okay. After we got out, she just … she just … passed out. *Everything* was fine before … I don't understand." He paused, shaking his head. "She has cancer, though." The words were hard to get out and he paused again, running his hand through his white hair and down his beard.

"I understand. I see the cancer on her chart here," Dr. Clark said before walking over to Alicia where he fixated on the monitors and scribbled down some notes. "Her vitals are good. Blood pressure is a little low. We need to run an MRI and an x-ray. The hospital in Spain sent her basic chart over. It says here that the cancer was the size of a marble the last time they looked, and in a tough spot too."

Teddy shuddered at the words "marble" and "cancer" in the same sentence, then the doc threw in "tough spot" just to set him at ease—his thoughts raced with fear. A marble might not be big for some tumors, but for a brain tumor in the wrong location, it was another story. The malignancy must be twice as big now, and Alicia was going to die. Yes, he would never see her again. Never kiss her again. Never see her smile again. He prayed to God to let him see her smile just one more time; to *let* her smile again, or maybe God wanted her on the other side or it was just her time—maybe she was ready to go home. In that case, it would be okay. The doctor's words jolted him out of his mind trip.

"Just relax, Mr. Dollarhide. We'll do everything we can to help her. We're having her full medical records transferred from Santa Maria in Seville, where she was being treated. I'll check back in later on. The nurse will be in shortly."

"Thank you, Dr. Clark. This means a lot to me."

"You're welcome," he said, and exited.

Teddy watched Alicia, hoping she would wake up; perhaps he could will her to wake if he focused on her hard enough. He sat in the chair, drifting away with her delicate hand clutched in his calloused grip. Suddenly, a slender nurse wearing a crisp white uniform marched in, waking Teddy up. She wheeled Alicia away for tests. Teddy begged to go, but the nurse snapped at him to stay. He followed them to the elevator anyway, where she left him with a cold stare and the scent of oleander from her shampoo. She didn't deserve to wear that tender flower, he thought. When the door closed, he just stood there, getting lost in the steel reflection. He put his hands deep in the pockets of his jeans and fumbled the change around. Staggering back to the waiting room area with his head hanging low, he bought some cheese nabs and an iced tea. After mowing down the package like a beaver cutting through a tree, he chased it with the tea. The cold liquid simmered his frustration a bit. He decided to call Joey again and see what he was up to and inform him Alicia and he were at the hospital. With the time change, he figured it must be around 8 am in California.

Teddy dialed and Joey answered after a few rings, "Hey pop," Joey answered half awake.

"Hey bud, just calling to check in. Alicia, my new sweetheart, fainted today while we were swimming at the pond."

"Oh no Dad, that's awful."

"Yeah, but I am okay. Just waiting to hear back from her tests until we can know more."

"Ah man, I am so sorry Dad. Hey, guess what?"

"What? Tell me."

"Ole Cos and me messed around and found Luke's treasure! We found the damn thing! Can you believe it!"

Teddy's eyes grew ten times in size and his mouth dropped open in disbelief.

"*Noooooo way!*" Where? I mean how? I mean you did? Come on....*really?*"

"Yeah, yeah!"

"Holy smokes! Congratulations man. Tell Cos I love him, I gotta do a round of high fives with the boys when we get home over this one."

They said goodbye without talking about if the money could help pay off Teddy's debt. Teddy didn't care and Joey didn't really know yet. It was too early to tell. The old man waited for hours, reading golf and celebrity magazines before his chin rested on his chest again in slumber.

This time he was on the makeshift deck of *La Gracia*, the rain glistening around him as it spilled over the wood. Staring off into the night, about to board a rescue boat, he thought about Alicia in Spain as the rain ran down his face. The tips of his fingers fumbled the moist gold in his pockets. Then, he was in the boat for a flash, and next, in a warm jungle where the sun came through a big elm tree; he was talking with many men, workers—giving them instructions. Behind the tropical foliage and near a warm pond, he sensed a few gators lurking and snakes slithering through the tall grass, iguanas crawling over stumps and parrots singing in the tall trees. He knew the exotic place must be Florida but didn't know what time. It was a Florida he had never known, still wild and free-untouched by the hand of industry and technology. The nurse shook him awake at 12:30 pm.

She led him to Alicia's room, where she lay awake. Teddy cracked a huge smile as he sat next to her. Leaning in, he kissed her forehead.

She was too weak to speak well. The nurse informed him that the doctor would be in shortly with the test results. Teddy thanked her. His stomach knotted up again at the thought of the cancer. Sitting by her, she motioned him closer. As he leaned in, she tugged down on his right earlobe. He cried, but she wiped the tears away with her weak, cold hands.

"I am sorry I am crying," he said.

"It's all right," she said softly. "Tears are just frozen emotions melting away."

He pulled on her ear and kissed her forehead.

Dr. Clark walked in. "Good morning, Mr. Dollarhide. I have Alicia's test results."

Assuming the worst, Teddy tried to figure out how much time they had left to try a new treatment. He could take her to Anderson in Houston, to Spain, to Lourdes in France, to the ends of the world, to a Godman in India, anywhere. He would do *anything* to cure her, to save her, to have forever with her. When Dr. Clark opened his mouth, everything became slow motion as Teddy waited on the precipice of the disaster that was coming.

"The tests all came back normal," the doctor said, flipping through them one more time.

"Really, what? Are you sure? I am so relieved!" Teddy hollered out loud.

Clark passed the results to him.

"Calm down Dr. Dollarhide. Dr. Gomez at Santa Maria says it's impossible, and, heeding his advice, I am considering having her retested. I find it hard to believe that a stage-four brain cancer patient with her condition could have been cured with no treatment."

Alicia's weak eyes grew with life and her mouth turned upside down in disbelief. "You mean the cancer on her brain stem is *completely gone?!*"

"If these tests are correct, then yes, she's cancer-free."

Teddy put his arms on the doctor's arms as if to shake him and then he bear-hugged him.

"Thank you so much Doc! Thank you!" He stood back. "It's the wine. *The wine cured her!* No, really, I am so serious about it. It cured her. For real." He looked astonished at her, then the doctor.

"Wine?" the doctor said confused.

"That's what cured the cancer. I can't believe it worked this fast, but it did," Teddy said, looking at Alicia, who shrugged her shoulders and smiled now.

"I don't know. Whatever you're doing, just keep doing it. I still think she should be retested."

"No doctor, I am fine, really, I feel really good now. I am healed," Alicia said, bright-eyed.

"Well, have it your way—it's really your choice."

"So if she doesn't have cancer, what's wrong with her? Why did she faint?" Teddy said, looking back at the doctor.

"Without a glucose smack test – the test for low blood sugar or hypoglycemia, we won't know for certain, but it seems she has pre-diabetic hypoglycemia and needs to be on a special diet."

"So, it was just her blood sugar?" Teddy asked.

"That's what we think."

"Well I guess the wine can't balance blood sugar, but who even cares about that."

"The nurse will bring in some dietary guidelines. You guys should make an appointment with an endocrinologist. She can rest a little while longer, but as soon as she's ready, she's free to leave," Dr. Clark said. Teddy hugged Alicia and she started to cry, which caused him to weep tears of elation. The doctor exited.

"What happened? How are you well so fast, baby?"

"The wine? Or maybe I was just—lovesick," she managed, studying his sweet eyes.

"Well, I'll never leave you," he said, studying hers.

After she rested for some hours, he walked her out into the sunshine, holding her hand.

GOLD IS IN THE AIR

BOOK 3

"Don't grieve. Anything you lose comes round in another form."

— RUMI

CHAPTER 1

In the high Sierras of California, the group divided the bounty of the chest up between the four internal frame backpacks, placing the bulk of the weight in the men's packs, dividing the weight as well as the risk. Then, they exited the boxcar.

The map indicated a crossing half a mile north—the only place for the next fifteen miles to cross the river that led to the north trail back to camp.

When they arrived, there was a sign reading, BRIDGE CLOSED nailed to a short wooden pole. The crossing was a primitive wood log, cut in half and balanced on either bank. The current rushed fifteen feet below and led to the vicious waterfall east of their old campsite about one hundred feet downriver, following the descent in the terrain.

"Bridge closed … damn." Joey put his foot down on it and pressed. It didn't give.

"But we *have* to cross here. If we go downstream, they'll be waiting," Belle said.

"I say we go back the way we came. Besides with have a Glock! What difference does it make when you have a firearm?" Joey said.

"I am crossing, we are heavy handed with these weighted down packs, gun or no gun," Belle insisted.

"No—wait, Belle." But before Joey could finish, she was already crossing.

In the middle, the wood plank gave a little, but the tree held. Joey shrugged and followed her, making it to the other side with only a little give in the board.

"Leslie, you go first," Cos said, but she was scared and insisted he go. Reluctantly, he crossed. Leslie was trepid because of her one arm—treading water was difficult for her, and if she fell, grabbing ahold of a rock would be very hard. Therefore, she proceeded with caution.

While crossing, the middle of the wood cracked and she slipped and lost her foothold. She went to one knee and Cos started to run down the tree toward her, but his weight made it give a little, so he retreated. She shook with fear, looking down at the rapids.

"Don't look down, Leslie!" Cos said.

She started crawling and a smile returned to her face. But after a few feet, the tree buckled hard in the middle—and she fell off the log. She managed to catch herself with her good arm on the stub of a limb, but the pack of gold went tumbling into the water below as she swung back and forth in the air. Belle, Cos, and Joey became hysterical. Cos started to cross the tree, but his weight sent an additional cracking through it that sounded like the earth opening, so he ran back.

"*Help!*" she yelled.

Joey sifted through his pack for something to throw, but there was nothing.

Leslie's grip gave and she plopped into the fast current.

"Leslie!" Cos screamed.

"Holy shit! What are we going to do? This is all your fault, Belle, for running out there," Joey said.

"Who even cares about that now, Joey! We gotta get her outta there, fast! Hurry! Do something, quick!" Belle yelled.

Leslie moved downstream, crashing hard into rocks like a pinball into bumpers. Dog tracked her along the ridge, barking. Cos grabbed a rope from his pack, looped it, and trailed her. She was thirty-five feet from the drop-off point. He tossed it in front of her, but she missed it. Calm and collected, he retrieved it, ran ahead a bit, and tossed it again. She managed to grab it. The strong current pulled him too. He jumped down to the lower embankment and, leaning back, managed to stop her from moving. Joey came up from behind and taking the rope one yank at a time, they slowly and forcefully got her to the river's edge, where they fell back, exhausted.

Leslie sat on the bank, shaking from the cold. Through her coughing, she thanked them profusely; the waterfall rushed in the background. They waited in silence for a moment; a hawk called.

After some time, Cos helped her change into dry clothes. Dog barked up the path a bit near the drop to the waterfall. When Joey went over, the gold heavy backpack was gone.

After some time, the four walked up a ridge to the forested north trail that headed back to camp. Leslie was free of injury, but still shaken.

The light air, birds, and blue sky played together like a symphony, carrying them through the day like a feather in the wind—a balm on the trauma. The day was unusually cold for that time of year in the Sierras, making it feel almost like late October. Joey's ears pointed up and he stopped them a few times, thinking he heard Skeet, but it turned out to be a rabbit hopping through the brush or a bobcat breaking a twig.

After some time, they stopped by a small stream and ate the rest of the jerky and trail mix. By dusk, they had passed through a clearing, and the path headed up a sharp incline toward a forest of tall trees, which led to camp about a mile away. They were exhausted, but they pressed forward.

The sun was gone and the temperature had dropped even further. They were all chilled and stopped to put on sweaters and fleeces. While changing, they heard an odd noise. Everyone kneeled; Joey raised the pistol forward, thinking it was Skeet again, or maybe Chuck even. Coming from a dense brush, the sound rose and fell like a teakettle simmering on and off.

Joey instructed everyone to stay back, but Belle insisted on going with him. As he moved toward the thicket, the sound intensified and his heart beat faster. When they reached it, Belle ducked behind his shoulder, peeking over. He moved the leaves away with his hand to reveal an old abandoned refrigerator with the whole top rusted out. He opened the door and the noise seeped out.

"Oh my," Joey said.

"Is that what I think it is?" Belle asked.

"What else could it be?" Joey said.

"Is he alive?" Leslie asked.

"I don't know," Joey said.

"How in the hell did he get all the way out here?" Cos wondered.

"This fridge must be his home base."

Against the shelfless wall of the old icebox, a grey ball of fat leaned back, head hung down, feet splayed out like a wino, locomotive snores vibrating a bulging belly and the black around his eyes gripping his head like a tight sleep mask. A sea of empty plastic wrappers and white rectangular boxes trashed the floor, evidence of an inevitable loss to the sugar and grease so foreign to a raccoon's wild diet.

"Bear Thirteen!" Joey called, but nothing happened.

"Let's bag him and take him back to camp," Belle suggested.

"Good idea," Joey said.

Joey retrieved the bear box from his pack and cut air holes in the black plastic bear box with his knife and dropped the top on the coon, whose eyes didn't even open. Scooping him up, he screwed on the box lid. They took him back and showed Cos and Leslie, who laughed.

They headed out again along the path that met a four-foot-tall dirt wall cut into a gigantic hill that rose up from the top of the wall to their left and dropped off to their right, falling down a sharp incline. They walked and chattered, high off the capture of Moon Pie, forgetting all about Skeet and Jethro.

After half a mile, a tree limb in front of Joey snapped; the leaves flickered once, and then again like it was raining. The startling realization of what was happening struck Joey and he cried out, *"Gunfire! Get down!"*

Everyone fell to the path, taking cover behind the dirt wall; bullets showered around them, the shots coming from on top of the hill and up ahead.

"Dammit! That's sniper fire!" Joey said.

"So, what do we do?" Cos said.

"I don't know. Let's wait here for now. You think it's Skeet?"

"I don't know," Cos said and threw a rock up in the air toward the fire and the bullets returned immediately.

Up the hill was Jimmy Clock, who had tracked the boys' cellphones through a hacker friend of his, so he knew their location. And he had finally snapped—the headaches increasing to a point that he was in terrible pain throughout the day, especially when he was in Latch, but they had stayed with him this time after leaving, and his noggin was full of traumatic painful tension.

Cos stood up and right as he did, gunshots from the hill whistled through the air, hammering the edge of the embankment in front of him, throwing dirt in his face. Cos startled and fell back down the sharp incline behind him where he landed on the ground ten feet down the hill—he held his arm up in pain. The ravine was too steep for Joey to climb down, so he tossed a rope to Cos, who grabbed it with his good arm while Joey hoisted him up. Reaching the top, he leaned against the dirt wall to rest—Dog ran over to his side, placing his paw on his arm. Leslie was more upset about Cos's fall than she was about falling in the water. Joey looked at Cos's arm, which was red and sore to the touch.

"I don't think it's broken," Joey said.

"Good, because I need it for baseball," Cos said.

"Who's shooting at us?" Leslie asked.

"I don't know," Joey said. "We need to have Cos rest soon."

"We need a distraction or something," Belle said.

"Oh my God, what are we going to do?!" Leslie said and broke down sobbing. Gunfire hammered the leaves and trees.

Joey reminisced about Jack and how special he was, then said to the group, "Jack said 'if you ask, a way will be made.'"

"I believe that too," Leslie said. So, they took hands and closed their eyes, asking for help with all their hearts.

Gunfire continued for five minutes at a closer range, the sniper was moving in on them. Then the wind blew hard with a frigid air. The wind picked up and a white and grey haze walked through the woods, curling around the trees, enveloping them as it passed, obscuring everything and traveling up the hill to where Jimmy was firing, reaching its arms higher and higher; gunfire continued in waves, firing over the embankment or hitting the grass edge just in front of it, spraying dirt up.

The path ahead of them followed along the dirt wall where openings of the hill dipped down roughly every twenty feet, making a passerby vulnerable to being sniped at those points. Dog led passing by one of the openings, motioning with his head for them to follow.

Joey took both his and Cos's backpacks, and they moved forward, kneeling down. Pretty soon, they made it past the first opening. They stopped and waited for the ladies at the other side. Belle and Leslie ran, but just before the first opening, bullets slammed the path in front of them. Through the thick haze, they could just see Joey and Cos kneeling on the other side. They waited and started to go again, but the fire returned.

"It's like he can see us. How can see us?!" Belle asked Joey through the fog.

"I don't know, he must have some sort of thermal imaging."

"Who is it?" Belle asked.

"I don't know," Joey said.

"What are we going to do?!" Leslie cried, her bleary eyes fixed on Cos across the way.

Through the haze, the gunfire continued in waves around them. More fog filled the forest and the temperature fell, followed by a drizzle. The gun up the hill fired through the moisture. After a minute, little bits hail fell from the sky.

"It's hail fog! He won't be able to see through this," Joey said to Belle. "After the next wave of fire, go!"

After five minutes, the hail storm was so thick that nothing and no one could been seen five feet ahead. They waited until the next round of bullets, which exploded some of the hail in the air, then they ran fast, going up the trail to the other side of the opening. Once Belle and Leslie made it across, Dog led Joey and Cos on.

When the group reached the next opening, there was no more fire as they had moved past where Jimmy believed they were. They headed further and passed one more opening; the rest of the trail was concealed behind the embankment, so they could walk upright on it until they reached the area where the land was flat and even again on both sides. All the while, the haze and hail continued. After thirty minutes, they came to the gravel road, which marked the boundary for Camp Big Bear. Haze and hail covered the grounds there too. It was 6 p.m.; they passed the gym where the chicken-mobile was parked and went up the path straight to Aspen's.

Aspen opened the door, inviting them in. They explained what happened, but Joey feared retaliation against the camp by the perpetrators if someone found out.

The springs on the spare cot creaked when Cos lay on it. Leslie sat next to him, holding his hand, still shaken from the gunfire, while Dog lay at the foot of the bed.

Aspen inspected the arm and confirmed it wasn't broken. A wave of relief washed over everyone. Aspen explained that the closest hospital was thirty miles away, but that he was a registered nurse and felt confident the arm was just badly bruised.

Aspen took Cos's vitals and found that his blood pressure was low.

Joey thanked Aspen and told him about the treasure, opening the top of his bag to reveal the gold, which glimmered in the incandescent light; he promised to send back the contracted amount after taxes. Aspen thanked him graciously; then, Joey remembered Moon Pie and went over to the bear box. He set the black box on the kitchen table, and Aspen walked over to look at it.

"What is it?"

"You'll see," Joey said, and unscrewed the top, just tipping it enough for a visual. "Look."

Aspen saw Pie's beady little eyes glowing in the blackness. "*Moon Pie!* Where'd you find him?"

"On the north trail in an old refrigerator just outside of camp. It was his hideout."

"Ha! Thanks! Tuck will be so happy. You have no idea."

Aspen insisted they stay with him. Joey refused on the grounds that it might endanger the campers since they didn't know where the sniper went or if he would return. Aspen reminded him the campers were out on a two-day overnight and would leave the day after returning to go home.

With Cos sleeping now, they relaxed with a game of poker, and when the night closed, Joey, Leslie, and Belle went to sleep in that counselor's more expansive cabin. The hail continued to fall on the metal roof, but much smaller and lighter now.

In the morning, the haze and hail were gone. Joey brought Cos a breakfast from the dining room. He expressed amazement to see his brother moving with less pain. Aspen explained that it was a minor injury and that the shock had weakened him.

Over the next couple of days, the group was truly alarmed by the possibility of Big Ham and Jimmy entering the camp, but fear of poaching the summer camp's grounds kept them out. Joey, Belle and Leslie played slaughterball and capture the flag while Cosby rested. And Moon Pie was back on the sidelines in his cage with a healthy new diet prescribed by the vet. After breakfast on the last day, Aspen and Tuck thanked them for catching Moon Pie and waved them off at the gym as they climbed into the wagon. Joey drove out of the campus, winding the headless warrior down the road to Bagby. They agreed to drive until Vegas, where they would stop for the night.

CHAPTER 2

With Alicia well rested from the blood sugar crash, she and Teddy set out on *Gold Lip* with the Pearlmakers to search for the Prince. The heat broke another record for the day.

Joey's call came to Teddy around noon in the captain's office. When he heard about the treasure again, he Frisbeed his Ecuadorian hat through the window to the ocean. Joey decided not to tell him about the sniper, but did say that he could possibly help with the foreclosure payments on Isabella with their finds, but was still unsure how much his and Cos's cuts would be; Teddy paused for a long time.

"Dad, are you there?" Joey asked from the passenger seat.

"Yes, I am here. It's no use, though." Teddy sat back in his chair and looked out the window through his aviators.

"What? But, I *saw* the letter."

"I owe more in back taxes than you can pay, and the state will seize the property at the end of the month and auction it off."

"But, if we don't give half away, Cos and I have that much easily."

"No. We have to keep the promise Luke made to donate half of the treasure to the people who helped him find it. It's the wise thing to do."

"But dad!"

"Things are different now. The legend of the diamond checked out, and it was on *La Gracia*. I am certain we'll find it."

"It checked out?! And it *was* on *La Gracia*. That's amazing."

"Doesn't that put pepper in your gumbo?"

"It really does, but you only have a week to make the payments, right?"

"Yes."

"So why don't you sell some of the land around the property? You could cover the payment by selling off some acreage." Joey said confused.

"No. I can't break Isabella up. She's a whole thing, you know."

"Dad, you're being completely irrational."

"No—we're going to find it."

"But Dad!" His voice rose.

"Let it go, son. We're literally sitting on top of the hull now." They both paused.

"Okay, okay."

"Thanks—so when will you arrive, and what's the itinerary?"

"We have a long drive from here to Vegas then to Santa Fe, and from there to Little Rock onto Goodchance and back home," Joey said.

"Nice! I look forward to seeing y'all soon. Drive safely. I love you and I am very happy with your find!"

"Thanks Dad—see you soon!"

Joey hung up, still shocked by how matter-of-fact Teddy was about the debt.

Teddy shared the news with everyone on the boat again and they all celebrated by jumping in the ocean. He hugged Alicia in the water and pressed his forehead to hers. Her skin was warm and sensitive from the sun and the sensation gave them both a wave of well-being. They kissed.

Teddy called Charlotte, instructing her nicely to prepare a dinner to celebrate. He invited everyone.

They combed over the area in hopes of finding The Prince. After a few dives, they found more boat debris—metal hooks for the sails, doorknobs, a little caked silver, and the remains of some old ragged holey clothes. Then, they breezed to the docks around sunset.

At the house, Alicia helped Charlotte prepare a meal of tapas, ceviche, gazpacho and homemade corn chips with freshly ground tomatoes, cilantro, and chilies for sauce. Teddy brought out the Chinese cloth lanterns, hanging them in the backyard around the pool. Then, he put tiki torches out and lit them. When the wind blew from the east, they almost forgot where they were for a moment and had the sensation of being far from America, far from civilization, far from trouble. The lightning bugs circled in the distance while the ladies set the table with a yellow floral cloth.

After eating and drinking a few bottles of red wine, Ty started to fiddle and they danced around the yard, spinning the ladies until midnight, then Ty and Patch stumbled out into the night, grinning senselessly.

Later that night, Dal gave Charlotte a pearl necklace that he'd bought from Alicia. She swooned over it for hours and even slept in it. She almost said I love you, but couldn't.

CHAPTER 3

The drive down to Palm Beach was easy. Alicia received a call from the jewelry store to say that they'd sold out of her necklaces and were having serious demands from countless customers, and they requested all ten she had as soon as possible.

After dropping the necklaces off and getting her commission check, she and Teddy spent the day looking at the historic architecture of Addison Mizner and Maurice Fatio; then, they dined at Mint on Worth Avenue in the evening to celebrate, sitting in the same table by the open shuttered window where they looked out onto the street and watched people busy by in the twilight.

While sharing some grilled octopus, they noticed an exquisite Japanese woman at the next table showing her necklace to her boyfriend. Her eyes smiled as he complimented it; in his eyes, a slow steady fire burned for her. Alicia saw it was one of her own creations —a natural blue pearl potato-shaped necklace with an ivory pendant of a baroque goddess. Alicia's eyes sparkled as she covered her mouth in amazement. She told Teddy the necklace suited the lady's personality. When he asked how, she explained that the woman was a little quiet and introverted, but beautiful, and she secretly wanted to be adored.

"Well, she is—that guy is head over heels."

"He is, isn't he?" she said, smiling. After the meal, they drove to downtown Del Ray, a little beach community on the Atlantic with an entertaining downtown, to listen to a live jazz band with a riveting black lady who had Billie Holiday's range and Aretha Franklin's mojo. After half an hour, Teddy bought a bottle of Monterey Pinot Noir from the bar and they headed back to Palm Beach. He turned onto Seaspray Lane and parked. They got out into the hot night, the royal palms craning in the breeze like they do in the Caribbean. Teddy tucked the star-spangled quilt under his arm and they made their way down the opulent road of historic homes. One caught his attention; he backpedaled to it with a craned neck.

"What is it, babe?" Alicia said, looking back.

"That house." He paused, watching it closely. "It looks very familiar."

"Have you ever been there?"

"No. I can't explain it." He paused again. "But it feels like home." She walked over and locked arms with him. The house was a grand 1920s Italian Mediterranean, like Isabella. The bottom floor was built out of stone rather than stucco, but it had a face and mahogany door identical to Isabella's. The features were more masculine, however: the windows squarer and the roof broader. The house was white and had a spiraling stone staircase that jutted outside and back up to a tower, like the Birdhouse. The vegetation was a dense Caribbean array of swooping green and blossoming flowers that produced a heady aroma.

"Oh, I really like it," Alicia said, looking on with him.

"I do too. I swear it's like I've been here before." He shook his head and started to walk away, noting the address in his phone before leaving.

Ignoring the POSTED HOURS sign on the beach, they descended into the hot sand, curling up on their quilt between two new dunes. Clouds moved in over the night sky and a light rain started, but they decided to stay and cuddled on the quilt with the water hitting them. When it ceased, they went swimming, and Teddy went back to the truck to get a Mexican blanket he had. They wrapped up in it on the sand and made love before falling asleep.

Back in Latch, Teddy took *Gold Lip* out the next day while Alicia crafted necklaces. The word of her special necklaces had spread fast through the coconut telegraph of Southeast Florida and she soon got a call from a jewelry store in Miami that wanted to carry them—as luck would have it, they also had a satellite store in St. Barts. Apparently, women who had worn the creations either fell in love, found their soul mate, or got married within a short time. When she told Teddy, explaining that nothing like that had ever happened before, he chuckled and said, "Our love is rubbing off on everything and everyone, baby."

"You better believe it," she joked. Their passion for each other grew with each passing day. They made love in the morning and the evening and sometimes during the day around the house.

The air conditioner at Isabella broke one night and nothing Teddy did could fix it. He even had an AC man come out and check it out—he said everything looked "A-okay." So all they could do was deal with it until another AC man showed up. During the hot humid nights, Teddy and Alicia swam, ate on the porch, watched funny classic movies, and made love—or when Dal and Charlotte were around, they played Scrabble or Trivial Pursuit. One night, during an intense game of Scrabble, the radio announced a tropical storm named Irene that had gained strength in the Caribbean, mimicking Eliza's path toward the northeast coast of Florida. That was a very unusual path to happen twice in one summer. The jockey reported that they had never seen this much tumultuous hurricane activity so early and so widespread.

The next day, Teddy picked up a whole pig from the meat market for the boys' homecoming and brined it in an apple cider vinegar and salt marinade for twenty-four hours.

CHAPTER 4

*D*ays earlier, the foursome were still out west.
They stopped at Bo's the previous night, and although the pain was still in Cos's arm, his range of movement was almost back, and they felt truly blessed he was okay.

Years of desert sun and dust had tanned the outside adobe of the Native American Cultural Center in downtown Santa Fe. Joey carried his heavy Gregory backpack slung snug over his shoulder as he came through the door.

The inside of the museum had white walls and a reddish clay tiled floor. Some sage incense burned on a wooden desk lined with brochures. Pictures and drawings of Indians, mostly Navajo, hung on the walls, and the main entrance opened into a room that contained more photos and paintings. Square pillars and boxes topped with glass cases housing artifacts and antiques from different tribes were in the center. He studied the cases for a moment; a grey cat wandered across the floor and meowed. The center was the most obvious place to give their donation in the name of Luke.

"Can I help you?" A deep soft voice approached. Joey recognized it and turned to see Tahoma, the man from his dreams.

"Hi, Tahoma," he said with a shocked look on his face.

"Hello." His smile crinkled his Sedona-colored skin.

"You were in the desert—you helped my girlfriend, Belle."

He smiled. "How is she?" he said, stopping in front of Joey.

"Never been better. She sleeps like a baby now."

"Very good. How can I help you?"

"I want to make a donation."

"Oh wow, that is truly special, dear man, thank you very much!" Tahoma said.

Joey walked over to the table where he set the pack down, the gold banging on the wood. He opened the top and took out a gold bar. Tahoma watched, his beautiful eyes gleaming. Seeing the quantity of gold, he wrapped an arm around Joey's shoulder and grinned.

"This will help our people, who are in great need right now. Thank you." Out of the bag, Joey gave him the gold Luke had promised the Native American so many years ago.

The next day, they followed I-40 to Oklahoma and onto Little Rock, where they stayed with Courtney. The rain fell so hard that the farm flooded with six inches of water. They told Courtney about the treasure hunt, and she popped a bottle of champagne.

Toward midnight, Joey and Belle went to bed on the side-screened porch with glasses of sweet tea. Cos and Leslie were still inside. He drew the curtains around it, but left a crack so they could watch the rain. They held one another on the twin bed, gazing out the crack. Through the water, Jack's church was almost invisible across the way, the lights in the windows a mirage in the haze. Joey's mouth was close to Belle's ear; he kissed the soft skin there a few times.

"Sweetheart," he whispered, and paused.

"Yes?"

"I've been thinking. Why don't we both move to Florida."

Her head moved forward and she pulled away from him.

"What? But what happened to California?" she said softly.

"My tribe needs me. Besides, I need them."

She stared at him, her facial expression twisting like a piece of paper being crumbled.

"But, you said you would be in California."

"I know. I am so sorry. I changed my mind."

She shook her head and rolled her eyes. He almost regretted the decision, but remembered Jack's advice to be true to himself.

"But, you encouraged me to go to Stanford. I can't believe this!" She got off the bed and backed away from him into the curtain like he had a contagious disease.

"Like I said, I am sorry. But I gotta follow my heart."

"But, what about us? Can you live without me?"

"I was thinking that … maybe you could come with me?" he fished.

"To Florida? *No way!* It will always be home, but I'm *not* moving back." She paused. "This *won't* work with us on opposite sides of the country either. Ugghhh! That's what I think about you. Ugghh."

"I want to be with you, Belle, but I gotta do this. It's the path I am on."

She turned and slid the curtain all the way open, looking out into the rain. Crossing her arms, she frowned.

"Well I am on a path too, and it's heading straight for California." She turned back to face him. "I've wanted to go to Stanford my whole life and now you're asking me to give it up after *you* told me to go."

"We can be together long-distance. I can stay faithful to you for as long as it takes."

She turned back.

"What if I never come back?"

He paused and said, "Well, that might a problem. Is this about rebelling against your father?"

She turned all the way around, angry now. "No! It's about my dreams!" She started to cry and rushed inside.

He fell back on the bed and exhaled deeply, wondering if he really was afraid of how much he loved Belle—afraid of getting hurt, afraid of losing someone else important, secretly running away to Florida to avoid that pain.

He didn't sleep all night. All he could think about was kissing Belle under the waterfall the last time they were here, and the painful awareness that when the sun peeked over the horizon, she wouldn't take his hand with her finger pressed over her sweet lips.

Everyone woke early. Joey commanded the wheel, driving south toward Jackson, Mississippi, where they cut over to Alabama through the country. Belle sat in the back, silent, throwing him an occasional angry glare through her aviators, but mostly she didn't look at him. He did his best to remain positive and engage her politely. Her distance tugged on his heart, which felt like a pitcher that had all the water poured out. Leslie and Cos sensed the tension; she asked what was wrong, but Belle shrugged it off as fatigue.

At 9 p.m., they arrived in Goodchance.

When they turned into Jim's driveway, a uniform white house with a crisp lawn resembling the eighteenth hole at Pebble Beach greeted them. There, as they climbed the steps to the clean porch, they could feel the neighbors' newfound happiness emanating from next door. Two sculpted ferns replaced the scuffed up trashcans that had been flanking the door. Food baskets and presents from relieved residents kneeled before the door in gratitude.

Jim answered with a big grin wearing a Henley and welcomed them in. Then, he hugged the boys.

"So?! Did you find anything?"

"No, not really," Joey said. He set the Gregory pack down and pulled out a bar.

"What?! But, you found it?! Hot dog!" Jim stomped on the ground. Then, he took the bar and bit it with his teeth for fun.

"Where was it? I just gotta know."

"Hidden on a natural nook in the dirt wall of the river," Joey said.

"No wonder ole Luke never found it. How did y'all, for goodness sake?"

"I actually fell in the river," Cos said, "And accidentally grabbed ahold of it. It was an accident! But ole Luke was there, I swear Granddad, he was there guiding us to it. We saw a big bear named Chuck who also helped out, sort of. Just like ole Sawtooth."

"Some luck, guys!" Jim said.

"Thanks, Jim," Joey said.

"The yard looks great by the way. *What happened?* You did all this in just a week?" asked Cosby.

"Yes sir! I figured it was time to clean up the mess here. So tell me, how are you doing by the way, Belle? What happened to your necklace?"

"Oh, I am so sorry Mr. Dollarhide, I lost it in the river. But I am sleeping *really well* now."

"Don't be sorry. I am just glad you're doing better. Did y'all see Tahoma?"

"Well, not for her nightmares, but we saw him to share some of the gold as an honor to Luke's promise," Joey said.

They talked, and Jim ushered them to sit for a dinner of Kumamoto oysters, black-eyed peas, lima beans, and okra. The Kumos were sweet and nutty and made them feel playful.

They settled down and Joey took the room with Cos. Leslie caught him in the hall on his way to brush his teeth.

"Joey, you *have* to talk to her!" she said, grabbing his arm.

"And say what?"

"Say you'll make it right. I have watched y'all on this trip, and you're perfect together."

"Okay I will."

"You promise."

"I promise."

"Okay, but I am holding you to it," Leslie said and pushed her finger into Joey's chest.

Jim called Joey into his room; the door creaking as he opened it.

"So, my son. How does it feel?"

"Great! I can't believe we actually found it." Joey walked in and crossed his arms, leaning against the wall.

"No, *not* the treasure, I know all about that. The *girl*—how does it feel to be in love? Tell me. I hardly remember."

"Good—I mean, it's really great and it's really bad. I mean, it's the best feeling in the world and it's the worst when it's off."

"Oh, that's a bunch of bull. Have you told her how you *really* feel yet?"

"Yeah, I mean—I told her that I loved her."

"Have you told her that the sight of her totals you?"

"No … but it does."

"What's going on with y'all? When you first came here you were like white on rice, now you hardly speak." His face became serious.

"We just had a disagreement, that's all."

"What kind?"

"I broke a promise to her. An important promise."

"You know, it's probably better to do anything than to break a promise to a woman."

"I am starting to see that." Joey slightly smiled.

"Tell her how you *really feel* and it will all work out."

"Thanks, Pa."

"You're welcome. Goodnight." He exited and went to sleep.

AROUND 2 A.M., they woke to clanging bells. Jim ran out of his room in his pinstriped pajamas and woke Palmer. They slipped on roper boots and jostled the group, instructing them to get dressed and meet them outside. Everyone dressed and hurried out to see what was going on. The porch bells rang up and down the street. Jim and Palmer waited in the truck, waving them on. Dog headed out first and hopped in the bed; the rest followed. The typically quiet road swarmed with vehicles.

They rode along the water for two miles before whipping into the marina and pier. There were no parking spaces—cars rested along the curb, going up the hill; trucks parked in the grass, creating a lot where there was none. Men, women, and children walked along the humid shoreline with big nets; the musk of fresh seafood blew in with a hot breeze.

Jim tossed Joey and Leslie a net. On the shore, fresh crabs, flounder, and other fish covered the sand, discoloring it. Their fins and scales piled on top of each other—the gathering spanned for miles, like an open fish market, but much larger. The town scooped up the jubilee of fish with nets, carrying the take to the coolers in their cars.

Jim led them to the shore, where they began filling their nets with fish and crabs. Belle and Leslie marveled at the event, asking where the fish came from. Palmer informed them it was a very unique combination of many factors that produced a lack of oxygen in the bay at certain times that caused the fish to act peculiar and have trouble swimming. Seeking more oxygen-rich water, they headed toward the shore, where they beached. Until recently, the event only occurred in one other place in the world, but now, these so-called jubilees had started happening in Southern California and Italy—although not with the frequency of Goodchance. Joey pointed out a crab trying to climb a tree, which he was able to pick up and drop in the cooler without any fight. With the cooler overflowing with seafood, they returned home, grinning. Through her elation, the sight of Joey still irritated Belle, which caused him to wait until the opportune time to tell her how he really felt.

That night, lying in bed, Joey thought that he was just like one of those oxygen-deprived fish without Belle—he was like that stupid crab, trying to climb a tree like a squirrel. He eventually went to sleep, hoping she would sleep well.

CHAPTER 5

Tropical Storm Irene was now Hurricane Irene. The news predicted she would make landfall the day after next, late in the evening or early morning as a Cat 2 or 3. Teddy called the boys to make sure they would arrive before it; they assured him that they would and they could help prepare. Then he walked out on the porch off the kitchen with his coffee. The cool breeze furled his opened button-down as he squinted out at the black and blue sky. An early warning, he thought.

Alicia sneaked up and wrapped her arms under his from behind.

"Good morning, sweetheart."

"Good morning. The storm is on its way," he said. "How are you feeling?" He cocked his head back, throwing an ear toward her.

"I feel a lot better sweetie. The diet and other things we bought really help my blood sugar feel balanced. I still get a little lightheaded if I have too much sugar, though."

"That's so great to hear," he said. "It takes time for these things to work." He kissed her hand.

"I know. I have to admit, I was starting to get sick of the taste of the wine though, *so strong*."

"I really think you should stay on it so you continue to get its benefits."

"Ugh! But okay. Drinking some wine during the day isn't that weird for us Europeans, but strange for you Americans, no?"

"Yep, sweetheart—not us, no way."

He took her by the hand, leading her over to the swing, where they sat and rocked.

"When do the boys get here?"

"Late this evening. It'll be just in time too. I can't wait to see them and examine the gold. I still can't believe they found Hodge's treasure."

"I know, it really is incredible!" she said, looking out. "Oh, I got a message from the jewelry store in St. Barts! They placed an order for twenty necklaces and said to send as many as I could the next time. At this rate, I could keep my parent's store open!"

"Oh, that's wonderful news, sweetheart." He paused. "Just wonderful. I knew it would happen that way."

They sat quiet for a moment, then Teddy said, "I'll go get supplies for the storm at the grocery and lumber yard."

He checked on the pig he had to set marinate the day before that he planned to roast for the kid's return, then headed inside, showered and took the truck to the lumber yard downtown. Buck's Lumber sat off Hibiscus Street in downtown. A brass bell on the door announced Teddy's entry and a man with a red work apron and a bushy gold beard like a terrier asked him if he needed help.

"Yes—plywood."

"Right this way, sir." The man walked like a Welsh terrier too, and if he had a tail, it would have pointed up in the air, firm and stiff. The terrier made a straight line to the back of the big warehouse, where different sizes of plywood were lined up against the wall on a metal shelf. He nodded, "Here you go."

"Thanks," Teddy replied and the man strutted off.

While placing an order for all the plywood he would need, Teddy noticed a familiar face in the employee hallway. He would have known that round head anywhere—it was Buzz Smith, his back leaned against the wall with his arms crossed. Looking up at the ceiling, he frowned. A gruff man with a red apron exited an office and got in his face, yelling. Spit flew. Buzz cowered and flinched. The man pushed Buzz's body hard against the wall and slapped him in the face. Then, he greased out of the hallway with a look of disgust. Seeing Teddy, he replied, "What the hell are you staring at?" Teddy looked straight ahead, and the man shook his head and kept walking. Due to his size, people rarely talked to Teddy in such a way and the behavior caught him off guard. Buzz hung his head, and after a moment, dragged off toward the restrooms. Teddy headed down the hall after him, catching him at the restroom door.

"Hey Buzz, I know you and my son Cos have a little beef and you stole my favorite hog, but I think we can let all that go and work together on a nice sailboat I have wanted to build for some time. Maybe you could help me on the weekends when you are not trimming trees. What do you think?"

"Sure Mr. Dollarhide, I guess so, I mean why not!" Buzz said, surprised by Teddy's offer.

"Alright boss, let's get er done," Teddy said.

Teddy didn't even have a way to pay for the boat's completion, but he didn't care anymore—he was going to start building his dream sailboat anyway for fun with the supplies he did have. Buzz agreed to swing by the farm later on to discuss the job, then exited with the plywood.

Teddy picked up nails and three rolls of duct tape. Buzz's dad checked him out.

"I saw you talking to my boy. You know he ain't right. He's been slow ever since he was little."

Teddy glared at him. "Seems fine to me."

"Well *you* don't know him like *I* do."

"No I don't. *Not like you.*" The man stared Teddy down as he left.

Driving to the grocery store, he thought about the scared boy in a young man's body, each desperate act a cry for help. Teddy considered Buzz's unhealthy relationship with his father and Teddy wondered what his own life might have been like with a different upbringing, and then he wondered what he might have been like if Sarah had lived. It started to hit him just how distant and rough he had been with his boys at times, and he realized that people's traumas sometimes leave an emotional tattoo that causes them to act against their true nature. He wanted to wash off his tattoos and be there for Alicia and his sons. No, he wasn't Buzz's father, but he also wasn't a redeemed George Bailey from *It's A Wonderful Life*. He would, *could* be different now.

At the grocery store downtown, Teddy loaded up on fresh fruits and vegetables. On his way home, he went to the marina and tied up *Gold Lip* for the storm. Not able to afford the steep docking fee to place the boat in the marina warehouse again, Teddy decided to risk taking his chances with the wind. Then, Teddy gave ole Bob Barclay a call to see what he thought about the weather since he had that mysterious gift.

Bob answered, "Hello Mr. Dollarhide,"

"Hey Bob, how have you been?"

"Been good, thanks for asking. Listen this storm is going to be a put a real first-class ass stomping on Latch, so you cats be safe now."

"Really, your head is telling you that now?" Teddy asked.

"Oh yeah, I got that feeling. You know I know. I was right about Eliza, wasn't I?"

"Yes," Teddy said, laughing. "You were spot on buddy."

"Alright, well trust me on this one too. I can help with your trees afterwards also if you need it."

"Sounds good. Thanks Bob. Let's talk soon!"

"Okay boss, take care," Bob said and hung up.

At Bob's news, Teddy crossed himself and kissed his pendant for good luck.

By early afternoon, a light rain had started, but it let up after a couple of hours. Charlotte and Alicia sat in the living room, chatting while sipping green tea. Teddy called the boys to check on them, and they estimated they would roll in around 8 p.m.; he got the brined whole pig and set up a rotisserie spit in the backyard; he trussed the pig's legs up and lit a fire under it. Having cooked many pigs, he knew he must start early to be done by nightfall. Leaving it to cook, he grabbed a bushel of oysters from the outside cooler, two oyster knives, and three empty plastic drywall buckets, and carried them to the yard. He flipped two of the buckets upside down on the moist grass and sat on one. Light punched holes in the gray clouds. He began to shuck oysters waiting for Buzz.

After a while, the old Dodge that had stolen Half Ton arrived at the gate, and Teddy let him in with the automatic clicker on his keychain. The Dodge clunked down the driveway where it parked and Buzz got out with a reluctant expression. Teddy motioned him over, gesturing for him to sit on the other bucket.

"Say hello to Half Ton first big boy." Teddy asked. Buzz edged over to the pen and waved at the pig before walking over to Teddy.

"Hungry?" Teddy asked, holding out an oyster knife and a rag.

"Yes, sir." He took the tools.

"Glad you came," Teddy said, shucking an oyster.

"Sure, thanks again for the offer," Buzz said in a reserved voice. He attempted to open an oyster, but the dull knife ran off, hitting him in the hand.

"It's nothing. Like this." Teddy demonstrated by placing his oyster knife at the point of the oyster and working it back and forth. "Try it."

Buzz worked it until the shell popped open.

"Good man."

"I love oysters, they're my favorite food," Buzz said, eating one. "I broke a record once at Cap'n Sams."

"A record breaker?! At Cap'n Sams! Wow, Buzzard, I've always wanted to do that, but never tried it. You know, they are *the best* food." The two faced out toward an open field to the right of the barn and Ton's pen.

"You see that spot where the sun is shining?" Teddy pointed with his knife toward a broad space in the yard. "That's where we'll build the boat." Teddy took out a small folded photocopy of his plans and handed them to Buzz, who studied them.

"Very nice. When do we start?"

"Next week, if I find some more of the hull at sea. And I will find more of the hull at sea! I already have the plans for the boat. I am just waiting on this money to come in. I had an engineer draw it for me a long time ago. I have to hunt the sea in the day, so I want to start early and work on the weekends only. Can you get here at 6 a.m. on Saturdays?"

"Sure." Buzz got the hang of the oysters, eating his third one. Eight empty shells lay in the bucket. "These are really good oysters. Big too."

"Glad you like 'em. They're live Pacific oysters. Most people only eat these after grilling because they're so large, but I'll have you know I am not most people when it comes to oysters."

"You know a lot about oysters, Mr. Dollarhide."

"Call me Salt or Teddy, or anything other than Mr. Dollarhide."

"Sorry, Salt."

"Thanks—well, I know a bit." Teddy held up an oyster in its shell, admiring it. "An oyster is a rare breed of aquatic creature. People associate them with food and pearls, but few folks know that the edible ones only serve one of those functions. Did you know that only one in thousands of oysters will produce a natural pearl? The pearls in stores are usually made in labs by implanting a piece of mussel shell tissue on the fleshy mantle of the oyster, where it produces mother of pearl." He paused.

"Interesting, I've always wondered about that, how they were made and all."

Teddy nodded, looking into the distance, his eyes narrowing. "People are like oysters too, you know. We can make pearls with the right mindset." He looked at Buzz and clanged another oyster into the bucket.

"I guess that's what I need to do with my life: turn the bad into good."

Teddy smiled, "Maybe so, so how about the job? What do you say?"

"Let's do it," Buzz said, looking at him and smiling.

"Good, I'll give you an advance on your pay."

"Thank you."

"See you Monday, Buzz."

Buzz put down the knife and rag to shake Teddy's hand.

"Thanks again for the oysters."

"Think nothing of it. Call me if you need to. Here's my number," Teddy said, handing Buzz his business card.

"All right."

Teddy looked off at the spot of land while Buzz headed to the Dodge and drove off.

Teddy visualized the vast ship sitting on the property. He finished off a few more oysters and went to check on the cooking pig in the backyard. Then, he went inside. The AC in Isabella dried the sweat on his chest and the windows dripped with condensation from the contrast. He walked from room to room, finding Alicia in the dimly lit sauna.

The sauna was Teddy's vision of the perfect water and heat experience. He had taken a rectangular room off the weight room, tiled it, and placed a huge hot tub, a dry sauna, two showerheads, a tufted leather massage table, and a steam room in there.

Alicia relaxed in the hot tub. Her hair was slicked back and sweat wetted her forehead. Miles Davis soothed through the overhead speakers, and the rose oil and flames from the candles lulled her into a daydream that was like a trance of waking sleep.

Teddy knocked and entered, "So you found my special place. What do you think?" He took a seat on the tiled side of the gigantic tub.

"Oh, I love it, baby. It's *so* relaxing."

"The sweating is good for your immune system and eliminating toxins," he said. "I'll give you a massage when you get out."

"Oh, do I *have to*?"

"It's too much for me to take. I am getting in with you, baby." Teddy removed his clothes and hopped in naked.

"Come on in," she motioned with her hands.

He eased into the hot water.

"This is so relaxing on my muscles." He sat on the underwater bench across from her. He found her wet hair attractive.

"So, who were you talking to outside?"

"A young man named Buzz. He's going to help me with a new project."

"How do you know him?"

"He's that boy who stole Half Ton."

"*What?* You're going to let *him* back here?" she asked, shocked.

"He's a good boy. I can see it in his eyes. He just has a bad father."

"What project?"

"I am going to build a gigantic wooden sailboat." He held his arms sideways.

"Really?" Her eyes widened. "That's great. Can we sail it to St. Barts and sleep on the beach? I haven't been able to stop thinking about it since Palm Beach."

"It's been on my mind all day. Sure, we can take it there. If I have the money," he said. They smiled at each other, wondering when the next time would be. Teddy's attraction to her was rugged, unmanageable, beautifully complex.

"Did you make any necklaces today?"

"Yes. I am making them so much better than I used to. It's amazing!"

"That's great. I can't wait to see them."

She swam over to him, wrapped her flushed wet arms around his long shoulders, and kissed him, placing her bottom lip in his mouth. Then, she sat next to him, rubbing his chest with her fingers. He tried to pull her back, but she purred and gently pushed him away.

"Tell me about this debt on the house? I overheard you on the boat the other day through the window, talking on the phone with Joey." His arms were splayed on the mantle outside the tub.

"I don't want to talk about it."

"No, tell me. I need to know what's bothering you."

"Why?"

"Because I love you," She backed off a bit. "I care about you. You can't be like this, always acting strong. You have to share your troubles with me. That's what a relationship is."

"But then you'll worry."

"So, we worry together. We laugh and we cry, but we do it together as a team," she insisted and he softened a little.

"Okay, you're right. Well, it's really bad."

"How bad? Tell me." She moved closer from the side and brushed his wet hair back.

He exhaled and adjusted the pendant on his wet chest. She straddled his lap and brushed the sweat off his forehead with her fingers.

"It's okay, baby. You can tell me anything. I am totally open to you. It's safe."

"Okay ... I owe a bloody hell in back taxes."

"Oh no," she said. "That *is so* bad baby."

"I know. My uncle's trust finally ran out a while ago. I could break the land up and sell some lots, but I promised Sarah I would never do that."

"But she would understand now."

"I know, but I don't want to."

"Well that's honorable, but circumstances change things. If you don't pay it, what happens?"

"The state will foreclose on me, probably."

"How long?"

"Five days."

"*Five days!* Until?"

"Eviction."

"You *must* sell some land right away. Call the agent now!" She moved off him.

"No, sweetheart. I'll find something within that time. Every day is a possible day for the hull of *La Gracia* to reveal her splinters of light to me." In his eyes, she saw a conviction that concerned her.

"You're crazy," she said, wading around the bubbling water. "You would lose it all to save your pride."

"No, it's not about pride."

"Then what is it?"

"I just know I'll find it. I have a feeling. The time doesn't matter."

"*In five days!* I hope you're right."

"I am."

She floated back to the other wall and leaned back, relaxing.

"So how does it feel to be cured?"

"You're changing the subject."

"I know."

She paused. "Well, okay then, *it's wonderful*. I feel reborn. After facing death, you're different forever. Everything is new. Doctors and nurses know about it because they see it every day, but ordinary people don't know unless they or someone they love gets sick and then gets well."

"Please give me an example of what you mean."

"Every breath is a precious gift from God. Every moment is a blessing. I won't take life or the people I care about for granted. I won't take *you* for granted."

"Nor I you, angel—I love you," Teddy said.

After twenty minutes of floating, Teddy gave her a massage on the table. Between the hot water and the rub, she fell asleep. He let her rest and took a shower in the room, then he got dressed and went out back to check on the pig.

CHAPTER 6

That evening, Alicia and Charlotte prepared mashed potatoes with gravy, corn on the cob, and a big field salad with walnuts and a vinaigrette dressing. Alicia glowed with well-being and love. The ladies got in a small food fight in the kitchen with the potatoes and couldn't stop laughing. Afterward, they set the porch table with a stark white tablecloth and lit candles on it, big fat ones and tall lean ones, buff beeswax ones. Teddy lit the Chinese lanterns again and the tiki torches, and added additional tikis along the whole front driveway under the tall palms to welcome the boys home.

Dal arrived dressed in white linen pants, black leather sandals, and a matching button-up with the sleeves rolled up. His gold diver watch wrapped around his ebony wrist. When Dal came in, Charlotte wrapped her arms around him and kissed him. She had on Alicia's pearl necklace. He smiled and then turned to go outside, but she reeled him back, giggling, and whispered in his ear, "I love you."

"But I thought we didn't use that word," he said and pulled her hands up, holding onto them tightly in the air.

"That was a stupid rule," Charlotte said looking deep in his eyes.

"Yes it was. I love you too, babe," Dal whispered.

As dusk approached, Cos called, informing Teddy that they were thirty miles out.

The porch smelled strongly of the cooking pig. Charlotte and Alicia put the finishing touches on the meal while Teddy and Dal drank a glass of Pinot Noir and pretended to monitor the spit. Around eight, they heard the familiar sound of shells grinding together under the weight of turning rubber. Teddy smiled when he saw the chicken covered in dead bugs and black gasoline dust as it breezed past the gate door. Cos hit the horn as they approached. The car stopped and they got out like fat men popping out of tight pants. Dog ran a lap around the land, searching the perimeter for dinner.

Teddy greeted his sons with big hugs and a huge smile, wearing a white cotton shirt with all the buttons fastened, his pendant still visible through the opening. He said hello to the ladies, congratulating them all.

"What on God's green earth happened to its head?" Teddy asked, searching for answers.

"Nothing really," Cos said with his hands on his hips. "It's in the car. Got knocked off out west. Can you help us put it back on pop?"

Teddy shook his head at the explanation. "Boys, boys, boys." He paused, studying them. "I am not going to touch this. Not this time. Just get this car cleaned up nicely. You can do it with the stuff in my shop. I reckon you could weld it back on for certain. Come into the backyard." He led them through the gate. "We have a pig cooking."

"I smell it. Sweet!" Joey said.

Joey and Cos had their packs slung over their shoulders—Belle and Leslie carried the cooler with the fish from the jubilee. They set the packs and cooler down on the stone back porch. Joey unloaded one of the Gregory backpacks, pulling out a gold bar, which he handed to Teddy.

Teddy held it in his palm, studying it with a keen eye. Then, he floated his hand up and down to feel the weight. "Well, it's about a pound of straight bullion." He paused. "How much was in the chest? Was it just the one?"

"One chest with probably over a hundred and fifty of these. It weighed a bloody hell, but we lost one of the packs on the trail back to camp," Cos remarked.

"I can't believe y'all actually did it!" Teddy's eyes sparkled. "You're giving half back to the Native Americans, correct? Some kind of institution to help their people. To keep Luke's promise, right?"

"Yep, we already found a center in Santa Fe and donated half of all the treasure."

"Good for y'all. Remember, nothing given is ever lost. It's our duty. And you should be thankful for your blessing."

"Thanks, Dad. We are," Joey said.

"Are you ladies happy with this?"

"Yes, sir!" Belle said. Her face lit up, watching him remove the gold. Her mood had greatly improved, although she was still ice water toward Joey.

"I think you girls are good luck. Pearlmakers like us." He paused. "Thanks for taking care of my boys. They didn't bother you too much, did they?"

"No, sir. They were gentlemen," Leslie answered.

"Good."

Teddy noticed the cooler. "Well, what's in the cooler?"

"Fresh fish from a jubilee in 'Bama," Cos said.

"You hit a jub, too?"

"Yep!"

"Hot damn! Y'all need to go treasure hunting with me now," Teddy said. "Luck is on your side. We got plenty of food prepared, so we'll freezer the fish and eat it soon. Dal, would you mind taking it to the garage?"

"Sure thing, Salt." Dal stood.

"Thanks." He paused as Dal lifted the cooler. "Y'all got back just in time. Hurricane Irene will touch down the day after tomorrow," Teddy said, slicking his hand through his hair.

"Yeah, we heard about it on the radio," Joey said.

"I just can't believe there's another 'cane coming!" Leslie exclaimed.

"I know, I know it," Teddy said.

Alicia walked out with the last plate for the table. When Teddy saw her, he motioned her over.

"I want y'all to meet my girlfriend, Alicia I told you about."

Alicia swished over and kissed them twice, once on each cheek. "It's so nice to meet you. I've heard *so much* about you all."

"So nice to meet you too, Alicia," Joey said.

"Nice to meet you," Cos, Belle and Leslie all said.

"So what caused y'all to get together?" Leslie asked.

Teddy watched Alicia with his arm around her, rubbing her shoulder.

"Let's just say we have a long history together," Alicia replied with a twinkle in her eye.

"Can you convince him to start wearing shirts in public again?" Joey said. "That would be a huge relief."

"Don't push your luck, Joey," she said, smiling.

"Give me a little credit. I've already starting wearing nice shirts and shoes again," Teddy gestured to his shirt. "*And* cologne."

"I think he puts a little bit of scotch on his wrists and calls that cologne," Alicia said and laughed.

He rubbed his nose to hers and then turned back to them, "So who's hungry?" Teddy boomed.

They all said "me" and took a seat around the table.

"One moment—I have a surprise," Teddy said. Going inside, he returned with a big bowl of shucked Louisiana oysters, seven shot glasses, cocktail sauce, cayenne pepper, minced garlic, lemon wedges, soy sauce, and a bottle of Tabasco. With the ingredients, he made Louisiana Charlie Wobbles—an oyster shot named after a famous oyster shucker from the 50s who worked at the St. Charles Street Cafe in New Orleans—and then passed them around.

"A Charlie Wobble shot to celebrate. Cheers!" Teddy said and everyone knocked one back together.

Teddy sat, smiling. "Please tell me what else happened in California. I want to know everything."

"Oh, I almost forgot," Joey said; he got up and removed the Moringa oil, seeds, and powder Bo gave him from the backpack.

Then, he handed them to Teddy. "Bo wanted you to have this. It's a plant called Moringa—apparently it's the most nutrient-dense plant in the world, capable of helping malnutrition."

Teddy studied the powder and smelled it.

"It's the most nutrient-dense plant in the world? Can't believe I haven't heard of it."

"That's what we said," Belle said.

"Can it grow in arid conditions?" Teddy asked.

"Yes, that's what Bo says," Joey said.

"Well, better late than never. I'll talk to him about it in depth. Thank you," he said. "Now tell me what else happened on the trip."

Charlotte came out with a bottle of red wine and filled the glasses. "Hey everyone," she said, and winked at Dal.

"There was a bear we had to get away from named Chuck, just like Ole Sawtooth!" Joey said.

"A bear! Just like Luke! I told y'all to be careful," Teddy roared. "What else? Tell me, how's Jim's gold making coming along?"

"Good, because he's done with it," Cos said, waving his arm in a sideways karate chop.

"*What?*" Teddy bellowed, almost exploding.

"That's what he says. He baked one last bad nugget and stopped. Finished construction on his house, too," Joey said.

"Finished that damn place!? I'll never believe it, really. Never!" He grinned, almost crying now. "What about Bo, how is he?"

"He's good too," Joey said.

"Oh good. How was the drive through the desert?"

"It was beautiful, especially around Santa Fe," Belle commented. "I slept *so well* there!"

"I love the drive out west," Charlotte added. "So wide open."

"Yes, so wide open," Teddy said. "Did anything else happen?"

"Well, yeah. Two guys tried to steal the treasure from us in the Sierras and that turned out okay, but someone fired at us on the trail back to camp and Cos had a bad fall," Joey said.

Cos nudged him under the table. "Why did you have to say that."

Teddy's expression changed. He lowered his glass and leaned forward, "*Fired?*"

"Shot," Joey squeaked, glancing at Teddy and looking back down in his lap while twiddling his napkin.

"It was nothing, Dad; I've had worse falls surfing. C'mon!" Cos remarked.

"Who was it?" Teddy demanded.

"We don't know. We escaped through a fog hail storm."

"Why didn't you tell me *right away?*" Teddy's voice rose.

"Because we knew you would overreact! It's no big deal. We got the treasure and I only have a bruise!" Cos asked. "We got out, clean slate."

"Yeah, but you could have been killed! Belle or Leslie could have been hurt, dammit!" Teddy got up and paced around the porch. "I wonder if the land sharks here could have had anything to do with this. I just wonder." Teddy paused, staring out toward the pool with his hands on his hips. "I told y'all those bastards stole that chest of gold we found. But it would be strange if the sharks went after y'all though. I mean how would they even know, right?"

"What sharks?" Belle asked.

"Land sharks. Bateman and Banks," Teddy said, craning his head enough to connect with her eyes before looking back at the pool. "The real estate company hired a gun to make me sell, but I refused. Maybe I shouldn't have. My love for this house is nothing compared to my love of my family. I've been a fool." Teddy hung his head.

Belle stared down, concerned, but said nothing.

"What are you going to do, Dad? What should *we* do?" Joey asked. Teddy turned and faced them.

"Keep a watch out for anything suspicious. The important thing is that y'all are safe. I will unlock the firearm case in my office. If someone comes, get a piece and call the police. I will call Catfish and report it now."

"Okay, Dad," they said.

Dal and Teddy went to get the pig. Dog and Bear circled around it for a handout. They cut off big chunks of the pork and placed them

GOLD IS IN THE AIR

on a serving platter, throwing scraps to the animals before passing the meat around the table. Teddy lightened back up; after a glass of wine, Joey and Belle loosened up a little around each other. Cos and Leslie stuck with sweet iced tea. Everyone at the table had firsts and seconds, and even third servings of the greasy pig. The boys went on to tell about their trip to see Teddy's brother, Bo, and his pet iguana, Popeye, and how he gave them the missing journal containing the key map, which marked the spot where the treasure was. They also relayed everything about Camp Big Bear and the racoon mascot, Moon Pie, and how they met with the camp's owner, Tuck Wallace, and created a contract with him giving them permission to hunt for treasure on Big Bear's land, offering him 10% of anything they might find. Teddy told them again about how ole Buzz Smith stole Half Ton, but that they were now working together after Teddy discovered Buzz's father was abusive. Leslie confirmed Buzz's father was a lunatic but that Buzz had a good heart, she thought. That was why she had dated him.

They asked Teddy how they could file the treasure, and Teddy offered to do it on their behalf, pay the taxes, and distribute the money in cuts, sending Tuck Wallace his share as well. The ladies trusted him and agreed. Teddy said he would call Catfish in the morning about the shooting in the Sierras.

He inquired as to what each would do with their take: Belle said she would finance her college tuition to Stanford, which saddened Joey, who said he would give all the money to Teddy to help with his taxes. Cos said he would pay the school back and help Teddy with the rest. Leslie wanted to give a lot to her parents to help Gooch's—and she also volunteered a portion to help Teddy. Alicia and Charlotte assured them their plans were noble; Teddy thanked them and toasted to all of their good fortune despite his financial woes.

When they finished eating, Dal opened the louvered doors and rolled out the baby grand piano from the den. Teddy smiled.

"Alicia told me you were playing again; haven't heard that sweet voice since Miami, Salt. Play something for us."

Teddy sat and started tickling a Smokey Robinson song.

"Good choice, Salt—Old Smoke, I love it!" Cos said.

Everyone started to dance as Teddy's voice filled the backyard. The wine had loosened Belle up. She danced with Dal and then Charlotte, and finally began to dance with Joey, with a reserved smile. She wore a white polo dress that cut just above her knees, showing off her legs and hugging her butt tightly—not too tight to be inappropriate, but just snug enough to drive Joey crazy when she moved. Her auburn hair was pinned up with two chopsticks in the back. And when she touched his shoulder, he thought she was on the way back to him. He moved her closer, but she pushed him away, insisting she had to go. Leslie said she needed to go too, and kissed Cos goodbye. They pulled on each other's right earlobes and watching them caused Alicia smile. Joey tried to follow Belle when she left, but she got in her Cherokee with Leslie, and this time she was not crying like she had done in Montana—she was angry.

Belle and Leslie left; Teddy, Alicia, Charlotte, Dal, Dog, and the boys went swimming in the pool. When they retired, it felt good to sleep in their own beds.

Teddy and Alicia knocked on Joey's door to the tree house, and he invited them in. Sadness misted the room. They pulled chairs up next to his bed. He lay on his back with his hands behind his head.

"Hey Son," Teddy said. "Alicia and I want to talk with you."

"I know we just met, Joey, but your dad and I can tell you're upset. Do you mind telling us what happened?"

"Belle wants to go to school in California, and I miss Florida." He looked at Alicia.

"What are you going to do?" Teddy asked.

"I don't know," Joey mustered.

"Agree to go with her, and maybe you can have Florida and California."

"How?"

"Who knows. See what happens. *Go for it all,*" Alicia said.

"She's right, Son; trust your instinct," Teddy said.

"Thanks, guys."

"Anytime. I got this for you to give to her." Alicia presented a pearl necklace; Teddy smiled.

Joey was speechless. "Wow, thanks Alicia, she's going to love it," he said, still uncertain that he would ever have a chance to give it to her.

"You're welcome. Get a good night sleep now. Tomorrow things will look different. Emotions are like the weather. They change constantly."

"Thanks, Alicia; that's a good analogy."

"She's right, Son. Every day, things are different," Teddy said. "Now get some rest."

"Thanks, Dad; goodnight," Joey said.

They exited and Joey placed the necklace in the bedside table before falling asleep.

CHAPTER 7

A baby blue sky puffed up with cotton-ball clouds and a burning sun that poked through them to hover above Joey and Wolly—Joey and Cosby's friend and teammate—as they played ball in the field to the right of the barn. Half Ton retrieved the hits for them. Cos walked up with wet hair sticking to his forehead, Dog jogging alongside with his tongue hanging out, his warm body dripping wet with the sea.

"Those are some salty dogs right there," Joey said at their approach.

"One *rich* salty dog!" Wolly added.

"Hey Wol!"

"How were those waves man?"

"Good, I am taking it really easy with the arm. Leslie joined us; I am teaching her how to surf and she loves it. We're both one-armed now."

"Ha! How does the arm feel?" Joey said.

"Pretty good. It's still a little sore."

"Good."

"I heard y'all got shot at?!" Wol said.

"Yeah, it was so crazy."

"Are you fixing the chicken today?" Joey asked.

"Yeah, and then I am taking it to Dan's."

"Hopefully he won't notice. Are you going to quit today?" Joey asked.

"No, I'll wait until next week."

"I knew you'd never quit," Wolly said.

"Next week—you just wait and see," Cos said.

"Sure," Wolly remarked.

Cos smiled and left to go put his board up. He walked over to the Dog House to spend the first part of the day repairing the top of chicken head and patching the bullet holes in the tail. When he finished, he changed the oil and washed the car with a hose and soap. Standing back, he admired how the body shone in the sunlight. *Good as new*, he thought.

Next, he dressed in the red polo shirt with the chicken head patch over the heart. The shirt was hard to get on, like it had shrunk in the wash. He put on the matching visor with *Dan's* in yellow cursive across the front. On the way to work, he stopped by a Firestone store and got the brake pads replaced and swapped the spare tire for a brand new tire and spare. He prayed Dan wouldn't notice the extra miles, the new weld job on the roof, or the Bondo on the pieces of the tail.

When he pulled in, Dan spotted him from inside the store and stormed out to the driver's window.

"Where the hell have you been, boy?" he shouted. His eyebrows hawked forward as he leaned into the window. Cos was afraid of Dan because he was a live wire and there *always* seemed to be water nearby. He'd never liked him, but he always had a certain level of respect for him—or was it fear, he wondered, looking at Dan's shiny pug nose and cascading chins.

"Answer me, boy!" Dan shook with anger. Watching him, Cos realized he didn't feel fear anymore, only sympathy.

"I told you I was taking two weeks off."

"Two weeks, not two and a half weeks." Dan grabbed him by his shirt, his hands shaking with adrenaline. "Bill quit on me and I had no other car. I called you a billion times. Do you have any brains in that big empty head of yours or are you too busy riding that stupid board with that dumb fleabag, you surfer freak!"

"I am sorry about the extra couple of days. I got sick."

"You think I am dumb, don'tcha?" Droplets of spit flew from Dan's mouth and splattered on Cos's face. Cos leaned back, but Dan's fingers gripped his shirt tighter, pulling him closer.

"Look, I said I am sorry, Dan, chill out, man!"

Dan was about to punch him, but the fear of a story in *The Grapevine* stopped him—landing on the front page would devastate his business. He loosened his grip and stood up, holding out his hand.

"Give me my keys and get inside. I want you to get to work on the dishes."

Cos got out of the car and held the keys out in front of him. "I quit. I've taken this abuse for long enough."

"Oh my *goodness!* You can't quit on me! You're fired!" Dan threw his arm in the air like an umpire calling an out. "As a matter of fact, give me my damn keys, you little prick!" As Dan's wide arm swung out for the keys, Cos dropped them on the ground and Dan's face lit up; he tightened his big fists and charged toward Cos. Bad press or not, he was going to hit him. Cos ran off and Dan followed, but his weight was no match for Cos's teenage fitness. After wobbling fifty feet, he stopped to catch his breath, leaning hard on his knees. While running, Cos heard a sound he had never imagined could come from Dan. Could it be? Could it actually be *sobbing?* Cos stopped at the edge of the parking lot and looked back to see Dan kneeling in the lot with tears pouring from his eyes, his whole upper body shaking. At first Cos thought it was a bluff, so he approached with caution, but the wailing continued.

"Are you okay, Dan?" he asked.

"Ohhh yesss—I am-sorry, I've-just [sob] been-angry [sob] for-so-long," Dan replied. "I wanted-to-be-[sob]-a-singer. I never wanted to be a cook-or-a-manager [sob]. When I was thirteen, Dad died and I took over the family [sob] business to support Mom and-my-sisters. My dream was to always be in the theater [sob]. I can't handle this stress any longer. Oh Jesus." Dan paused with a bewildered look in his eyes. "What are we supposed to do when we have to sacrifice our dreams for our duty until we practically forget them? Huh. You're not so bad, are you, you little surfer freak with your little surfer freak dog."

Cos watched stunned. Was Dan asking him for advice on life? He knew he had to say something, but what?

"Maybe you could sell the restaurant and go for it. There's always tomorrow."

"No! It's too late [wailing]. I am too old. I am too tired. Look at these hands, would you?" He held out his opened palms. "They're all calloused and rough. Worn out. Do they look like an actor's hands to you?" He looked up at Cos with needy eyes, seeking approval.

"Well, hands never carried a tune, Dan. Your voice is good, it might not be too late. You should try it. Look, Dan, I gotta go. We're getting ready for the storm back at the house. The car is there and the brake pads are fixed."

"Maybe so, I hope so. I really hope so."

BACK AT THE FARM, Wolly pitched balls to Joey. Ton and Dog retrieved them in the outfield. Joey was so distracted about Belle, he couldn't get a bat on any of them. He decided to call her. He took a deep breath and pulled out his phone as he walked away from Wolly, who picked up the bat and hit some balls for Dog and Ton. Joey dialed her number, his heart thumping in his chest. Her voicemail answered, and that voice, oh my goodness: she talked like a little bluebird sang.

"Belle, it's Joey. Look, it was wrong for me to change my plans without asking you first. I know I put you in a hard spot. I hope we can work this out. I love you. Please call me. I'll be around." He hung up the phone and picked up his bat.

"I feel better already," he said to Wolly.

"Good." Wolly fired one down the middle. Joey ripped it to the right field area of the land. After looking like it was going to disappear into one of the cotton-ball clouds, it returned to earth, getting lost in the top of the short trees. Wolly tossed a breaking curve; Joey line drove it right for his head. Wolly ducked, and Joey grinned at him. Dog and Ton both bolted after it. They hit balls for a long time, alternating positions. When they got tired, they penned up Ton, packed into Wolly's CJ Jeep with Dog, and drove down Route 1. In a few miles, they came across Cos. Wolly pulled over.

"Look at that stray dog," Wolly said.

"What are you doing, Cos?" Joey asked.

"Coming back from Dan's. I just quit!"

"Well it's about time," Wolly said, smiling. "Did he find out that the chicken got shot up?"

"No. He was ticked off about my missing extra days of work, and then he had a sort of epiphany that he wanted to sing on Broadway, so be it. It was kinda weird. I didn't know whether to scream or yell 'hey, way to go!'"

"Wow, I can't believe big ole Dan wants to sing musicals," Wolly said and laughed hysterically.

"Yeah, I swear," Cos said.

"Well, hop in why don't you? We're going to see a movie," Wolly said.

"Right on," Cos said.

"Well, I am proud of you for quitting though," Joey said.

"Thanks, Jojo. I did it in style, I guess."

They went to *The Searchers* with John Wayne at the old timey Aquarius theater downtown. They tied Dog up outside and enjoyed the show.

On the way home, Joey checked his phone for the third time, but there were no messages. He was quiet.

"Shake it off, bro," Cos said, patting him on the shoulder from the backseat. The salty wind blew their hair back. "You know what we always say, if a girl doesn't want you, let her go."

"I know Cos, I've just never felt this way before. It's like she's a piece of me."

"Give it some time. Time is a salve."

"You're messing up my mood, Dollarhide! I swear. I bet if we were hitting balls, you wouldn't get a bat on it. You're going to have to walk home if you don't stop sulking. I can't be around this," Wolly said. Joey smiled. "Got it?" Wolly looked at Joey in the passenger seat.

"Got it."

"All right then, so who wants to head down to Cap'ns? I could use some oysters and a cold beer. You know, anybody over the age of 15 with a big chin can get served at Cap'ns. It's old school like that. And besides, talking to some nice ladies will do you plenty of good, Joey."

"Yeah, let's go!" Cos said.

"Okay," Joey said harshly, and then eased up, "I guess I am in."

"That's not cutting it, Jojo. We're talking about oysters and a million-dollar view. The CJ needs some enthusiasm to get going."

"I am in!" Joey yelled.

"Good, let's go dominate a bar." Wolly whizzed South on 1 while Cos called Leslie, who agreed to meet them there a little later on. They rode past the marina and Guana State Park. Then, they sailed past Banana State Park, marked by its large array of banana palms.

Cap'n Sam's was the beach beer dive right on the water, south of Latch, just outside of tiny Spanish Palm, right next to the Seabreeze Motel where Jimmy liked to stay when he was in town. The owner of the joint, Sambo Fletcher, was raised in Mississippi before he migrated to Louisiana to run a shrimp boat. After making fast money on some stock tips, he decided to move to Florida in 1965 and open a beachfront restaurant. Ever since, Cap'n Sam's had been a hidden jewel of the Southeast coast. Off the tourist grid, locals slammed it daily. The menu, which made memories, was a piece of paper featuring five items: raw oysters on the half shell, seafood gumbo, a fried catfish po'boy sandwich, fried pickles, and shrimp etouffee—and Sam had had his share of all five.

People always said, "You meet ole Sambo's stomach before you meet him," and it was true—when he walked, his belly wagged out in front of him with the rhythm of a samba dancer. He had ruddy skin, blue eyes, and the whitest teeth. When people asked how he kept those pearls so white, he replied that it was the oysters, but with Sam, *everything* good was due to the oysters.

Cap'ns did well through Eliza, being so far south of where the biggest surge hit, plus it was raised off the ground and up to hurricane code. A fallen tree rammed a hole in the back porch, but other than some debris, that was the only damage. The parking lot was packed, so Wolly pulled in next door at the Sea Breeze motel. Whipping the CJ into the hard sand lot, he took the last available spot. They leashed Dog in the back of the Jeep. Joey noticed the tag on the truck next to them and laughed. The New York plates on the orange F250 truck read *GNSLNGR*. Inside, people packed the wood walls to capacity. A rumble of laughter and chatter filled the air along with the smell of cologne and perfume. Joey had a strange feeling Belle was there. He looked through the audience for Belle's red hair, but only saw a fake ginger dye job on a brunette. The three guys sat at the bar and a waiter came over.

"We want oysters on the half," Joey said.

"What kind?"

"What kind do you have?"

"Any kind you want." He pointed up to the chalkboard. "We have them shipped in from the West, East, and Gulf Coasts almost daily.

They looked up at the huge chalkboard, which had oyster after oyster written in chalk with the price per oyster with a slash and then the price per dozen after each name. Their mouths watered as they read: Beavertails, Deer Creek, Apalachicola, Blue Points, Louisiana, Texas, Mystics, Naked Cowboys, Kumamatos, Hog Neck Bay, French Kiss, Discovery Bay, Hood Canal, Duckabush, First Light, Lady Chatterley, Cuttyhunk, Martha's Vineyard, Point Julia, Fanny Bay, and on and on. Then, below those, the shooters were listed, with the Louisiana Charlie Wobble last on the board.

"Holy smokes," Cos said, pop-eyed.

"Why don't we get one of each?" Joey said.

"All right, you want them in shot glasses? We can open them and you can shoot them right here."

"Sounds great!" Joey said.

"Excellent, I'll bring some Tabasco and lemon wedges," the waiter replied.

"No thanks, we like 'em straight up unless it's a shooter," Cos said.

"Yeah, all that stuff just waters 'em down, but do bring us a round of Charlie Wobbles first," Joey added.

"All right. I'll have the shucker come out and serve you while he shucks."

"Thanks bud," Cos said.

"One check?"

"It's all on me," Cos said. "I am, like, rich now—it's weird."

Joey and the group chatted while they waited. Someone plugged "Hushabye" by the Beach Boys on the juke. A brunette down at the end of the bar stared at them. Wolly noticed.

"That brunette is really giving one of us the eye." They all craned.

Joey saw it was Belle's friend Natasha from the beach. She looked away and talked with her pal, shooting glances out of the side of her eyes toward him.

"I swear that stone fox is looking at you, Joey," Wolly said, leaning his big frame to look at her.

"Yeah, I am afraid so."

"Afraid so?! What's gotten into you?"

"It's Natasha, Belle's friend."

"*That* Natasha?! Oh man. You should go talk to her."

"No, I am not interested."

"I swear you're dumber than a second coat of paint, Dollarhide. It's your loss. I want her number then," Wolly said.

Intrigued by their order, Sambo came over. He sat a shot glass in front of each of them and started with the Charlie Wobble shooters. Then, he began to pull oyster after oyster out of the metal bins under the bar. After shucking each one with the speed of lightning, he placed it in one of their shot glasses and they shot it, savoring the different flavors.

"Thanks, Sambo," Cos said.

"How'd ya know my name?"

"Are you kidding? Everyone knows you."

"I guess you're right." He smiled and wiped his hands on a rag at the bar. He had small eyes poked into a round head and appeared weathered like an antique carriage that was left out on the range in the hot sun.

"Oysters keep you healthy. It's a crying shame that young folks don't have a taste for 'em anymore. They think they'll get sick or that they taste gross." He shucked another oyster and dropped it in Wolly's glass. "That's a Naked Cowboy," Sambo said.

"Not us, we eat 'em like candy. Our father gets bushels by the hundred from the docks and keeps them in a fridge outside," Cos said.

Sambo's eyes lit up and he grinned, showing his pearls. "You sound like my kind of people." He dropped an oyster in Joey's shot glass. Joey knocked it back.

"Thanks, Sambo. That was delicious!"

"Tell your father to stop in—I'd like to meet him."

"You probably know him already. Teddy Dollarhide?"

"*Old Salt*? Why of course I know him. He and Sarah used to come down here all the time, but I haven't seen him since she passed. How's he doing?" Sam said, while shucking.

"He's really good. He has a new girlfriend," Cos said. They continued to eat as he shucked.

"So glad to hear it. Tell him I said hello."

"We will," Cos said. A shucker came over, taking Sam's place.

"This is Bill. Just let him know if you want any more after he completes your order. By the way, if you break the record, the whole bill is free." He slapped a swinging wooden chalkboard with his hand and kicked his head back, gesturing to it. It read *BUZZ: 232*. "But, if you stop at 232, you still have to pay."

"That's a lot of oysters. No one could eat that many," Joey said.

"Most can't. Buzz has the stomach of a whale," Sam insisted.

"Is that *Buzz Smith*?" Cos asked.

"Yep," Sambo answered.

"We know him; he used to date Leslie," Wolly said.

"You're a better man for knowing him. Used to come down here when he worked this way." Sambo scanned the bar and saw a friend approach. "Good chatting with you boys. I gotta run."

"You too," remarked Cos and Sam walked off.

They ate the oysters. Sitting at the bar made Cos and Wolly feel collegiate. They finished the final oyster, and after taking in the minerals and life from each saltwater area of North America from Washington to Florida, they felt that they had in some way been to those places and felt happy, calm, and content, the way good oysters make people feel.

Natasha approached Joey, hopping onto the vacant stool next to him. Joey greeted her surprised, as if he hadn't seen her ogling him. He asked if she had seen Belle, and she replied that she thought she went to a party at Zach Watt's beach house in Latch. They made small talk and she edged closer to him. She was nice, but her talk bored him, and when she placed her hand on his upper thigh, his heart recoiled and he realized he must pull himself away. She puckered her lips and sipped a mojito while holding his gaze. He thanked her for the talk and excused himself to the restroom. She blocked him with her knee and tilted her head to the side, asking in a high voice if he would come back.

"Sure," he lied.

"I gotta go too sexy." She called his bluff and followed him. She lightly grabbed the back of his shirt while walking to the restroom and locked her arm into his.

In the restroom hall, Belle exited the *Ladies' Room* and saw the arm lock between her friend Natasha and Joey. She stormed away into the bar, wiggling between people. He pulled his arm away from Natasha and headed after her, calling for her to wait. She went onto the back porch and to the beach. He caught her near the water.

"Wait Belle! It's not what you think!"

"*What is it then?* She had her arm around you, dammit! *You jerk!* That's supposed to be one of my good friends." She marched down the beach as he followed.

"Some friend! She has been hounding me all night, and when I went to the restroom to escape, she grabbed my hand. When I asked where you were, she said you were at Zach's beach house!"

"No, no, no, she's lying!" She stampeded away as he ran after her.

"Just listen to me sweetheart. Give me a minute." But she didn't stop. He called out to her, "I'll go to California with you."

She stopped and turned slowly, looking at him. He approached.

"Really?" She paused with her hands on her hips.

"Yes. Anything to be with you. You see, I can't live without you."

"You would do that *for me?*" she asked.

"Yes, I would do anything for us."

He took her hand. She smiled reluctantly.

"Well, you don't have to, because I'll go to Florida. You see, I can't be without you."

"That's great, babe, but what do *you really* want?" Joey said.

"I want *to be* where *you are.*"

"But what about your dreams?"

"I've been thinking about it, and I think Florida is better. Cos and Leslie will be here and we can start that treasure hunting business in our spare time."

"Is that what you *really* want?"

"At first it wasn't, because I've always wanted to go to Stanford, but after hunting in California, I realized that it's like you said—dreams really do change."

"So you caught the gold bug just like Old Salt?" he asked.

"I guess I did," she said, and smiled.

"What about your dad?"

"He'll never be happy, even if I go to Texas."

"Let's start with Florida, and maybe we can have Florida *and* California."

"How?"

"I don't know, let's just see what happens. As long as we're together, it doesn't really matter. I mean, we can-"

She interrupted him, *"I think you need to kiss me right now."* He didn't argue with her, but gently grabbed the back of her neck and pulled her hair up in his hand as he cradled her head and pressed his lips to hers; they fell to the warm sand and their tongues and lips touched again and again; she bit his bottom lip gently and kissed his top lip.

"Being away from you was terrible," he whispered.

"I know. I couldn't breathe all day," she said.

"I couldn't either, I felt just like one of those dumb crabs at the jubilee," he said. She smiled. "Do you want to go back to the farm and play Scrabble?" he asked.

"Will your dad know we're spelling?" She smiled.

"No, he never comes over."

"All right, I'll stay, but no funny business with him so close by."

"Not even first base?"

"Didn't you sit the bench anyway in baseball?" She laughed.

"Oh that's a low blow girl."

"I am just joking. I am yours."

She kissed him. They left out the back and headed to Belle's Cherokee as he texted Wolly that he was leaving.

IN THE TREE HOUSE, Belle went to the bathroom and Joey took off his shirt, flipped on some Duke Ellington, lay down on the thick plush mattress and stared at his huge map of the world on the ceiling. Silver stars marked his bucket list places: Italy, Provence, St. Barts, Scotland, Ireland, South Africa, Switzerland to name a few. With the money, he could travel.

He lit some candles on the bedside table. The candlelight waved a little in the ocean breeze blowing through the screen. He popped a mint.

In a bit, Belle came out of the bathroom wearing canary-colored panties and reached her arm up the doorway, caressing the frame with her hip stuck out to the side. With her stretched arm and strawberry hair flowing in waves across the front of her chest, she looked like a polished sculpture. Want was all over them.

She slinked over with a smile on her face, looking up at him with her head tilted forward. She got on the bed on all fours and they touched gently. Then, they teased each other with quick kisses and flicks of the tongue. He traced her body with his finger and she brushed the tip of her hair against his chest; her body was warm and the Aqua de Parma on her neck smelled graceful. He nibbled her earlobe; she smiled and then kissed his ear. They kissed over and over again. After a while, they forgot where one ended and the other began.

They watched the ceiling as he held her. When he glanced at her, he realized how much better it was now than it would've been when they were younger.

He leaned over and took the pearl necklace Alicia gave him out of the bedside table drawer. Then, he put it around her moist neck and fastened it. She caught it with her hand and looked down, surprised.

"You'll always be my pearl, Annabelle. This is for you. Alicia made it."

"Oh my! I love it! It's just *soooo* beautiful! Is that a sapphire?" She touched the stone in the center of the pendant.

"Yes."

"Oh, I love sapphires! They're my birthstone."

"*Really*! Oh wow! I didn't know. What a coincidence."

"Yeah, I know. It's like, meant to be, right? Thank you so much."

"You're welcome."

"It can replace the rose necklace," she said.

"Of course."

"Why do you think I no longer have the dreams even though I lost the necklace?"

"I think the necklace broke the spell."

She kissed him and rubbed his chest. After blowing out the candles, they fell asleep in each other's arms.

So the sea had finally risen to cover the sand, and they were one.

CHAPTER 8

They woke to a rooster crowing at the break of day.
"Damn bird," Joey said.
"No, this is perfect; I need to get home anyway." She put on her clothes and adjusted in the mirror. Admiring the necklace, she modeled it for a moment.

"I just love this necklace! *Please* thank Alicia for me."

"I will. It looks great on you. *Stay.* Last night was amazing."

"I know." She smiled up at him while slipping on her pink New Balance running shoes. "I want to, but I have to go." She walked over and kissed him, her breath sweet. "Take care in this storm. It's supposed to be serious."

"I will. You too. I love you," he said.

"I love you too—call me."

"I will," Joey said as she exited.

Falling back on his pillow, he went back to sleep. When he woke, the clouds had moved in to block out the sun. He stared up at the map and thought about Belle again, her scent like lingering morning dew on the pillow. He buried his face in it and breathed deeply, grinning ear to ear. Rather than fight sleep, he rose and went to the main house for breakfast.

Joey poured some fresh juice there, drank it, and looked out the bay window at the sky. He decided to go surf. With the approaching storm, the waves would be huge. He finished the drink and went outside.

Grabbing Cos's board, he biked down the deserted road. When he arrived, the beach was a desert of white sand stretching for miles with no one in sight. The sky swirled with grey-blue tones and the sea roared with life. Some six-footer waves broke. He rolled out a session, cutting and flipping in the salty froth. When he got back to the farm, everyone was up. He found Alicia in the kitchen drinking coffee.

"Good morning, Alicia."

"Good morning, Joey!"

"How are you doing?" he asked, leaning on the long island.

"Great, now that I am healthy again."

"I am so happy for you. Teddy told us about your recovery. That wine is a miracle."

"Yes it is. I am very very grateful for it," she said. "You're glowing, by the way! What happened?"

"I am?"

"Like a lantern."

He gave a big grin. "I gave Belle the necklace last night."

"Really? What did she say?!"

"She loved it and wanted me to thank you!"

"I am so glad. She's very welcome. Did you tell her you would go to California?" she asked. He crossed his arms.

"Yeah, but she wants to go with me to Miami anyway, so we decided to just see what happens."

"Oh good, you two look so right for each other."

"Thanks, Alicia."

She sipped her coffee and walked to the window, staring out at the sky. "Some storm coming in," she observed.

"Yeah it is."

"I've never been in a hurricane before. What are they like?"

"Ah, kinda like a washing machine," Joey said, smiling.

"A washing machine?"

"Yeah, the first time is bad, but after a few loads, you get your sea legs." He smiled, looking out with her. "We've been through a bunch, but I've never been as scared as I was during Eliza."

"I heard it was bad. Hopefully this will be better."

"Hopefully."

"I am going to go take a shower; will you be around?" Alicia asked.

"Right here."

"Great."

She walked away, but stopped at the door and turned.

"Joey, thank you for accepting me," she said. "I know since your mother passed, there hasn't been another woman."

"Oh, of course. I should be thanking *you*. It's been too long now. Dad needs to move on. Believe me, we're all *very* glad you're here."

Alicia smiled. "That's so sweet of you."

Cos walked into the kitchen and greeted Alicia before she exited. Teddy strutted in wearing floral swim shorts, cologne, and a crisp shirt—even the big room felt crowded by his jolly presence.

He still barked out pre-storm orders for the boys, but he did it with a smile now: "Good morning. I love you boys. Glad you're home. Need you to lock up the barn, feed the animals, board up the windows, go to the store, and pick up gasoline for the generator." He informed them Buzz would be over shortly to help.

"What?! Not Buzz! How can you do this to me? You know he used to date Leslie, right?" Cos exclaimed.

"Now, shut up, Cos. You're going to try get along with him. He's trying to change. He's helping me build my boat."

"*Is he really trying to change?* Okay, I guess. Whatever you say, Dad."

They agreed, and Cos threw a toy for Half Ton outside while he waited for Joey. In a little bit, Buzz arrived, and the three boys headed into town to complete Teddy's list. They got along fairly well with Buzz—nothing was said about Leslie. They both silently decided to let it go.

When they got back, the University of Miami called for Cos and offered the full baseball scholarship. Joey hugged him. They boarded up Isabella and the barn, and by late afternoon, the whole house was secured except for the indoor pool room, where the glass was thick and would have been very difficult to cover anyway.

Dark blue clouds covered the sky as a trickle started. Teddy placed Half Ton in the indoor sauna. The boys put the chickens and horses in the barn, on the second floor this time, then everyone hunkered down inside. Buzz's home was too delicate to ride out the 'cane—he had ridden out the last one inland at a hotel—so Teddy invited him to stay.

The wind whistled a tale about the angry sea.

BACK AT BELLE'S HOME, she found her father in the den watching the news, sipping a scotch out of a bubble-shaped glass with his initials, W.B., frosted on the side. She told him she needed to speak to him. He turned down the news.

"What is it, honey? How was the school, by the way?" he asked.

"I didn't go. I went to California with Joey Dollarhide. We found a treasure."

He nearly spit out his drink as he jerked forward. She had his full attention now.

"*You what?!*" Leaning forward, he stared at her wide-eyed.

"I am a woman now, Dad, and I can do what I want with whom I want."

"Joey Dollarhide is the offspring of that…that sea rat! I don't care if you think he's good looking, his family is trash!"

"No they're not! They are the sweetest people, and I love Joey!" she said with a raised voice.

"You don't even know what love is. Love is two people who are right for each other, who come from the same backgrounds—who were raised the same way. That's the kind of love that lasts."

"But we're so much closer than you think. We were raised similarly and connect on many levels. I am going with what I feel here, Dad."

"That worked out really well with TJ, didn't it?" He raised his voice and stood.

"That was different. *Joey* is different."

He shook his head and walked over to the window, watching the rain in the backyard.

"I am not asking for your permission, Dad—*I am telling you*. I found a lot of money in California, and Joey and I are going to buy a boat to start a little offshore treasuring hunting business in."

"What kind of half-cocked idea is that? What is this treasure?"

"We found it in the Sierras. It was a Dollarhide family secret."

"Did you report it?" He looked at her from the side.

"Mr. Dollarhide is going to."

"You'll never see any of it again." He looked back out the window, sipping the drink. "*If* you found it. Are you lying to me about this, this treasure thingy?"

"No, we found it, all these gold bars in a trunk. This is about your dad and the fact that you never went to college, isn't it?"

"This is about keeping you from throwing your life away! I never had the opportunities you've had!"

"So you want me to live your life, then? Maybe I should drill for oil and marry a girl!"

"That's not what I mean," he said. She shook her head and stormed out of the room, stopping at the open door to the kitchen.

"Sometimes I can't believe we're related. You associate with criminals for money and call honest people dirt. *Who* are you? *What* are you?"

"What criminals are you talking about?" he snapped.

"We think Bateman and Banks hired a *hitman* to harass the Dollarhides. They stole his gold and shot at his son!" She waited for his response, but he just stared at her and then sat back in his chair.

"Ugh!" She threw her hands down and ran away to her room.

He leaned back and turned up the news again, exhaling a long breath before closing his eyes. The sound of the anchor's voice massaged his brain. He loved those sound bites and voices. Distant. Always thought out. Never erratic, like Belle. Why couldn't she be more like those voices? He thought about the last thing she said. What *the hell* was she talking about? Then, an image flashed in his mind of the orange truck and men dressed in black on Sand Piper Street that night he'd been out driving late. He opened his eyes. What if what she said was true?

My goodness, he thought.

CHAPTER 9

Charlotte decided to stay with Dal downtown. Teddy, Alicia, Buzz, and the boys packed into Isabella's living room with the weather channel on. The weatherman tracked Irene, now a Cat 2, with his finger—an orange circle spinning across an enormous screen. Teddy rose and began to pace, stopping at the beverage cart to pour a glass of tea.

"This is bad," Teddy said, and sat, putting his arm around Alicia on the couch and rubbing her shoulder as they watched the television.

After five minutes, he said: "I don't feel like dancing this evening. Maybe for our celebration, we'll just have a cigar. What do you say, boys?"

"Sounds great," Joey said, lying on the coach.

"Fire 'em up," Cos added, leaning on his arms on the rug.

Rising again, he went to the office, opened a box of Zino Chubby Tubos, and passed it around.

"You want one?" he asked Alicia, but she held her hand up in protest, rolling her big eyes.

He held out the black box for the men, who each took a Zino. They drank tea and smoked the cigars, which tasted like chocolate cognac.

Teddy moved around like a lawyer in a courtroom, chewing on the leaf stick.

"How's the arm, Cosby?" He glanced at Cos.

"Never felt better, Dad." Cos patted his arm.

"I swear you're about as tough as wilt leather, boy."

"And about as thick, too," Joey said.

"Watch it, now," Cos said to Joey. Teddy bellowed.

"Hey Dad, Sambo Fletcher told us to tell you hey," Joey said.

"Old Sambo? Oh yeah, how's he doing?"

"Great! Still dealing oysters. They've got tons of oysters at Cap'n's," Joey said.

"I know. I need to go down there again. The po'boys and gumbo remind me of the Gulf Coast. Tastes like home." He paused, drawing on the cigar.

"Cap'n Sams? That's where I broke the oyster record," Buzz added from the floor on the other side of Cos.

"Really, Buzzard?" Teddy asked, smiling.

"Yep."

"Yeah, we saw the chalkboard last night," Cos said, giving Buzz an equal respect for once.

"Glad to know it's still standing."

"Ole Sambo was singing your praises," Cos said and Buzz grinned with a closed mouth.

"Tell us a story while we wait, Dad," Joey said.

Teddy paused. "I don't really feel like it, Cos."

"C'mon, Dad," Joey begged.

"Oh, all right, what do you wanna hear?" Teddy stood in front of the mantle now, the Zino in his fingers.

"Tell us about the eye in Key West," Cos said.

"You want to hear it, babe?" Teddy asked Alicia.

"Sure, why not?"

"Okay—Tom and my buddy Justin were living way down south in Key West or *caya hueso* as the Spanish call it, that means bone island by the way. And we were down there in a mobile home when a bad 'cane rolled through. The eye rolled over us and they bet me two hundred bucks to walk out in it. I was young, witless, and very broke, so I did it."

"What's the eye?" Alicia asked.

"The force of the hurricane creates a wall around the center called the eye, which blocks the wind, so it's silent and motionless inside."

"I see."

Smoking the Zino, he paced around the room. "Needless to say, I got my money, but the other side of the hurricane came through a half hour later, lifted the top off the trailer, threw it a hundred and fifty yards down the road, and knocked the walls clean off. Tom and I were thrown into the barn. Justin was on the toilet at the time. We thought for sure he had gotten Toto-ed to Oz, but after it passed, we walked out, and lo and behold, he was still sitting there on the porcelain throne holding the Arts and Leisure section of the *Miami Herald*. We had to pry him off and lead him into the barn until the weather passed." Alicia and the group laughed, while Teddy showed his teeth and chuckled.

"What happened to Justin?" Joey asked.

"Oh, he's fine now. But it took a lot of time on a shrink's couch before he could go to the bathroom without closing his eyes." They laughed.

The rain thundered outside. All traces of light had vanished behind a wall of black clouds. The wind ran up against the house. Teddy turned the volume up on the weather channel, which showed the outer wall of the storm about sixty miles offshore, fifteen miles south of Latch, near Spanish Palm.

"Wow, it's headed straight for Cap'n's!" Joey said.

"Let's play Scrabble. It'll help to pass the time," Alicia said. Dog was curled up against her side; Bear was on the top of the sofa.

Teddy broke out the board; they extinguished their cigars. As they played, Buzz dazzled everyone with his expansive vocabulary, which allowed him to tile out twice in the first half of the game.

"So how d'you know so much, Buzz?" Joey asked.

"I used to read a lot to get away, and it kinda became a habit. I read everything, really: how-to books, mystery novels and serious literature. It puts my mind at ease."

"That's pretty cool man! I would've never known it," Cos said.

Buzz didn't reply, rearranging his Scrabble letters with a closed-mouth grin. He tiled out again with *"quixotry"*.

"Again?!" Teddy said.

"Quixotry? Is that even a word?" Alicia asked.

"Yes ma'am, it means extreme idealism in action or thought. It's from the classic novel, *Don Quixote*."

"Not so fast Buzzard," Teddy said. "Let me look this bad boy up real first before you run away with another big one." Teddy glanced at the Scrabble dictionary, "Wait a minute, wait a minute. Damn! It is a word!"

"You're a boy genius, Buzz," Joey added.

"Thanks."

"Anyone want some wine?" Cos asked.

"Only one glass, Cos, I want y'all clear headed when Irene shows up," Teddy said.

Cos agreed and went into the kitchen. Opening the glass cabinet, his stomach purred when he spotted the Cab Sav. He reached for it and a loud zip shattered the door in front of him. A bottle of Ron Zacapa rum next to the wine exploded, and the syrupy maple alcohol sprayed all over the inside of the cabinet and out the door into the kitchen. Dog barked in the background. Blue, caged in the dining room now, croaked "Danger!" Cos's heart skipped a beat and he jumped back with his mouth and eyes wide open. Ducking down, he took cover and skirted in a low position toward the living room. Another shot followed, hitting the doorframe behind him, dislodging a chunk of wood.

"Crap!" Cos yelled. "Someone is shooting at me!" He darted into the living room.

Teddy stood up with the unlit cigar stub in the side of his mouth, his face intense. Thinking for a moment, he ordered Joey to retrieve two guns and commanded everyone else into the library, explaining that it would be safe because there were no windows. "We should have boarded that one up," Teddy stated. Still startled, Cos was the first one up the stairs, with Buzz, Dog, Bear, and Alicia behind him.

CHAPTER 10

Teddy headed into the office, where Joey loaded a .22.
"No Son, not enough stopping power there."
"Maybe the Remington .243?" Joey said.
"The Dakota, it's a long-range rifle used for hunting big game at a distance."
"All right." Joey grabbed it.
"I have a feeling we're dealing with a real cockroach here. No reason to go soft with our firepower when we have the main squeeze." He grabbed a box of ammo and stuffed it in his khaki pocket.
Watching his father, Joey realized that he had never been afraid for his dad's safety—Salt had always been a survivor—a lion. But this was different. Whoever it was, this assassin was patient, cold, executing. He had tracked them in the Sierras and here he was again, a faceless shapeshifter who wasn't afraid of being out in a hurricane; he had fired on them in the Sierras, and Joey was certain he would shoot them all given the chance.
Teddy handed Joey a loaded rifle and a box of ammo; Joey's hands shook as he gripped the gun.
"Gentle, Son. Only shoot if you have to. Don't draw attention to the room, okay?"

"Got it," Joey said, hugging his father.

"This is probably the same sniper who stole my gold and tracked y'all. When you escaped in the mountains, I bet he took the next flight back."

"I was afraid that might happen," Joey said.

Teddy followed Joey upstairs to the library, where they found everyone sitting on the big leather sofas. Teddy went up the circular stairs to the second floor and then to one of the small circular windows in the corner. He dialed 9-1-1, and spoke to an operator who said no one could come until the storm was past.

After hanging up the phone, he opened the window. An overhang sheltered it, keeping the rain from obscuring the view. He could see the auto court, tree house, barn, and workshop past it on the left. He looked for movement, but it was still.

"Cosby, do you have any idea what angle that shot came in through the kitchen window at?" Teddy hollered.

"A little elevated and to the left. Maybe from on top of the barn or the tree house." Teddy squinted out and repositioned the cigar with his tongue to the other side of his mouth. He studied the yard like it was the first time he had ever seen it, scanning every surface.

"No, I reckon he must have been on the tree house porch. The barn would be too high. But I can't see him now."

"What about our gold?" Cos asked alarmed.

"It's in the safe here." Teddy paused. "I knew better than to store it in the preservation room again. I had a hunch this guy would return. Just not in a 'cane." He grabbed the gun, slung it around his shoulder, went down the stairs and to the door, where he stopped and instructed Joey to watch the hall and fire on anyone who tried to come up other than him.

Alicia begged Teddy to stay.

"You and the boys are all I have left, and I am not going to lose you. I'll be fine," Teddy said, and pulled down on her earlobe. She started to cry and wrapped her arms around him, begging him to stay. He lifted her chin up and interrupted her tears with a kiss; then, she tugged on his ear.

"Not like this, Teddy," she said, touching the gun. "Like this." She placed her hand on his heart. "Stop resisting. We can hide and they'll go *away* when the storm arrives. They'll never find us in this big house."

"No, I am not hiding babe, I have to take care of you," Teddy said, and walked away.

Joey caught him at the stairs. "Let me go with you Dad!"

"No, it's too dangerous son."

By Teddy's tone, Joey knew he meant it, so he waited a minute and tossed the gun to Cos before following his father downstairs anyway.

As Joey left, Cos remarked to the group, "Why is Dad leaving us up here? Isn't the smart move always to wait in a protected room with a gun pointed at the door. That way the assailant comes to you? I just don't get it!"

"I don't know. Teddy always seems to know what he is doing," Buzz said.

"I guess."

Downstairs, Joey caught Teddy in the living room.

"What did I tell you son? Go back upstairs now!"

"No Dad, I am staying with you whether you like it or not."

Teddy paused and looked at his rifle.

"Well, I guess if you're gonna stay you'll need a gun."

"Sweet!"

Teddy took Joey to the office to get another gun—the Remington.

"Stay close behind me."

They could hear the storm roaring outside through the broken kitchen window.

The power went out. The other boarded-up windows blocked all slivers of light. Teddy cursed their luck and stumbled over to find some candles in the living room. Lighting ten, he handed a votive to Joey. They made for the garage to flip the generator on. Teddy raised his gun in firing position as they crept through the dining room. He moved a bit around the corner in the kitchen and waited for gunfire. Nothing. They passed through the dining room and into the back hall toward the inside poolroom.

Glass shattered. Bullets came through the open door leading into the poolroom, decorating the wall in front of them—they took cover behind the doorframe. The shots were fired from an elevation, probably from the oak tree in the backyard. Teddy blew out the candle.

"He must have moved around back. He's fast like a roach too—can't take your eyes off him."

Teddy pulled his gun around and stuck the barrel past the corner of the door with one eye in the scope, but he couldn't see anything.

"Must have been perched on one of the low thick branches to the left of the pool," Teddy stated. He fired. The bullet penetrated the glass wall, cruising into the night. In a minute, shots fired back, hitting the stone in front of him.

"We'll save my gun. Give me yours." Joey handed him the gun and Teddy fired off round after round through the hole in the glass wall. Shots fired back, but he and Joey were very well protected by the door wall with almost no part of his face showing, so they all missed. Teddy kept firing, eventually running out of bullets and switching to his own gun.

In the poolroom, a huge chunk of glass broke and a small steel container hit the floor, dispersing a thick grey stream of smoke. Covering his mouth, Teddy ran out and kicked it into the pool. With the kick, the box of ammo flung out of his pocket and clanged on the floor like wind chimes, spilling and rolling. He reached down to pick some of the shells up, but shots descended, forcing him to take cover —the bullets followed his trail—smoke clouded the pool.

"Dammit!" He ducked back behind the doorframe. Lying on the floor, he took the remaining bullets out of his pocket, and shook them in his hands counting them.

"Two, three, four ... six left."

"You dropped the bullets?" Joey said, his voice shaking.

"Yes."

"What are we going to do?" Joey said, his eyes full of fear.

"We'll figure something out."

"That's your answer, Dad?"

"My son, you're the one who insisted on coming along." Teddy looked back at him.

"Yeah, but that was then. Things are different now."

"Things are always different. You gotta go with the flow. We're going to fire back. Besides, don't you hear that storm outside? It's a toad strangler. He'll be a treed coon soon. We got the upper hand. Plus, we still have six bullets, and he can't stay up there forever." Teddy paused, listening. "You hear that? It's howling now."

"Yeah, I hear it."

"I don't wanna shoot him anyway, we're just keeping him at bay."

CHAPTER 11

Teddy put the cigar plug in his pocket. Then he fired a shot through the larger hole in the wall. The storm escalated and the branches of the tree swayed in the wind. They waited, listening.

Teddy thought about what Alicia said and began to hold forgiveness in his heart toward Bateman and Banks, even the sniper, and tried to let his anger toward them go. Closing his eyes, he let it all wash away for a moment and felt a huge relief, but he stayed alert.

Meanwhile, Big Ham, Jimmy's right hand man, had entered the house by ripping the planks off one of the boarded-up downstairs bedroom windows and proceeded up the stairs to the second story. Cos, Alicia, and Buzz heard the footsteps and Cos could perceive by the rhythm that it wasn't Teddy. "I knew Teddy shouldn't have left. Dammit!" Cos whispered.

Cos shuffled everyone, including the animals, into the secret passage behind the wall. Then, they crawled over to the faux iron return air grill where they could see out. The door kicked in and a towering figure with boulders for shoulders dressed in black entered with an automatic weapon drawn. Dog barked loudly at the sound, and Big Ham swung around in their direction of the air grill as Cos frantically wrapped his hand around Dog's mouth to muzzle him. Big Ham fired. Gunfire penetrated the plastered wall between Alicia and Buzz. Bear cried out, his cat eyes large. Cos and the group crawled forward toward the interior-exterior wall passage that turned right to the next bedroom. Ham kicked in the grill and fired to the left into the dark, but they had already rounded the corner. The grill was too small to squeeze through and Ham couldn't find the entrance.

The storm rolled in harder. Downstairs, the gunfire ceased. Teddy sensed a presence and looked through the partially shattered glass to see a figure standing outside in the rain. Dressed in black with black goggles, Jimmy's face was obscured by a tight hood and a dark grey matte metal mask over his nose and mouth; he cradled an automatic assault rifle as he faced toward the door, his fingertip caressing the trigger like he was stroking a gerbil.

"Dammit. We're checkmated. If we run down the hall, we have nowhere to go, and if we go back through the dining room, he's got a shot through the pool room windows," Teddy whispered.

Jimmy broke his way through the glass wall of the pool room after firing a round of ammo at it. Teddy and Joey darted for the dining room, but he fired through the poolroom window into the living room, forcing them to retreat.

Teddy fired the last of his ammo around the corner into the indoor poolroom, but Jimmy dodged the bullets by hiding in the corner of the poolroom next to the living room window. Teddy and Joey took the opportunity to run again, but Jimmy fired through the window and Teddy stopped in the dining room, holding his hands up in surrender.

"I'll sell!" he yelled. "Whatever you want."

"Where's the treasure?" Jimmy yelled through the shot-up poolroom's window glass, his gun pointing straight at Teddy and Joey who stood in the living room. At that moment, he was struck with another severe cluster headache and grabbed his temple in pain.

Teddy and Joey took the opportunity and ran. Jimmy squeezed the trigger—a bullet soared. Joey jumped into his father, pushing them both down.

Lunging down the hall from the sauna where he had busted the door down, the herculean hog rounded the corner into the pool room and charged straight for Jimmy who fled out the broken glass wall into the yard to get away. Ton torpedoed into the rain after him and nailed him from behind, knocking him to the ground hard where his face slammed into the wet mud.

Teddy and Joey leaned up from the dining room floor and watched the spectacle with amazement, cheering their big friend on. Jimmy rolled over as Ton backed up like a bull before revving forward. As he neared, Jimmy fired three shots that pierced Ton's feet and lungs, but the hog kept coming, crashing into Jimmy's side before dropping his chest on Jimmy's arm. Jimmy screamed in pain and fired five more shots into Ton's shoulder with the gun in his free hand. Ton squealed one last time as his snout crashed into the mud with a thud. Jimmy pulled his arm out and rose, looking at the pig for a moment. His arm felt broken; he chased away into the night, leaving Big Ham in the house.

The force of the wind pushed Teddy back when he stepped out into the yard. He tailed the black figure into the mad wind, but Jimmy was far ahead of him and vanished into the brush at the edge of the property.

The ferocious storm pounded Teddy so hard he almost fell to the ground. He dropped down near Ton, placing his hands on his friend's warm body. Blood ran into puddles of rain on the ground. He closed his eyes. Joey watched from the poolroom.

After a moment, Teddy stood and, fighting the wind, returned to Isabella, entering through the shattered glass.

"He got Half Ton?" Joey asked.

"Yep," Teddy said with a somber tone and paused. Then, he looked at Joey in the eyes. "Thank you very much for what you did, Son, it took a lot of courage."

"Sure, I am just glad you're okay."

"I am fine. Let's go." He placed his hand on Joey's shoulder.

As they walked away, Teddy saw the wall in the dining room splattered with a deep red and the five remaining bottles of *La Gracia* wine lying broken on the console along the wall.

"The wine!" Joey exclaimed.

"Dammit!" Teddy said, shaking his head. "I think I may have a little left in the lab. But Alicia's well, and that's the most important thing."

"Yeah, but it was an elixir."

"I know. Can't win all the wars Son."

Upstairs, Cos and the group took the ladder to the Birdhouse through the interior wall ladder passage and waited patiently. Big Ham received a text via his burner phone from Jimmy to abandon ship, so he went out the way he came in, meeting him at the edge of the property.

Joey and Teddy headed upstairs and down the hall to the library. Isabella warmed and protected them.

Teddy opened the library door, but it was empty inside. Alarmed, he ducked back out into the hall with his gun up in the dark. He heard clatter in the Birdhouse and took the spiral staircase to the loft, where he found the group spread out on the bed.

Alicia jumped up at the sight of Teddy through the dark and met him at the door; she squeezed him. Pressing her head to his chest, he kissed her hair.

"We heard gunfire and we didn't know—I am so glad you're all right."

"What happened?" Cos asked.

He explained, suggesting it was best to stay in the library for the evening; they all went down. Bear waited at the closed and busted library door, pawing at the bottom. Dog sat behind him, turning his head from side to side.

"Look," Cos said. "It's like Bear knows."

"Let him out and see what he does."

Joey opened the door and Bear barreled down the stairs with Dog on his heels. They went after the animals as they cantered straight for the dining room. Bear sat at a windowsill that looked out at his friend and stared. Dog sat next to him and whimpered. The wind picked up and the group left the two sitting there.

CHAPTER 12

*U*pstairs, Teddy asked Joey to select a book to help everyone relax. He read from a collection of Foxfire stories by candlelight.

In a short while, Irene arrived, shaking Isabella so hard it felt as though she would crumble like a gingerbread house in the hands of a hungry fat man. They heard a few booms in the distance like bombs going off in a neighboring town, but no trees or limbs fell on the house. Teddy figured Bob—his tree man—and Eliza—the previous hurricane—had taken care of all the weak vegetation near Isabella.

Joey's soft voice lulled everyone to sleep. The wind still howled and the rain hit the roof, but Irene passed faster and easier than Eliza. After a while, Joey's eyelids became heavy and he thought about Belle. His thoughts trailed into a dream where they baked in the hot sun. He kissed her and the golden light from the sun swirled into them.

Meanwhile, Teddy found himself in a dream sitting in a beautiful green field with Sarah. She looked angelic. He felt peace and grace emanating from her. She didn't say anything, but he heard her thoughts and intentions.

"My dear Teddy, I am so glad you found love again. Marry Alicia, she's your present and your future. You'll have happiness together."

He tried to interrupt the transmission by asking a question, but the message was stronger than his will. When he woke in the library, the good feeling was still with him. He couldn't see Sarah, but he sensed her presence.

The rain had stopped and he went to the window where a violet green brushed the early morning sky. The sun was not yet up, but there was light. The house was still. While putting on his jeans, T-shirt, and emerald green slicker, he decided to wait until he returned from going to Sarah's grave to call the police again.

Before leaving, he went into the office, opened the gun case, and took out a Glock in case the sniper reappeared. He walked by the lowboy in the entry and picked two robust red roses out of an antique blue Chinese vase. Walking into the yard, there was no flood, just light rain damage.

Irene must have slowed down to a Cat 1 before making landfall, he thought.

He walked over to where Half Ton lay, finding Bear and Dog crouching near him with sad eyes. Ton's eyes were closed and he looked satisfied. Teddy placed the rose on the furry white and brown back. Then, he exited. Bear followed.

They both got in the truck with leaves covering the hood and top.

Driving south along Route 1, they found a few limbs were down and some fallen trees lay in yards, but nothing blocked the road. Teddy surveyed the damage, keeping a lookout for any people. A BP sign leaned over to the side.

He turned down Mangrove and passed through downtown, going out towards the country. Spotting Stone Garden Drive, he took a left and drove down the long street. When he reached a stone wall with buttercup flowers along the base, he stopped and entered through a black iron gate, wiggling down the paved drive that took grieving visitors through the cemetery. He came to a stop at Sarah's plot—they had inherited the plots from Red along with Isabella. Taking the rose, he got out with Bear. A five-foot-tall piece of cut marble marked her tomb. The Prayer of St. Francis of Assisi was engraved on it. He placed the single red rose on top of the stone. Instead of breaking down like he thought he would, he just smiled.

"I guess we need to catch up, Sarah."

Teddy and Bear stood there for a moment, then Teddy started to tell her about Cos and Joey and how they were growing up nicely, becoming men instead of boys, his love for Alicia that knew no bounds and how his love for Half Ton had softened his hardened heart. He realized that somehow, maybe, everything, even the cancer, was a learning experience for their growth. When he finished, he left.

Teddy headed toward the ocean and reached Route 1. On the radio, a DJ reported that the electric companies were working to resolve the power outages before confirming Teddy's suspicions that Irene was only a Cat 1 when she touched down. The sun got a leg up on the clouds over the horizon. He decided to go to the marina to check on *Gold Lip*.

Continuing south along the bay to the marina, a post-hurricane sun came out. As he approached the marina, he saw boards stuck up on the dock. One boat had skipped its space, landing sideways on a neighboring boat.

Yikes, Teddy thought as he parked. He took the Glock in case Jimmy was lurking around, put it in his pocket, and went to the marina. Bear followed.

He saw a young man leaning on his knees and attempting to dislodge the nose of a large sailboat that had wedged under the dock. The sailboat tilted to the side, but wasn't taking on water. Irene had snapped the mast in half and left the top dangling from an upright stub. Teddy offered to help, and the man—who said his name was Clark—welcomed his strength. Together they managed to get the nose out, which had a small crack, and the body showed some mild damage. Clark's face drooped with disappointment, but he seemed relieved it wasn't worse and thanked Teddy. After Clark turned, Teddy saw him spin the top of his watch one way and then the other. He walked back over.

"What did you just do?" Teddy said, remembering Admiral García Díaz from his dreams doing this very thing on La Gracia.

"Spinning the knob of my watch? It's just something I've always done."

"Why?"

"I don't know. My father did it, and so did his father. For good luck, you know. I think it's an old sailor thing. Why do you ask?"

Teddy looked deep into his eyes and smiled.

"No reason. Great meeting you, Clark."

"You too."

Teddy strolled around the marina, inspecting the damage. A few more boats had broken masts—others were thrown into pilings. When he reached *Gold Lip*, his heart sank. All that was left of her was a pile of rubble rammed up against the docks, broken into three parts. He looked on baffled and bewildered, his hopes for finding *La Gracia* now dashed. He couldn't afford to buy another boat, and without one, it didn't matter how close they were. The tears began to fall down his face as he stared dumbstruck at the wreckage. Bear looked on and let out an empathetic meow. Teddy walked over; Bear found his mini captain hat on the dock around the boat, picked it up in his mouth, and brought it to Teddy.

"I should've put her in the warehouse, Bear," he stated, "Somehow, but oh well, I couldn't afford that this time either." Teddy kneeled and another tear fell. He hit his hand on the dock. "Dammit!" he said.

Suddenly, up the coast, he saw a huge grey cloud approaching, getting larger and larger as it did. He wiped the tears away and squinted to make it out, and as it neared, he recognized the seagulls. He hadn't seen the birds since many years ago, back when he and Sarah were together. They were on another mission this time, flying like a squad of B-52 bombers. When they reached the marina by the hundreds, the whole area came alive with the sound of their wings and squawking. Clark looked up, stunned. They headed north along the bay and up the sandy coast. Teddy followed them, heading out of the marina along a path through the park. The path ended and he headed over a dune to a tiny wooden bridge to the beach. Bear sprinted forward onto the beach; Teddy followed. Smiling, he slipped off his flip-flops and sank his toes into the plush sand. The gulls flew ahead and turned around, coming back toward him. An elegant brown pelican perched near the water's edge, taking flight as Teddy approached. Pieces of driftwood, sea moss, and shells speckled the wet mica more than normal. The gulls passed back over him, and then, turning around, headed back up the coast. He wondered what they were trying to tell him. This time, when the gulls reached a certain point, they darted to the right and headed off over the ocean to the horizon again.

Teddy saw Bear digging in the sand up ahead about where the gulls had turned. He went over and kneeled by Bear; a shell stuck out of the sand; he ran his hand along its rough surface; Bear dug around it. He observed that it was very square. Pulling it out, he set it on the sand. His eyes blossomed when he saw that it wasn't a shell at all, but a thick crust covering a small rectangular metal box. Scanning the distant shoreline, he spotted the lighthouse, the onshore marker for where Cos had found the pistol.

Must have washed ashore with the storm, he thought. Bear watched.

He surveyed the area for people. Seeing no one, he picked up the box and carried it back to his car. At the marina, Clark was pressure-washing his boat; he waved at Teddy and Teddy waved back before jumping in his truck and peeling out to the farm.

Back at Isabella, Cos woke. Shirtless, he picked up the .22 before shuffling downstairs to get breakfast. Setting the rifle on the counter, he prepared some steel-cut oatmeal and topped it with butter, honey, and blueberries. The yard seen through the shattered glass was a mess. He called Leslie at once, but his call went straight to voicemail. With the gun in one hand and the oatmeal in the other, he strolled down the hall toward the indoor pool to observe the damage.

In the poolroom, he saw the broken glass on the floor where puddles of warm rain had collected. The smoke from the bomb left a chalky murk in the pool, and the stone floor in front of the door was busted from the gunshots. Through the shattered wall, he saw leaves and limbs littering the outside. Then, his eyes went to Half Ton, lying on the lawn with the single rose resting on his back. The scene saddened him and he walked back to the hall. There, golf-ball-sized slug holes in the antique floral wallpaper caught his eye. He raked his finger in one. As he moved closer, he spotted a tone of French blue among the plaster.

He couldn't make out what it was, but it sparked his interest. He took a bite of oatmeal before withdrawing his Swiss Army knife. Unfolding the smallest blade, he picked at the wallpaper, removed a big chunk, and pulled it back about five inches. What he saw next astonished him.

Behind the wallpaper, instead of a plain plastered wall, there was a painting of a man working in a field. The sky was baby blue, the field of golden wheat. He couldn't believe his eyes and tore back more of the paper—the more he removed, the larger the image became. Through the uneven tears, he could still decipher a small house on a hill in the country. He ran upstairs to wake Joey and Buzz, who came down with him.

Joey called to check on Belle, who answered quietly. She was alarmed by Joey's news and wanted to see him at once, but he told her to wait.

When Joey and Buzz saw the discovery, they both looked amazed. Buzz knew how to remove wallpaper, so following his instruction, they started to spray the wall with water to moisten it. Then, they got a scraper from the garage, and very gently scraped the wallpaper so as to not damage the mural.

In the meantime, Teddy and Bear returned to the farm, going straight to the preservation room with the box. Dog greeted them in the yard. Teddy unlocked the door and they entered. After examining the box, he began cutting through the crust.

Back inside, the longer the young men scraped, the larger the image became. After a while, they were awestruck, staring at a seven-foot-tall by ten-foot-wide fresco spanning the edge of the dining room to the entrance of the spa. Joey hurried off to get some towels to clean it.

When it was dry, they wiped the sweat off their brows and admired it. Broad fields rolled along hills, a house perched on one of them. The man plowed the land around it, which traveled to the edge of a cliff that dropped off on the left side into an ocean with wooden fishing boats floating in the sunshine. Two lovers with ruddy skin gazed at each other in the foreground.

"What do you think it means?" Joey asked Cos, his arms crossed over his chest.

"It's just a painting, I don't think it means anything."

"No. It's about love, the everlasting kind," Buzz said, studying it.

"Well, do you think it's worth anything?" Cos asked him.

"Absolutely, but it's a mural, so it kind of goes with the house," Buzz said.

"Yeah, I guess you're right. Pretty cool we found it, though."

"Yep," Joey said.

"Salt will like it," Buzz said.

"Sure will!" Cos said.

Alicia came downstairs, walking over to where they were gathered. She told them good morning with a smile, but as she approached, she covered her mouth at the sight of the mural.

CHAPTER 13

In the preservation room, Teddy buzzed the crust off the luminous metal box in about twenty minutes, but had been working the lock for the last forty. He couldn't seem to pry it open or unlock it with a universal key of any sort. Bear and Dog watched, attentive to his every action.

Finally, he sat against the wall, staring around the room; his gold gone, his boat destroyed, his pride tarnished. What if the box was empty or contained an item as pitiful as that plain ring, he thought; then the bank would seize Isabella and Bateman and Banks would destroy the rugged Florida coast. Charlotte would be out of a job. The Pearlmakers would have to break up. On the verge of giving up, his eyes came to the boxes of water, and there, beside the cannon, he saw the antique pistol Cos had found while surfing. He got up, reached in, took it out, and dried it off with a cloth.

All that's left is this stupid gun, he thought—another dead end. He twirled the gun around. He could probably get forty thousand for it, maybe. *Who were you for?* he thought. *Did you ever kill a man? No, too ornate for fighting. You're royal like a gun made for a king or a prince. A prince.* He paused for a short moment. *That's it.* He fully extended the long octagonal piece on the end of the gun that appeared to be designed to be used as a belt tie—his hands shaking all the while—and tried to fit it into the lock of the box. With a little shake, it turned and clicked. His smile expanded. It must have been the Admiral's gun, aha.

He lifted the lid and the light in the room ricocheted into a thousand pieces off the largest diamond he had ever seen, perfectly fit into tufted velvet that was a little rugged, but still preserved.

"A big star splinter!" He held it up. "We're rich, we're rich boys, we're really rich!" He picked Dog up, kissed him on the mouth, and swung him around. "I mean we're really rich boys, like really, really rich!" He put Dog down and petted Bear, looking at him: "You did it Bear, *you found it*! You really were a Pearlmaker all along. A cat that likes water couldn't be anything less!" Bear smiled and meowed. Teddy picked up the diamond and, feeling like Santa Claus at Christmas, skated to the main house. "Six years of searching and dreaming finally paid off." He paused, fiddling with his keys.

Teddy walked inside with Bear and Dog on his heels, locking the door behind them. Going through the living room, he saw the boys and Alicia talking in the hallway. Grinning, he almost knocked over a side table as he headed toward them.

"Good morning everyone!" he said, holding his arms up.

"Good morning, Dad. You're not going believe what we found!"

Teddy was a little taken aback, and snapped, "No, *you're* not going believe what *I* found!" As he approached, however, he saw the painting in the hall.

"What is this? *A mural?*" Teddy asked as he walked up and touched it. And for a moment, he forgot about the diamond.

"We found it underneath the wallpaper," Cos said.

"Oh sweetheart, don't you see?" begged Alicia. "It's the dream you told me about, the dream about us. It's just like your drawings."

He recognized the lovers in the middle.

"Oh my, it most certainly is. Why, I can't even believe it." He backed up and rubbed Alicia's shoulder, smiling. Then, he turned and kissed her on the forehead. "But how did it get here?"

"We have no idea," Alicia said. "We thought you might know. It looks very old."

"Do you know the history of the house?" Joey asked.

"Only so far back, but I can find out. But first, I also found something that beats the hell outta this." He paused and opened the box containing the illustrious Prince.

"You found it?! But-but how?!" Alicia asked.

"My old friends the seagulls came back and pointed the way to it. Technically, Bear found it. It was washed up on the beach. Good thing, too, because the storm totaled *Gold Lip*."

"The little Manx! He's a Pearlmaker after all," Joey said.

"I am sorry about the boat. But oh my goodness! I just can't believe it!" Alicia said, shaking her head.

"But I have something even better than that to give you, Alicia."

"What could be better than all this?"

He fell on bended knee and removed the plain ivory ring he had found many moons ago while searching for La Gracia from his pocket and presented it to her.

"What do you say to *forever?*" Teddy asked, beaming.

"Yes! Yes! Of course! But of course." The two hugged and kissed on the mouth with closed lips. Joey, Buzz, and Cos hugged the future husband and wife and reached around to get a better look at the diamond.

"Wow, that's the biggest diamond I've ever seen," Buzz said.

"And it's the biggest one you will *ever* likely see. And we have Cos and Joey to thank for it. Joey told me about the legend, and the pistol belt tie was the key to the lock."

"It was? Sweet," Cos said. "Had to be something, you know."

"Best of all, we don't have to sell Isabella!" Everyone clapped. "And Buzz, I want you to become a Pearlmaker after we build the ship and continue the hunt for *La Gracia*."

"Thanks. Count me in."

"There's still wine down there, and gold, and rubies, and all sorts of stuff. It's like the biggest bounty ever, you know."

"Okay, sounds good," Buzz hollered.

"Now let's make sure we put this diamond in a *real* safe in case the sniper comes back. I have a secret safe upstairs no one knows about. It will be safe there."

They carried the diamond upstairs. Teddy called 911 to report the incident with the sniper and the lady informed that him an officer would be out shortly.

Walking behind the desk, he opened a gold-trimmed landscape of Tuscan cows to reveal a safe. He carefully placed the diamond inside. While setting it down, he noticed Red Dollarhide's file in a bison leather-bound folder, and laid it on the desk. They gathered around as he flipped through black and white photos and newspaper clippings. At the end, he came upon an article praising Red for saving a drowning child's life one day while visiting Isabella. The article reported the incident before describing him as a good man who worked in real estate and who had bought Isabella as an investment. The house was built and named by the Spanish merchant Álvaro Ramos in 1687.

Teddy sat back and thought for a moment. In his lucid flashback dreams on La Gracia, he remembered being called by the name "Ram" —he knew it was a nickname, but never knew what it meant. Ram … Ramos:

"My goodness, it was *him*," Teddy exclaimed.

"What do you mean?" Joey asked.

"The man who built this house, Álvaro Ramos, was the person I dream about. When he got shipwrecked, he must have used the swiped treasure to open a trade and built a house afterward. This house. Then, it was added onto over the years." He looked at Alicia.

"Really? That's amazing!" she said.

"So who is Isabella?" Cos asked.

"Perhaps it was the name of the woman you dream about. How sweet," Alicia said.

"Yes, and I bet he had the painting commissioned. Over the years, someone must have covered it up," Teddy said.

"That's incredible, y'all!" Joey said

"Can we know more about these people?" Alicia asked.

"Yes, with a name we should be able to find out more. I'll call

Patch. He knows how to really hunt Google. I need to tell the Pearlmakers about the diamond anyway."

The power was down, but their cell phones worked. Teddy got Patch, who gasped at the news of The Prince. He agreed to do research on the house and Ramos on his laptop and bring it over when he was done. Teddy set down the phone; the doorbell rang; he closed the safe but left the papers on his desk.

The group settled down in the living room and he went to the door. In the peephole, he saw Catfish in uniform. He opened it and greeted him, offering him coffee. They made small talk about the storm before Teddy came to the sniper incident.

"We had a little rodeo here last night. Before the storm, some wacko started shooting at us. Let me show you where it happened." Cat took out a pad and they walked from the living room to the kitchen. Teddy showed Catfish the kitchen window and then took him into the poolroom, detailing how Half Ton had saved them but died in the process. Staring out at the fallen hog, Cat couldn't believe his eyes.

"You had this hog all along?" Cat said.

"Yeah, he came knocking during Eliza and there was something in his eyes, you know—I just couldn't shoot him."

"I've never heard of a feral hog being anything other than wild. Well, we'll have to do a full investigation on a crime like this. Do you have any idea who the sniper was?"

"No. I just know the sharks did it. The same ones who stole my chest."

"I understand, Teddy, but without evidence, we've got nothing. We have to get the shooter. Do you have any clue as to what he looked like or what kind of car he drove?"

Teddy thought hard. "No. Just that he was tall and thin."

"Without any leads, it's going to be really hard to find him. There's nothing from the first time?"

Teddy thought. "Can you remind me of the day again?"

Cat looked at his pad, "It was June sixteenth."

Teddy thought back to the day, "No, nothing."

Cat shook his head. A knock occurred at the front door; Teddy excused himself to answer it. In the peephole, he saw Will Burns and opened it.

"Yes Mr. Burns.?"

"Hello Mr. Dollarhide, it's Will Burns—Belle's father."

"Hey Will," they shook hands. "What can I do you for?"

"I was on the board of directors at Bateman and Banks. I heard they've been harassing you."

Teddy's smile flipped. "Harassing me, that's an understatement. They practically killed me!"

"That's so terrible. I heard about it."

"Well you're one of them, as far as I am concerned."

"Not anymore—I resigned this morning and sold off my shares. They've always been tough on people, but I didn't know anything illegal was going on until yesterday. I couldn't be a part of it. I may have some information that could help you, too."

"Okay Will, why don't you come on in," Teddy said.

Will walked in and Teddy introduced him to everyone.

"Officer, my name is Will Burns. I was driving up Sand Piper Street late at night to check out Mr. Dollarhide's land and see what all the fuss was about when I saw an orange F250 on the side of the road."

Catfish took notes down in his Moleskine. "What time was it?"

"I guess it was around 11 p.m.," Will said.

"Go on, Mr. Burns."

"Two men were loading a chest into the bed. I found it odd, but thought they were workers and didn't find it suspicious enough to warrant a call. But when my daughter told me that Bateman and Banks had hired a someone to harass this family, I immediately thought of it."

"Do you remember the date?"

"Let me see." Will whipped out his Iphone and scrolled through the calendar. "The sixteenth."

"Thank you, Mr. Burns," Catfish said. "That's the date we have. Did you catch a plate or exact color of the F250?"

"No, I didn't see the plates, but it was orange all right, like a pumpkin."

Joey and Cos rested on the couch tired from the previous night—almost asleep, Joey jerked up at the words *orange F250*.

"Wait—Cos and I saw an orange truck like that at the Sea Breeze motel the day before the storm. We were going to Cap'ns. The license plate caught our attention."

"Do you remember what it was?" Cat asked.

Joey thought hard. "I was so distracted that day I can't remember."

"I'll never forget it, though Joey," Cos said. "'Gunslinger,' spelled G-N-S-L-N-G-R on New York plates."

"Oh yeah, gunslinger! Ha! What an idiot, putting that on his plates!" Joey said.

Cat shook his head in amazement. "This bozo is flying a flag right there on his plates, just asking to get caught. Let's take some samples of the bullet shells and see if we can match them if he is carrying a gun. He may even be at the motel. Guys like this are risk-takers. And they have a habit of getting away. We'll see."

"Great! Good work boys," Teddy said. He thanked Mr. Burns sincerely, patting him on the back. Catfish went outside with Teddy and examined some of the shells.

"They look like armor-piercing bullets for an automatic long-range assault rifle—should be easy to match. I'll head to the Sea Breeze right now. Do you want me to send an armed guard here?"

"Thanks for the offer, Cat, but we'll be fine."

"Okay, keep all your doors locked. I'll call you with any news," Cat said.

Teddy thanked him, sending him away with some of Charlotte's homemade apple pie.

Will walked over to Joey at the sofa.

"Joey, I am sorry about what I said to you at our house. I realize now it's wrong to make assumptions about people. I've been bullheaded. Belle got herself into a dangerous situation and I became overprotective."

"Thank you sir," Joey said, looking at Will. "I understand. You know I love her."

"I can tell you do and I hope it works out for y'all. I really do."

With that, Will Banks left. Charlotte and Dal passed him on the way out. Teddy hugged them, relaying everything that happened with the diamond and the sniper; then, he showed them the mural. Dal giggled like an idiot over the diamond as Charlotte went into the kitchen and began to work her magic around the damage. The smell of black-eyed peas and beef began to spill out into the house. Their stomachs carried them into the dining room where they ate, conversed, and laughed.

Toward the end of the meal, a knock occurred. Charlotte went to answer it and saw Ty and Patch through the hole. She welcomed them in and asked if they were hungry. They followed her into the dining room, greeted everyone, and pulled up chairs by Teddy. They all looked at The Prince, examining it over and over again. Then, they celebrated with hugs and congratulations. And with the whole crew present, Teddy popped a bottle of his finest champagne. After toasting, Patch presented his research—Alicia moved her chair over as he directed them to a photocopy of a letter penned on parchment paper in formal cursive from Álvaro Ramos to a friend in Spain. Teddy asked Alicia to read and translate it aloud. She read:

Dear Rodriguez,

Our ship was wrecked in a storm off the coast of the New World. Some of the crew and I took a boat to the shore, but it capsized close to the beach and the strong waves overtook many men. Only three others and I survived, landing in a place called Florida near San Agustin. It is wild here, but tropical and pleasant. Things grow well and we've had no trouble with the natives. But there are wild beasts and odd insects. At first I was lonely, but I have befriended some countrymen. As the ship was sinking, I salvaged some gold and managed to set myself up as a merchant. As my business flourished, I employed the other survivors. With God's help, we have done well, and I built a nice house near the ocean. But I long for my homeland. I miss my family. And most of all, I miss Isabella. I would like to pay for her to come live with me or for her to wait until I can find a way home. Please deliver this to her.

 Your Humble Servant & Friend,
 Álvaro Ramos

"That's unbelievable," Teddy remarked, "Did they ever get together?" he asked Patch.

"Well, I thought so at first, but I don't think so. Look at what I found here." He pointed to the second letter penned in Spanish and had Alicia translate it as well.

My Dearest Sister,

 My heart and soul have been in pain ever since La Gracia went missing and I lost Álvaro. I have wept until everything inside of me is gone. I want to stop, but weeping is the only thing that makes me feel better. At times, I have wanted not to go on. The suitors come night and day. What they want with a tailor's daughter, I cannot understand. I reject them all, but there is one man, the Prince of Spain, Felipe García, who sits with me and listens when I speak. He is soft and reminds me of Álvaro and he is very modest to be a Prince. I can't say I do not find him charming. Since he is royalty, I think I should have no choice but to marry him, however, he says he won't force me. He insisted I must be in love with him and want to engage. When I am with him, I am able to let go of the sadness for a time. I am considering marriage, but feel like I will be letting go of Álvaro. Dear kind sister, lend me your wisdom, what should I do?

 Yours Truly,
 Isabel

Teddy placed the letter down.

"Oh, it's just so sad. Is this story for real?" Alicia replied.

"Well what happened?" Charlotte demanded.

"Look at this," Patch said, pointing to a scanned photo of a painted portrait of a prince and his bride. The woman had dark skin, a long straight nose, black hair, and large, round amber eyes, not unlike the woman painted on the hallway wall. Underneath the painting, it read in script, *Princess Isabel García*.

"It's Isabel," Alicia remarked.

"That's also the woman I see in my dreams. It's like a whirlwind of weird for me. Like looking into the mirror of my dreams with all this stuff," Teddy exclaimed, pointing at the image.

"So, she thought Álvaro was dead and married the prince. She either never got his letter or when she did, it was too late," Alicia said.

"Yep, but I think she never got it," Patch said, pointing to an old envelope printed off the internet from Florida with the words "Adriana Ramos" on it.

"It seems that by the time he wrote, she already had married Prince Felipe and most likely his friend didn't deliver it. When Álvaro didn't hear back, he married Adriana. The dates are snubbed out on the letters, so there's no way to know."

"Perhaps he even covered the mural himself," Teddy said as he and Alicia studied the document. "Well, at least, it's good to know the whole story."

"So let me understand this clearly: Prince Felipe commissioned *La Gracia* to be built and he was also the one who pursued Isabel and demanded the diamond, which was given to him by the country of Africa, to be presented to Isabel who was a beautiful tailor's daughter in Seville, Spain, as a wedding gift? And Felipe and Isabela got hitched in Spain, and our man Álvaro Ramos wound up marrying this other Adriana woman he met in Florida after being shipwrecked from *La Gracia?*" Teddy asked.

"Yes, well, I hadn't thought about it all until now, but it would have to be that way," Patch said.

"So, the diamond he sent with the ship was for Isabella, but she never received it?" Dal asked.

"That's my guess," Patch said. "I am having trouble wrapping my mind around all of it."

"I think we're all a little baffled by it," Teddy said. "I can't thank you enough though, Patch. You did excellent research this time, thank

God these people were royalty so we were able to find out all of this about them on google."

"Anything for you, captain!"

"Stay and celebrate with us! There will be dancing!" Teddy said.

"No thank you, I have to clean up. My yard was hit pretty hard."

"C'mon! You don't wanna watch a big man move? I'll teach you some tricks."

"Thanks, Salt, but I gotta go."

"All right. Well I am giving lessons at the Holiday Inn every Monday, Tuesday, and Thursday if you change your mind," Teddy joked. "As soon as we auction off the diamond, you'll receive a handsome bit, and we're going to keep searching for the rest of the treasure. This is just the tip of the iceberg."

"Thank you, Salt."

Teddy leaned over and kissed Alicia. Cosby and Joey wandered away upstairs to shower. And Buzz went back home to rearrange his life. Patch exited and Charlotte tailed him, locking the door after him. The group ate and drank into the evening with Teddy playing the piano and Alicia singing. As it grew dark, Charlotte, Ty, and Dal left, and Teddy and Alicia retired to the living room, where they both read until Teddy's phone rang. He answered.

"Hey Teddy."

"Hey Cat, what do you know?"

"We found the sniper. When we went to the Sea Breeze, his orange F250 was there. He was laid up in his room with broken ribs and a bummed leg. That hog busted him up good." He laughed. "We got the weapon, and the bullets will probably be a match. He was hurting so bad, I think he was glad to see us."

"Amen!" Teddy yelled. "They got him!" he barked to the house. "Hallelujah! Thanks, Cat. Any sign of my chest of gold, though? I could really use it. You know, it saved my life, finding that. I have debts, you know."

"Not yet, I am sorry. Looks like he sunk it or something. Not a word edgewise will come out of him about it. He won't even speak for a reduced sentence."

"Dammit. Well—thanks again, I guess. I just wish he would cough up that gold. Without it, I am broke until I cash in this new find!"

"We'll try, but probably not. He said he never took it. We still need to do a formal investigation. I'll send an officer and forensics expert over and they'll take your statement. After that, I think we're done."

"Okay, thanks boss!" Teddy said.

"Sure, later my man."

Teddy hung up the phone. He studied Isabella's walls, marveling at her humble beginnings and how she was added onto over the years. Someone in town always told him that a New York tycoon spent a fortune in the Flagler golden days, renovating Isabella to resemble the Fatios and Mizners of Palm Beach, suggesting that was what gave her the grandeur and grace. And perhaps they were right about her grandeur, but Teddy now knew her grace came from somewhere much deeper—Álvaro Ramos, a humble Spanish sailor's love for his dream girl, Isabella, back home in Spain.

Joey and Cos entered asking if it was safe for them to go to an open-air movie at the high school football field now with their respective girlfriends since the sniper was gone. Teddy waved them on with a jolly grin and Alicia fluttered in and landed on his lap. They smiled and kissed.

CHAPTER 14

The next day, Jimmy exposed Stern Banks in a bid for a reduced sentence, and Banks, in turn, squealed on Sheriff Waterhouse. He also revealed where the stolen treasure was, and the chest was recovered and returned to Teddy.

Teddy wanted to give Half Ton a proper funeral. After reflecting on it, he decided to bury the giant at the Willis Plantation, to protect the place from bad spirits.

He called Bob Barclay. Bob arrived that afternoon towing a small piece of equipment and hoisted Half Ton up in the air by a canvas belt with its crane, loading the body into the bed of his truck.

On a ninety-nine-degree day with a white sky, Teddy trailed Bob out to the Willis Plantation. When they entered the gate, the temperature dropped fifteen degrees and the white sky disappeared behind dark foliage. The wicked trees watched them and the air reeked of wet wood and rotting vegetables. Even Bob acted uncomfortable on the property, digging as fast he could with the mini Caterpillar.

After half an hour, Teddy felt a fever coming out of nowhere. He waited and watched as Bob lowered the hog down into the enormous grave and then covered the hole. The two men packed the dirt down with the backside of the shovels. Teddy took one of the *Bateman and*

Banks: Lot for Sale signs from his truck, broke it up to create a small white cross, and stuck it at the head of the grave. In black Sharpie, he wrote "Half Ton" across the horizontal plank and dropped a bouquet of gardenias he'd picked up on the way from the young boy at the Ball neighborhood vendor's stand.

Teddy said a long prayer—Bob removed his hat and recited his own prayer when Teddy finished. The prayer rambled on for an eternity—Teddy eventually had to stop him, and paid him—then they left.

TEDDY CALLED the bank to inform them about the diamond, and he was able to borrow money to pay off his debt on Isabella until the stone could be inspected and auctioned. A week later, Teddy sent The Prince diamond to an appraisal agency used by the best auctioneers in New York. They informed him the process would take five weeks.

By mid-July, the heat had risen to epic proportions, breaking 106 degrees. That wasn't dry desert heat either, but Southern fire with 92 percent humidity.

And for the first time in years, Teddy's dreams about the sunken galleon were gone.

On July 20th, Latch hosted its annual Mutt Parade and Classical Symphony at Lover's Bay Park. Everyone gathered around, some on lawn chairs and others on quilts, to watch the show and dine with picnic baskets full of goodies like tuna salad sandwiches, cheese, and red wine. Around 1 p.m., a troop of dressed-up dogs trotted in the parade—one like Deadpool, another dressed like a pirate, and so on. Following it, the Jacksonville Classical Orchestra performed in chairs facing the water. Afterward, the young boy with the flower stall came running through the crowd wearing a nice suit with the legs rolled up, his feet skipping.

"*Come look, come look! Everyone come look!*"

"What is it?" a middle-aged man with trimmed blonde bangs and a golf shirt on asked.

"*You'll see. Come look, come look!*"

"Where?" a young lady asked.

"Follow me, I know the way." He waved them after him, hopping up and down with a wide smile. A crowd began to rise and move toward him. He ran out to a vintage red truck and hopped in the passenger seat; then, his uncle drove away slowly. People headed to their cars, pulling out in a line.

Teddy, Belle, Joey, Cos, Leslie, Dal, Charlotte, and Dog piled into Teddy's Ford and its bed and drove off. The red truck hustled into the country for miles, eventually turning down the gravel road to the Willis Plantation. Up ahead, everyone saw something in the air. As they got closer, they recognized that above the trees, hundreds of butterflies were filling the sky, rising like a symphonic hot air balloon.

Teddy and Alicia watched slack-jawed. Joey, Belle, Cos, and Leslie craned around from the bed of the truck, squinting their eyes through the dust from the road. Even Dog looked forward to see what all the excitement was about.

The cars parked along the side of the road. When people got out, they headed after the boy as he hurried toward the forested property. Some of the butterflies sailed out over the crowd, while others hovered above the trees. One came toward Belle, landing on her shoulder; another hit Teddy's windshield and he observed that it was a queen butterfly, not a swallowtail.

They followed the crowd up the gravel road. As they neared the tree-lined property, they saw that the once dark and twisted limbs had grown straight, glowing with a lush green, vibrating with life like something that had just been born somewhere special.

When they entered, it was warm inside the land, but not too hot, and there was a steady breeze from somewhere. The people gathered in awe, standing and watching the beautiful insects floating out from the open windows of the manse. The peeling paint on the white house had repaired itself and the once dark windows sparkled with sunlight. Teddy's attention was drawn to Half Ton's grave to his left, now covered by a bed of brilliant white gardenias that grew up and around it, the cross hidden behind their blossoms. A lush garden of various flowers expanded out from the grave, the petals vibrant and the scent like a potent perfume. Teddy held his hand on his forehead in amazement. The residents of Latchawatchee were speechless as they watched the whole spectacle.

The young boy went to the door of the house, and some people gasped. Teddy walked ahead of the group toward him. Barclay tried to stop him, suggesting it might be dangerous, but he pushed on.

Taking his hand, the boy led him in. The house was empty of furniture, but the walls looked freshly painted and the old wood floors seemed new and polished with fresh beeswax. Butterflies perched on the white walls and danced in the air. They walked through them to the upstairs, and a few of the delicate winged creatures hitched a ride on them. A luminous ray shone out of one room. The boy entered, and Teddy followed. Many butterflies were there, too. In the corner, a book titled *The Willis Plantation History* sat on a wooden table.

As Teddy opened it, he expected to find a detailed description of how runaway slaves and their helpers were killed, or something horrible to that effect. But as he turned through the pages and read, the ink began to disappear right before his eyes and all the pages became blank. The boy stood beside him.

"What does it mean?" the boy asked. Teddy paused for a moment.

"It means that whatever violence happened here is over now, and all the memories of tragedy are gone from this place."

"Good. Can we go?"

"Yes, my dear friend."

They exited, walking down the stairs with some of the butterflies following them. The crowd strolled the grounds, admiring the flowers, eventually entering the house to see the spectacle for themselves. After a while, Teddy and the group returned to Lover's Bay Park to continue the celebration.

AFTER THAT DAY, things were different in Latch. The city no longer let things go like it had with the Ball neighborhood, and with a little help from local volunteer groups, the neighborhood rebuilt itself with new houses all raised to hurricane code. Ignorance was less—instead of gossiping about what other people were doing wrong, people focused on improving their own lives—others stopped envying people and shifted their attention to what they could do to improve their own circumstances. There were still some problems and a few bad eggs, but things were better. Buzz moved into the Willis Plantation, bought by Teddy, and managed the property on Teddy's behalf. And with the help of world class horticulturalists, it became a nationally recognized garden and historic estate.

Butterflies covered the grounds of the place and the flowers continued to grow where no seeds were planted. Species grew that shouldn't grow in a Floridian climate, and the vegetation never wilted when the seasons changed, not even one petal. A young girl with leukemia was cured after picking a gardenia off Half Ton's grave, and the news spread like wildfire. Within a few months, it became known as a place for healing like Lourdes in France, Chimayo in Santa Fe, New Mexico or Mount Kailash in Tibet, and people from all over the world flocked there to see the gardens and butterflies. Some got well, others didn't, but everyone said that they received a sense of peace from their visits. The tourism caused the stores in town to flourish. Butterflies were abundant in the green spaces of the town as well as in Lover's Bay Park.

Sadly, ole Bear was never the same after Half Ton died. He became depressed, and one day, the cat ran away. Teddy looked everywhere for him. A week later, he received a call from Buzz that the Manx had shown up at the doorstep of the Willis estate, refusing to leave. He said the ole manx would run the grounds and then just sit in front of the hog's grave to keep his old friend company. Teddy just laughed and said he could have the old tiger.

CHAPTER 15

Teddy had the Hodge's gold reported and cashed in by the end of July and distributed to each shareholder. Joey declined his job in Yosemite, and he and Belle spent August on their boat, docking in Key West where they loved to explore the artsy downtown, eat Cuban sandwiches and Cuban cortadito coffees (a double espresso with a dollop of cane sugar, topped with steamed milk) at the Cuban Coffee Queen's stand by the marina, and gobble down as many slices of key lime pie as they could on Duval Street. Their connection strengthened with time, flowing deep and strong like the saltwater in the Gulf Stream.

Cos paid off his debt to Latch High. Then he, Dog, and Leslie went to Miami together so Cos could start practicing with the University of Miami Hurricanes while Leslie volunteered in the Everglades until classes started. They bought a boat and rented a dock slip in the posh Miami Beach marina. Dog loved it because he could swim and surf as much as he wanted.

By mid-August, everyone was eager to hear about The Prince diamond. Teddy had been checking his mail twice a day and his email ten times a day. When the news came in that the diamond appraised at a staggering 450 million dollars, Teddy decided to strike while the iron was hot by sending it straight to auction. The auction was an invitation-only soiree in South Beach of the wealthiest players in the world. Bidders who couldn't be there were allowed to place real-time bids online. All the major news outlets had live coverage, and the Pearlmakers' story got international attention. After aggressive bidding, The Prince sold for 550 million to a Japanese billionaire. Uncle Sam took his small share without even rolling up a sleeve, but Teddy walked away with a large chunk of change. He knew exactly what he wanted to do with it, too. Hell, he had spent years floating around the sea, making plans.

The first thing was to pay the Pearlmakers their shares. Ty and Patch each got 10 percent of the total, while 25 percent went to Dallas. After paying them, Teddy bought a lot of the property around Isabella. And he and Buzz finished the wooden sailboat. Then, he and Alicia financed her parents' business and her own, which she named *The Pearlstringer*, setting up an online shop and a storefront in the French West Indies Island of St. Barthelemy. Teddy and Dal bought houses on the same street in St. Barts within walking distance of the store. The lots sat right on a majestic sparkling harbor, where Teddy docked his boat.

Teddy donated a big piece of his money for a non-profit to be founded in order to repair the homes of the families dispersed from the Ball neighborhood in Latch.

After calling the other lab that was supposed to be running tests on the wine, he learned it had been mysteriously lost. So, he let it go, and funneled the rest of his money to setting up a nonprofit called *Sarah's Dream* dedicated to feeding starving communities via the use of the Moringa and many other things as well.

In mid-September, Joey and Belle visited St. Barts to see Alicia and Teddy. From the moment they set foot in the French West Indies, they felt alive. A stream of vitality flowed into the people, food, plants—everything emanated like it had been touched by heaven. And after a day of sun, two mojitos, and a meal of wild caught fish, the two lovers stumbled into the crescent moon-shaped harbor lit by paper lanterns strung along the beach. After burrowing in the white sand beside a beached sailboat, they agreed to stay there forever. The next day, they bought a dock slip and decided to hunt for sunken galleons in the Atlantic. Belle agreed that California *and* Florida no longer mattered, they were free now!

Alicia and Teddy chose Alicia's birthday, which happened to be his favorite holiday, Christmas Day, for their marriage. On Christmas Eve, everyone they cared about traveled to St. Barts for the wedding: Alicia's father, Hugo, brother, Jose, and mother, Sofia crossed the pond; the Pearlmakers showed up to be Teddy's best men. Even Catfish made it. Teddy placed them all in an open-air hotel overlooking an ocean so clear they could see the bottom from their balconies. Lavish wreaths appointed the candlelit white-washed rooms full of teak furniture. The weather was seventy-five degrees and a nice breeze blew all the time. Abundant presents flowed out from the base of Teddy's penthouse, blocking the doorway. Each person, including Dog, had at least ten.

On Christmas Day, Alicia's birthday, they opened presents with Joey, Belle, Cos, Leslie, Ty, Patch, Dal, and Charlotte, and the gifts were luxuries they had never imagined being able to give each other. They ate lunch on their balcony with the ocean crashing upon the sand below. Afterward, everyone traveled down a long, sandy road to a nearby clapboard church tucked in between a forest of lush green plants. Alicia radiated love and health, and her dear mother, Sofia, couldn't stop crying at the sight of her healthy daughter.

Teddy had a special perfume made for her, choosing the essences he thought reflected her true nature. With notes of peony, vanilla, and musk, he named it Isabella and gave it to her the night before the ceremony along with a pair of earrings fashioned out of two coins he had found from *La Gracia*.

For the eloquent ceremony, she wore a white driftwood pearl necklace, the perfume, the plain ivory ring and the earrings. He asked why she chose the driftwood-looking pearls out of all her necklaces, and she said she didn't know why, but perhaps it was because she kind of drifted to him from the ocean. Old Salt just grinned and called her a mermaid.

Dog was the ring bearer, so Colt suited him up with reindeer antlers. After an elegant ceremony, they proceeded to a French Caribbean restaurant down the road for the reception. A calypso band carried them through a musical journey of love and joy as the guests got tipsy. A grey monkey with emerald eyes from the surrounding jungle sneaked in and picked up half-empty drinks left on unattended tables. Within a half hour, the drunken monkey staggered onto the dance floor. Teddy's mouth hung open when he saw the Oscar lookalike from his dreams about La Gracia, and he let Dog loose, who drove the drunken monkey back into the green vines.

Everyone tossed rice at the bride and groom as they left. They retired to the hotel room where they made love under the mosquito netting to the sound of the jungle and roaring ocean. When they slept, they both had another dreamless night and woke the next morning refreshed. The next day, Teddy and Alicia stayed in St. Barts to be around their families. St. Barts already was a honeymoon destination for them.

IN FEBRUARY, Teddy turned Isabella into an historic site and the land around it into a park. He and Alicia bought the house that had caught his attention in Palm Beach and divided their time between there and St. Barts. He and Will Burns became fishing buddies; Will came down to St. Barts to see Belle and they all went bonefishing together. After a while, Will joined the Pearlmakers part-time, going out with Ty, Patch and Buzz as they searched for the missing pieces of *La Gracia* still hiding in the deep waters. Teddy returned to Latch every year for some months to join them. While he was in Florida, he always picked up two red roses: one for Sarah's grave, and one for Half Ton's. At the plantation, Bear came over to greet him, and Teddy swore he looked a little younger each time.

When Teddy stood back to admire all the pearls he had made, they seemed too round and beautiful to have come from a man with such a rough oyster shell like his own, but he knew that he had been helped by the ocean, his dear friends and family, and from Alicia and Sarah. And he realized that true love and abundance wasn't just about the single pearls he had made over the years, but what they could all do when they were strung together shining brilliantly in unity as one beautiful, complete whole. A string of everlasting pearls from a true Pearlmaker.

APPENDIX

I. PEOPLE & ANIMALS

Adrianna – A professional surfer in Malibu, California and the former girlfriend of Joey Dollarhide.

Adriana Ramos – Merchant and sailor. Álvaro Ramos' wife in Latchawatchee, Florida in the 17th century.

Admiral García Díaz – The Admiral on the Spanish galleon La Gracia.

Álvaro Ramos – aka Ram. Álvaro was the sailor on La Gracia that Teddy Dollarhide can't stop dreaming about.

African Khalifani – The African King in the 17th century who sends the Spanish Prince García a massive diamond as a gift for his military protection.

Alicia – Teddy's Spanish love interest, whose eyes resemble the Spanish woman from his recurring dreams.

APPENDIX

Andy Matthews – An elderly black male resident of the Ball neighborhood who is ill with a parasitic infection from a pipe that busted during the flood caused by Hurricane Eliza.

Annabelle Burns – aka Belle. Joey's red-headed crush since high school. She recently graduated from The University of Texas at Austin. A little country, but still polished, she can skin a buck with a pocket knife, while wearing a pair of high heels.

Aspen – Joey and Cosby's old camp counselor at Camp Big Bear in the High Sierras.

Bateman & Banks Realty – Stern Banks and Walker Bateman's aggressive real estate company in Latch that keeps pressuring Teddy Dollarhide to sell his historic estate, Isabella, and her surrounding land.

Bear – Teddy Dollarhide's pet Manx cat who recovered from feline AIDS with the magical wine from La Gracia.

Betsy – Cow mascot for Latchawatchee High School who is used by some mischievous seniors as a prank when they put her on the top floor of the Biology building.

Big Buck Hunter – A strong muscular guy who is playing the old Big Buck Hunter game at Wild Bill's. He ends up saving Cosby from Skeet Boomer.

Big Ham – Assassin Jimmy Clock's right-hand man.

Bill – Oyster shucker at Cap'n Sam's. The fastest shuck in Latch County.

Billy, Bob and Steve – The crew of misfit handy men who pull the Dollarhide's garage into their massive swimming pool.

APPENDIX

Bob Barclay – Teddy's psychic tree man who has two crooked feet and a camouflage fire truck he uses to work on trees. He also likes to play music out of the truck's megaphone.

Bo Dollarhide – Teddy's brother who lives in Santa Fe, New Mexico on a ranch called The Wrangler's Roost. He trains bulls for the rodeo circuit and grows the Moringa plant.

Brawny – Bo Dollarhide's rodeo bull.

Buzz Smith – A Latch senior who works for the tree man, Bob Barclay. A football jock and terrible bully, he is Leslie's former boyfriend.

Cosby – aka Cosmo or Cos. Teddy's youngest son who likes to surf, play baseball, chase girls, and drive around in Dan's chicken mobile. He works at Dan's World Famous Fried Chicken joint.

Caramel – Teddy's brown quarter horse.

Charlotte – The Dollarhides' maid and Dallas' love interest. She used to be a model in Paris and can make the best homemade lemonade.

Chuck – A renegade grizzly bear in the High Sierras that has a taste for gunpowder.

Courtney – Belle's oldest sister who lives outside Little Rock, Arkansas.

Dallas - aka Dal. A former student of Teddy's and linebacker for The University of Miami. A black marine biologist and member of The Pearlmaker crew.

Crazy Legs – An albino alligator that gets loose in Latch after Hurricane Eliza.

APPENDIX

Dan – The owner of Dan's Fried Chicken who hails from Beaux Bridge, Louisiana. His fried chicken recipe is world famous—even swanky New York chefs have heard of it.

Dog – The Dollarhide's pet Jack Russell. He prefers varmint over dog food and has been trained to smell gold.

Donna - Leslie's mom.

Dr. Clark – Alicia's doctor in Latch.

Dr. Gomez - Alicia's doctor in Valencia, Spain at Santa María Hospital.

Dr. Wyman - Teddy's hypnotherapist.

Earful – Teddy's white Arabian horse.

Felipe – The general of Spanish Prince García's army.

Five Alarm – Teddy's brahma bull.

Fleetwood – aka Baby Fleet is the fat cat at The Pantry restaurant in Latchawatchee who has a hollow leg for corn on the cob.

Half Ton – A mystical white and brown spotted enormous wild hog with a $25,000 reward on his head from Will Burns.

Hog Kong – A legendary wild hog that was almost as big as Half Ton.

Hugo – Alicia's father.

Hurricane Frank – A rodeo circuit bull that injured Bo Dollarhide when he used to be a cowboy.

Jack – A wise preacher in Little Rock, Arkansas who helps Joey.

Jasmine Hope – Jack, the preacher's wife.

Jean Lafitte – A famous French pirate who worked in the Gulf of Mexico. Teddy and his father, Luke, used to search for Lafitte's treasure, which is supposedly hidden at Fort Morgan, Alabama, when Teddy was young.

Jethro – Skeet's half-deaf friend and accomplice.

Jimbo Dollarhide – Teddy Dollarhide's father, who is a hobby alchemist at his home in Goodchance, Alabama.

Jimmy Clock – A gun for hire.

Joey – Teddy's son, UCLA college graduate with wheat-colored hair, who used to be a big baseball star. He has an unending crush on Annabelle Burns.

José – The foreman on La Gracia and good friend of Álvaro Ramos.

Jospehine – A red-headed cowgirl who took control of Luke Dollarhide's mine. She was later the founder of Camp Big Bear in the Sierras.

Indians, The – Latchawatchee High's baseball team

Leslie – Cos' summer crush. A tomboy with only one arm, she lost the other in a car accident when she was younger.

Luke Dollarhide – California gold miner and relative of Teddy's, he hunted for the John Hodges Treasure in the Sierras, but never found it.

APPENDIX

Lulu – Belle Burn's grandmother.

Melvster, The – A high school student that crushes Virginia.

Mary-Jo White – An old lady who runs a ride share service for drunk drivers called Mary-Jo-Goes in Goodchance, Alabama.

Miss Jimmy – Cook at The Malt.

Miss Leavers – A mean teacher who harasses Cosby.

Miss Judy - The nurse at the Latch convention center who helps people from the Ball neighborhood with their infections.

Moon Pie – Camp Big Bear's raccoon mascot who has an insatiable hunger for Moon Pie sandwiches—marshmallow concoctions of sugar.

Natasha – Belle's friend and former college roommate at The University of Texas, Austin.

Officer Catfish – Teddy's best friend, and a police officer in town who has an insatiable appetite for fried catfish.

Old Blue – Teddy's royal blue macaw.

Ole Sawtooth – The legendary grizzly bear that harassed Sam and Luke in the High Sierras. He has a taste for gun powder.

Ooljee - aka Moon. Bo Dollarhide's Native American girlfriend.

Oscar – Admiral García Díaz' trained pet monkey.

Paige – Belle's youngest sister and Wolly's girlfriend.

Palmer – Luke Dollarhide's roommate and fellow alchemist.

Patsy Burns – Belle's Mother.

Pearlmakers, The – Teddy's four-man team of treasure hunters: himself, Patrick or Patch, Ty, Dallas, and—let's not forget—Bear, their Manx cat mascot.

Peter Bergman – CEO of Ore Dog, a Switzerland operation that trains canines to hunt for precious metals. Teddy used this technique to train his Jack Russell Dog to sniff for gold.

Popeye – Bo Dollarhide's pet iguana who likes to fart.

Prince Felipe García – Prince who commissioned La Gracia to be built in the 17th century in Seville, Spain.

Princess Isabella García – Prince García's wife.

Red Dollarhide – Teddy's uncle. A late real estate investor who left Teddy the estate of Isabella in his will.

Sam Boxfly – A Coast Guard officer and friend of Teddy's.

Sambo Fletcher – The oyster king of Florida and owner of Cap'n Sams.

Sarah Dollarhide – Teddy's late red-headed wife who died of cancer. She owned a landscape gardening business. She tried to help end world hunger.

Shadow – Tuck Wallace's English pointer.

Sheriff Waterhouse – Crooked Sheriff in town who takes payoffs

APPENDIX

from Bateman and Banks Realty to keep quiet about their illegal activities.

Skeet Boomer – A rodeo rider who gets in a fight with Cosby Dollarhide at Wild Bill's in Goodchance, Alabama over Leslie. He ultimately follows the boys out West.

Sofia – Alicia's mother.

Tahoma – A friend of Bo Dollarhide's, he is an enlightened Navajo Indian and chef at Gourmaize in downtown Santa Fe, New Mexico.

T-Bone – A man who lost his mind after visiting the haunted Willis Plantation.

Teddy Dollarhide – The leader of The Pearlmakers, father of Joey and Cosby, husband to the late Sarah and owner of Isabella, he often goes by the name "Old Salt" and is plagued by dreams of being a sailor on La Gracia, a Spanish galleon that went down in a hurricane in the 17th century.

Tommy Thompkins – Cos' Physics teacher.

Tuck Wallace – The owner of Camp Big Bear.

Ty – The best diver, and member of The Pearlmakers.

Vanilla – Teddy's white quarter horse.

Virginia Matthews – An attractive senior at Latch High.

Will Burns - Belle's father. A Texas high school dropout who made over a hundred million dollars drilling for oil in Texas and retired early to Latch.

Wolly Boone – One of Cosby's best friends and teammates on the Latch Indian baseball team.

Zack Watts – A fellow Latchawatchee High classmate.

II. THINGS

Antique Long Nosed Pistol – An engraved gold-finished long nosed pistol from La Gracia that Cosby finds one day while surfing.

Bagby Jail – Jail in Bagby, California where Luke Dollarhide was thrown after a bar fight at The Bear Claw Saloon in old town. In his cell that first night, he heard about The John Hodge's Treasure from fellow Native American cellmate.

Ball Neighborhood, The – Poor neighborhood in Latch that was badly flooded during Hurricane Eliza.

Bear Archery Carnage Bow – Belle's bow and arrow.

Birdhouse, The – The tower at Isabella.

Camp Arrowhead – The sister camp of Camp Big Bear where Belle Burns went as a child.

Canadian Maple Leaf – A Canadian one-ounce gold coin.

Cap'n Sam's – Sambo Fletcher's world-famous oyster dive south of Latch along the ocean.

Casablanca – A cheesy 150 million condo development Bateman and Banks Realty plan to build on top of Teddy Dollarhide's land.

APPENDIX

Chicken Mobile, The – Dan's Fried Chicken's delivery vehicle, it's a 1972 Pontiac Grand Safari wagon that is lipstick red with a yellow chicken head mounted on top and a matching tail feather on the back with a rooster call horn.

Dan's World Famous Fried Chicken – The best fried chicken in Florida, where Cosby Dollarhide works the fryer.

Diamond Symbolism – Teddy says diamonds are often called *star splinters.*

Dog House, The – Teddy Dollarhide's workshop.

Eagles Nest, The – The Dollarhide boys' cabin at Camp Big Bear.

Eastern Tiger Swallowtail Butterfly – The famous Latchawatchee butterfly that purportedly was all over the town until the tragedy at the Willis Plantation.

Foxfire Stories – Folktales and legends of Southern Appalachia.

Fox Hollow – A cabin at Camp Big Bear.

Goodchance – Teddy Dollarhide's hometown on the Mobile Bay in Alabama.

Gold Lip – The Pearlmakers' treasure hunting boat.

Gooch's – Leslie's father's outdoor store in Latch.

Honey Burn – Honey is set to burn in a tin can on a fire until a thick black smoke rises up from it, luring bears to the area. Once it has boiled, it can then be painted on trees with a brush in the area to entice bears.

Hub, The – The town square in Latch.

Hurricaine Eliza - Category 2 hurricane that devastates Latchawatchee, Florida.

Isabella – Teddy Dollarhide's historic Mediterranean estate in Latchawatchee, Florida built by the Spanish merchant and sailor Álvaro Ramos in 1687. It was renovated and added onto in the 1920's in the Italian style.

Ivory Ring – A curious ring from La Gracia that Teddy finds.

Joey's Treehouse – An elaborate sprawling tree house built by Joey Dollarhide on the grounds of Isabella in Latchawatchee so he could live in a tree like a monkey.

John Hodges – The leader of The Triangle of Ghosts, a group of thieves in the Wild West who robbed countless banks and trains. Their treasure is apparently buried in the High Sierras.

Jubilees – A special time of low oxygen in the sea that causes all the fish to swim toward the shore, where they beach on the sand. It only occurs in a few places in the world, with South Alabama being one of them.

La Gracia – A Spanish galleon that sank off the coast of Latchawatchee, Florida in the 17th Century with twenty-five hundred pounds of gold and silver, chests full of emeralds, pearls and valuable antiques on board.

Latchawatchee – A small historic town on the ocean in Northeast Florida. Founded by Ponce de León, Teddy Dollarhide lives there near the ocean in his estate Isabella.

APPENDIX

Lover's Bay Park – Latchawatchee park on the Bay where the annual high school graduation ceremony and after party are held.

Louisiana Charlie Wobbles – An oyster shot developed in New Orleans and favored by Teddy Dollarhide and his boys.

Malt, The – An airstream trailer café in downtown Latch where Miss Jimmy is the chef.

Mantiques – Manly antiques.

Moringa – Grown by Bo Dollarhide, it is also known as The Tree of Life, being one of the most nutrient dense plants on earth.

Mudbugs – Crawfish.

Oregon Duck Hunt Video – A famous video on YouTube of Joey Dollarhide riding his bicycle into the Oregon Duck mascot.

ROV or Remote Operated Vehicle - An underwater robot for treasure hunting; controlled by The Pearlmakers with an iPad.

Pantry, The – A Georgian soul food restaurant Teddy loves to frequent. Baby Fleet, an oversized cat, is often seen wandering the floors for corn on the cob, his favorite dish.

Pearlstringer, The – Alicia's famous pearl necklace store.

Preservation Room, The – The Pearlmakers' treasure hunting room on the property of Isabella in Latch.

Pulling on the Earlobe – Teddy and Sarah's way of saying "I love you."

Rose Necklace – Gemstone necklace for protection that Jimbo

Dollarhide gives Annabelle Burns after she tells him about her nightmares.

Sand dollar Symbolism – Teddy says sand dollars are thought to be lost coins from the city of Atlantis.

Seagulls – A flock of seagulls that visit Teddy from time to time to give him encrypted messages about La Gracia.

Searat – Someone who spends too much time on the ocean.

Smoke Ship – An ancient treasure ship that is thought to be only a legend.

SS Central America – The Ship of Gold that sank in a violent hurricane off the Carolina coast in 1857. Ty worked on the excavation when he was younger.

St. Nicholas Pendant – Teddy's St. Nicholas pendant which represents both Father Christmas and the patron saint of sailors. He kisses it for good luck.

Teddy's Birthmark – Teddy has a birthmark on his leg in the same spot where a canon landed on Álvaro Ramos' leg in Teddy's dreams.

The Great Star of Africa – The famous 530-karat cullinan diamond.

The Prince – An extremely rare oversized diamond that was on board La Gracia.

Vitamin R or Red – Slang for crawfish

Wild Bill's Saloon – An open-air Wild West style saloon near Goodchance, Alabama.

APPENDIX

Willis Plantation – A haunted plantation that plagues the whole area of Latchawatchee. One day, slaves and workers just vanished from the place—and to this day, no one knows why.

Wine Elixir – 12 blue bottles of 300 year old wine from La Gracia that seems to cure various maladies.

III. PEARL SPEAK

A fistful of manners – Correct someone by force.

Bad juju – Bad energy or bad vibes.

Bird-dogged – Stay on top of.

Bull butter – A lie.

Can't hear a gun go off if he was in the barrel – Very deaf.

Cowboy up – Step up to the challenge.

Thieving yellow-bellied scoundrel – A cowardly, deceitful individual.

Dangerous as a tank full of rubber banded lobs.ters – A dangerous thing that has been neutralized

Don't complain if you fall asleep with dogs and wake up with fleas – If you place yourself in a bad situation, bad results will occur.

Jealous tongues tell jealous lies.

Like white on rice – Stick to something.

Muleskinner stare – A look of pure ignorance.

APPENDIX

Nervous as a cat's tail in a room full of rocking chairs – Very afraid.

Put pepper in the gumbo – The final ingredient that finishes it off.

This ain't chicken shit boys, it's chicken salad - Something very good.

This data is like a good dog, it hunts.

IV. MAP

ABOUT THE AUTHOR

Duke Tate was born in Flowood, Mississippi in 1980 to Ken and Charme Tate. He is married to the lovely Wiphawan Tate and the couple have two sons, Chirayu and Phiraphat.

The author of 12 books in 4 languages, his book *The Alchemy of Architecture: Memories and Insights from Ken Tate* was released in 2020 and selected for The Times Literary Supplement's 2020 Books of the Year List. It has also been featured in Mississippi Magazine's Heritage & Culture section, The Clarion Ledger and The What We Are Reading Today section of the mass circulated Arab News. Selected by Amazon as a "Great on Kindle" book, it is a #1 Bestseller in the Architectural Firm category, and has reached #1 in three additional categories.

Duke attended high school at the Kent School, located in the lush Housatonic valley of Connecticut. His constant essay writing in his English classes there eventually shaped him into the writer he is now.

Duke penned his first novel, *The Opaque Stones*, in 2014. After many subsequent edits, it has since been re-released as *The Pearlmakers Trilogy*. He has since gone on to to write three books about his time studying under Sufi masters in The Tradition, called the *My Big Journey* series. He has also written two fantasy adventure novellas in his *Big John* series. He likes to write about magical realism, life, spirituality, and health. He lives in Thailand for part of the year with his amazing wife, their sons, and their dog, Sugar.

You can visit his author website here: https://www.duketateauthor.com/.

- amazon.com/Duke-Tate
- goodreads.com/9784192.Duke_Tate
- facebook.com/duketateauthor
- twitter.com/duke_tate

ABOUT PEARL PRESS PUBLISHING

We are a unique publishing company that produces books of a superb quality across all genres. Our mission is to empower authors with the freedom to speak their minds fully without the censorship traditional publishers often employ.

ALSO BY DUKE TATE

WITH KEN TATE

The Alchemy of Architecture: Memories and Insights from Ken Tate

BIG JOHN SERIES

Big John and the Fortune Teller

Big John and the Island of Bones

MY BIG JOURNEY

Returning to Freedom: Breaking the Bonds of Chemical Sensitivities and Lyme Disease

Gifts from A Guide: Life Hacks from A Spiritual Teacher

TRANSLATIONS

Gifts from A Guide: Life Hacks from A Spiritual Teacher - Spanish edition

Gifts from A Guide: Life Hacks from A Spiritual Teacher - Dutch edition

Big John and the Fortune Teller - Thai edition

COMING SOON

Big John and the Hitcher

The Architect

The Clockstopper Series: Book 1: The Wordsmith

The Clockstopper Series: Book 2: The Cobbler

CPSIA information can be obtained
at www.ICGtesting.com
Printed in the USA
BVHW080907040421
604027BV00005B/8/J